Lottery

Lottery

Anita Burgh

MACMILLAN

First published 1995 by Macmillan

an imprint of Macmillan General Books
Cavaye Place London SW10 9PG
and Basingstoke

Associated companies throughout the world

ISBN 0 333 62927 2

1 3 5 7 9 8 6 4 2

A CIP catalogue record for this book is available from the British Library

Phototypeset by Intype, London
Printed by Mackays of Chatham PLC, Chatham, Kent

For my daughter Rebecca, with love

PART ONE

February
&
March

Chapter One

On Sundays Peggy woke at exactly the same time as she did on every other day of the week. It was annoying, especially when the alarm was not even set. Each Saturday night she promised herself a good lie-in in the morning but at seven on the dot, like clockwork, her eyes opened. Dan, her husband, never had the same problem, and lay gently snoring beside her.

Peggy changed her position hoping she might, just might, go back to sleep. Even as she did so she knew it was a forlorn hope for she was one of those people whose mind, once awake, becomes irritatingly active.

With no one to talk to and no radio burbling beside her, she knew it was only a matter of time before she found something to worry about. She could no longer remember what it had been like, that time long ago, before the children were born when she hadn't had a care in the world. These days Dan called her a compulsive worrier, but deep down she knew she was no different from other women: it was as if worrying and motherhood came together. She could never be sure what her mind would choose to agonize over – the state of the world, or the nation, maybe the size of the electricity bill or whether the joint would be tough, or perhaps what was happening to the ozone layer would bother her. Her worries were, to say the least, catholic. She knew she was better off with a good, solid subject to fret about, for once, when she woke up she had found she wasn't concerned about a thing. This had sent her reeling into a mega-attack of angst: if she wasn't worrying, why not? What was wrong? What was fate setting up for her?

She itched to turn on her radio but this was guaranteed to annoy Dan. However, on weekdays he was up at six thirty and what she did and listened to after that was her own affair. Her bedside radio was constantly tuned to Radio 4 even though she only half listened to it. She used it more as background noise, to ensure that she was not lonely. She did not give it her full attention because the news was generally too depressing and only fuelled her anxieties. It also made her feel woefully unimportant for she felt that what governments did here, or anywhere, come to that, had nothing to do with her – they would do it anyway, no matter her opinion. Who would listen to Peggy Alder? – age forty-five, a bit overweight, suburban mother of three and a shop assistant, though she had now learnt to say 'in retailing'. No, she was totally insignificant in the scheme of things. Then, if she didn't listen to the news, why not have music instead? She loved music, but not early in the morning. That was why. It was the soothing effect of the voices that she liked. There was, she was convinced, a Radio 4 voice: it had a pleasant tone, a human voice, not too posh like Radio 3, not too screeching and mind-numbing like the others. It was a tone that lulled her into a sense of security and kept away the gremlins of unease.

Sitting up, Peggy turned her pillow over on to the cooler side, lay back and sighed. She wished she had not always made such a fuss about people smoking in her bedroom, then she could have had a fag.

To take her mind off the cigarette, she looked intently at the ceiling, and worried if the hairline crack that snaked across from the window to the light-fitting was any longer or wider than yesterday. And just look at the dust on that lampshade!

She must stop smoking! She had decided that months ago. It was an easy decision. 'I'm going to give it up,' she had told everyone, including her doctor, as if by saying it she was half-way to doing it. Well, in a way, she supposed she was. Didn't they say deciding to give it up was half the battle? Now she was saving up for the patches. 'When I get them, I'll do it,' she said. But it was taking an age to save enough money for the whole course. Dan had pointed out that what she saved each week in smoking she could spend on patches, so instead of popping into the tobacconist's she should pop into the chemist's. Peggy didn't trust herself to do that. She wasn't convinced they would work on her and then she'd have no money left over for fags. It was how she saw

4

it – complicated, in other words. Like everything. Why were the patches so expensive? Had the Government levied a tax on the nicotine they contained, too? 'I wouldn't put it past them. Mean sods,' she said aloud, without intending to, and Dan muttered, turned over and his right hand searched for her. Peggy slipped down in the bed and moved closer to him. But she sighed as she felt his hand suddenly fall limp and heavy on her, its searching over as he settled back into an even deeper sleep.

What if it had been the man in the car beside her? she thought. The man she saw nearly every working day. She shuddered quite violently, making a conscious effort to force that idea out of her head and away. 'We don't want to think about *him*,' she told herself firmly.

Dan turned over and she found herself looking at his back and longing for him with an uncomfortable nagging ache in her nether regions. She slid down the bed and snuggled closer to him. His body responded, nestling into the curve of hers. Emboldened, she slid her hand down the inside of his pyjama bottoms, searching for his penis, which she found, tucked neatly between his thighs like a small, soft, hibernating mammal. She began to stroke it, gently enjoying its soft silkiness. Perhaps he needs a bit of encouragement, she thought. Why should it always be him making the advances? His hand found hers. She realized she had stopped breathing in anticipation. He covered her hand with his, both of them holding him. 'That's nice,' she whispered. Then, quite deliberately, his hand lifted hers, moved it across his hip-bone and dropped it the other side.

She felt ridiculously close to tears. It was stupid of her. He was asleep, he did not know what he was doing. Or was the fact that he didn't know even more significant? She turned away from him and lay on her side, her back to him.

Being middle-aged was a right bitch, she had already decided. When younger, what with her job, the house *and* the kids to care for she had so often felt too knackered to encourage Dan's sexual advances. Now, when she would quite like him to, he did so less often. As her interest in sex was being reignited his seemed to be waning. Right mess God had made of the libido of the middle-aged, was her studied conclusion.

She slid her hand under the duvet and felt her soft flesh. Gone to pot, she had. A relaxed body – too relaxed. Her stomach appeared to have slipped, giving her a roll of fat which made it look as if it was grinning at her – that was, when she felt brave enough to look at herself naked in the mirror. Still, her boobs were not too bad and had not sagged like those of some of her friends. Why, Suzy, a friend at work, had confessed she had to be careful not to tuck her nipples into her waistband with her blouse. Peggy grinned at the cracked ceiling. Dan moved on to his back and his snoring took on a new momentum.

Nothing was fair. Why was it women worried so much about how they looked, and men rarely? And felt such guilt if their figures had gone when men just shrugged good-naturedly at their faults. How many men did she know who dieted, whereas every woman did? And why had God – His fault again – made it possible for men to impregnate women and stay slim while all hell broke out on a woman's body if she was not vigilant.

She levered herself up on one elbow the better to study her husband. He was not the handsome young man, a shade like James Dean, whom she'd married – he'd long gone. In his place was a rugged-faced individual, whose wrinkles gave his face interest and whose silvering hair added distinction. Even his bit of a paunch was attractive in an odd way, almost endearing.

Middle age should be fun; she flopped back on the pillows. But what had happened? Just as you thought there might be more time for a lark the aches began. Dan's knee played him up something rotten, especially if it rained. Peggy's back was none too reliable these days and she dared not lift anything heavy; she knew she had to have an eye test. She would soon be holding the newspaper the other side of the room to read it. What was that Bonnie Tyler song which summed it all up? She racked her brain . . . She began to hum inside her head, 'Turnaround. Every now and then I get a little bit nervous that the best of all the years have gone by . . . la la . . . Every now and then I fall apart . . . la la.' Those were all the words she could remember, but she was sure there was another bit, something about need. She was sure that was what *she* needed – for him to need *her* as she did him.

She half sat up. This was getting her nowhere. What had she to feel so down about? Not enough sex? Heavens, just look at all the times they had made love over the years. And when compared with all the other good things in her life what did sex amount to? It wasn't *that* important, not any more, not at her age. She had a sudden image of the red car, and experienced a surge of excitement, like the one she felt when she saw it approaching the bus stop.

Money, she thought hurriedly. Maybe Dan was worrying about money. She had read that worry put men off sex faster than anything. Well, there was an odd thought. Did that mean that no young man ever had one single worry? She smiled at her ceiling.

Money? That could be it. The last electricity bill had been horrendous and the car had needed new tyres to pass its MOT. Now that two of the three children were off their hands, and both her and Dan were working, things should have been easier. So why weren't they? Why were they still juggling bills, putting up with their old car, delaying having the crack in the bedroom ceiling fixed and not having the holiday in Italy they had been promising themselves for years? And still worrying.

The ability of money to disappear so fast was a constant mystery to Peggy. Of course, they had helped their son Paul with the deposit on his house, and they were still recovering from the cost of Carol's wedding over a year ago. Peggy moved in the bed as if uncomfortable – her body was not but her mind was. Whenever she thought of that wedding a lump of anger grew behind her sternum, like trapped wind. She sat up and fumbled for her cigarettes and lit one. Sod it, she thought, as she broke her own rule. She could still remember every detail of the whole do.

Neither she nor Dan had objected to Carol wanting a big white ceremony.

'Course you can have the works. Nothing but the best for my Princess,' Dan had said with a soppy grin. Peggy, a placid woman normally, often had an irrational urge to hit him when he called their daughter 'Princess'. She was never quite sure why: was it just because she thought it silly or because he never called her anything but Peggy?

The problems had arrived in a rush when what Dan and Peggy thought was best did not coincide with what Daphne Webster, Carol's future mother-in-law, considered right and proper.

7

Thinking of Daphne made the lump swell so that Peggy found herself rubbing her chest hard.

'You all right, Peggy?' Dan mumbled from below the duvet.

'Just caught myself thinking of Daphne.'

'Oh, that old cow. Then don't think.'

'I can't stop.'

'You're smoking.'

'She made me.'

'Any excuse . . .' Dan said, with the smugness of one who had given up two years ago. He turned over, dragging an unfair share of the duvet with him and burrowed back into his pillow.

She inhaled deeply on her cigarette and found she was enjoying it more than usual, probably because she should not have been smoking in bed – a bit like a quick puff behind the school bike-sheds when she had been a tearaway fifth-former. Pleasure was cheap then, she mused.

Nothing was cheap now. Over the years they had put money aside for both their daughters' weddings. But Carol's had swallowed Stephanie's share as well as her own, plus an overdraft they had negotiated for the event and which, try as they might, with the interest piling up never seemed to diminish. Dan was convinced he would go to his grave in debt to the bank. What was most annoying was that they had never been in debt before – not to anyone.

Peggy had budgeted for the wedding at the local church with a nice sit-down meal at the Central Hotel, which, by anyone's standards, did a good spread. Well, anyone normal that was, which did not include Daphne Webster . . .

'I know you mean well, Margaret. I may call you by your Christian name?' Daphne had smiled archly over her tea-cup at Peggy who, not wishing to let the woman feel left out of things, had invited her round to discuss the plans.

'It's Peggy, actually. And I don't see what's wrong with the Central. Dan's company always have their Christmas party there, they do them proud.' She had meant to be firm but realized she had managed only to sound as if she was whining.

'It's a touch impersonal, though, don't you think? I always like a nice marquee myself, more select,' Daphne pressed on. 'Of

8

course you wouldn't have room here, would you?' The small pale blue eyes, pink-rimmed as if she had been crying and which reminded Peggy more and more of a pig's as the conversation continued, glanced dismissively out of the patio window. 'Too small by far,' she said. Peggy looked out at her garden, which until now had always seemed adequate.

'A marquee? You're joking.' Peggy found herself sitting upright in the chair, her indignation making her spine more rigid. She gave a half-laugh, fully aware that no joke was intended and wondering why she had been so unfair to pigs, pleasant creatures that they were. She decided Daphne's eyes looked more like those of a ferret.

'The conveyance. Have you decided on that?'

Peggy paused on this one until she had worked out that the woman was talking about vehicles and not legal work.

'We thought of hiring a white Rolls-Royce.'

'Bit of a cliché, wouldn't you say? *Everyone* has a white Rolls. I think a nice coach and pair would be so much nicer for our Sean and your Carol.'

'But the church is only round the corner! By the time you'd geed the horses up they'd be there.'

'That's another thing, Margaret, my dear. The church.' Peggy found herself sitting even more upright for, with her eyebrows arched and her lips pursed, Daphne was giving full notification of disapproval to come. 'Your church . . .' she sucked in air, which whistled past her teeth, ' . . . I mean, these modern churches, all red brick and no stained glass.' Daphne paused, picked up her tea-cup and glared at Peggy over the rim so that for an insane moment Peggy almost apologized as if she had built it herself, brick by offending brick. 'I suppose such a place of worship is all right if you *like* that sort of thing, but if you ask me' – which Peggy had not – 'you can't beat a nice *old* church with a lichen gate.'

'Lych gate, actually.' Peggy felt inordinately smug with this correction.

'Which brings me to the point,' Daphne completely ignored Peggy's interruption, 'we, of course, have a wonderful garden.'

'Of course.'

'Plenty of room for a marquee there and a really nice *old*

church just across the way. The happy pair could walk through the *lichen* gate – so pretty. Of course, if it's a matter of cost Cyril and I are only too happy to help you out . . .' And Daphne, with the sensitivity of a fully armoured tank, rolled on, dominating the rest of the conversation. Finally Peggy accepted Daphne's invitation to tea at her house in return; curiosity had got the better of pride. But Daphne had hardly clambered into her Rover before Peggy was rootling in the garage to find the metal ruler and was measuring the garden.

If they sacrificed the vegetable patch for this year and took down the garden shed as a temporary measure, and if the marquee opened off the patio doors, they could just squeeze one in. It would mean a pond in the middle of the marquee, but that might look quite nice – different certainly, and with any luck old Ferret Eyes might fall in.

Carol had told her mother that the architect of Sean's parents' home had stormed off the job in a temper. Getting out of the car and looking up at the newly built house Peggy could imagine why. It was almost impossible to be certain what the original plans for the house had been for it was battlemented, urned, porticoed, half-timbered and lattice-windowed. It was such a mélange of styles that the architect's primary concept was now invisible.

'How on earth did they get planning permission for that?' Peggy exclaimed.

'Oh, I don't know. I rather like it,' Dan answered. Peggy looked at him with dismay and had one of those savage urges, which lasted only a second, to push him into the ornamental pond on the forecourt with its water-spouting cherubs. Instead she pushed the bell button and Dan nodded approvingly at the muted sound of a carillon which they could hear through the heavily studded oak front door.

'Ah, Margaret and Daniel,' Daphne gushed, and Dan blinked since he had not been called that since his christening forty-eight years ago. 'Come in, do.'

If it was unclear what style the exterior of the house was supposed to be, inside was in an even worse state of confusion. The hall, with a Black Watch tartan carpet and artificial coals in a fireplace large enough to stand up in, was evidently Daphne's idea of Scottish baronial, whereas the drawing room, with its abundance of gilt furniture and gilded cornices, was a good crack at French nineteenth century – Peggy knew because she'd seen the style in a book she had. She liked to know about antiques and things, even if she was never likely to own any.

It had cost, that was for sure, Peggy thought as they sat in the ornate room awash with occasional tables inlaid on every possible surface, each one laden with knick-knacks and photographs, mainly of Sean, in silver frames.

'Done himself well,' Dan whispered to Peggy, as Daphne left the room to collect the drinks tray.

'A bit over the top for my taste. Too many dust traps,' Peggy answered practically. 'Just look at all those heavy gilt frames.' She nodded towards the paintings on the wall which, with piercing reds and blues, were either very new or had been over-cleaned within an inch of their lives.

Dan, looking about him with the wide-eyed stare of the doubly impressed, worried Peggy: she feared he might be intimidated by these surroundings, and Daphne, and be bulldozed into agreeing to anything. So she squared her shoulders, planted her feet firmly on the Chinese hand-woven carpet – more bedroom than lounge, she thought – and prepared mentally to do battle, if necessary.

Peggy need not have worried. Daphne overplayed her hand and was just a shade too disapproving about the size of their house and garden. Dan did not like that. What man would? He had worked hard to give them a decent home. Their estate, its executive housing with integral garages and respectable people, was a far cry from the Victorian terraces where they had both been brought up with only the street to play in.

'That won't be necessary,' Dan said stiffly, rejecting Daphne's offer of her house and garden for the wedding. 'A girl should marry from her parents' home. Any other arrangement would look odd.'

'I was only trying to help,' Daphne fluttered.

'No doubt, and both Peg and I appreciate your intentions but we could never accept.' Dan stood up abruptly.

'If there's anything I can do, then?' Daphne leapt to her feet with arms and eyelashes flapping and spoke almost with anguish as she saw disappearing fast her dream of herself in total control of the wedding.

'I'm sure Peg will appreciate any help you can give with ... whatever,' he said, all at sea in the feminine world of weddings, and unsure what would be involved and what Peggy was willing to relinquish.

'Bossy cow, isn't she?' he said as, five minutes later, they drove away from the house, both smiling and waving politely and Peggy mouthing, 'See you soon.'

'And Sean's so quiet and amenable.' She turned in her seat to speak to him.

'You can see why now. He must be doing it for a quiet life.'

'I mean, how dare she muscle in on our Carol's do?'

'Don't you think this marquee business is a bit over the top?'

'I've got used to the idea now,' she said hurriedly. She liked the plan and was not prepared to give up so easily.

'Expensive.'

'Still, she did agree to buy the champagne.'

'She did – that was generous. What's her husband do?'

'She says he's a financial adviser.'

'They used to call them insurance salesmen,' Dan said with a snort.

That had all been over a year ago and it still rankled, especially the champagne. Buy the champagne – there was a joke! Peggy thought as she slid her legs over the side of the bed. Oh, they bought the champagne all right – eighteen bottles for ninety people. Stingy so-and-sos! She felt for her slippers with her feet. She had had to send Paul out to the off-licence to buy more with a cheque she prayed the bank would not bounce, which had only added to their financial burden.

Still, no point in dwelling on that. 'What's done's done,' as her own mother was fond of saying. She quietly padded along to the bathroom, washed and dressed in yesterday's clothes – she would change later.

Once in the kitchen she fed the cat, put the kettle on, got the joint out of the pantry and looked out at her winter-depressed garden.

Her best friend's husband always took Hazel out to lunch on

a Sunday. Peggy would have liked that. After all, it did not cost an arm and a leg to get a nice roast and two veg at the Lion and Lamb up in the village.

'When I'm married, Mum, and sorted out we'll take it in turns – you come to us one week, we'll come to you the next.' That's what Carol had said. Long bloody time it was taking her to get sorted out – she and Dan had not been there for Sunday lunch once. Still, what was she about, complaining? She should be thankful she had a daughter who still wanted to come home each week, even if her father did insist on calling her Princess.

The whistle on the kettle trilled at Peggy, and she made herself a cup of tea – the best one of the whole day.

Chapter Two

A couple of hours later, breakfast eaten and cleared away, Peggy was well advanced with her lunch preparations. As she rolled the pastry over the apples in the pie-dish and fluted the sides she thought of how many pounds, or would it be tons, of pastry she had made over the years. She might dream of Sunday lunch in pubs, but would she have it any different? She smiled to herself. Probably not. She had heard an Italian chef on the television say that food should be prepared with love and that's what made it good, which was what she was doing, every Sunday, every Christmas, feeding her family, showing them she cared.

'Hello, Mum.'

'Paul! What a lovely surprise,' said Peggy, as her son's head appeared around the back door. 'We don't see nearly enough of you. Come in. Your dad's just popped out to get the car filled up and the tyres checked. He'll be back soon.'

'It was you I wanted to have a word with.'

'Coffee? I was just about to have a cup,' she said, as the kettle whistled on the hob.

'Lovely. Smells good.' He nodded in the direction of the cooker.

'Bit of pork – beef's too pricey,' she said, as she spooned the instant coffee into the two mugs. 'You're welcome to stay – there's plenty.'

'Thanks, but I can't. Candice is cooking a chicken.'

'That's nice,' said Peggy, when in reality she would have preferred to say, 'Surprise! Surprise!' Candice was a pleasant enough girl but lazy. She and Paul spent far too much on take-aways for Peggy's full approval. 'So, what is it you want to talk about?' she asked, as she cleared the debris of her pastry-making, placed the

14

coffee mugs on the kitchen table, and motioned him to sit down. Paul looked about the kitchen with a trapped expression. He looked all ways but at her.

'Well?' she asked patiently. She saw her son take a deep breath. Hurriedly she sugared her coffee, aware she was holding her own breath as to what he was about to say, and instinct telling her she wasn't going to like it.

'I wondered if I could come back here.'

'Back here?' Peggy repeated inanely.

'Yes – live here for a month or so until I sort myself out. It's Candice and me. It's not working out,' he said, still not looking directly at Peggy.

'It's worked out well enough for one child and another on the way so far,' Peggy said sharply.

'I know, I know. Don't get me wrong. I've thought long and hard about this. I made a mistake, Mum. I should never have married her in the first place.'

'But you did, didn't you? It's done – you can't just walk away from Candice because you think you made a mistake.'

'I'm not. Candice agrees. She wants me to go, too.'

'What on earth for?'

'We've nothing in common. We bore each other rigid.'

'Pity you couldn't have found that out sooner.' With a jerky movement she spooned more sugar into her coffee.

'And we've no money to do anything.'

'I'm sorry about that, but who has?'

'But the point is I think we'd be happier if we split up.'

'Don't talk bloody daft. Divorce is a rich man's hobby.'

'Listen, Mum. If I left, if I just pissed off, she could get income support. I could send her money on the side.'

'Oh, yes, and how long for? How long before you meet someone else and want to set up home with them? Then you couldn't afford to send to Candice. What then? Honestly, Paul, I don't think I've ever heard such a load of rubbish in my life. If you're here in the same town, and working, you don't for one minute think the Soc are going to pay Candice? And what about the Child Support Agency? Think straight, son.' She was stirring her coffee so energetically that it slopped over the side and left snail trails on the surface of the brightly coloured mug.

'I'm not working.' He looked long and hard at his hands with their slim, tapering fingers.

'You got the sack?' She had stopped stirring and sat, spoon in hand, a shocked expression on her face.

'No, nothing like that. Yesterday John closed the shop down. There's no money around for the sort of computers we sell.'

'Then you'll get redundancy.'

'He's gone bump, Mum.'

'Gone bump? What's that when it's at home?'

'Bust. Bankrupt. There's no redundancy money.'

'Oh, my God! Paul, I'm so sorry, you were doing so well.' Peggy absent-mindedly pleated and unpleated a tea-towel which was on the table. 'Why only last year you hoped to be made manager of the new shop he planned. This is so unfair. Why did he raise your hopes like that? He must have known – he must have seen this coming.'

'Exactly. And, like a fool, I believed him. I relied on the extra money I'd be earning. That's why I changed the car. Can't keep the payments up now. And Christ knows about the mortgage.'

'Now, calm down, Paul. There's ways and means. The Soc pay for things like that. Being made redundant isn't reason enough to break up a marriage. What a load of old cobblers!' She was almost laughing – almost, not quite.

'You don't understand, Mum. Candice doesn't want to know any more. She's fed up. The house is too small, Lance is playing her up, and she feels sick all the time.'

'So? It's temporary, she'll get over it. She was like that last time she was pregnant.'

'She doesn't want me.'

'She's cooking you a chicken.'

'We don't love each other – it's gone.' He put his head in his hands. Her instinct was to go to him, to hold him and comfort him, make everything right for him, tell him that she loved him.

'Pull yourself together, do!' she said instead. 'Of course you don't love each other like you did – you didn't expect to, did you? If so, how naïve can you get? Love changes. You can't keep the white heat of an affair going for ever, it's an impossibility. Just day-to-day living sees to that. Every morning that you face them

16

bleary-eyed at breakfast it fades a little. Every burp, every fart, every time you hear them on the bog then a bit of romance gets chipped away. But love, real love, *that* can stay, but it changes. It becomes calmer but it's longer lasting.'

He looked up at her. 'Is it?'

'Of course it is. Dan and I haven't mooned over each other for years, but it doesn't mean we don't love each other. Heavens, if everyone got divorced after the first romantic flush had gone no one in the world would stay married.'

'I don't want this kid.'

'A bit late now.'

'She tricked me. Said she was on the pill and she wasn't.'

Peggy sighed with exasperation. 'Now why would she trick you if she didn't want to stay with you? Come on, talk sense.'

'Me losing my job was the last straw. We had one hell of a row.'

'It's not your fault.'

'You tell her that.' He snorted what she presumed was meant to be a laugh.

'Look, Paul,' she leant across the table and took hold of his hand, 'you'll get another job. Sign on and keep looking. It's lack of money's brought this on, nothing else. Wait a mo . . .' She stood up, went into the dining room and from her handbag on the sideboard took her cheque-book and wrote him a cheque for a hundred pounds. She'd have to phone the bank manager in the morning, explain what she'd done. She thanked heaven she had her own account so that Dan need never know. She returned to the kitchen and her heart went out to the dejected figure of her son huddled over the table. It was such a short time ago that he was just a kid bursting into her kitchen near to exploding with excitement that he had been picked for the team. Look at him now.

'Paul, take this – tide you over a bit. And here,' she gave him a five-pound note, 'on the way home, get a bottle of wine to go with your chicken. Doesn't Candice like that Blue Nun stuff?'

'Liebfraumilch.'

'Yes, that's it. Well, get a bottle of that. Lock Lance in his room, or bring him round here if you like, and then bonk some sense into the girl.'

'Mum!' Paul was shocked at her even knowing such a word

17

and, like most sons, doubly shocked that she might, from experience, know what it meant. They heard the slam of a car door. 'Mum, it's—' he had just begun to say but clammed up as he heard his sister call from the hall. 'I'm off. I'd rather not see them. Sean gets on my wick – he's always so bloody smug. Bless you, Mum.' He kissed her cheek quickly. 'You sure you can afford this?' He waved the cheque in the air.

'Of course,' she lied.

The back door slammed as the kitchen door opened.

'Wasn't that Paul?' asked Carol.

'He had to get back to Candice.'

'Charming! He might have waited to say hello.'

'That smells good, Mum.' Sean sniffed the air appreciatively.

Peggy tilted her head to accept kisses from them both. She sometimes wished Sean would not call her Mum, since she was not and he had one of his own. But then, come to think of it, with a mother like Daphne was it any surprise he should want another? 'How's your mother?' she asked as much to his surprise as hers.

'Fine, thanks – well, she was last time I saw her.'

Peggy, with a mother's antennae that noticed even the minutest change in her children, registered that there was an edginess between these two this morning and wondered if she should comment on it or let it simmer. Best not to interfere, she told herself.

'And what do you mean by that?' Carol snapped at her husband, as if to prove Peggy's fears.

'That's a nice outfit, Carol,' she said brightly, sharply changing the subject with the practised ease of one who often arbitrated.

'You like it? Miss Selfridge,' Carol said in explanation, patting the smooth skirt smoother. She was a smart, neat young thing. Peggy could not imagine who she took after, certainly not herself. Peggy had never managed to look bandbox fresh when she was young – always in too much of a hurry. She was better now; she had forced herself to be tidier in her appearance. She'd had to, or else she would not have become the successful section manager she was.

'Very smart. Shift your bot, Sean, I need to check the meat.'

She playfully pushed Sean away from the cooker.

'Sean's mum does lamb with garlic and rosemary,' Carol volunteered.

'Does she now? Your dad wouldn't like that. He can't stand garlic.' Peggy began to coat the apple pie with an egg glaze.

'Don't you get bored always cooking the same thing?' Carol asked innocently.

'There wouldn't be much point if I did. It's still got to be done, hasn't it?' Peggy said, not meaning to sound as sharp as she did.

Carol looked at her with a surprised expression. 'You needn't snap at me like that.' Her lower lip trembled and tears tumbled from her large blue eyes. 'I was only making conversation.'

'Don't be silly, Carol, I wasn't snapping.' Peggy turned from her task to see Carol beginning to cry in earnest and Sean to shuffle sulkily from one foot to the other. 'What on earth's the matter?' she asked almost wearily. Evidently the basinful of bad news from Paul was to be augmented.

'It's Sean, he's been a real bogeyman, frightening me rigid, and now you're *tempered* with me.' Carol lapsed into her childhood way of talking. It always worked wonders with her father but irritated Peggy.

'What's going on?'

'I had to explain a few things to Carol, Mum, and she didn't like it.'

'What things?' Peggy asked, afraid of what they might be.

'Like we might lose the house at Highwinds. Like I've got to wait for a baby. Like his dad's worried sick about the business. And I'll have to keep my crappy car . . . and continue to work,' Carol added, almost as an afterthought.

'Anything else?' Peggy asked, unaware of how sarcastic she sounded.

'You don't understand either. It's not fair.' She gulped between her sobs. 'Not fair.'

'Life rarely is fair,' Peggy said patiently.

'Everything we planned for seems to be going out of the window. And I don't understand why it's happening.' She blew noisily into the handkerchief Sean handed her.

'I'm sorry. I've tried,' he said, looking guilty and helpless at the same time.

'We all know that, Sean. No one has worked harder than you.'

'Thank you, Mum,' he said, his own voice thick with emotion.

Oh dear, thought Peggy, I do hope he's not going to cry as well. Peggy never knew where to put herself when men cried.

'Times are hard, Mum. Real bad.'

'They say on the television the recession's over,' Carol said grumpily.

'They've been saying that for years. It's taking time to circulate down to us ordinary people. Why, look at . . . the shop.' Peggy quickly stopped herself saying, 'Look at Paul's company,' and changed it to her own experiences. 'Things just aren't picking up as quickly as everyone said.'

'Paul and Candice are having a baby and they're not as well off as us.'

'Only because Candice forgot to take the pill,' responded Sean.

'Typical of a male! Go on, blame the woman.'

'It's true. Paul told me. Twice he's been caught.'

'This is no way to be talking. What's done is done,' Peggy said, and found herself thinking of how often she spoke in clichés, but what useful little things they were. 'And your dad's worried about business?' she asked Sean, as she placed the apple pie in the centre of the oven, moving the roast to the bottom and the potatoes to the top. Here, she was in a quandary for her heart fairly sang at the thought of Daphne getting her comeuppance, but then the better side of her nature remonstrated with her for being so mean-spirited and unChristian.

'I feel so sorry for him. He's worked hard for years to build the business up. We'd enough fat to weather the recession – we did, we made it. But what with their new house . . . well . . . things have got to pick up a bit faster for us to survive.'

'Oh, I am sorry,' Peggy said, hearing how false her voice sounded. 'Well, then, Carol, you're just going to have to adjust and wait for all the things you want, aren't you?'

A weaker soul might have reeled back from the look of sheer venom Carol gave her, but Peggy was used to such looks from her daughter and hardly reacted.

'There's your father,' she said with relief, looking up as she heard Dan's car being driven on to the hard standing in front of the garage.

'Dad!' Carol flung the back door open, allowing a burst of the cold damp late February morning to waft in. 'Oh, Daddy!' She clung to him.

'How's my best Princess, then?' Dan kissed her enthusiastically. Peggy caught herself looking at Sean to see how he reacted, if he found Dan's attitude to his daughter as annoying as she did. But Sean just looked blank – he often did. 'What's this? Who's been making my Princess cry?'

'It's nothing, Daddy,' Carol said bravely.

'Anything you want to talk about?' he asked, glaring at his son-in-law.

'No, nothing. Sean and I had a silly tiff.'

'Oh! One of those.' Dan laughed.

'Shift, everyone, if I'm to get this meal on the table,' Peggy said, with mounting irritation. That was so typical of Carol. She would burden her mother with her problems, but her daddy must always be protected. Peggy was fully aware that it was not an indication that Carol loved her more – the opposite, probably. They'd never been really close, even though she had tried, and she'd never understood why. She loved her daughter, that she never doubted, but she felt she didn't understand her and now never would.

'Where's Steph?' asked Dan.

'Upstairs.' Peggy nodded at the ceiling. 'Homework,' she said in explanation.

'Skiving more like,' said Carol.

'That's not fair, Carol. They're swamping the poor girl with work. Her exams are only a few weeks away. She never complains, though.'

'I can't see the point of it all myself. She'll only get married and have kids like everyone else does,' Carol said, sugar-sweet, smiling at her father as she spoke.

'You never spoke a truer word.' He looked at his watch. 'Have we got time for a pint, Peggy?' he asked, as he did every Sunday.

'Just the one,' she replied, as *she* did every Sunday.

'I'll come too. I fancy a bitter lemon, if you don't mind, Mum,' said Carol, as she also did every Sunday.

'No, off you go, all of you. I'll get on faster by myself.'

'Am I to pick up either of the grans?' Dan asked.

'Neither. My mother's out to lunch with friends and Jean has gone on an OAP outing. We're on our own for once.'

'That's nice,' said Dan, slamming the door behind them.

Peggy leant against the kitchen table, lit a cigarette, and looked vacantly into space. She didn't want to think about Carol and her problems, not yet awhile. Neither did she fancy thinking about Paul. She couldn't take in his news, not yet. So stupid. So selfish of them. She shook her head with disapproval. She'd think about something else.

Dan was so hard on Steph. Why? She had never given them a moment's worry – not like Carol who at sixteen had had a rather wild period and a very unsuitable biker boyfriend . . . It couldn't be because Steph was not as pretty as Carol, that would be insulting to Dan. But then Steph's looks had a charm of their own, a shy diffidence of expression which Peggy found appealing even though her hair was darker than Carol's blonde curls. She hadn't inherited Dan's clear blue eyes as Carol had but had hazel ones like Peggy's. People said that Steph looked like her, although she could never see it herself, but there was a lot of Dan in Carol. That was a trite reason for him to favour her. No, it was more complicated than that. Sometimes, and it was only sometimes, for Peggy did not feel happy with the thought, she wondered if he was not jealous of Steph's ability, that the girl's cleverness frightened him.

Poor Dan. Peggy was sure that he had always had a bit of a chip on his shoulder that he had failed the eleven plus and Peggy had not. It was only lack of funds that had made it necessary for her to leave grammar school before joining the sixth form with her good clutch of O levels. At first it had hurt that she had to work in a shop and would not be able to go to college. But then she'd met Dan, a trainee draughtsman in the local engineering works. They had fallen in love and that had taken the sting out of the unfairness of fate. Since then she had always played down her intelligence. As her mother was fond of repeating, no man liked to think his wife was brighter than him – not a reasonable concept but, given the times, one she had taught herself to accept. She read a lot – it was a family joke, 'No good talking to Mum, she's got her head in a book.' It was true: give Peggy a book and she was lost to the world. Her taste was wide and if she could not afford to buy many she was a devoted member of the library.

A couple of times in her marriage she had started night classes, once for A level English and once for history, but with a young family to care for, and a part-time job into the bargain, she hadn't been able to keep up with the work. She had promised herself to return to them when the kids were older, but by then she'd needed to work full-time to bring the money in. She could honestly say she hadn't minded, her family came first and always would. And she hadn't given up – she was now learning conversational Italian for the dream holiday they had been planning for years – or, rather, she had. She wanted to go to Rome, Venice, see the paintings in the Uffizi; she had an idea that when they eventually went it would be a case of browning on a beach and a knees-up every night, but never mind, she would be abroad. And, as Hazel had pointed out to her, you couldn't get a nicer bum than on an Italian bloke.

'What's the joke?' Steph said, entering the kitchen.

'Not for young ears,' Peggy grinned. 'How's it going?'

'Not bad, though I don't think GBS and I are ever destined to get along. As soon as these exams are over we're parting company, I'm seeing him no more.'

'Shame. I rather like *Man and Superman*,' Peggy said.

'Mum, honestly! Give me the romantics any day. They all down the pub?' Steph asked, pinching a carrot from the saucepan on the draining board. 'Shall I lay the table? What's for afters?'

'Apple pie and custard. What else?' Dan would sulk if he didn't have his pie.

'Don't you ever get bored with the predictability of it all, Mum?'

'That's the second time I've been asked that this morning. It *is* boring and yet, you know, I find a lot of comfort in the same solid routine. It's safe,' she answered, but not sure what she really meant.

'Sounds as if you're persuading yourself,' Steph answered, but before Peggy could ask her what *she* meant, Steph was saying something else. 'By the way, Mum, later this year I've a chance to go fruit-picking in France once the exams are over. Would you mind?' Steph often changed the subject in the abrupt way of youth as if otherwise there wasn't time to say and do everything.

'Why on earth should I mind?'

'I thought, I won't need much while I'm there and I could save towards college and help and . . . if I get in.' She tapped the wooden table for luck.

'You'll get in. All your UCAS choices will be begging you to join them.'

'Mum, it's not too late.' Steph suddenly looked serious. 'I need not go. It's going to be hard financially, even with my grant. I could try for the Civil Service, if you like.'

'Don't talk such rubbish. What have I always said? You're going to university. You'll be going for me, too. I can learn from you. We'll manage.'

'You're sure?'

'Of course,' Peggy said, with no idea of how the hell they would.

Hot and frazzled, she finally had the lunch on the table. Peggy sat at her end, the one close to the door and the sideboard, and looked down the length of the table at her family chatting and laughing. She was lucky. Her children all lived within easy visiting distance; they were a close unit. They had the odd crises, usually associated with money, and the lack of it, like Paul today, and their preferences for each other changed back and forth – but liking was one thing, loving was another. Peggy had no doubts that their love for each other was strong enough to withstand anything – and that went for all of them.

Chapter Three

If she was irritated when she woke early on Sundays, Tuesday was her worst day of all. On Tuesday she went back to work and on those mornings she found it hard to get going. She was always more tired on that day than any other and Monday was to blame. On Monday, the shop was closed all day to give the assistants a semblance of a weekend. Some weekend! Peggy's, like most of the women she worked with, was devoted to catching up on all the jobs not done, ignored or pretended did not exist in the mad scramble which was the rest of her week. The only consolation was that when she left for work on Tuesday she knew she was closing the door on an ordered house. Each room had had a good going over, the laundry bin was empty, the linen cupboard was full and Dan's shirts for the week were neatly folded, with his hankies and socks, in his drawers.

'You do too much, Peggy,' Dan often said. But that was as far as it went. His idea of helping was occasionally to do the drying up. She often thought he would die in front of a full refrigerator rather than open the door and sort something out to eat. She supposed that if she got hit by a bus one day and went to the great kitchen in the sky he might then learn to boil an egg. More likely he'd move in with his Princess and she would take over the nanny role. Peggy always chided herself when she had that particular thought. Even if true, it struck her as spiteful and petty.

What Peggy never understood was Dan's pride in his inability to cope. She had often heard him brag that he did nothing about the house. She had heard him sneer at men who donned rubber gloves and pinny and helped their wives. Peggy thought his attitude grossly unfair since she earned an integral part of their budget. Not that she ever said anything: for a start she doubted that it would do any good and she'd only be accused of nagging; and she was of a generation that accepted their lot a little more acquiescently than their daughters were prepared to do.

Female writers in books, magazines and newspapers could rant on about equality, liberation and the success of women in the workplace, of crashing through the glass ceiling, of modern man and his more caring attitude. Changes such as this had passed by Peggy and her like. Despite owning more domestic machines, in their world the role of women had not changed much since their mothers' and grandmothers' day. The roles remained the same, there were women's tasks and men's tasks and never the twain should meet. None of it was bloody fair and when she felt herself whipping up into a good old moan she thought of the waste-bins and congratulated herself. She had managed to con Dan into regarding emptying and washing out of waste-bins as man's work. That usually calmed her down.

Although their house was in the village of Marton it was no longer a true village, but one that the ribbon development of the city had swallowed up. The tiny centre with its pub, village store and a few cottages was all that was left. The rest had been smothered by the new estates built to house those who could not afford to live in the city.

Luckily for Peggy she had only to walk a couple of roads to the bus stop and the bus which took her to the centre of town, and an even shorter walk to the store. Just as well on a cold, wet February morning as this was.

She stood huddled under the Perspex bus shelter, into which the sharp wind gleefully whipped, among the group of commuters who, although they daily caught the same bus, merely nodded to each other and never spoke. There had been a time when Peggy, to amuse herself, had made up stories about the other travellers, built imaginary lives about them, but she'd long ago given up doing that. They all looked so boring and all she could come up with was equally boring lives for them.

She pulled up her collar and tried to kid herself that she wasn't looking out for a certain car. She was ashamed that she took such an interest in that red vehicle and its occupant. The guilt had been there from the beginning, but had become worse when at night, if she couldn't sleep, she'd started to make up stories about 'him' which had turned into stories about 'them'. With Dan lying beside her the shame was even more acute. It was almost, she'd decided, like verbal masturbation. Each time she allowed herself to do it, she vowed never again.

Then she saw the car inching along Byron Road towards her. She tried not to watch its approach and looked away, only to glance up again immediately. It was stationary now as the traffic lights just along from the bus stop were at red. She sighed, almost with relief. That meant he'd shoot past in the traffic when they turned green. The hardest and yet the best and most exciting mornings were when he got stopped by the lights alongside her bus shelter. Then they looked at each other – and just recently he'd smiled.

The lights changed, the red car went by, yet she was certain it slowed fractionally as it approached the queue. And then it was gone and the excitement was over for the day.

The bus shuddered to a halt and she clambered on with the others. They were never fast enough for the disgruntled driver: there was always one who hadn't got their money ready or not the exact amount. She longed for the good old days of a friendly conductor. She loathed damp ones like this when the bus quickly reeked of wet clothes and hair. She consciously set aside the thought of the Peugeot driver and concentrated for the rest of the journey on planning what to have for supper that night, and mentally juggling bills and how they were to be paid.

She flicked her card into the time clock with the expertise of years, checked her shopping bag into Security, pocketing the numbered disc she was given in return, and joined the crowd of women and a few men who were moving towards the staff entrance. She did not bother to look out for Hazel, who worked for a make-up company with a franchise within the store. Hazel was not subject to the same rules and regulations and turned up for work when she wanted. Peggy fell into step with Phyllis, from Women's Shoes, who thought her husband was having a ding with a girl from the haberdashery counter of the rival department store in the town.

'I could understand better if she was pretty, but she looks like the back end of a bus,' Phyllis moaned, as they hung up their coats in the staffroom. With handbags over their arms, they made for the lift and their various floors and Phyllis continued to confide. Poor Phyllis, Peggy thought, she was not much of a looker. How puzzled and confused she must be, endlessly asking why he had strayed, where she had gone wrong.

Phyllis got off at the first floor and as the lift slid down to the ground, and her own department, Peggy tried to imagine how she would react if Dan ever played around. She often joked she'd cut his goolies off if he ever did. But, seriously, how would she be? Would she storm out, or kick him out? Probably she would have a moan and put up with it, as Phyllis was doing, for fear of being alone. Still, she thought, as the metal cage of the lift shuddered to a halt, it was not something that she felt she need worry about too much. Where would Dan ever find the energy to have an affair in the first place? And, judging from his performance of late, would he ever be interested enough?

She greeted the other assistants in her department, who were already dusting the shelves and the stock, then crossed to the office, as small as a cupboard, tucked away at the back behind gloves and scarves.

'Good morning, Viv,' she said to the department's manageress.

'What's good about it?' said Viv, from her minute and cluttered wooden desk where she was opening mail. She looked up at Peggy with eyes sunk into skin which looked as puffy as rising dough. Her powder sat, obvious, on the claret-coloured mottling of her cheeks. Oh dear, thought Peggy, she's hung over again.

'Nice weekend?' Peggy asked, with forced cheerfulness.

'Not particularly. You?'

'The usual.' Peggy shrugged her shoulders.

'There's a complaint here – looks as if Karen was sharp with a Mrs Fox, an account customer.' Viv pulled a face: she hated account customers on principle. In her opinion they were a stuck-up lot who were more demanding than people who paid in cash. 'Will you see to it?'

'Can't Personnel cope with it?'

'And get fat-arsed Jenkins involved? No, thanks. We'll deal with this ourselves,' said Viv firmly. Her loathing for John Jenkins went back over forty years to a staff party when they were both junior shop-floor assistants. He had groped her in Soft Furnishings and had ignored her the following day and every day thereafter. Now he was the smooth-suited, smooth-chinned general manager of the whole store and Viv hated him even more.

Peggy took the letter reluctantly. The rules were laid down: complaints went straight to the personnel manager, who dealt with them unless they were so horrendous that they had to be referred to Mr Jenkins. Worse, Peggy was sure she knew Mrs Fox whose husband was rich. She was one of those women who believed that their husband's success gave them the right to be awkward and rude, especially to shop assistants. Peggy's life was full of that type.

Poor Viv, she thought as she unlocked the showcase and considered having a word with the window dressers about redoing the display in a more springlike way. People laughed at Viv behind her back, especially the juniors, but Peggy understood a little why she had become an old soak and felt sorry for her. Viv had worked at Sadler's since she had left school at sixteen. She had once confided to Peggy at a staff party, when really the worse for wear, that she had longed at one time for marriage and children. Instead of a husband she had to care for an ageing, incontinent mother. Instead of children she doted on a somewhat smelly Pekinese, of which, she'd told Peggy, her mother was jealous, so every day she worried for her 'baby's' well-being. Viv had once brought the dog round to Peggy's for tea and after they had gone Peggy had emptied a whole can of Forest Glade to get rid of the smell left by the flatulent Peke. Such a depressing life, with so little hope two years off retiring, all Viv had to look forward to was the carriage clock which was every departing departmental manager's farewell present. No, with a life like that Peggy reckoned she would have been in detoxification or have topped herself years before.

Her luxury handbags clean and gleaming, her till float counted, her various docket books lined up, her pen working, Peggy was waiting ready. At one minute to nine she watched the porters open the large plate-glass doors with as much ceremony as if the ravening January sale hordes were about to pound in.

Instead only a trickle arrived: a few pensioners used to rising early and wandering around to fill their days, a couple of harassed-looking young mothers who had, no doubt, just dropped the kids off at school. No great spenders – they would come later. Peggy had a fantasy about her richer clients: they breakfasted in a leisurely way off bone china, giving instructions to the char before showering and deciding what to wear from their extensive wardrobes. Then they rang a friend, arranging a lunch appointment, before driving off in their spanking new cars, given them as a birthday present by their adoring husbands. She could not be sure if this was true or not since she did not know anyone remotely like that, only Daphne who didn't really count since she'd been born two streets from Peggy and had attended the same primary school – something she preferred to forget.

Just as the first customers hit the shop floor, Hazel arrived, smartly suited in her red and navy blue uniform with crisp white blouse supplied by the House of Pompadour for whom she worked. Pompadour was owned by a large American pharmaceutical company – not that the customers were aware of that for the aura of Paris shrouded the four-sided glass box in which were displayed the expensively packaged creams, colours and perfumes that Hazel spent her day successfully vending, pandering to her customers' ever-hopeful dreams.

Peggy admired Hazel: she had recently reached forty, not that anyone would guess as she could easily pass for a sophisticated thirty-year-old. She was always beautifully groomed, and she was slim as a reed. Peggy liked to remind herself that Hazel had no children so her shape was more thanks to that than discipline. They had known each other for fifteen years, ever since Hazel had joined as an assistant in the perfumery department. Now she was the House of Pompadour's manageress in the shop within a shop, with the best set of sales figures in the country.

Hazel and her husband Bruce were Dan and Peggy's best friends. Outwardly they had little in common. Bruce had his own building firm and was well off, while Dan worked for a large engineering company and never had enough money, but they shared a passion for cars. Hazel was houseproud and a compulsive cleaner whereas Peggy hated housework and only did it out of a sense of duty and fear of the shame she would feel if she did not. Peggy smoked and Hazel never had. Peggy liked reading and art, Hazel never opened a book and pictures were for going to. Dan was faithful while Bruce was an out-and-out bastard. They were complete opposites – and yet their friendship worked.

Peggy waved at Hazel across the aisle, the other side of Costume Jewellery and Stockings. Hazel waved back, pointing to her watch, and Peggy gave her the thumbs-up that they would meet over coffee in the café opposite. They both liked to get out of the shop and away from the carping which was the norm in the canteen.

Peggy slipped away five minutes before Hazel: she had to walk through the back of the large store because only manageresses were allowed to use the front door to the annoyance of everyone else.

Peggy had got the coffees in and was already half-way through a cigarette before Hazel arrived.

'Try this,' said Hazel, plonking a bag on the table. She slid effortlessly into the banquette opposite. Peggy tried to avoid sitting on banquettes: her bottom always seemed to stick to the plush velveteen of the seat and she felt clumsy squeezing into it. Not so Hazel.

'What is it?' she asked curiously, peering into the familiar green and yellow striped bag of the shop.

'New gunge. Pompadour's marketing it in a serious way. Lipids and all that crap,' said Hazel, who, although plastered with her firm's cosmetics when on duty, preferred at home to wash her face in soap and water and to use a little light moisturizer. Still, she had been blessed with fabulous skin – her mum's genes – and had no need for the constant care and cosseting that Peggy, a bit late in the day, went in for.

'Fantastic! I read their advert in Carol's *Tatler*.'

'What on earth does she take *Tatler* for?'

'I don't know. It's a good magazine these days, mind, masses of interesting articles.' She knew she sounded defensive. 'Is it a free sample?' she asked anxiously, hoping it was, for Hazel was liberal with her company's products and it worried Peggy that one day she might come a cropper.

'Yes, it is, and I've filled the docket in as a freebie so you've nothing to fear from Security. You *are* an old worrier, Peggy.'

'I don't want you, and certainly not me, to get into any trouble. I don't know what we'd do if I lost this job.'

'Still bad, is it?' Hazel asked, concern in her voice, and Peggy nodded. 'It was that damn wedding, wasn't it? I'd still ask that mean old bitch Daphne for a contribution – at least towards the extra champagne you had to buy. Their lot guzzled enough.'

'It's not just that, it's Paul, too. He's threatening to leave Candice, says he's bored.' Peggy rolled her eyes heavenward.

'Can't say I blame him. She's always struck me as dead from the neck up. All she talks about is that kid of hers and her washing – she's a washing advert come to life.'

'But that's not the point, is it?' said Peggy, in a quandary, feeling she ought to rush to the defence of her daughter-in-law but at the same time knowing she was in total agreement with Hazel. 'There's the kids – they'll soon have two,' she added. They should be the main problem to be considered, not Paul's whinge-ing or Candice's whining.

'Worst reason for staying with someone I've always thought. What will they do when the kids are grown-up and they're stuck with each other and still bored rigid?'

'That's easy for you to say. He's responsible for them, too.' Peggy sounded self-righteous. It was all right for Hazel to go on, with no kids of her own. What did she know about it?

'So how does a hiccup in Paul's marriage rock your financial boat?'

'Well, that's half the problem, isn't it? No money, no fun, just graft and the telly. Poor kids.'

'You've been giving them hand-outs?'

'I can't just sit back and watch it happen without trying to help.'

'Who helped you and Dan when you were young?'

'No one.'

'Then why should you beggar yourself now?'

'For a start I'm not beggaring myself, and in any case things were different. The young these days have greater expectations than we did.'

'So we mustn't disappoint the poor little darlings. Honestly,

Peggy, you're too soft for your own good. If I'd had children, and thank God I didn't, I would have told them to stand on their own feet.'

'You wouldn't have, you know.' Peggy smiled at her friend who, even if the world thought she was tough and sophisticated was generous to a fault. Peggy knew that if she ever asked Hazel for a loan, she would give her her last penny and then take a loan herself to give her more. It was one reason Peggy would never ask for the price of a coffee – she might end up with a three-course meal.

'No Italy this year again, then?'

'No chance.'

'You know what would be fun? You and me go – on our own – leave the husbands behind,' Hazel said enthusiastically at this sudden thought.

'Oh, I could never do that.'

'Why not?'

'It wouldn't seem right. Dan needs a holiday as much as I do.'

'But does he really want to go to Italy?'

'He says he does.'

'Bet he'd prefer a knees-up on the Costa with Bruce while you and I soaked up the culture in Italy.'

'You? Culture?' Peggy snorted.

'Well, that and the lovely little bums!' Hazel giggled.

'Like Lendl's.'

'The very same.'

'Nice idea.' Peggy shook herself nervously. 'Gracious, what am I thinking?'

'What any woman married as long as you thinks.' Hazel glanced at her watch and picked up her handbag ready to move on.

'Oh, shut up! Here, did you see the *Sunday Planet*? They're running a bingo in the *Daily Planet* – a million quid prize. I got it yesterday and three of my numbers came up, the same today. What say we take turns buying the paper and enter it together? It'll be more fun.'

'We never had any luck with the pools. Just think of the money we threw away on that.'

'This is different. It's only for a month. It won't cost that much

33

if we share,' she explained and wondered fleetingly why Hazel, of all people, should be concerned about the cost.

'Oh, all right then, I'll get tomorrow's, but don't raise your hopes.'

Back at the shop, trade was slow. Peggy gazed into space, and thought about what it must feel like to own half a million pounds. She considered confiding in Hazel about the bloke in the red Peugeot, but realized how silly it would sound since there was nothing to confess – just dreams, unattainable dreams, much the same as dreaming of winning half a million.

'Yes, madam, can I help you?' She stepped forward smiling pleasantly, eager to be of assistance.

Chapter Four

It was an uneventful week. Trade was slow. The Government, the newspaper and TV pundits might be saying that the green shoots of recovery from the recession were popping up all over, but, so far, the seeds were lying fallow in Peggy's High Street.

After coffee with Hazel on the Tuesday, Peggy plucked up the courage to telephone Mrs Fox to tell her how sorry she was that a member of her department had been rude to her. Peggy had the small satisfaction of knowing she was right and Viv wrong to try to apologize when she reeled from the tongue-lashing she received from plummy-voiced Mrs Fox. By the end of the lambasting she felt nothing but solidarity with Karen. After the call she reported back to Viv who then insisted she write the woman a letter.

'But, Viv, it won't do any good – she'll still witter on. She's enjoying it. I reckon she's a stuck-up bully.'

'A correctly worded letter *might* work. Try it,' Viv said dismissively, returning to a column of figures which just would not add up.

Peggy wrote the letter, showed it to Viv who okayed it, and then went straight to where she should have gone in the first place – Personnel. They hauled in Karen, then Viv, then alerted Complaints and thanked Peggy.

Viv didn't. Viv was incandescent with rage at the undermining of her authority and stormed out of the shop early leaving Peggy to cash up and be late home.

Over a supper of fish and chips from the shopping precinct – there hadn't been time to prepare anything else – she told Dan and Steph of her scrap at work.

'Viv was right. Always try and sort things out yourself before alerting the guv'nors,' Dan said, pouring tomato ketchup liberally over his cod. It wasn't the answer she had expected but, then, he hated fish and chips, so maybe he was venting his disappointment on her.

'It would have been a waste of everybody's time. There are some people you can never placate.'

'Perhaps Viv's feeling insecure in her job and that's why she was so angry. You made a decision over her head – one she knows she should have made herself,' Steph volunteered, as she neatly dissected the black skin from the underside of her fish. Peggy smiled at her warmly. Such a wise head – far more mature than she'd been at seventeen.

Dan was bolting his food – she and Steph were only half-way through theirs when, his plate pushed back, he was on his feet.

'I'm going down the snooker hall for a couple of hours.'

'But I thought there was a football match you wanted to watch.'

'It's not tonight. I promised Bill Witherspoon a game. Don't wait up,' he said from the door.

'I won't,' she said, a mite sharply, but she need not have bothered for she doubted if he had heard.

'He never used to spend this amount of time playing snooker, did he?' Steph asked.

'Oh, he's always liked the game. Maybe he sees himself turning into another Steve Davis and he'll save our fortunes.' She was amused at the idea. 'It's nice for him to get out with the blokes.'

'And what about you? Apart from your Italian classes, when do you get out?'

'Where would I go?' she said briskly. 'I don't mind, I quite like the peace and quiet. I can watch what I want on TV or read or just go to bed. Lovely.'

'When I'm married – if I marry – I won't tolerate anyone like Dad. If my husband wants to go out three nights a week then I'll go out three too.'

'Some marriage, with one night at home together. If you've a job you couldn't go out that number of times, you wouldn't get everything done.'

'If I'm working he helps, it's only fair. We'll share the jobs, otherwise they won't be done.'

'Dear Steph, I'm afraid you're in for a shock. I've got friends whose husbands "help".' Peggy made the sign for inverted commas in the air. 'But some help – except only when they feel like it, and rarely anything done properly. My friends say it's easier to do everything themselves than to rely on *them*.'

'I think this is probably a generation thing, Mum. It'll be different for me.'

'Yes, dear. I expect so,' agreed Peggy so as not to hurt her daughter's feelings.

With the dishes cleared away, the kitchen worktops wiped down, breakfast laid and Steph working in her room, Peggy contemplated the evening ahead with satisfaction. She would have liked to read the new paperback novel she had bought last week and hadn't yet had time to start but made herself get out her Italian grammar books instead. She'd read the novel later, in bed, if Dan was late.

Before she settled to her study she turned on the TV and channel-hopped on the off-chance there was something she might want to watch. Her quick flicking through the programmes paused as on one channel she was just in time to see a Spurs player score a goal.

That was odd. She frowned. Dan must have made a mistake about which night they were playing. He was an avid Spurs supporter – he'd never have missed a match on TV.

Wednesday dawned bleak with bitter, lashing rain. Peggy was late and, even though she ran, missed her bus. The next one was crowded when it finally came and she had to stand the whole way into town.

The atmosphere at work was equally chilly since, it was soon apparent, Viv was not speaking to her. Peggy was mildly irritated by this and somewhat amused at how Viv, while not speaking, managed to make her presence felt with judicious sighing and huffing and puffing. Stupid woman, thought Peggy, as she picked up her yellow duster to buff up her crocodile leather bags.

At mid-morning, Viv, with no explanation, left the shop floor, which made Peggy late for her coffee break.

'I should have waited to get your coffee in. It must be stone cold by now,' Hazel fussed.

'It's not too bad.' Peggy sipped it.

'I got the paper.'

'Have you checked the numbers?'

'You've got the card.'

'Of course, silly me.' Peggy dug into her handbag and retrieved the large gold-coloured card. There was silence as she concentrated on the numbers. She sat back and looked astounded. 'Bloody hell, Hazel. We've got three more numbers!'

'I don't *believe* it. Let me see. Sure you've got it right?' Hazel held out her hand.

'Of course I haven't made a mistake. I'm not thick.' She laughed excitedly and on the strength of nine correct numbers she ordered two more coffees and threw caution to the wind by adding Danish pastries to the order.

'How's it work?' Hazel asked.

'I told you.'

'I've forgotten.'

'This week and half of next we've got to get three numbers a day right – twenty-seven in all. Then it changes to two for the following week and half which makes eighteen, and then the last five days one number, making fifty in all.'

'I wonder what the chances of winning are?'

'God knows.'

'And there's the one prize of a million?'

'Yes. Usually there are payouts during the competition. You know, if you get a straight line, that sort of thing. But this one hasn't.'

'It's a bit like bingo, then.'

'Exactly, only the card's much bigger.'

'Just think, Peggy, what would you do if we won?'

'Me? I haven't thought. It seems pointless to. But . . .' she paused ' . . . well, I'd get our Paul and Candice sorted out, clear his mortgage, set him up in a little business. Same for Sean and Carol, I suppose. I'd make sure Steph's education is secure. I'd get Dan a new car.' Her face was glowing with happiness at the game they were playing.

'What about yourself?'

'Heavens, I don't know. A month at a health farm.' She patted her hips good-naturedly. 'And then? I'd tell Viv what she could do with the crocodile and patent leather handbags and I'd find myself a nice cottage in the country, beamed and thatched. I'm a predictable sort. And you?'

'Oh, I'd probably blue the lot.'

Thursday was dry and the members of the bus queue even nodded to each other. As the Peugeot drove past, slowly this morning, the driver waved, or so it seemed. But then, Peggy told herself on the ride into town, he could have been scratching his nose.

She and Hazel didn't wait until the break to check the numbers, but did them the minute Hazel arrived. They had another three correct ones – twelve in all! Viv still didn't speak. The coffee break was spent mainly in planning Bruce's birthday party on Saturday.

'Would you do your guacamole dip for me? Yours is always better.'

'Of course. How many are coming?'

'I can't remember. I just keep asking people and then forgetting who I've asked and who I haven't. Probably about fifty.'

'Fifty! You'll never get them all in. And he's no idea?'

'None at all. Luckily, on Saturday he's out playing golf all day. We'll meet you and Dan in the pub as arranged. I'll leave the key with Jennie, and the food and booze. She and the others will whip all the stuff in while we're away.'

'How are we going to get back to the house without him getting suspicious?'

'I'll say I've forgotten something – my credit cards. That's it, I'll leave them and then say I can't pay for his slap-up meal without them.'

'Brill.'

She didn't see the car on Friday, but she didn't mind. They now had fifteen of the numbers and spent the coffee break trying to work out what percentage that meant – and failing.

Peggy felt excitement gnawing inside her, which she felt she should keep under control. It was stupid of her. The chances of them . . . Still, the dreams were so lovely, such fun to have.

She kept it all to herself, though. She didn't want Dan and Steph to know – there was no point in raising their hopes, too. One person disappointed in the family was enough.

Friday had its moments, mainly when Mrs Fox swept into the department, complaining loudly that the handbag Karen had sold her was faulty. Having to wait her turn agitated her further and she began to shout. Karen was hiding in the stockroom, Mary was lurking by Stockings, intent on not letting her customer go, and of Viv there was no sign. That left Peggy to absorb the outrage full frontal.

Peggy inspected the bag. There was nothing wrong with it that she could see but *Madam* insisted the clasp was faulty. Would *Madam* like to exchange it for another? *Madam* would not. Peggy would have bet money that would be the answer. *Madam* wanted a full cash refund. Peggy understood her game. She'd needed a new handbag for some do or other. By now she'd been to the function flashing the patent-leather, gold-chained, close-approximation of a Chanel bag to her friends and had no further need of it. Peggy handed her the refund and all she could do was grit her teeth. Company policy: where possible, the customer was always right even when you knew she was a lying, thieving, fraudulent bitch like Mrs Fox.

Friday evening Dan was out again, Steph had taken time off from school work and had gone to a disco, so Peggy cut her Italian class and made her dip for Bruce's party instead.

Dan was late and she was reading her Mary Higgins Clark paperback when he returned. 'You're mad, reading this late,' he said as he undid his tie.

'I can't put it down. I've been scaring myself witless with it. In any case, I wanted to be awake when you came back.' She giggled nervously and thought how silly she was after all these years together. 'Steph's sleeping over at Moraigh's. And I thought . . .' She moved languorously, she hoped, in the bed and stared suggestively, she also hoped, at her husband now in his underpants.

'You've got to be joking. I'm knackered,' he replied, as he climbed under the duvet, switched off his light and curled up, his back to her.

She placed her book neatly on the bedside table, turned off her light, and lay flat gazing wide-eyed at a ceiling she could not see. No, she had not been joking. She had meant it. She'd lied to him. She hadn't been reading all the time. She'd been lying there planning how to seduce him, how to get him to make love to her – it had been so long since he had. She hadn't meant to blurt it out quite so clumsily; she hadn't meant to be so coquettish – at her age it must have appeared grotesque. She should have been more patient, more subtle. But, oh, how she needed him to make love to her, to make her feel wanted, to reassure her she was still attractive. A single tear escaped her eye and slid silently down her cheek. She did not seem to notice as tear followed tear.

Chapter Five

In the morning, Saturday, Peggy was glad Dan was up and away before her. She would have been embarrassed to face him after her clumsy attempt at seduction the previous night. She had forgotten he'd said he had a car to fix, which he'd promised faithfully to do and hadn't been able to fit in during the week. An old couple living outside the city, he'd explained, who depended on their car to get their shopping – there was no doubt Dan was good-hearted to the elderly and needy.

She packed the dip for Bruce's party in a basket and left a note for Steph, asking her to pop into Tesco to do some shopping. She put two twenty-pound notes under the salt cellar and hoped it was enough. Even as she did so she remembered how much food forty pounds would have bought just five years ago and, not for the first time, wondered where it would all end.

Viv was speaking to her, which was a relief – if only a slight one. She kept an eye open for Hazel who was later than usual. By Peggy's coffee break there was still no sign of her, so she went to the canteen. There she checked their card with the numbers in the newspaper. They had another three correct. It was all she could do to stop herself cheering out loud. On the way back to her department she stopped at the Pompadour counter.

'She phoned in ill,' one of her assistants said.

'Ill? Today? Oh, no. What about the party?'

'I don't know anything about a party.'

'It's her husband's birthday.' Peggy could have kicked herself – Hazel never invited anyone from the shop other than herself. 'I don't want that lot knowing my ins and outs,' she'd explained one day to Peggy who, at the time, had thought it odd. What did it matter? And if she'd had a lovely modern home, all gleaming

42

parquet, picture windows and split levels like Hazel's, she'd want everyone to see it.

In the gift department she found the ideal present for Bruce: a decanter encased in a gilt and ornately tooled leather book. It was more than she had intended paying and not something she particularly liked. But then, she told herself, as she dithered over it, one bought a present that the recipient would like not what one wanted oneself, and she was certain Bruce would love it.

Saturday was the busiest day of the week and passed quickly as it always did – there wasn't time for clock-watching or even time to think of aching feet. As she cashed up it was to find that this Saturday was the highest turnover so far this year. That pleased her, though it often surprised her that after all these years she could still get worked up about takings that weren't going into her pocket.

Because she had Bruce's present and the basket to take to Hazel's she rang home to ask Dan to pick her up. Steph answered. He was still out, she told her mother, but she had got the shopping in.

A long bus ride later as she arrived at Hazel's house, which was in darkness, she could have kicked herself for not telephoning first. She still rang the bell but there was no response. She went next door.

'I've been expecting her,' Jennie said, inviting her in.

'Is she ill?'

'Ill? No. She looked all right as she left for work this morning.'

'She didn't turn up.'

'No? She probably felt like a day off.'

'Can I leave this here?' Peggy asked, feeling a whisper of irritation towards Hazel.

'More grub? Oh, great. Best put it in the kitchen with the rest.'

It was an uncomfortable, overcrowded two bus rides home from Hazel's and her mood was not improved by finding Dan still hogging the bathroom.

By a quarter to eight, miraculously, she was ready, if still flustered from the rush.

'How do I look?' She twirled round to show off her grey crêpe suit with its satin lapels and toning camisole.

'Is that new?' Dan asked.

'No,' she replied, exasperated. 'I wore this to Carol's wedding but then, feeling the way you do, I suppose you didn't notice what I had on.' She could feel the previous mild irritation begin to swell into anger at his male insensitivity.

'What's that mean?' he asked defensively.

'You know,' she said sharply, but not feeling any better for giving way to her aggravation.

'I don't.'

'Then think.' She shut her eyes as if blotting out last night's humiliation.

He shrugged his shoulders, then brushed at his sleeve, as if he did not care, as if he had no further interest in this exchange. She'd like to have said to him, shouted at him, '*Because you don't make love to me any more*', but she didn't say anything. His rejection had hurt her enough without her having to verbalize it as well and risk making even more of a fool of herself. What was the point? And by being angry with him she risked pushing him further away.

'Ready?' She flashed him a smile, a false one, but he seemed to accept it as genuine.

'At your disposal.' He bowed mockingly as Steph appeared in the open doorway.

'You look great, Mum. Just one thing . . .' Steph raced up the stairs two at a time and returned carrying a long turquoise silk scarf that Peggy had forgotten she owned. 'Needs a touch of colour, Mum, otherwise you look a bit washed out.' She knew her daughter meant well, but all the same she wished Steph would learn to be a little more tactful.

Hazel and Bruce were already in their local, the Bush and Nail, with drinks lined up on the faux marble-topped table in front of them, awaiting their arrival.

Hazel, dressed in a black velvet suit with a short skirt and a shiny black and white polka-dotted blouse with a cravat style neckline, looked wonderful. Her long black-stockinged legs were twined effortlessly one around the other like ivy clinging to a tree.

Peggy always envied her being able to do that, never sure if her own inability was caused by having plumper legs or shorter ones.

'Christ, Hazel, you look a bloody knockout,' Dan said, leaning over the table to kiss her – and holding on to her hand for longer than was strictly necessary, Peggy thought. Bruce kissed Peggy in welcome but nobody told her she looked great so she sat down, resigned to Hazel getting all the fuss as usual.

Bruce had on a new wig, which Peggy felt was a bigger mistake than the last one. At least that had been a believable brown shade whereas this was tinged with a russet colour which hadn't quite worked. Neither had the wig fitter's skills for it looked so incredibly wig-like that all Peggy could hope, for his sake, was that anyone seeing it might think that no one would wear a wig like that so it must be real, but she was doubtful. She was glad it was a reasonably calm night since even the faintest of breezes, she was sure, was likely to lift it off his head. Poor, vain Bruce, she thought, as she pressed the gaily wrapped gift into his hands.

'Oh, Peggy, you shouldn't have,' he said, with the satisfied expression of one who was very pleased she had.

'It's from both of us. Hope you like it. They'll change it if not – I checked.' Peggy knew she was burbling, but giving a present always made her nervous because she so wanted the recipient to like it.

'Wow, Peggy, how did you know? I've seen these and thought how super. Look at that, Hazel.'

'It's very nice,' Hazel replied in a tight little voice, and sat stiffly as if stopping herself from shuddering with displeasure at the gift. Peggy should have guessed Hazel would loathe it.

'Thanks, both of you. Right, another drink?' he asked.

Peggy, sipping her gin, watched the others joking with each other and thought how lucky they were to have such good friends. If the chips were down – totally, as opposed to the present almost – then she could rely on Hazel and Bruce to come galloping to the rescue. Okay, so Hazel had been thoughtless today, but no doubt she'd had her reasons and Peggy knew she was excited. Hazel always got over-excited at the prospect of a good party – it was normally one of her charms. No doubt she'd just forgotten and as soon as she saw Peggy's food laid out at home she'd be full of mortified apologies. She smiled at the punch-line of one of Bruce's shaggy-dog stories to which she hadn't been listening. Even though Bruce was a bastard to Hazel it was difficult not to like him. Success hadn't changed him one iota. He had the aura of a strong, dependable man, the sort she often thought she'd like to be close to if there was ever a war, knowing that he would cope. If he had a fault, apart from the awful wigs and his womanizing, she supposed it was that he could be a bit too noisy – as now, while he excitedly listed to Dan the presents he'd received, making everyone else in the pub look in his direction and not necessarily with a benign expression. That and his taste in clothes – he was always just a little too smart, a little too colour-coordinated for comfort. Smooth-looking bugger, Dan called him behind his back, but she was never sure if that wasn't jealousy talking.

'I wanted a shindig – it's not every day one gets to fifty, but Control here said no.' Bruce grinned at his wife.

'I just thought a quiet dinner with our best friends would be nicer.'

'And more suitable for an oldie – don't want you getting too frisky,' Dan teased from the comfort of his forty-eight years.

'Bugger off.' Bruce aimed a playful fist at him.

'I said to Peggy to get you a gold-plated zimmer frame, but she said it would be too expensive.'

'Oh, Dan!' Peggy joined uncertainly in the laughter.

'Peggy, you can be so thick at times. Dan's joking,' Hazel shrieked.

'Of course I *knew* he was,' Peggy said sharply. The unpleasant angry feelings of earlier in the evening were still lurking just under the surface. 'Where did you get to today, Hazel?' she asked, and knew she did so in an attempt to embarrass her.

'What do you mean?'

'Your assistant said you were ill.'

'Don't be silly. I told you. I said I was going to skive off. I'd things to do.' She arched her eyebrows meaningfully. 'And I went to the hairdresser's.'

'Oh, I see,' said Peggy, and wondered why she didn't believe her and why she was behaving in this rather unpleasant way.

46

'How did we do on the numbers?' Hazel asked pointedly, changing the subject. Peggy frowned at her. She hadn't wanted to discuss it with Dan around, but it was too late.

'What numbers?' he asked.

'In the *Daily Planet*. I wasn't going to say anything but we've got eighteen numbers up – three each day this week.'

Hazel squealed with simulated girlish excitement. 'Incredible!' she said, clapping her hands. 'You two had better pull your socks up! We could be on our way to winning a million and might just piss off and find ourselves a couple of toy-boys.'

'What's this?' asked Bruce. Hazel explained. 'Oh, sweetheart,' he said, his good-natured face creased with concern. 'I don't want to piss on your fireworks, but you're the fifth person today I've heard that from.'

'What? They've all got eighteen correct numbers?'

'That's right.'

'But we can't all win,' Peggy said miserably.

'Exactly, Peggy my love.'

'So how is it so many have the same numbers?'

'It's a con,' Hazel said angrily.

'No, it was on the news, didn't you hear? A cock-up at the printer's – all the same numbers have been printed on the cards.'

'No!' both women exclaimed in unison.

'What a disappointment,' said Peggy, and although she knew it was silly to have pinned any hopes on winning she felt cheated.

'You're not telling me you hoped to win something, Peggy?' Dan looked at her with amused disbelief.

'You do the pools,' she replied defensively.

'That's different.' He bridled.

'What's different about it? Don't they say you stand more chance of being murdered than striking it lucky?'

'You need skill to fill in the coupon.' Dan patted the side of his nose with his finger.

'Skill be blowed! You've used the same numbers for years, I know you have. At least Hazel and I have only wasted pennies, you lay out pounds,' Peggy said heatedly and, as she did, asked herself again why she felt so edgy tonight. Was it just the bingo in the paper? Unlikely, she was fairly realistic. Then what?

'Bloody hell! Guess what I've done?' Hazel was making a great fuss of emptying her handbag on to the pub table. 'Left my credit cards behind, that's all. We'll have to go home and fetch them.' She winked at Peggy who thought she had never seen such a useless bit of play-acting in her life.

'Some treat.' Bruce patted his jacket pocket. 'No need to worry, hen, I've got mine.'

'No, no. I said I'd pay and I will. We've got to go home.' Hazel was already on her feet and for once hadn't reacted to being called 'hen' which she usually did.

They travelled in convoy, or rather Dan succeeded in catching up with Bruce's powerful Jag when the car stopped at traffic lights.

'You're very touchy tonight, Peggy. Why?'

''Cause I feel like it,' she said shortly.

'It's not like you.'

'Probably not, but I am and that's that.'

'I was just interested. What brought it on all of a sudden?'

'Why can't I be a bit moody? Why do I always have to be a bloody equable saint? You have enough moods.'

'Oh, come on, Peggy, we're going to a party.'

'Yes, and what will happen? You'll get pissed down one end of the room and I'll stay sober at the other so I can drive us home. Great!'

'You don't like drink.'

'Who says? You, because it suits you.'

'Sorry I spoke,' he said, in an exaggerated imitation of Larry Grayson.

Peggy huddled into her coat and glowered in the half-light. This time instead of querying her frame of mind she relaxed and let the crabbiness wash over her. Everything had made her testy. For a start she didn't like parties, she never had but never quite had the courage to say to Dan, 'You go, I'll stay at home.' She hated the noise, the standing about, which always made her back ache, and the trying to be nice to total strangers she wouldn't meet again.

There was another reason for her moodiness, though, and one of which she was not proud. When she thought about it she felt childish and stupid. Peggy had realized the last few times when out with the husbands that she was becoming fed up with Hazel getting all the attention and compliments. It was quite ridiculous of her. It wasn't surprising things were as they were: Hazel *was* more attractive, more scatterbrained, more feminine than she was. Sometimes when she was with her friend Peggy felt totally colourless, as if she wasn't there. She dug her hands into her pockets. But, then, Hazel had more time, more money with which to make herself more feminine. She felt her cigarettes. She'd have liked one but Dan, like many reformed smokers, loathed anyone to smoke in his car.

They drew up outside Bruce's dark house, piled out of the car and walked up to the Jag.

'Don't be bloody daft! What's the point of us both getting out and freezing our nuts off?' Bruce said.

'Speak for yourself.' Hazel tittered. 'Oh, come on, Bruce, come with me. I hate going into an empty house.'

'Take Desperate Dan here – I'll keep the engine running.' Hazel looked at the others in desperation.

'Come on, Bruce old man. I'm gasping for a snort. How say we have one here before going on to the restaurant?' Dan suggested.

'Inspired idea, mate.' Bruce replied to everyone's relief, switching off the engine and slowly, it seemed to Peggy, swinging his legs out.

They tripped up the path in a crocodile. Bruce opened the front door and felt for the hall light. Nothing happened. 'Bloody bulb's gone. Hang on, I'll put the lounge light on.' His hand was outstretched when the door suddenly swung open. Light flooded into the hall.

'Surprise! Surprise!' forty voices shouted.

'Cor, bugger me.' Bruce grinned.

Chapter Six

As parties went – and this one was still going strong at three in the morning when they left – Peggy assumed it had been a success. Judging by the noise, the quantity of alcohol consumed, the amount of food demolished, it was a great success. As she had driven a befuddled and snoring Dan home, she had wondered how many of the other wives had enjoyed it since as far as she could see most of the men were drunk.

She had dragged him out before the end not because he could barely stand, was being a mite obstreperous, but because suddenly there was a lot of whispering and giggling.

'What's going on?' she asked Jennie, who was standing beside her.

'They're planning a key party,' Jennie replied, her eyes shining with excitement.

'What's that?' asked Peggy.

'Where you been?' Jennie laughed. 'The men throw their keys into the centre of the room and we women select a bunch and go off with whoever they belong to.'

This had frightened her rigid while at the same time fascinating her morbidly. All the years she'd lived in suburbia and she'd never even come close to a wife-swapping party. In the past she had heard rumours of them taking place, but that was all – just gossip and rumours. But this time, Peggy was sure it had been for real.

Half of her wanted to run in panic, but the other half, to her shocked horror, would have liked to stay. Only, she'd told herself, to see who got off with whom. But then, as she drove along through the deserted streets, she admitted to herself it was far more complicated than that. She'd found she liked the dark-haired quantity surveyor, Mark, who worked with Bruce. She had surreptitiously watched him most of the evening and would have been interested to find out who he'd ended up with. She felt a frisson of regret that it wasn't her. If she had been two stone lighter, without the spare tyre and the cellulite, she had a nasty idea she might, with the help of a stiff brandy, have stayed! At this idea her foot pressed down on the accelerator, she shot a red light and raced at speed for home and safety, away from such wicked demons.

Ten frustrating minutes later she gave up trying to wake Dan, who had slumped even further in the car seat so that most of him was now on the floor. She garaged the car, banged the door with annoyance and went to bed.

The following morning she awoke to find Dan beside her, asleep, naked except for his socks. She sat up in bed, clutching her nightdress to her, looked down at him and experienced a dreadful rush of guilt. How could she have had such thoughts last night? Even thinking such a thing was, to her, almost as bad as actually doing it. She felt sick to her stomach.

Quietly she got up, dressed, went down to the kitchen and made herself tea. With a cigarette in her hand she sat drinking it, more miserable, more guilty and sick with every passing minute. What had got into her? First the man in the car and now the unsuspecting surveyor. A 'hiccup' in her sex life with Dan and she was leering at other men. She didn't often give sex much thought these days, apart from the occasional regret that it was so infrequent, but when sexually active she had never given another man a second glance, let alone fantasized about him. Fantasize! She shuddered. That was the word, though. She had read in magazines that women fantasized in the same way as men; that when making love to one man it was quite common to pretend it was someone else, like Tom Cruise. She never had, not once. And even if she had, it wouldn't have been Tom Cruise. Steph was always teasing her that she never had the vaguest idea who the film stars were these days. To Peggy they all looked the same.

'Not like James Mason or Dirk Bogarde or Gregory Peck. You never mistook them for each other – they all looked different.'

'No, they don't. I can never tell one from the other,' Steph had said, and Peggy had marvelled at discovering yet another difference in the generations.

She spooned some more sugar in her mug. Odd how your mind fluttered about this way and that when you let it. She idly stirred the tea, the spoon clinking against the china. She frowned – she'd got a headache, a nasty one, she must have drunk more than she thought. Instead of depressing her this thought cheered her. *That* would explain a lot.

The problem was, she gazed pensively out of the window, how could she face Hazel? How could she look her in the eye? How could they ever be the same again, with Peggy knowing what shenanigans they'd got up to last night?

Shenanigans. One of her mother's favourite words. Just thinking of Myrtle made everything seem worse again. Hell! She could just imagine *her* reaction to last night. Myrtle didn't approve of sex at the best of times and would have been much happier in a world without it.

'Pity we can't lay an egg, none of that nastiness,' she'd often been overheard saying.

There was much about Myrtle that Peggy, if she was totally honest, didn't like, and yet she always felt guilty when she admitted this, even though it was only ever to herself. Myrtle said they were close but Peggy was none too sure. Peggy tried to please but nothing she did was ever quite right for her mother. There was a sharpness, an edge to her, which when alone with Peggy was always present but which disappeared when they were with others. If Peggy had complained, no one would have known what she was going on about.

Everyone else loved Myrtle and said what a sweet old dear she was. What a perfect grandmother, who always had time for the children and a secret store of sweeties for them and jelly on the table whenever they came to tea. But Peggy knew of another, hidden, side to her mother. She was a woman who considered life had been unfair to her, and continued to be. But she did not overtly complain. She hinted, she sighed, she apologetically suggested when she needed things. Peggy thought her manipulative and sly. The only other person who had seen through Myrtle was Peggy's father and he was long since dead.

Peggy much preferred her mother-in-law, Jean, who was easy-going and open. She rarely wanted or needed anything, but if she did she didn't beat about the bush but asked outright if it was possible. Her house was lived-in and welcoming. She never said a bad word about anyone, always seeing the good, reasoning why people behaved the way they sometimes did. The nearest Jean had got to being nasty was when she told Myrtle that her daughter had christened her first-born Willow.

'Odd thing, naming a child after a tree,' Myrtle had said, somewhat sniffily.

'Better than being called after a bush,' Jean had snapped back promptly, and that was the closest to being bitchy anyone had ever heard her be.

It was a cause of much guilt to Peggy – yet another wodge of the stuff which seemed to clog up her entire system – that whereas she'd be quite happy to look after Jean, should she become ill, she would be only too happy to shove her own mother into a home. Now, was that natural?

But even Jean with her logical fair-mindedness and her somewhat ribald sense of humour, would, Peggy knew, have had difficulty in accepting last night's shenanigans. Still, it was a lovely word.

'What a pleasant surprise. What have I done to deserve this?' Dan asked when, five minutes later, she took him a tray of tea and toast.

'You looked sweet lying there asleep.'

'I thought I was in for a good old bollocking after last night. Sorry I disgraced you, Peggy.'

'Oh, you didn't, most of the men were smashed out of their minds,' she said stalwartly, determined to minimize the goings-on at the party.

Dan shook his head and immediately regretted it. 'Christ, what got into me?'

'It was those stupid champagne cocktails they were serving – I'd said to Hazel they were fatal.'

'Did anything, you know, funny-like happen?' Dan looked intently at her as he gingerly sipped his tea, having confessed he wasn't quite up to the toast.

'What do you mean?' she asked, picking up and nibbling at a

piece, which she hadn't meant to, determined, after feeling such a lump last night, to get down to some serious dieting.

'Well, those cocktails, they were intentional, Bruce told me. He wanted everyone to get pissed out of their skulls.'

'Bruce? But he didn't even know he was going to have a party.'

'Of course he did,' Dan scoffed. 'Hazel couldn't keep it secret.'

'Then why did she pretend she had?' She moved uneasily on the bed as if her thoughts were making her physically uncomfortable. What was Hazel's game? Why do one thing and pretend another? She felt foolish with the two of them aware that Bruce knew about the party when she was not. It made her feel left out, not part of the circle.

'Search me.' Dan carefully placed his cup and saucer on the bedside table. 'Anyhow, did they do it? The keys?'

'You knew?' Momentarily she felt sick. How could he have taken her there, knowing what was to happen? She was pretty certain that had she been aware of the plans she would have refused to go. 'You knew . . . And you still . . . took me there?' Peggy sat bolt upright on the bed, almost unable to speak from hurt feelings combined with a touch of indignation. 'That's bloody disgusting.' Indignation had triumphed over hurt. She slapped the toast back on the tray.

'Oh, come on, Peggy, it was just for a laugh.'

Peggy jumped off the side of the bed. 'And who were you hoping would pick up your keys? Eh? Answer me that. Hazel, was it? Was that who you were hoping for?' She stopped, shocked. Her words had taken her by surprise. Why should she have said that? Why Hazel? And then suddenly, like fog lifting, she felt she was staring the truth in the face. Of course. How stupid she had been! How blind. When he went out so often, was it to her? When he went to mend a friend's car, was it an excuse to see her?

'Peggy, honest, I didn't think any of them would go through with it.'

He was lying, she was sure he was. She was shaking now, angry, disillusioned. 'It didn't stop you hoping they would, did it? And what about me? Did you hope I'd refuse? Or didn't you care if I went off with another bloke?' Peggy was shouting, standing with hands on hips, hurt making her look belligerent. 'God, you

make me sick – *men* make me sick! Why can't you all grow up?'
And she stormed from the room slamming the door as she went,
unaware that the crack in the ceiling widened just a fraction.

Peggy thundered down the stairs. In the hall she grabbed her
coat and as she struggled into it, searched for the car keys, which
she found on the sideboard. The front door crashed behind her as
did the car door. Slamming doors was supposed to be a satisfying
experience. It wasn't she found, merely noisy.

She had not finished with noise yet for she over-revved the
engine and then grated the gears, searching for reverse, before she
juddered backwards into the road. The car straightened up, she
put her foot down and roared up the road, making net curtains
twitch on every side.

She drove furiously and dangerously until she found herself
out on the by-pass. A narrow miss with a juggernaut was as
sobering to her anger as a bucket of iced water and she slowed
down to a reasonable speed. She could not go back, not yet, that
was for certain – a right fool she would look. If one was going
to make a scene one had best make a good one. She drove to the
local National Trust property, the grounds of which were open.
She parked the car and walked for some time in the gardens,
whose plants were starched by winter.

Would they manage without her? It was Jean's turn to come
to lunch: would anyone think to go and pick her up or would
they put her off? Who would cook? Carol should have been able
to but Peggy very much doubted if she could or would. Steph
might have a stab. She hoped they didn't try to do it together: it
would only end in them rowing. These thoughts she found quite
cheering – she would be missed, for once she would not be taken
for granted. *Did* they take her for granted? Is that what she really
thought? They always thanked her nicely enough but sometimes
she had to admit it was as if it was done on some sort of verbal
auto-pilot. She sat huddled on a bench watching the ducks on the
elegant ornamental lake. These thoughts occupied her, keeping at
bay the others, which she did not want to contemplate. Despite
herself she began to think about Dan and Hazel. In her mind's
eye she saw them together . . . Suddenly she stood up and began
to walk purposefully towards the car park. She knew what she

would do. She'd drive a little further and she'd treat herself to a Sunday lunch out.

Peggy finally decided on the Blue Pig, a liberally horse-brassed pub on the outskirts of town. It had once been a comfortable slightly shabby, but traditional pub until the brewery had mistakenly decided to tart it up and ruin it. She ordered a gin and tonic, and found a seat at a corner table. Muzak seeped from a speaker above her head. Soulful, sentimental, violin-dominated sounds certain to make even the happiest soul doleful. She looked around the crowded room, full of families congregating for a pint and Sunday lunch, half-heartedly trying to control over-excited children, and suddenly felt lonely.

She sipped at her drink and shuddered: spirits on an empty stomach were not a good idea. She scooped up a handful of peanuts and munched them quickly to give her stomach a chance and then lit a cigarette, inhaled deeply and immediately felt so dizzy she found herself hanging on to the table for support. She stubbed out the cigarette quickly and wondered what was wrong with her. That had never happened before. Was she ill? Was it nerves? Under the table she felt surreptitiously for her pulse: she was no expert but it felt steady enough. Perhaps she could again blame having had no food. She lit another cigarette apprehensively, but this time nothing happened. She was relieved – she might be planning to give up smoking but now was not the ideal time.

So much was going on, so much that was new. Why had she made that accusation about Hazel to Dan? It had never crossed her mind before that they even fancied each other. 'No.' She shook her head, unaware of a little boy who watched her with interest. 'No,' she said, and the little boy tugged at his mother's jacket and pointed out the funny lady talking to herself. Embarrassed, the woman dragged away her son. Hazel was her best friend, she wouldn't do anything like that with Dan, just as Peggy wouldn't try anything on with Bruce. Still, that was easy to say – she didn't fancy Bruce. But maybe Hazel did fancy Dan! Peggy was always the first to admit how attractive Hazel was for a woman of her age. Why, she was even proud of her friend and the way she looked. Had she fallen into the trap of so many married women of being too smug, too confident of their relationship even to think that it could be threatened? If she faced it square on, wasn't she the last person to be that confident? Dan didn't fancy her any more. Even though until now she had been blaming herself, she'd also been half blaming their age, presuming Dan's libido was slowing down. But was it? Maybe he didn't make love to her because he couldn't – because he was too 'knackered' from doing it with someone else.

Peggy shivered and clutched her heavy coat to her in the overheated room. She downed the rest of her drink in one and, without stopping to think if she should have another, wove her way through the crowds to the bar.

'You eating?' the barman asked brusquely, as he sloshed in the tonic water.

'Maybe,' she replied uncertainly.

'Make your mind up quickly. We fill up fast. Want a dekko at the menu?' He held out his hand for her money.

'Thanks.' She took the maroon leather folder with a heavily embossed gold pig on the front and, drink in her other hand, excused and sorried her way back through the throng to her table. On it lay her handbag. Her heart jumped into her mouth – she'd never done anything as silly as that, ever, she thought, as she quickly checked the contents and, with relief, found everything still there. She'd been lucky. She opened the menu and began to read ... Of course, she'd been stupid about other things, too. How many times a week did Dan go to the snooker hall these days? He'd never spent much time there before. And he was always out helping people with their cars. Still, he'd always done that, if the car was an old one and interested him. But, then, a whole day to help one couple? And wasn't it odd that it should coincide with the day when Hazel didn't turn up for work? She felt blind panic rising within her.

'You ready to order?'

Peggy looked up vaguely at the blue-skirted waitress with a jacket like a guardsman. What had that to do with Blue Pigs? she thought irrelevantly.

'Yes, thanks, I—'

'You need more time? We're filling up fast.' The waitress's toe was tapping.

'I'll have the beef.'

'Starter?'

'No, thanks.'

'You have to, it's in the price.'

'All right, then.'

'Well, what?'

'What is there?'

'Pâté de chef, fruit juice, smoked mackerel, prawn cocktail, soup de—'

'Orange juice.'

'Pudding?'

'I don't know if I want pudding.'

'It's in the price.'

'Can't I decide when I've had my beef?'

'Nope.'

'Well . . .'

'Apple pie with or without custard, ice cream, vanilla, strawberry, chocolate chip, chocolate mousse,' the waitress recited, eyes glazed with boredom.

'Vanilla ice cream.'

'Table two, five minutes.'

'Thanks.' She sagged in her seat and remembered that this was what she had longed for: the Sunday lunch in the rural pub she had dreamed about. It wasn't what she had expected – she felt pressured, as if she was on a conveyor belt of lunchers. She did not know why she'd ordered lunch, was unsure if she wanted to eat, or even if she could.

Fifteen minutes later she knew she could not. The orange juice had been all right but faced with the large plate of roast beef, stodgy Yorkshire pudding, unsatisfactorily roasted potatoes, frozen peas and Brussels sprouts, all covered with a thick custard-like gravy and jockeying for position on the plate, she knew it had been a mistake. She stood up abruptly, leaving her money on the table, and quickly left the noisy restaurant.

It was a relief to be outside in the cool air, of which she took huge gulps before getting back into the car. Coffee, she needed coffee. The gins had made her woozy and the orange juice slopping about in her stomach was not helping. The two coffee shops she knew of were closed. Then she thought of the station. The buffet would probably be open.

It was. She sat for some time over a coffee and a Danish pastry, which her stomach was grateful for. Maybe she was overreacting and being stupid. Maybe she had been hung-over and therefore over-sensitive this morning. She hoped so – she hated feeling like this, empty and frightened as she'd never been before in her life.

On the way out she stopped at Smith's, bought a couple of newspapers, splashed out on *Interiors* magazine. She enjoyed frittering the money away – it made her feel better, doing something she would never normally do. She walked quickly across the concourse towards the automatic doors, but paused in her step when she saw the instantly recognizable blue and white fingers-crossed logo of the lottery company.

'Come on, love, take your chance, save a stately home,' the young man in charge called cheekily to her. *'It could be you.'*

Why not? thought Peggy, delving for her purse. 'Maybe I will.'

'Good on yer. Someone's gotta win, after all.'

'Yes, and why not me?'

'How much are you going to spend, then?'

'Twenty pounds.' She laughed at her recklessness. She took the cards he handed her to the small desk and began to fill them in. The first card was easy to fill using a combination of the birthdays and ages of her family members. It was harder after that to think up numbers with a particular relevance and soon she was filling them in at random.

'You should win something with that lot,' the man said, as he began to slip her coupons into the computer terminal.

'I sincerely hope so,' she replied, not feeling quite as confident as she parted with twenty pounds.

Chapter Seven

The following day, Peggy was polishing the dining table vigorously as if it had to be punished. She was working hard in an effort to blank out the previous day. If she kept moving and concentrating on chores, hopefully the memory of a day she could not regard as an unmitigated success might be kept in check. But she failed . . .

Peggy had returned from the railway station to a sulky brood still sitting around the debris of their lunch. From the silence that ensued at her appearance she could only presume they'd been talking about her.

'Hello,' she said from the doorway, somewhat inanely. 'How was the joint?' she added. 'I'm—'

'Where the hell have you been?' Dan asked angrily which, since the words of apology for her absence had been on the tip of her tongue, was a tactical error.

'Out,' she said, shortly.

'Evidently.' Dan sneered more than spoke.

'We were worried sick, Mum,' Steph said, beginning to stack their pudding bowls.

'I'm sorry about that, Steph. There was no need. I just popped out. I felt I needed . . .' Her voice trailed off. She needed what? But whatever it was, was her business and nobody else's. So she set her mouth firmly to stop herself explaining anything to anyone.

'Would you like something to eat?' Carol asked, standing up and turning towards the sideboard on which stood the remains of the joint, its fat already beginning to congeal and look unappetizing.

'No, thank you, I've had lunch,' she half lied.

'Where?' Dan was standing now, his large hands flat on the table, head jutting forward aggressively.

'The Blue Pig, if you must know.'

'And who with?' Dan blustered.

Peggy stared at him long and hard, unaware that everyone else in the room was holding their breath. 'Really, Dan, don't be so ridiculous.' She clutched her newspapers tightly to her chest, head held high, and walked from the room and into the lounge.

The cheek of it, she thought, as with one foot she kicked the door shut. Trying to put her in the wrong like that. She took off her coat and folded it over the back of a chair. She eased off her shoes, twiddling her toes with relief – those shoes pinched – sank back into the corner of the large, soft white four-seater sofa they had bought last year in Leatherland and which she knew, in her heart of hearts, looked completely wrong in this room. She flicked through the sections of her newspaper searching for the colour supplement. Idly she turned the pages but could find nothing of interest. It was full of arty photographs of people she'd never heard of and, judging by their looks, didn't want to know.

With the remote control she put on the television, which, with the sofa, seemed to dominate the room, and pressed buttons hoping for a black and white movie, Bette Davis preferably. When she didn't find one she switched off and sat gazing into space, wishing the others would go and that Dan would come and talk to her.

Carol and Sean popped their heads round the door. 'We'll be off then, Mum.'

'Have you helped Steph clear up?'

'She's all right.'

'She's not all right, Carol, she's got homework to do. You help her for a change.'

'What does that mean?'

'What I've said.'

'You implying I don't help?'

'I don't *have* to imply.'

'Well, that's a relief.' Carol flounced from the room, and Peggy sighed over her poor, dim daughter.

'You all right, Mum?' Sean asked diffidently.

'Yes, I'm fine. I just felt like a bit of a break.'

'We should all do that from time to time.'

'Yes, Sean, we should, shouldn't we?'

'You all right, Mum?' It was Steph's turn.

'I do wish you'd all stop talking to me as if I had an illness.'

'We're not used to you doing a runner, Mum,' Steph said. 'Did you and Dad have a row?'

'I wouldn't call that a row. A bit of a raised voice, that was all.' Peggy was quiet for a minute. 'Did your grandmother come?'

'No. Dad put her off.'

'How is he?' she asked, as nonchalantly as possible.

'He's gone out. Says he's going to fix somebody's car,' Steph replied.

'Again! Bloody marvellous,' exclaimed Peggy, and wished she had a large box of chocolates to wade through.

It was late evening and she was in bed, unsuccessfully trying to read, when he returned. She lay in bed listening to the familiar noises of Dan shutting up the house, noises which, normally, made her feel comfortable and safe as he put the cat out, followed by the milk bottles. She heard the sound of the bolts on the front door slamming shut and Dan resetting the central heating timer, which was wonky and had to be helped manually. She could hear him checking the catches on the windows, putting the guard in front of the fire, clicking off the lights, and the noise of his heavy tread on the stairs. She lay rigid, almost afraid to see him and angry with herself for that – *she'd* done no wrong. She waited for the door to open, but it didn't. Instead she heard him rootling in the linen cupboard next to the bathroom, heard the plop of linen fall, a soft curse and then Dan padding back down the stairs. She could imagine him huffing and puffing as he made up a bed on the sofa in the lounge.

Not used to rowing, Peggy was at a loss what to do. Should she go and say sorry, tell him not to be so silly? She was half out of bed when she decided against it. Why should she? Let him sulk. She puffed up the duvet round her. It wasn't she who had been paralytic. Not her who had known all about the keys-in-the-circle plan and done nothing about it. It wasn't her who was in the wrong.

Angrily she thumped her pillow. She felt guilty just because of a fleeting moment of attraction towards the dishy quantity surveyor. A thought, that was all. Surely a thought could not be so wrong? It didn't mean anything – or did it? She loved Dan, no one else. What was it she wanted, then? She twisted about in the bed trying to find somewhere new to lie as if that would help her escape these unwelcome thoughts.

Perhaps in the morning she'd cook him a fry-up. He'd like that. She'd do it, not to say sorry but to get him in the sort of mood so that they could talk and iron out a few problems.

She thumped her pillow again for good measure, sank back on it and felt happier. But then – like a bucket of ice water – a new idea came. Where the hell had he been all this evening?

In the morning Peggy overslept. Dan had left for work. An unresolved row, she decided, was an unpleasant thing to be carrying around with her, hence the little house was on the receiving end of a cleaning it would remember for a long time. Peggy felt wretched. She hadn't slept at all well but had lain in the dark mulling over the past few months, Dan's constant absences from home, putting two and two together and reaching some nasty conclusions, which ensured that the windows on the ground floor were cleaned until they sparkled like crystal. God, she'd been such a fool. If only she'd been less smug she'd have seen the writing on the wall a hell of a lot sooner. What a bloody fool she was! The woodwork in the sitting room was swiftly wiped down as she muttered angrily to herself.

So, what was she to do? Peggy sat back on her haunches as she wrung out her sponge into the dirty water in the bright yellow bucket. What *could* she do?

Kick him out? Where would that leave her? Half a house which, in any case, wouldn't be half a house once the mortgage was paid back. And half of this wouldn't buy her a rabbit hutch the way house prices had soared since they'd bought it.

What would she live on? Even if the courts gave her an allowance it wouldn't be much, not now, not with the kids grown-up. There was Steph, of course, but anything she got for her would go to her – she'd be needing it. There was no way she could survive in this house on what she earned at the shop. Take in a lodger? She supposed she could, though she hated the idea. Maybe she'd be better off in a small flat, just her and Steph. Could she afford even that? What about the council? Maybe she should put her name down. Oh, *why* had they blown all that money on Carol's wedding and taken on the overdraft? If they hadn't she'd have had a nest egg to fall back on.

She could feel panic and desolation building inside her. That this should happen to her! After all this time! All she'd ever been was a good wife and mother. It was so unfair, so bloody unfair. She clutched the damp sponge to her breast, and a great moan escaped from her and echoed round the empty room. She felt so frightened, so alone.

The doorbell rang.

Peggy jumped and dropped the sponge, got quickly to her feet and in her haste almost kicked over the bucket of filthy water. She ran her fingers through her hair. She must look a mess. Who could it be? She tiptoed along the hall, shaking as she put up her hand to open the door. Not once had it crossed her mind to leave whoever was there to ring and go away – she was too polite to do that.

'Peggy, love, got time for a coffee?'

'Hazel!' She wanted to slam the door in her face, had every right to do so. 'Come in,' she said, holding it wide and apparently welcomingly.

'When you didn't call for a good old natter about the party as you always do . . .'

'I was going to drop you a notelet.'

'Yes, well, that would be nice. But then I thought I should see you.'

'Of course.' She led the way along the hall.

'We've got things to talk about.'

'Yes,' Peggy said limply.

'Things to put straight.'

'We have?' She felt her heart plummeting even further when she thought it had fallen as far as it could. 'Do you want tea?'

'No, no, nothing like that. Got an ashtray?' In one fluid movement Hazel had sat down, wound her legs elegantly around each other, opened her handbag, put a cigarette to her mouth and flicked a gold lighter.

'You don't smoke,' Peggy stated, as she placed a large crystal ashtray on the coffee table in front of her.

'I do now.' Hazel laughed, a deep, throaty and very sexy chuckle, which angered Peggy. It was all right for her to laugh! 'Want one? Aren't they elegant? See, got my initials on. Did you know you can have your own cigarettes done that way? Costs a mint, of course.' She sucked deeply on the cigarette as if she were a long-term opium addict.

'How long's this been going on?' asked Peggy, meaning the smoking.

'Weeks. I'm amazed you hadn't twigged,' replied Hazel, meaning something else.

'I can usually smell it. Perhaps my hooter's packing in along with everything else,' she said dismally.

'Smell it? Hooter? Peggy, my sweet, what are you going on about?'

'Your smoking.'

'Oh, that,' Hazel squealed girlishly and tapped her ash towards the large ashtray, missed by a good three inches but apparently did not notice as it fell on the carpet. Good, thought Peggy, she needs specs too. It was a measure of comfort, if not much. 'Have you got a drink? I'm gasping for one, especially if this is Confession Time.' Hazel exaggerated the last two words.

'I think I've a bottle of white wine.'

'Super.' Hazel kicked off her shoes, curled up on the sofa and looked a picture instead of the lump Peggy became when sitting in that position.

Peggy went into the kitchen to collect the wine, glasses and a corkscrew and allowed herself to seethe with rage. What a cheek! And what a wimp she was being, not giving Hazel a piece of her mind. She would! She clattered the glasses onto the Ratner's silver-plated tray, which she rarely used nowadays after the hurtful remarks made by Ratner's chairman. But she'd nothing else and, the way she felt about Hazel right now, it was all she deserved.

'Look, Hazel, I'd like to say a thing or two. I'd like things out in the open.'

'Of course you would. You're upset about it, I knew you would be.'

'Of course I'm bloody upset.'

'I warned Bruce, I said it was going too far, that you'd hate it.' Hazel stretched out her hand, her expression serious and took Peggy's. Peggy snatched it away as if she was being contaminated. 'Peggy, love, what is it? Please don't be this cross, this upset. It was a stupid game, that was all.'

'A game?' Peggy snorted with derision.

'Well, not even that, really. Nothing happened. Nothing at all.'

'Nothing?' Peggy was puzzled.

'No, everyone was too pissed. There wasn't a man there who could get a hard-on – well, there was one,' she amended almost secretively. 'But there you are, no one else could. Everyone just collapsed in giggles. The party folded soon after you'd gone.'

'The keys? You're talking about the keys.'

'Yes, that's right. What did you think I was talking about? Are you ever going to open that wine? I'm dying of thirst here.'

'Sorry,' Peggy said, reeling with confusion as she attempted to operate the corkscrew which was not easy given the way she was shaking.

'Here, let me. Peggy, what is it? What's got into you?' Hazel asked, as she took the bottle from Peggy who relinquished it with no resistance.

Peggy put her hands to her face. The tears she'd held back, dammed by the anger she'd been feeling towards Hazel and Dan, burst free and she began to cry. But, not being used to crying, not knowing how, she made an ugly rasping noise as the tears flowed and she gulped for air.

'Heavens above! What's happened? Look, have some wine. Have a hanky. What's going on?' Hazel drummed her fists on her knees with frustration.

'I need to know,' Peggy choked out, the words broken up between sobs.

'Anything, darling. Ask away.'

'It's Dan—' Peggy felt bile rising in her throat.

'Yes?'

'And you—'

'Me?'

'Is it true?' She tried to swallow as the bile seeped into her mouth.

'Is what true?'

'Are you ... you know ... are you and he ... No!' Peggy slapped her hand to her mouth. 'I can't say it.' She tried not to gag.

'Say what, love? What are you trying to ask me? Are Dan and I having an affair?'

Mute and miserable, Peggy nodded.

'Oh, sweetheart, what an idea! Whatever or whoever put such a notion into your head?' She was laughing so much that tears began to roll down her cheeks, but tears of a different calibre.

'Is it true?'

'Would I lie? You think I'm a liar?' She wiped her eyes with her hanky. 'Oh, Peggy, honestly, what do you secretly think of me? What sort of person do you take me for? Come on, calm down, do.'

But Peggy couldn't calm down. First, she had to apologize for thinking the way she had of her best friend, of all people. She was happy, elated almost that it wasn't Hazel, but the euphoria lasted only a minute.

'Well, if it's not you, who is it, then?'

Chapter Eight

Peggy's words seemed to hang in the air. 'Who?' she repeated. 'Who's he doing it with?' She still could not bring herself to say that one dreadful word – *affair*.

'Are you sure? Dan? I can hardly believe it.'

'What else am I to think? He's always out these days. Why, last Saturday he disappeared for the whole day, some cock-and-bull story about mending an old couple's car.'

'Oh, that was true, he did. I heard him talking to Bruce about it, but then he started talking about sumps and things and my attention wandered.'

Peggy was not nearly as relieved as such news should have made her. 'There's something else. It's difficult. I mean, I don't think I can explain even to you.' Peggy's eyes darted about wildly, and she wished she hadn't even said that.

'Sex?' Hazel said.

'How did you know?'

'It always comes down to sex. If the sex is fine there's rarely any problem. With a good sex life anything is surmountable. I tell you, all marriage break-ups start in the bed – it stands to reason.'

'He doesn't want me,' Peggy said miserably.

'I'm sure that's not true.'

'Well, not as often.'

'There you are, then. Maybe he's just slowing up. Perhaps he's worried about something and that's upsetting his libido. It happens to men, you know. It's not you – look at you, you're still an attractive woman.'

'Oh, come off it, Hazel. Don't fib. I'm fat, my hair's a mess, I'm boring.'

'My, my, don't we hate ourselves this afternoon?' Hazel's tone was kind. 'I never think of you as being overweight.'

'It's all right for you. You never think about weight, probably. No need to.'

'I know I'm lucky, but I'm sure you're not nearly as fat as *you* think you are. But if you begin to think you're unattractive, then I promise you, you'll start to look it.'

'Thanks a bunch.' Peggy freed a laugh, but knew that every word her friend said was true.

'Why don't you—'

'Oh, Hazel, for God's sake, don't even say it! I'll scream!'

'So what was I going to say?'

'You were going to suggest I went and had my hair done, bought a new dress and made a special dinner.'

'So what's wrong with doing that? It's what I'd do. Men are suckers for the candlelight and sloppy music technique.'

'It's not me, though, is it? I mean, he'd immediately be suspicious. He'd probably think I'd done something wrong and was busy distracting him.'

'Then *make* it you.'

'Why should I do something so false? It's not me who's up to tricks. It's him,' Peggy said indignantly.

'True.' Hazel lit another cigarette. 'But are you certain? I still can't believe it.' She shook her head. 'I mean, good old Dan, he's straight as a die. Dependable. Always the same. No, I'm sure you're mistaken.'

'God, I hope you're right. I didn't twig for ages but then, when I suddenly thought, everything seemed to slot into place and so neatly.'

'Ah, well, then, he isn't. Nothing ever slots in neatly when an affair's in the offing. I know.'

'Of course you do,' said Peggy sympathetically, remembering the times without number when she'd consoled Hazel over Bruce's misdemeanours.

'No, I didn't mean Bruce,' Hazel said. 'I meant me.'

'You?'

'Yes. I've done it at last. Forget Dan, it's me. I'm having an affair.'

69

'Since when?'

'Three months.'

'I never knew.'

'Exactly.' Hazel winked at her.

'Well I'm blowed. Who?'

'Did you see a rather dishy bloke at the party? Quiet, tall, dark, horn-rimmed specs?'

'Mark someone . . .'

'North. That's him. Lovely bum.'

'But he said he was a quantity surveyor. That means he works for Bruce.'

'That's right.'

'That's awful.'

'What's awful about it?'

'It's disloyal.'

Hazel shrieked with laughter. 'Peggy, you're a scream. When the old pheromones react there's no loyalty or disloyalty. You just go for it.'

'I'm sorry. I can't agree. I know Bruce has been unfair to you . . . but all the same . . .' Peggy pulled a face. 'It's tacky.'

'Life's tacky, my sweet. Or haven't you learnt that yet? If not, bully for you,' she said, quite sharply. 'Any more wine going?'

Peggy filled her friend's glass and, seeing that her reaction had upset her, thought it best to change the topic of conversation.

'By the way, now the bingo thing in the newspaper is out I bought some lottery tickets. Want to go halves?'

'Sure, how much?' Hazel opened her handbag.

'Well, I'm afraid I went a bit mad. I spent twenty quid.' Peggy winced as she remembered her rashness.

'*How* much? Have you gone bonkers?' Hazel shut her handbag smartly.

'I *felt* bonkers. I bought them yesterday. I suppose I wasn't thinking straight.'

'It'll have to wait, I haven't got a tenner on me,' Hazel said briskly, and Peggy thought that must be the first time she'd ever known Hazel short of cash.

'No hurry. In any case, give me a fiver if you think it's too much or a quid, I don't mind. We won't win, anyway. Where are you and Bruce going for your holiday this summer?' she asked to keep her mind off other things.

Hazel stayed another half-hour and they talked of this and that, Peggy preferring now to skirt all talk of emotional entanglements. After she'd gone Peggy went into the kitchen and opened the freezer, contemplating what to cook for supper. Maybe Hazel was right: maybe she should make a bit of an effort. Tonight would be ideal: they were alone – Steph had gone to Anglesey on a field trip and wouldn't be back until Wednesday.

She felt wired up and ridiculously shy as the time approached for Dan to return from work. She'd washed and blow-dried her hair twice before she was satisfied with the effect. She made up carefully and took ages to decide on a pair of black velvet trousers and a long crêpe blouse that covered her waist and hips most satisfactorily.

During all these preparations she had decided she was going to ask him. Outright. It was the only way. They'd never had secrets. Their marriage had been based on their openness with each other . . . until just recently. The sex thing they hadn't been able to talk about – sex was always difficult to get to grips with – but all that was going to change.

At the sound of his key in the lock, Peggy's heart fluttered. She giggled to herself: she was acting like a teenager.

'What's the celebration?' Dan asked from the dining-room door as he watched her trying to fix a candle into a holder that was too big for it. His presence made her feel all fingers and thumbs and she dropped the pretty pink candle on to the table, cracking it. 'Sorry, did I make you jump?'

'No, just me being clumsy,' she stammered.

'So what's the big occasion?'

'Us,' she said simply.

'That's nice.' He stepped into the room.

'I missed you last night.' She looked down at the candle, not at him.

'That sofa's bloody noisy to sleep on. It made farting noises every time I moved.'

'I warned you about that when we bought it,' she said reprovingly.

'Peggy, don't let's be so stupid again.' He was beside her now and tentatively put up his hand to stroke a strand of her newly washed hair. 'You look nice.'

'Thanks.' She was blushing. She could hardly believe it. She turned to face him. 'I love you, Dan.'

'Me too.' His arms were round her, holding her tightly to him. 'I'm sorry I was bad-tempered.'

'I'm sorry I swanned off like that without saying where I was going.'

'That's all right, then. I've hated today, it felt odd – you and me quarrelling.' He kissed the tip of her nose before letting her go.

'We've too good a marriage to fall out over something as stupid as Bruce's party, especially when nothing happened. Hazel was round. She said everyone was too drunk to do anything.'

'It did cross my mind that that might be the case.'

'And guess what? She's having an affair with that Mark North.'

'Never! That four-eyed, rather boring-looking bloke?'

'The same, though I don't think I'd describe him in quite the same way,' Peggy replied archly.

'Well, don't you start getting any fancy ideas about our friend Mr North.' He lunged at her and playfully patted her bottom which made her giggle and jump skittishly around the table. 'Hope the grub lives up to all this.' He nodded at the pink candles, the matching tablecloth and napkins, their best crystal glasses, the small vase of snowdrops and violets.

'Prawn cocktail and then chicken breast in a tarragon sauce.'

'Sounds fabulous. I'd best go and have a quick shower and change.'

The evening was a greater success than Peggy had dared hope. Dan, entering into the spirit of things, had popped out to the off-licence and bought a bottle of white wine, which had made the meal perfect. And he'd splashed out on a bottle of Drambuie which he knew Peggy loved. They sat curled up together on the giant sofa sipping their liqueurs, Simon and Garfunkel on the stereo, the lights subdued.

'Steph should go out more often,' Dan said contentedly.

'It's nice, isn't it, just you and me?' She snuggled closer to him. 'Dan?'

'Um . . .' he replied sleepily.

'Dan, there's something I've got to ask you.'

'Ask away.'

She sat up and regarded him, sprawled back on the white leather, his face a picture of contentment as he lay eyes closed, half asleep.

'Dan, are you having an affair with someone?'

'Am I what?' His eyes snapped open, the contented expression replaced by one of astonishment. 'What sort of question's that?'

'I had to ask. I have to know. Are you?' she asked, her voice strained.

'Of course I'm not bloody having an affair. For God's sake, when would I have the time for one? Even if I wanted to, which I don't. Honest, Peggy, I feel hurt you should even think such a thing.'

'Dan, I'm sorry, but I've been going mad thinking you might be. I've been so miserable and afraid.'

'Since when?'

'Well, for some time. But I only thought you might be having an affair yesterday – it didn't cross my mind before. Then I began to think what a fool I'd been, how complacent – God, I've been so afraid.'

'But you said "some time".' He was sitting up now. She felt stupid and silly and thoughtless, and wished she'd never started all this. 'So why "some time"?' he persisted.

Peggy examined her hands, picked at her short nails. She twisted her wedding ring and the small solitaire engagement ring Dan had given her all those years ago. How many? Need she ask herself? It was their silver wedding anniversary this year.

'You haven't answered me.'

She took a deep breath, sat up straight and virtually lunged into words as if she would not get them out if she spoke normally.

'You don't seem to want me these days. We used to – you know – regularly. Now you hardly ever touch me.' She was bright red now, blushing to the roots of her hair. They had never talked like this before, ever. 'I'm sorry,' she said, waving her hand ineffectually, tears pricking behind her nose. 'Is it me? I mean, is it my fault? Don't you fancy me any more?'

'Oh, Peggy, I'm sorry. It's just I get so bloody tired what with work . . . Come here . . .' He pulled her towards him. 'Of course I fancy you – what a daft thing to say. I'll always fancy you.' He put his hands either side of her face and brought his own close, his lips searching for hers. They kissed for a long time, a deep, satisfying kiss, the sort of kiss they had once given each other several times a day but now rarely. 'I guess I should prove it then, don't you?' he said, breaking away from her lips. She felt his hands sliding inside her blouse, heard herself whimper with pleasure as he touched her nipples, felt the familiar charge of pleasure that shot from her breasts down her body to her vagina.

'The hot line's working, then?' He chuckled, using their words for her easy arousal.

'You always could make it work just like that.'

'And she says I don't fancy her?' He undid her trousers and proved to her there on the big leather sofa, in the glow of the fire, to Simon and Garfunkel, that he loved and needed her.

Much later, she lay contentedly in his arms, her head resting on his chest. 'Whose car is it you mend?' she asked.

'What? The old Citroën? Marvellous vehicle. You expect to see Maigret sitting in it.' His voice rumbled deeply in her ear – a comforting sound.

'Who owns it?' she persisted.

'Bloke called Greentree – used to work for the company years ago. Nice old boy, but he's got arthritis in his fingers and can't fiddle with the engine as he'd like. Why all the questions?' He lifted his head to peer awkwardly at her.

'Oh, nothing. Just curious.' The last little niggle of doubt was laid to rest.

Chapter Nine

That Tuesday Peggy had no problem getting up. She felt happy again, full of joy and energy.

'I'd say you look like a cat that's had the cream.' Hazel had materialized at the glass-topped counter making Peggy, who had been beside the back shelf, jump.

'I was miles away,' she said.

'Everything's all right, then – you and Dan?'

'Does it show?'

'You glow, my love, literally a peaches-and-cream glow that none of my creams and lotions could ever give you.'

'We talked,' Peggy said simply.

'And the other. I do believe, old friend, that you're blushing. Anyhow, I just popped over to say I've got to skip coffee this morning. I've got to go to the bank.'

'In the middle of the morning?'

'Bruce has some papers I've got to sign – something to do with the business.'

'Maybe lunchtime?'

'Yeah, maybe.' She turned to leave.

'Hazel, you couldn't let me have that tenner you owe me, could you? I stupidly left my purse at home.'

'How did you get to work, then?' Hazel said, somewhat brusquely.

'Dan brought me in – he was late today.' Peggy was beaming. 'We got a bit delayed this morning and, well, it was all a bit of a rush and I'd changed handbags over the weekend and picked up the wrong one.'

'Sorry, I haven't got it now. I'll have to give it to you after I've been to the bank.'

'Fine. Fine,' Peggy said, puzzled and not sure why as she watched Hazel's retreating back.

Viv suddenly popped out of her little office. When she did that, with no warning, she often reminded Peggy of a mole suddenly appearing from its burrow. 'Peggy, you're wanted in Personnel at eleven thirty.'

'What for?'

'Search me,' said Viv, popping quickly back into the safety of her lair.

Why Viv was in retailing was a mystery to Peggy; she did everything possible to avoid contact with the customers, whom she loathed. It was probably as well that she did hide away since she found it impossible to conceal that loathing. But while Viv's big bottom was safely installed on the office chair Peggy never stood a chance of being departmental head. She supposed she could apply for China and Glass, which she knew was coming up next autumn, but it was unlikely she'd get it; there was an excellent section manageress who'd worked that department for twenty years and whose knowledge of the products was encyclopedic.

The morning dragged on. Of Hazel there was no sign. Customers were few – the lousy weather, no doubt, it was tipping down outside. She'd lunch in the canteen today; Hazel would have to lump it. There was no way she was going out in this.

By eleven fifteen Peggy had sold two cheap handbags and, in the juniors' coffee break, one pair of woollen gloves and a scarf. Even umbrellas which, in a downpour like this, should have been walking out of the store, weren't shifting. Business was bad.

Before going up to Personnel Peggy went to the staff cloakroom and tidied herself. She wasn't nervous, she was doing it out of principle. Office staff loathed shop-floor staff and vice versa – no rhyme or reason, it had always been that way and probably always would be. Tucked away behind the scenes, and rarely seen by the customers, the office workers were not expected to wear the house uniform of dark green skirt and cream blouse. They looked a motley crew in their home-knitted jumpers. Shop-floor staff took pride in making them look even scruffier in comparison.

'I've got an appointment, I'm not sure who with or why.

Name's Peggy Alder, Handbags and Accessories,' Peggy said to the young girl who opened the glass partition in answer to her ring, and scowled out at her.

'Miss Oliver's waiting for you. You know where her office is?'

'Yes, thanks.' Peggy walked down the narrow corridor between the glass and white-painted wood-partitioned offices, peering in curiously. Up here as much space was devoted to the running of the huge shop as downstairs. She stopped at a door on which was a sign: Miss Iolanthe Oliver. If she had a name like that she'd make damn sure no one knew, she thought as she knocked.

A voice bade her enter. Miss Oliver, young and efficient, power-suited and heavily made-up, sat behind a desk on which were a telephone, an appointment diary, a file with Peggy's name on it and nothing else. This office, given Miss Oliver's senior position, had no windows into the corridor, only one which gave onto a roofscape and the outside world. There was a large year-planner on the wall, a rainbow of coloured pins stuck in it, but no pictures, no pot plants, nothing else. Bleak, thought Peggy as she took the seat offered her by Miss Oliver.

'Peggy. I may call you Peggy, may I? Though we haven't met in the six months I've been here.'

Peggy nodded, though she would like to have said, 'Only if I can call you Iolanthe', but she didn't and was struck by her lack of courage in the silliest of things.

'Good, Peggy, I prefer Christian names – more friendly, isn't it? And it makes one's task easier.' She flipped open the file. 'I'm sorry to have to tell you but I'm this day issuing you with a month's notice. Of course, since you're paid weekly we would be within our rights to give you a week's notice. However, although we're not obliged to do any such thing, given your long and excellent record here the management decided a month would be fairer.'

Peggy felt her mouth open slackly, her stomach contract, her heart turn over, and wanted desperately to go to the loo. She shook her head as if she hadn't heard right.

'I beg your pardon?' she said.

'We are terminating your contract of employment.' Miss

Oliver smiled brightly, her large pillar-box-red lips heavily glossed and gleaming. With a firm hand she slapped Peggy's file closed and pushed it from her as a diner pushes away a plate after finishing a meal.

'Why?'

'Rationalization.'

'Why me?'

'Someone has to go.' Her facial muscles geared up and the scarlet lips were instantly in smile mode again.

'But I'm a section manager, I'm senior. Why not my assistant? She only joined us a year ago.'

'These decisions are always hard, Peggy.' The smile flashed as if programmed to do so at the end of every sentence.

'Harder for me. I've never been sacked before.'

'You're not being sacked, Peggy. Whatever next?' Miss Oliver trilled, as though she found the idea funny. 'Your position is being made redundant. We shall not be refilling it. And, of course, we shall be paying you redundancy money and there will be no problem over excellent references.'

'Too right. So who's going to do my work?'

'No doubt Viv will train your assistant.'

'What? Pay her an assistant's wage for doing a section manager's job? The union would love to hear about that, I bet.'

'But you're not a member of the union, are you, Peggy?' The smile was different this time, less pleasant.

'No, but I'll make damn sure Karen is,' she said, with immense satisfaction. 'Did Viv know about this?' Miss Oliver did not answer. 'Then she did.' When Peggy thought of the number of times she'd covered for Viv when hung-over or a bit pickled . . . 'Do I have to stay the month?' She stood up.

'In the circumstances we thought we'd leave it up to you.'

'I'm going now, then. You can send my cards and money on to me. And by the way, I'm not Peggy to you, I'm Mrs Alder,' she said, cloaking herself in her name, emphasizing the Mrs as if it protected her, as if it gave her back some dignity. She walked towards the door.

'In view of your long service, Mr Jenkins will wish to see you to say goodbye.'

Peggy swung round. 'You can tell Mr Jenkins he can stuff his job, and this store.'

'Well, really! Reacting like this isn't going to help, is it?'

'Probably not, but it makes me feel one hell of a lot better.' And Peggy was out of the door and controlling an urge to slam it.

She raced from the administration floor and, not bothering to wait for the lift, ran down the stairs to the staff locker room. It was empty. With relief she sank on to a bench, dug in her handbag for a cigarette and, ignoring the No Smoking sign, lit up. Her heart was racing, her mind reeling. The last thing she had expected. The last thing they needed. *How* was she to tell Dan? After the happiness of last night this was doubly cruel. Maybe she need not say anything? Maybe she could get another job and tell him then? She stubbed out the cigarette under her shoe and immediately lit another – more to annoy than because she needed one.

She splashed her face with water, ran the cold tap over her wrists and still felt awful. She looked at herself in the neon-lit mirror. What a mess.

Oh, to hell with it – with them!

She crossed to her locker and quickly stuffed everything into the bag she kept at the bottom. She put on her overcoat and walked through the shop to the ground floor. She arrived at Handbags and Accessories just in time to see Viv spot her and scuttle quickly into her office, which had no door. Peggy walked purposefully towards it. Viv was trapped.

'You could have told me,' she said angrily, standing at the entrance.

'I was too embarrassed.' Viv was taking a great interest in her stock sheets.

'I bet. Did you help them choose me? Was it because of Mrs Fox and her complaint fiasco?'

'Don't be silly, Peggy. As if I'd do something like that.' But she looked sufficiently shifty for Peggy to know she'd hit the nail on the head.

'It's going to put you out, though, isn't it? You're going to have to get off your fat bum and do some work for a change.'

'Well, really, what a thing to say!'

'I haven't finished. Who's going to cover for you now, Viv?

When you come in pissed? When you can't think straight because of your hangover?'

'You've never seen me like that.'

'Oh, no? I feel sorry for you, Viv. You needed me and – Oh, Karen, come here a minute.' She called across the department and waited patiently for her young assistant to join them. 'I've been given the push, Karen.'

'Oh, Peggy! No! What for?'

'I'm warning you, Karen, they want you to do my job on your assistant's wage. Join the union if you haven't already.'

'I'm a member.'

'Good. Then take my advice. Shaft them.'

Peggy swept away from the office, over to her desk, packed up her pens, scissors and other odd paraphernalia she'd collected over the years; the motions of her arms, hands, her whole body were of anger.

'Hi! Peggy! What's the matter?'

'Hazel, am I glad to see you! I've been sacked.'

'You're joking?'

'Wish I was. They gave me a month's notice. I decided to get out now before I smash the place up.'

'Understandable.'

'Have you got that money for me? I'm going to have to get a cab.' Peggy indicated her bag – fat with its contents – at her feet and the bulging shop carrier in her hand.

Hazel's perfectly manicured hand shot to her mouth. 'Oh, my God, Peggy. I forgot.'

'You mean you haven't got ten quid?'

'No, I'm sorry. It was so boring and long-winded at the bank that—'

'Oh, forget it. I'll have to pay the cabbie with a cheque.' This was the last straw. Peggy began to walk to the back of the shop and the staff entrance. On all sides there was whispering, and oblique glances shot her way – news travels faster in a department store than anywhere else. Sod them, she thought, and marched purposefully towards the large, sliding plate-glass doors. She'd go out in style. She'd go out of the front entrance. As she marched towards the doors what started as a ripple of applause swelled as the assistants clapped and wished her well. Customers caught up in the demonstration looked puzzled, confused and then joined in. At the door Peggy swung round, raised her fist in salute to her comrades, dived out into the pouring rain and, fortunately, a waiting taxi.

Chapter Ten

On the following morning Peggy got up and left the house before Steph, as usual, as if nothing had happened. With her exams coming up soon, the last thing Peggy wanted was to worry her unduly.

Once out of the house she didn't know what to do with herself. She should have checked with Steph what her plans were; as a sixth-former she was allowed to work at home some days. If Peggy was to keep up this charade she'd best take a squint at Steph's timetable and learn when she could safely return home.

Peggy started walking in the direction of her mother's house. She hadn't seen her for a couple of weeks and by now Myrtle would be wondering what was up.

'No work? What a surprise!' Whether a nice one or not it was difficult for Peggy to tell from the tone of her mother's voice, as Myrtle opened the door of the small terrace house close to the football ground where Peggy had been born and raised.

'No, day off,' Peggy lied, and followed her mother's bulky steps along the passageway.

'Cold enough to freeze the brass knobs off a monkey, isn't it? And with coal the price it is . . .' Myrtle White was rubbing her hands to keep them warm, even though a large fire burned in the grate.

'Back boiler working well?' asked Peggy, referring to the fireplace that she and her brother had installed a couple of years back, which was enough to run the heating for the whole house. The house was as warm as toast.

'It's all right,' Myrtle said grudgingly.

'Tea?' Peggy asked.

'That would be lovely.' Her mother sighed as she spoke.

82

'How's the hip?'

'Playing up something rotten – it's the cold.'

Peggy didn't want tea, but she knew her mother: if anyone popped in at any hour of the day or night, she'd expect them to brew up for her.

Peggy stood in the kitchen and waited for the kettle to boil. The room needed redecorating, she thought, looking about her. Barry, her brother, had painted it every other year, but two years ago he'd been sent to Canada by his firm. She'd have time to do it now. Years ago they'd taken out the old copper and furnished the corner with work units and a sink with a tiled surround. Barry had stripped the dresser of fifty years of gloss paint, back to its original pine. Compared with the dark, inconvenient room of her childhood it was lovely, she thought, staring out of the sash window to the whitewashed back wall. In the spring she would hang pots of red geraniums where, as a child, the yard broom and tin bath had hung. Now the little back bedroom had been fitted out with a primrose-coloured bathroom suite.

'I fibbed actually. I've been given the push from Sadler's,' Peggy said, as she returned to the living room with the tray of tea.

'What did you do?' Myrtle asked suspiciously.

'Nothing.'

'You must have done something. Why else would they want to be shot of someone with all your experience? Did you find the digestives? I like a biscuit with my tea,' she said unnecessarily.

'They're here.' Peggy handed her the plate and poured their tea. 'They're cutting back. They're hoping to get someone else to do my job for less pay.'

'Still, you'll get redundancy money, won't you? That'll be a tidy sum.' Myrtle's eyes glistened at the thought.

'It won't last long, not with our commitments.'

'Pity you spent all that money on Carol's wedding.'

'I know. We were stupid there.'

'I said at the time.'

'Did you?' This was news to Peggy.

'I did – trying to keep up with Sean's parents. Pride, that's what it was. Throwing money away.' Myrtle, speaking with her mouth full of biscuit, sprayed crumbs in all directions.

'Yes, Mum,' Peggy said patiently. 'Still, it was a lovely wedding.'

'I've had my electric bill in. Shocking. How we're supposed to get by on our pensions, I don't know . . .' Her voice was raised at the end of the sentence making it far more a question than a statement. Peggy's heart sank. As if their own bill wasn't enough to pay.

'Where is it?' Peggy said in a resigned voice, knowing that if she didn't it was only a matter of minutes until her mother started the after-all-I've-done-for-you speech, which she always did when she thought she was not going to get her way. She took the bill down from behind the clock on the mantelshelf and got out her cheque-book, wrote a cheque and put it under the pepper and salt pots on the table.

'Can't you take it down to the showroom for me? You've precious little else to do now,' said Myrtle, starting on her second cup.

Suppressing an irritated sigh, Peggy picked up the cheque and put it in her purse. 'I've got to begin looking for another job,' she said pointedly. If she didn't watch out her mother would find daily errands for her to do.

'What's Dan say?' Myrtle looked up from her tea.

'I haven't told him. I didn't want to worry him.'

'Why ever not? He'll be next, though. It said in the local paper last night that they're expecting redundancies at Fairling's,' Myrtle said, her voice laden with doom, picking biscuit from her teeth.

'But that's the shop floor. Dan's in the planning department.'

'If they sack the buggers who make the things it stands to reason they'll sack the buggers what draw them in the first place, doesn't it?'

'If that happened we'd have to sell the house.'

'And who would buy it just now?'

'Mum, I came round here to be cheered up,' Peggy said with forced brightness.

'What's there to be cheerful about?' was the mournful reply.

Once she'd washed up the tea things, wiped the bathroom floor and run round to the corner shop with a list of groceries that, mysteriously, she'd ended up paying for, it was noon. Fortunately for Peggy it was a Meals on Wheels day, otherwise, no doubt, she'd have had to cook lunch as well.

She could no longer remember when she'd decided she didn't like her mother, she thought, once she had escaped and was walking back through the almost deserted park. She supposed there hadn't been a specific moment; rather, the conclusion had been a slow dawning. Once acknowledged, it was something that concerned her about herself which she carried with her various parcels of guilt. Others, she knew, moaned about their mums frequently, but nearly always such lapses were rounded off with a 'Still, for all her faults, I love the old girl.' Peggy could never say anything like that, or pin down the cause of her dislike. It was a mélange of discontent and querulousness which, rarely verbalized, was always lurking below the surface of any contact she had with Myrtle. Her mother made her feel in the wrong all the time; that whatever she did it was not enough, and never would be; that the way Peggy had turned out was a bitter disappointment. She'd never discussed it with Dan, who would have been shocked out of his boots. Dan loved his mother, worshipped her. In Dan's book, if you didn't you were no better than a two-headed monster.

She had tried once to explain it to Steph.

'Nan's old. What can you expect?' she'd said, with the tolerance for the old that the young frequently display.

'But she was always dissatisfied. It's got nothing to do with her age.'

'It's because how she is *now* colours the past, too, Mum.'

'No, I don't think it's that. I don't like her, you know, Steph, and I begin to think I don't love her either.'

'Oh, Mum, don't be silly. Of course you do. When Nan croaks, you'll be heartbroken,' Steph had said confidently.

Peggy was not so sure, but loving one's parents was too ingrained in Peggy's psyche to be easily displaced. Everyone loved their mum, no matter what. And if she didn't, then what was wrong with her?

'You're a million miles away! I've been yelling fit to burst.'

'Jean!' Peggy said with delight to her mother-in-law who, puffing from running, was standing beside her. 'I'm sorry, I was miles away.'

'Phew! My marathon days are over.'

'You shouldn't run like that,' Peggy said, concerned now at Jean's bright red complexion.

'I'll be right as rain in a minute.' She fanned herself with a glove. 'Not at work?' she asked, once she'd fully regained her breath.

'I've been given the push.'

Jean stopped dead in her tracks. 'Oh, Peggy, no. I *am* sorry. When? Why?'

Peggy explained. 'I haven't told Dan,' she said, grabbing hold of Jean's hand. 'I don't want him to know, yet.'

'Why not?'

'What's the point of two of us worrying? I might get another job tomorrow. I'll tell him then.'

'You tell him now. Good gracious, you need his love and support at a time like this, not having to soldier on alone. Go on, the great lump can shoulder it.' Jean smiled sympathetically. 'And it won't be long. Someone with your experience will soon be snapped up.'

'Well, there aren't that number of jobs come up – not at my level.'

'Then you'll have to lower your sights a bit, won't you?' Jean said, but not unkindly. 'Tell you what, let's get some fish and chips and you come back with me to eat them.'

Jean lived in a terraced house, too, the opposite side of the park from Myrtle, but with no back boiler or new bathroom. She had no central heating, and although Dan and his sister had bought her electric oil-filled radiators, she tended to use paraffin stoves since she couldn't run to the cost of the electricity. She told them it was because the radiators dried the air and made her cough.

Her kitchen was nice, however, and Jean was proud of the job Dan had done with the MFI units, the pretty floral wallpaper and matching curtains. Peggy knew why everything was done on the cheap. Jean would never want anyone put out, anything would do to satisfy her so, good-natured as she was, she got second best whereas Myrtle always got what she wanted. It was all so unfair.

For all that, Peggy preferred this house. There was always a nice cosy clutter – Jean liked to read and usually had half a dozen books on the go. She pursued hobbies, too, and no sooner had she started one than she'd begin another. At the moment her sitting room was littered with the debris from making crêpe-paper flowers and building doll's-house furniture.

'You need a bigger house.' Peggy swept up a pile of magazines and unfinished tapestry from a chair.

'Even if I had one, I'd still be in the same muddle,' Jean said as she divided the fish and chips between two plates.

'When I win the pools I'll buy you a fab bungalow.'

'By the seaside? I've always wanted to live by the sea.' Jean grinned.

'And collect shells, I suppose,' Peggy added. 'To add to the clutter.'

'And seaweed. I didn't know you did the pools.'

'I don't.'

'Then I won't hold my breath.' Jean was laughing.

After her lunch with Jean, Peggy felt much better and cheerful enough to go to the Job Centre. She had a feeling it might be a depressing experience that should only be approached in a happy frame of mind. She was right.

There were retailing jobs but she was too old for any of them. All were in the youth-orientated shops where, she knew, even the managers were in their early twenties. Still, she consoled herself, as she popped into Sainsbury's on the way home to buy some supper, would she be happy selling tat merchandise? Probably not, when she was used to selling the best.

Steph wasn't home when she let herself in. Of course, on Wednesdays she went to the drama club. She did too much, that girl – she should drop some of the out-of-school activities. She dreaded telling Steph what had happened. Her grant would never cover everything she needed, and how would they help her out now?

Peggy made some meatballs in tomato sauce with spaghetti for supper – Best start economizing now, she'd told herself as she had wandered the well-lit aisles in the supermarket, ignoring the temptation of the wonderful produce on offer. Gone were the days when she'd rush in, grab a trolley and throw in what she thought they might need. She'd never regarded them as well off before – not until now, that is.

'Smells good.' Dan's head was peering round the kitchen door in a fair imitation of a Bisto kid.

'Dan, is it true they're laying off people at Fairling's?'

'It's a rumour that pops up with depressing regularity these days,' Dan said seriously. 'The order book's looking a bit thin. I suppose if they don't get something soon . . .'

'But you'd be safe?'

'Love, once they start laying off, no man's safe, and that even includes the board these days.'

Peggy shuddered. 'It's so unfair, isn't it? You work hard all your life, and you should be allowed the privilege of feeling secure in your middle age.'

'Peggy, what is it? What's happened?'

'Hi, everyone.' The back door opened and Steph, eyes shiny, pink-cheeked from the cold, bounded in. 'Guess what? I've got the lead. I'm to play Portia. Isn't that something?'

'Absolutely wonderful.' Peggy held up her arms to hug her daughter. Over her head she frowned at Dan and shook her head. Later would be time enough. 'Are you sure you're not taking on too much, Steph? It's a large part to learn.'

'No hassle, Mum. We did *The Merchant of Venice* for GCSE so I know it off by heart already. I need this relaxation. It helps, you know, to make a complete switch from books and studying.'

'Well, you know best.'

'That smells ace! What is it?'

'My concoction. Off with you both and wash your hands. It's ready.'

It wasn't until after supper, with the washing-up done and Steph upstairs studying, that they were able to recommence their talk.

'I wasn't going to tell you, but Jean said I should.'

'You're pregnant?'

Peggy looked up, assuming he was joking, but his face was serious. 'No, nothing like that – thank God.'

'Oh, I don't know, it might be nice . . .' His voice trailed off.

'It would be awful. Screaming babies at *our* age? You have to be joking! In any case, I shouldn't think I could conceive now. If you're so keen, *you* have it!'

'Then what is it?'

As she told him she felt about to cry. It was only as she talked that she realized how hurt she was by the shop's attitude. She'd been angry up until now, but regret had begun to take its place. Thinking she was close to tears he gave her his handkerchief.

'Well, we don't tell Steph for a start, do we?' was the first thing he said.

'No, I decided that.' She blew her nose into his handkerchief – she never had one of her own when she needed one, but she was determined not to cry, it would only make Dan worry more.

'I sometimes think that poor kid is loaded with guilt as it is,' Dan said thoughtfully.

'I don't see why, do you?'

'Perhaps because she's the only one to go on like this – to college, I mean.'

'We're going to be pushed, Dan.'

'I know, but we'll manage somehow.'

'I'll keep looking for work.'

'Of course you will.'

'And we've all got each other.'

'Exactly.' He patted her hand comfortingly.

Chapter Eleven

Peggy found the oddest thing about not going out to work was that she was constantly pushed each day to get everything done in time. She always seemed to be racing against the clock, and the house, which had always been clean and tidy when she was working at the shop, was rapidly becoming a mess.

Last week, before she had lost her job, she had done her chores as quickly as possible to get them out of the way and didn't have much time to think what she was doing. Now she had time, after only a few days she was bored witless and her speed had slackened. What was frightening was that this was only her first week as a full-time housewife, something she had occasionally thought would be paradise rather than the juggling hysteria her life had become. Already she remembered her working days wistfully.

Still, she decided, putting on the kettle to make herself her mid-morning coffee, this was no way to think – it would get her nowhere. She needed to be more positive. She switched on the radio to catch *Woman's Hour*, as she began to prepare their supper. While she worked she kept an eye on the clock for Steph who, since it was Friday and she had a free study afternoon, would be back shortly after noon.

The vegetables finished, she changed into a smart suit and set off for the Job Centre. She'd been advised to try to pop in each day to keep an eye on the boards advertising jobs since the best ones were snapped up almost as soon as they were displayed.

She'd only been unemployed four days and already it felt like a few months, she thought, as she stood at the bus stop. Strange, how things could change so quickly in one's life. Here she was, and if a red car should drive past she wouldn't even notice, not now, not when things were going well with Dan. Still, perhaps the driver had noticed she was no longer at the bus stop. Did he miss her? The bus arrived and put an end to such thoughts.

Jobs were available, but none that she was willing yet to take. The redundancy money would have to go before she would do waitressing, washing up or cleaning. But, she supposed, when it had all gone pride and finger-nails would have to be sacrificed.

As she walked up the High Street and saw the plate-glass façade of Sadler's her steps faltered. Her instinct was to turn round and go the other way, but that was silly – this was her home town, and she couldn't spend the rest of her life avoiding the larger of the two department stores.

It was a good feeling to be striding in the front way and not skulking round the back, she thought, as the revolving door swallowed her up, swished her round and ejected her on the other side.

'Peggy! Hi! I've been meaning to call you but you know how it is.' Hazel greeted her from her glass box.

'New promotion?' Peggy indicated the tricolour streamers.

'Yes. A new anti-wrinkle cream – it's great stuff. I'll let you have a sample.' Hazel knelt down behind the counter and rummaged with a small blue-, white- and red-striped box which she slipped into a bag. 'How's things?'

Peggy raised her eyebrows. 'Could be worse, I suppose. We could all get the plague.'

'Nothing turned up?'

'I could wash up at the Blue Pig or waitress at the Coach and Horses.'

'Oh, Peggy, I'm sorry. What's Dan say?'

'He's been a brick, very supportive.'

'Well, that's something.'

They both stood and looked at each other, and Peggy felt uncomfortably awkward with no idea what else to talk about and waited hopefully for Hazel to say something.

'Well, I'd best be getting on,' was all she said.

'Yes, of course,' said Peggy, feeling as if she had a contagious disease. Maybe she had, in a way – if someone as senior as her had been given the push perhaps they were all running scared, wondering who'd be next.

She was about to move off but stopped. 'Hazel, that money for the lottery ticket?'

'You've caught me on the hop again.' Hazel's highly glossed lips stretched wide in a smile.

'Look, forget it, it doesn't matter. It was stupid of me to buy it.'

'You sure?'

'Positive,' Peggy said. She needed the money, but she couldn't face constantly asking for it, as if she was in the wrong. 'We'd never win anyway. It's my loss.'

'Well, thanks.'

'Love to Bruce.' Peggy almost bumped into Karen who, seeing her, had left her crocodile handbags to say hello. 'Karen!' They fell into step and crossed the small amount of shop floor to the handbag counter. Karen took up her position. Peggy felt jealous to see someone else in her place.

'How's things?' she asked, casting a professional eye over the shelves and noting, with satisfaction, that nothing had been changed.

'I did what you said. I went straight to Stella Pauline, the shop steward, about them using me. She went straight to Personnel and I got a rise, all thanks to you.' She smiled triumphantly at Peggy.

'That's good.' She nodded. 'Viv helping you?' Karen gave a dismissive little grimace. 'Don't let her use you either. Tell Stella if she works you too hard.'

'I will, Peggy. Thanks.'

It was ridiculous, really, putting someone as inexperienced as Karen in charge of such valuable handbags. How could she even begin to sell them when she probably didn't even know which skins they were made of? Viv should be there, not still skulking in her bolt-hole.

'Hello, Viv,' Peggy said, as she tapped on the partition and put her head round the curtain. Viv was, as she had suspected, sitting at her desk, bolt upright, but apparently asleep judging by the jolt and the bleary eyes which looked up at her.

'Peggy! I didn't expect to see you here.'

'I came to apologize. I shouldn't have spoken to you the way I did. It was spiteful of me.'

'It was.' Viv patted the fat row of curls which hung unfashionably at the nape of her neck.

'Yes, well, I said I'm sorry. I just wanted to put things right.'

'Harder to do than you might think. I was deeply hurt.'

'Oh, Viv, for goodness sake, I was upset, I was lashing out.'

'Why me?'

Peggy sighed. 'Because you ditched me – but I understand why you did it. In your position I'd probably have done the same.'

'And what position's that?' asked Viv, all dignity and ruffled feathers.

'Oh, you know, your mum and everything.' She would have liked to add, 'And the booze, *and* that you're an old maid.' 'I'm not alone to cope with it,' was what she said instead.

Viv looked as if she was about to bite off Peggy's head but the small ferret eyes, already red-rimmed, filled with tears which slopped over the edges and ran down the mottled cheeks, plopping on the over-large cardiganed bosom below.

'Viv, what is it?' Peggy asked, quite expecting her to be crying because she had missed her.

'My canary died.'

'Oh, I'm sorry.'

'That canary loved me.'

'I'm sure it did.' She patted Viv's bulky shoulder. So much for being missed, she thought.

The weekend seemed interminable. It rained on Saturday, so Steph's hockey match was cancelled and she was at home all day. She asked if Peggy could lend her some money for a new pair of jeans.

'Steph, I'm sorry, not this week. I'm short.'

'It doesn't matter,' Steph said, but Peggy saw the look of disappointment on her face. Such things mattered so much to the young. Peggy could remember the disappointment she had felt as a teenager when she had not been able to buy a skirt she had set her heart on. She owed the girl some sort of explanation.

'I've done a stupid thing, Steph. I blew twenty quid on lottery tickets – I don't know what got into me.'

'Gambling in your old age!' Steph laughed. 'I'll wait for your winnings, then I'll buy a dozen pairs.'

'You'll have a long wait.' Peggy was pleased at how reasonable her daughter was compared with some teenagers she knew. 'Next week, I promise, I'll make sure I juggle things.' Peggy gave her word, but even as she did so, she knew she was being unfair.

Peggy visited Jean who told her she was a fool to pretend and that Steph had more sense than they were giving her credit for. 'And, you know, I'm not so sure she wants to go to university,' Jean said, turning Peggy's coat in front of the fire where she was drying it.

'Jean! Of course she wants to go. She's always said how much she wants to study and get a degree.'

'And how much of that is because she thinks it's what you want to hear? You couldn't go, and so she can go in your place.'

Peggy played with her hair, remembering the times she'd said just that to Steph. 'That can't be true,' she said hurriedly, in an attempt to smother such thoughts. 'Steph's too intelligent to do something like that.'

'Intelligence doesn't come into it when you're talking about love and loyalty. You're going to have to tell her something – you can't keep clomping about in the rain like this. You'll be down with pneumonia before you know where you are.'

Later that day in the library, which smelt horribly of damp clothes, Peggy forced herself to go over what Jean had said about Steph. One sneaky thought persisted, despite her efforts to stop it coming into her mind: what a relief if Steph didn't want to go to college, think of the money they'd save. Money they didn't even have! She left at four with a pile of books, beaten by the smell of sweaty bodies and wet clothes. She let herself into the house, calling out as she did so.

'You're home early.' Steph appeared quickly from the sitting room. In the background Peggy could hear the noise of a football match on television.

'Your dad home?' she asked, sloughing off her soaking coat like an unwanted skin and jerking her head towards the sound of the match.

'No, he's gone to fix that couple's car.'

'Again? He must be rebuilding it, I hope they're paying him well. You watching football then?' she asked, curious.

'No, I've got a friend here – didn't think you'd mind.'

'Why on earth should I mind?' Peggy stepped into the lounge in time to see a tall, dark-haired young man hurriedly piling cushions back onto the chairs. 'Hello.' She smiled.

'Mum, this is Nigel.'

'How do you do, Mrs Alder,' he said, politely enough, but Peggy thought he looked a bit flustered. She shook hands with him and it occurred to her, not for the first time, that Steph's male friends must all be allergic to shampoo.

'Nigel's home for the weekend from college, aren't you, Nigel?' Steph prompted him.

'Yes. That's right.'

'They let you out of the cage occasionally, then?' Peggy asked brightly.

'Yes. That's right.'

'You're home early?' Steph asked again, as if to take her mother's attention away from Nigel, who seemed incapable of further speech.

'Yes, it was so slack I left Karen in control.' The lies tripped out effortlessly. Nigel stood awkwardly, looking more ill-at-ease than ever. 'I think I'll go and make a cuppa. Anyone else want?'

'No thanks,' said Steph.

As the door shut Peggy heard a burst of laughter from the other side. She stopped in her tracks. Had she walked in on them at an inopportune moment? Steph, of all people! She'd always been in a crowd up until now, never anyone special. Thinking of Nigel's lank, greasy hair, torn jeans and crumpled T-shirt with its message of youth, Peggy felt she could have done better for herself. Or did all mothers think like that? She hadn't about Sean: she'd liked him right from the start and still did, despite his mother. But then, he was conventional, normal, you knew where you were with Sean. With someone like Nigel she doubted if she'd ever know what to talk about. She pushed open the kitchen door. As she got the tea things together, she supposed it had to happen one day. She just hoped Dan wouldn't find out – he hadn't liked it one little bit when Carol had first started going out with boys, but she was his little Princess. Maybe he'd feel different about Steph. Pray God, she thought, as she hurled the tea-bags into the pot, that her daughter was on the pill.

That evening Dan suggested they drive out into the country for a drink at a nice pub. Peggy didn't want to go: she'd hoped to watch the lottery draw and results on the glitzy show that went out on the television each Saturday. But she couldn't tell Dan that or she'd have to confess to wasting twenty pounds on tickets.

'Is it the weather for a drive?' she asked.

'It's stopped raining. You're always saying I don't take you out enough.'

'Am I? I don't think so,' she said, perplexed. 'Of course we'll go.' She felt his remark was not worth arguing about. It would be silly to stay in. What were her chances of winning? The odds were hundreds of thousands to one against even the small prizes.

Peggy and Dan had discussed cancelling the normal Sunday lunch but Peggy had vetoed the idea, convinced it would alert Steph faster than anything else that things were not as they should be.

It was an interminable meal with many unanswered questions hovering in the air.

'Anything wrong, Mum?' was said by all.

'All right, Dad?' was echoed by others.

'Nothing. Everything's fine,' Peggy and Dan said, almost in unison.

'You're sure?' was repeated too often for comfort.

A sharp-voiced 'What is the matter with you all?' from Peggy seemed finally to reassure them.

The following Tuesday she had an interview. Afterwards she returned to the house feeling old – she knew she hadn't got the job. Oh, they'd said, 'We'll let you know', all the usual polite things, but Peggy had known the minute she stepped into the shop, which was fashionably cluttered and noisy with raucous music. The shop assistants were Steph's age and the manageress wasn't much older than Carol. What made it worse was that although, right at the beginning, Peggy had said, 'Look, I'm obviously wrong for this,' the young manageress, no doubt wanting to be kind, had replied, 'Oh, no, how do you know? Let's talk.' She had made coffee in her office and had explained the routine and workings of the shop. Peggy liked her, liked the system and would in all honesty have liked to be offered the job. Certainly it would have been different from any other shop she'd worked in. Wanting the job had made it even more painful to know that she was far too long in the tooth to get it. She went straight to the Job Centre intending to give the woman who had sent her a piece of her mind for wasting everyone's time. That was her intention, but it was a limp effort when it came to it.

'I was too old for them.'

'Oh, surely not. They asked for someone with experience.'

'It was a waste of time.'

'I'm sorry . . . I really felt . . . Look, Mrs Alder, don't keep trudging in here. I'll give you a ring if anything turns up, and that's a promise.'

'Would you? Thanks a million,' Peggy said, with real gratitude.

On Wednesday it snowed which, with Steph at home all day, couldn't have been more inopportune. Peggy left, maintaining the charade that she was going to work. At the bus stop everyone stamped their feet and shivered exaggeratedly at each other, but still no one spoke. The red car passed but Peggy did not even notice it.

The library was warm. She'd brought her Italian language books and spent the morning studying them. She hadn't been to her night class for weeks now – she'd be miles behind if she didn't do some work.

At lunchtime she called into the shop but Hazel was away sick. She should go and see her and offer to look after her if necessary, but that remained just a thought – the long journey out to Hazel's village was too daunting in this weather. She'd phone instead. Over coffee and a sandwich, she wondered how long she could go on playing box and cox with Steph. Not for long if this cold spell continued.

When she returned home and picked up the telephone to call Hazel she discovered it was not working. No one fancied going out in the cold to the telephone box down the street to report it. 'I'll do it when I get to work tomorrow. Who's going to phone at this time?' said Dan, settling down in front of the television for once, rather than going out.

Thursday dawned and Steph left at seven for a school trip to London. Thank God, thought Peggy as she looked out of the window at the snow. She made herself tea and toast, scuttled back to bed with her radio and settled back on the pillows with a contented sigh to wallow in the unfamiliar luxury of a mid-week lie-in followed by a long, leisurely bath. Trying once again to call Hazel she found the telephone was still not working. She dared not go out in case the BT men came, so she spent the day making a special meal for her and Dan. It had worked last time, she told herself. Maybe after a nice meal and a bottle of wine, he'd want to make love to her again. She produced Cornish pasties with baked stuffed apples to follow. To some, she knew, it would be a mundane meal, but not to her Dan: both were particular favourites.

It wasn't until he came home and Peggy thought to mention the telephone that he clapped his hand over his mouth, rolled his eyes to heaven and confessed he'd clean forgotten and then ranted on about a rush job. 'When I go down the snooker hall after supper, I'll do it then, I promise,' she heard him say, disappointment mounting in her.

'I hoped you'd stay in. Steph's not back till late.'

'Sorry, love. Can't make it. There's a tournament. I promised. What's for supper?'

'Cornish pasties.'

'Fantastic! My favourite.'

'Maybe I could come with you and watch you win,' she said hopefully.

'What? And cause a riot? No, love, not the snooker hall. It's no place for you. There's no women there for you to natter to,' he said, and she heard how patronizing he sounded. She felt too disappointed to bother to argue with him and remembered how often, over the years, he'd spoken to her in such a way and she, for the sake of peace, had let it go.

But he forgot the telephone as Peggy discovered when she picked it up before going to bed at nine. It was annoying: there was always a slight chance the Job Centre *might* phone.

On Friday Peggy reported the phone when she went to check on jobs.

'Oh, Mrs Alder, I've been trying to call you for two days,' the young woman said, the minute Peggy walked through the doors and into the searing heat of the Job Centre, on whose wall, incongruously, was a 'Save Energy' poster from the Department of the Environment.

'A job?' Peggy looked eager.

'It would have been perfect for you.'

'Would have?' Peggy said, aware of the wobble in her voice.

'In the handbag department at Thistle's,' she said, referring to the second largest department store in town. 'But they filled the post late yesterday afternoon. And that boutique rang back and said they wanted you to start on Monday, but when we couldn't reach you they took their second choice.'

Peggy slumped into the chair on the client side of the desk. 'And you've nothing else?'

'Sorry. I did try,' the woman said.

'I'm sure you did. Thanks. The phone was on the blink – I've reported it now.'

Peggy, feeling lower than she had since she'd been given the push the week before, started to walk towards the library. Suddenly she turned on her heel and made for the bus depot. She would have to risk Steph being at home – she couldn't face another day of wandering about. She sat on the bus deep in thought. What the hell were they to do if she couldn't get a job? The prospect made her stomach lurch. A thin film of nervous sweat sprang out on her forehead. It was going to get worse too. Already the mail was something to be feared rather than anticipated, each buff envelope to be scanned with nervous apprehension.

A car was parked outside the house, which was odd. Especially since it wasn't a car she recognized. Still, she rationalized, maybe it was just parked there and the owner was visiting someone nearby.

She put her key in the lock, but had barely pushed at the door when it was opened wide by an excited Steph. 'Mum! Where the hell have you been? I called the shop I don't know how many times and they sounded very cagey, said you weren't there. What's going on?'

'Did they? I took a shopping day and . . .' She began to lie as she took off her coat and then thought, What's the point? Steph had to know. She couldn't go on like this, she was too tired to keep up the subterfuge. 'You see, Steph, it's like this . . .' She started to explain but Steph grabbed her by the hand.

'Tell me later, it doesn't matter now. Come into the lounge. There's a couple of blokes want to talk to you.' Steph could hardly contain her excitement.

'For goodness sake, calm down, do,' Peggy said, as she allowed herself to be led from the hall. Pausing in the lounge doorway she saw two strange men sitting, drinking coffee.

'You shouldn't have let them in, not being alone here,' she whispered to her daughter.

'Oh, go on, Mum, they look respectable enough,' Steph replied, failing miserably to suppress a giggle.

'So did Jack the Ripper probably.' Peggy entered the room, her movements as unconfident as the expression on her face. After the knocks of the past week, she expected the worst, but did not know what it could be. At the sight of her both men leapt to their feet.

'Mrs Alder?' the older one asked.

'Yes,' said Peggy hesitantly, as if she doubted her name.

'Ah, Mrs Alder, I'm Bill Hodges, this is my associate Colin Renfrew. I'm sorry to barge in on you like this but when your daughter phoned us with the good news . . .'

'What good news?' Peggy almost snorted at the idea of such a rare commodity involving her.

'The numbers, Mum, in the paper. I did it – I checked them.'

'What paper? What numbers? No, that was all a mistake, the newspaper complained.'

'Mum, will you just *listen*?'

'Mrs Alder, we're from Camelot, the lottery company.' The man called Colin looked at her expectantly.

'Yes?' Peggy's heart pounded, but she made herself take a deep breath. If she had won, it was sure to be one of the minor prizes.

'When prizes aren't claimed on the night, we put the numbers in the newspapers throughout the following week in the hope that people will see them. Your daughter checked your tickets.' He paused. 'Mrs Alder, I've some very good news for you.'

'You have?' Peggy asked politely.

'It's my great pleasure to tell you that you are this week's winner of the State Lottery. Mrs Alder, it's the big prize. Well over a million pounds.'

'Oh, that's nice,' she said quite calmly.

Chapter Twelve

'That's nice! *That's nice!* Is that *all* you can say, Mum? It's absolutely mind-blowingly, bonkingly brill!' Steph was literally jumping up and down and reminded Peggy of when she was a little girl and wanted to go to the loo badly. She smiled at her and the memory, but stopped when she realized she must appear half-witted.

'It's a bit of a shock,' said Peggy, sounding as if she'd had no shock at all, but absentmindedly picking up one of the men's coffee cups and sipping from it. He said nothing to stop her. She sat down. 'Has anyone got a cigarette?' she asked, but no one smoked and she was out of them. 'A million, you said?'

'Well in excess of.'

'Good gracious, it really is a lot of money,' Peggy said vaguely and stood up but her legs felt woolly, as if they were made of marshmallow. She walked to the door but felt she had floated there. 'I'd best call your dad. If you'll excuse me,' she said politely to the men.

In the hall she looked at the telephone and touched it but didn't pick it up. What could she say to him? How could she break the news so that it wasn't too big a shock? She couldn't, that was the answer. She couldn't tell anyone. She suddenly felt dizzy and then sick. She ran noisily up the stairs, shot into the lavatory and sat on the loo lid, her arms wrapped about herself, to rock back and forth and found she could not stop; if anyone had asked her she would have been unable to say if she hugged herself from joy or from some other, as yet unidentified, emotion.

'Mum, Mum, you all right?' There was a hammering on the door.

She looked up abruptly not seeing, only registering from familiarity, the poster of *Loo Rules of the House* Blu-tacked on the back of the door. 'I'm fine.'

'You don't sound it. Are you crying?'

'Crying? Why should I be crying?'

'Shock.'

'Oh, Steph, don't be so silly.' She rattled the loo-roll holder.

'Did you call Dad?' Steph asked.

'No.'

'Shall I?'

'Please.'

She heard Steph run down the stairs, heard the clicking noise as she punched in the number, heard her ask for her father's extension, listened to Steph cutting through the polite preliminaries. 'Mum's won the lottery, Dad,' Steph said baldly. So much for Peggy's concern at how to break the news. She prayed his heart was up to it. 'Yes, you heard right. The top prize . . . Marvellous . . . Here, now – they're very nice . . . Come sooner than that, can't you? . . . Bye, then.' The telephone pinged. 'He's coming straight over,' Steph yelled up the stairs. 'Did you hear?'

'Yes,' Peggy shouted. Her head jerked up. She stood up and banged the wall with the palm of her hand. 'Bloody hell,' she said out loud. 'Me, a millionairess!' She leapt in the air whooping with delight, and in the confines of the lavatory she did her own little dance of joy. She began to laugh until her sides ached and she thought she would never stop. They were rich!

Within an hour chaos reigned in the lounge of the Alders' semi-detached. Steph had not stopped phoning so that Carol appeared, followed quickly by Sean. Paul arrived and hugged Peggy till she thought she would burst. Steph had called her best friend Frances and her second best friend Moraigh, and Nigel came – though why he was never at college was odd, Peggy reflected. The neighbours from both sides were in, and someone, though Peggy never found out who, had produced champagne. Bill and Colin, the two men from Camelot, were calmly understanding. They took Dan on one side and suggested that an hour or two of this uproar might be enough and for him and Peggy to detach themselves. He and Bill would drive them away to a nice quiet bolt-hole to get their breath. Dan was dubious, he felt like partying the night away and so did Peggy, he said – just look at her and the fun she was having. He pointed across the room to where Peggy, her cheeks pink with excitement, was chatting and seemingly unable to keep still. Colin and Bill, who had seen it all before, simply nodded and said they were ready when he was.

Myrtle arrived in a taxi, which Paul had thoughtfully ordered for her. She was 'all of a flutter', she said, and felt as if she'd won the money herself – which reminded her that she'd left her purse behind, so Paul dug in his pocket to pay the cab. When asked how she was she'd said fine, despite the bumpy ride, in one fell swoop offending the taxi driver, who'd joined them for a drink, and making everyone with a car feel guilty that they hadn't gone to pick up the dear old lady. She refused champagne, saying it gave her indigestion, that she supposed if there was nothing else then juice would have to do. She sat down because, as she said, her hip was killing her, but then she got left out of the general swing and, for once not pretending that she was a sweet old thing, sulked openly and sat like a malevolent witch in the corner, just like the bad fairy at the Princess's christening.

Jean, in contrast, had paid off her taxi before anyone else could get a hand in their pocket. She entered into the spirit of the occasion, knocking back the champagne, and was soon wanting music on so that she could dance the night away. She was quiet for a few minutes when she told Peggy not to do anything daft and to get someone else to open her mail for her. Peggy agreed, even though she didn't know what Jean meant. And she was subdued when she took her son, Dan, on one side and told him to watch Peggy and to get her away somewhere quiet and restful for the weekend.

'You've both got a lot to come to terms with,' she advised him.

As the noise level rose, word spread along the street so the throng grew larger, the house seeming smaller as it did so.

'Has anyone called Hazel?' Peggy suddenly asked.

'I did. She was really odd,' Steph answered.

'She's not been well, that's probably why.' Peggy, champagne glass in hand, made for the phone. 'I've got to talk to my best mate, haven't I?' She dialled the number and waited. 'Hazel, it's Peggy. Have you heard the good news? When are you coming over? I'm so excited I could burst.' The words tumbled from Peggy in a muddle.

'Bully for you,' Hazel replied. The line went dead and Peggy stood, the receiver in her hand, a puzzled look on her face.

'We've been cut off,' she said to Steph, who stood in the doorway of the lounge watching her.

'I was, too. I think she's miffed.'

'Why? That's really odd. Still, if that's how she wants to be that's her choice. Perhaps it's shock – it takes people different ways.' Peggy shrugged her shoulders as if she hadn't a care in the world. She turned round as the bell chimed and opened the door to find Daphne and Cyril outside, Daphne carrying champagne and Cyril looking sheepish behind a large bouquet of flowers.

'We simply had to call and wish you well on this night of your good fortune, Margaret my dear.' Daphne swept in dramatically but, given the smallness of the hall, had to retrace her steps before she damaged herself on the hatstand. She slipped off her fur coat which she handed imperiously to Steph, who was still standing in the lounge doorway. Steph dropped it immediately as if it had scorched her hands. 'Clumsy, clumsy,' Daphne trilled, standing over the fur, expecting Steph to retrieve it.

'I'm not touching *that*! It's against my principles.'

'Oh, really? Tedious things, principles.' Daphne bent and retrieved her coat. 'Sean called with the news. We felt as we're family we should join you.'

Peggy longed to say, 'Since when?' but managed to refrain.

'*My* Cyril here thought he might be able to help you.'

Since there was no other Cyril there, Peggy wondered why it was necessary to say 'Cyril here', and since he was the only one why was it necessary to claim him as hers quite so ostentatiously?

'Oh, yes, Cyril. In what way?' Peggy smiled kindly at him, for even though he verged on the pompous and self-satisfied, Peggy had always felt his heart was in the right place, whereas she became more and more convinced that Daphne had been born without one.

'Investments, pension funds, all the sort of things you'll have to be thinking about now,' Daphne answered for her husband. 'Best, Cyril here looks after your affairs for you. Who can advise you better, look after you, than someone in the family?'

'Someone outside the family?' Peggy said, laughter bubbling in her voice.

Daphne looked uncertainly at Peggy, then Cyril and back to Peggy.

'Oh, you're joking,' she said, with a sigh of relief.

'Am I?' said Peggy, the champagne making her feel reckless now. 'It's kind of you, Cyril, but I don't think now's the right time, do you?' she said, politely enough.

'You can never act too soon, can she, Cyril?'

Cyril managed, this time, to get his mouth open, but he paused just a micro-second too long.

'That's what my Cyril always says,' and Daphne had spoken for him. His moment had passed.

'Champagne?' Peggy suggested.

'Lovely,' said Daphne, passing regally into the lounge.

'Congratulations, Peggy. It couldn't have happened to a nicer person.' Cyril spoke! He handed her the flowers, a little awkwardly.

'Thanks, Cyril, how kind of you.' Peggy planted a kiss on his cheek. 'Come on, before the buggers drink the lot.' She took his hand and led him into the throng.

An hour later Peggy felt as if somewhere inside her a plug had been pulled out and all her energy was draining away. One minute she was on a pinnacle of happy excitement, the next she could feel herself slithering down a steep, steep slope to exhaustion and that funny feeling of fear she'd experienced in the loo.

Colin was by her side in a trice as if he'd been waiting for this. 'Mrs Alder, we've—'

'Peggy, please.' She flapped her hands weakly at him.

'Thanks. Peggy, then. We've the car outside and we've booked you and your husband into a nice quiet hotel.'

'Have you? Why?' Peggy frowned, puzzled.

'Because you've had a shock, and need to assimilate it, and because there's always the risk the press will find out and be pounding on that front door of yours. You don't want to deal with them now, do you?'

'Heavens, no!' Peggy looked up at him with eyes like a frightened doe. 'But I'll need some things.'

'All seen to, Peggy. I had a word with Steph. She's packed an overnight bag for you both. It's for the best,' Colin said, aware that Peggy was beginning to dither.

'Yes, I'm sure you're right. And Dan?'

'We'll just slip out quietly. No goodbyes, it's easier.'

'Yes, of course.' Peggy made for the door, grinning from ear to ear. Steph was in the hall.

'You'll be better off, Mum. A nice quiet dinner with Dad. Make some plans, have an early night.'

'Yes, I do feel suddenly very tired. But it seems a shame – your dad loves a party.'

'But I'm quite ready to leave this one. Come on, Peggy. Let's get going.' Dan spoke from behind her, his arm hugging her tight. 'Who's a clever girl, then?' He lifted her off the ground.

'Oh, don't, Dan, you'll get a hernia – a big lump like me.' She was laughing but felt humiliated too.

'You're perfect to me as you are,' Dan said softly, and Peggy didn't know what to do with herself: he never normally spoke to her like that.

Colin opened the door of the large Jaguar for them, and Peggy and Dan got in the back. Peggy sniffed the smell of leather upholstery appreciatively. 'Lovely smell,' she said.

'Lovely car. I'd love one like this.'

'Nothing to stop you now, Mr Alder.' Colin turned in his seat.

'Oh, I don't think so. I don't think I could ever spend what these cost – not on a car, it would seem wrong somehow. In any case, *I* haven't got that sort of money.'

Peggy looked out of the window only half listening. The powerful motor was switched on. She waved at Steph, Carol and Paul all standing together on the garden path. The news had spread even further: neighbours on adjoining streets had braved the cold to stand in their doorways waving them goodbye, shouting out their good wishes.

'Gracious me, I feel like the Queen,' Peggy said, as she waved at them all. The car purred up the slight incline of the close. She looked out of the back window. 'Do you think things will ever be the same again?' she asked Dan.

'Of course! Why shouldn't they be?' he said cheerfully.

Peggy settled back in the unaccustomed luxury, content with his reassurance.

PART TWO

March

TO

December

Chapter Thirteen

The hotel was an old mansion set in its own grounds. In the headlights Peggy could not make out if it was genuinely Elizabethan or a rich Victorian's caprice.

The car halted and, as if on cue, the front door opened, a shaft of light flooded the steps and gravelled driveway, and a man dressed as a valet ran lightly down the stone steps, past the moss-green stone lions, and opened the door before Peggy had time to find the handle.

'Welcome to Five Oaks, Mrs Alder,' he said, helping her out as if she was a geriatric.

'Five Oaks?' said Peggy, surprised. It sounded more like the title of an Enid Blyton novel than an ancient manor house. It was probably Victorian, then.

In the hall a log fire burned welcomingly, a grandfather clock ticked comfortably and oak furniture shone, and smelt enticingly of lavender. No sooner had they got their bearings than a tall, corpulent man bore down upon them, red-faced, fully moustached, with a huge hand held out in greeting. His impeccably cut dinner suit was somewhat marred by the bright fuchsia-coloured silk bow-tie and matching cummerbund, which only drew attention to the massive size of his stomach. Peggy's hand was crushed in another welcome by Reginald Fortescue – Captain.

'Navy?' asked Peggy with interest, since her own late father had been a chief petty officer.

'Army,' was the proud reply.

They proceeded up the wide, blood-red-carpeted stairs, past a dolorous collection of portraits, about which Captain Reginald was magnificently vague and made rumbling remarks as to the memsahib knowing their full history. He opened the door of their room with a flourish. 'The Queen Elizabeth Suite', he announced as if addressing his troops.

It consisted of a large sitting room, well furnished with antiques and comfortable chairs around another log fire, a bedroom with a four-poster bed, and a bathroom over which Peggy was in raptures. It was decorated in white with sprigs of flowers worked in the enamel, gold-plated taps but of the old-fashioned type. The floor was carpeted, the lighting subdued and flattering, and the towels, white and soft, were piled high on a shelf. Beside the bath was a collection of bath and body lotions.

'Oh, this is perfect.' Peggy clapped her hands with approval.

'I'm glad everything's to your satisfaction, Mrs Alder. If there's anything we can get you, just pick up the telephone and we'll be here in a trice.' Despite his gut he bowed his way out of the room.

'Gawd, I bet this costs an arm and a leg,' Dan said, lifting a bottle of Pol Roger champagne out of an ice bucket to inspect the label. 'Do you think this is courtesy of the management or do we pay for it?'

'If it's free we still pay – probably worked into the price for the room.'

'Who's paying? Us or Bill and Colin?'

'I don't know. Didn't they say?'

'Not a dicky bird.'

'Still, one thing's for sure – we can afford it now.' Peggy still found it almost impossible to believe.

'But can we? I'm up to the limit on my Barclaycard and I doubt if the bank would be too happy with a cheque for this place – not at the tail end of the month. And do we know when you get the loot?'

'Straight away, I thought. But I suppose the cheque has got to clear. Oh, Dan, I don't know . . .'

'No champagne, then?' he said wistfully.

'Go on, open it. If the cheque's going to bounce it might as well really bounce,' Peggy said recklessly. She was startled by the telephone ringing with a rather twee bird-like sound. Dan answered it, said a lot of yeses and put the phone down.

'That was Bill. He suggests we meet in the bar in half an hour, then dinner.'

112

'I've nothing to wear,' she said. 'I can't go.'

'Don't be daft. See what Steph's packed.'

When opened the case revealed her grey silk outfit and Dan's best suit, white shirt and polka dot tie. 'Steph's been organized, for once,' he said.

'Mine's got a bit creased, I'll hang it in the bathroom, and maybe the steam from the bath will straighten it.'

'Have you got time for a bath?'

'I'm going to make time.' She ran the water, deciding to use a Floris bath oil. 'Why don't you call Colin? Say we'll be an hour,' she called, amazing herself at taking the initiative.

Bathed and perfumed, wrapped in one of the large white towels, she padded back into the bedroom. Dan was in his boxer shorts on the bed watching a TV he had discovered hidden in an oak chest. He looked up as she entered the room.

'Come here,' he said, patting the bed beside him. She sat down. Slowly he unwrapped the towel and his hands stroked her back and then searched for her breasts. 'Do you think they'll mind if we're late?' he whispered in her ear, which he promptly began to lick with the tip of his tongue.

It wasn't just the money, things were looking up in other directions too, Peggy thought as she lay back eagerly in his arms.

The next morning they both awoke feeling pretty grim. It wasn't just the champagne – though they had consumed enough of that. It was, they decided, the fault of last night's dinner, which had been too rich and too much.

Captain Fortescue had contrived a menu of perplexing length, each dish requiring a paragraph of rhapsodic description. There appeared to be nothing that was not fried in butter and doused in cream, wine and brandy. And dishes which did not require the *flambé* trolley were few and far between.

Settling on an avocado pear followed by a fillet steak – grilled – they felt they were safe. But the avocado arrived with its flesh mixed into a cheesy cream sauce containing prawns and slivers of smoked salmon, all covered with more cheese and grilled.

They had asked for their steak to be cooked plainly, but this obviously hurt the Captain to the base of his pendulous stomach. 'No steak Diane? No steak *au poivre*? Tut, tut, what next?' he boomed so that all the diners in the room turned and looked at them. 'I recommend the speciality of the house, our Steak Rosita.' His eyes seemed to plead with Peggy as if a rejection would mean the end of his life.

'All right, then, but only a small one,' she said, weakening.

Her spirits sank lower and lower as she looked at the Captain's *flambé* trolley when it was wheeled towards them. She apologized to her heart at the huge slab of butter which was divided between two chafing dishes. In one went shallots, peppers, chunks of fresh pineapple, a chilli, and all were expertly tossed and teased. The fillet steak went into the second pan, while whisky was added to the vegetable mix. All was then tipped over the sizzling steaks, and double cream poured in.

'And now, *voilà*, the *pièce de résistance*, my special touch.' And the Captain delved beneath the cover and came up with a grater and a slab of chocolate which he proceeded to scatter over the mixture, now artistically arranged on plates. Peggy thought she might throw up. She eyed Colin's and Bill's steak pie and thought they'd made a wise choice.

'You're honoured. The Captain only *flambé*s for special customers.'

'But he doesn't know us,' said Dan.

'He does now.' Bill winked.

Rather than hurt the Captain's feelings, and still unsure if Colin and Bill were paying, they had both felt duty bound to eat the concoction. Oddly it did not taste nearly as bad as it looked and they had expected, but the richness was a killer and their bodies were telling them so even as they forced it down.

At least, Peggy consoled herself, she need not have a pud. But that fond notion also flew out of the window when the Captain appeared with a young woman, who looked Malayan, carrying a large ice-cream gâteau with 'Congratulations, Peggy,' iced on the top.

'Mr and Mrs Alder, I'd like you to meet this dusky maiden of mine, my wife,' he said ceremoniously, and Peggy had to kick Dan not to laugh.

After all that, brandy was drunk, not for pleasure but for medicinal purposes.

Their breakfast was, of necessity, Alka-Seltzer which they found in the bathroom, orange juice and coffee. After dressing sluggishly they forced themselves out into the frost-rimed grounds of the hotel. After ten minutes' brisk walking they both felt marginally better.

'Last night taught us a lesson, didn't it? No matter how much money you get we can't cope with rich food,' said Dan, hands dug deep in his pockets, his early-morning grey pallor slowly changing to a healthier pink.

'Too right. Pretty grim, wasn't it? And isn't this an odd place?' she asked, her own arm linked comfortably in his, their stride neatly matching. 'Captain Fortescue is too much. And I thought army captains didn't use the rank in Civvy Street? Bet he's Catering Corps.'

'Peggy Alder, you sound like a real snob.' He pushed her teasingly.

'He strikes me as false, like the furniture in our room. I think it's all reproduction. The drawers work too easily to be genuine, and I peeped at the back of that chest the TV's in and it's plywood.'

'You're joking!'

'No, I'm not.'

'Still, repro or not, the effect's pretty. And he seems to be doing well.'

'Bit too pretty for me, all that chintz – it's over the top. I think it's a shame – it's a lovely house.'

Dan stopped in his tracks. 'You're amazing. Last week you'd have thought this place perfect. You only learnt yesterday afternoon you're rich and just listen to you – nothing's right.'

'I didn't mean to sound like that. You make me sound horrible. I'm just being honest and the house isn't. And I think I'd have recognized it all as fake last week.' She felt affronted and sounded it.

'Okay, keep your hair on, I was only joking.' He began walking again, and Peggy had to hurry to catch up with him.

'What do you think about what Colin and Bill said last night?' she asked.

'About using the lottery company's financial advisers? We could – or rather you could. It's your money, not mine.'

'Don't be silly, it's ours. Haven't we always lived that way? Why should it change?'

'A million reasons.' He grinned at her. 'We could do worse than use them, I suppose. I mean, they're used to dealing with people like us. We need some advice, that's for sure. It would be easy to fritter it all away and we've got to think of the future.'

'We *couldn't* spend that much.'

'You reckon? Then you'd be wrong, love. A house, a couple of cars, a few holidays, help the kids, answer a few begging letters and you'd soon see a bloody great hole in it.'

'Oh, Dan, don't be so practical. Not just yet. We could do so many things. We could take the whole family round the world on the *QE2*.'

'Or an African safari,' he said, joining in her excitement.

'We could buy each member of the family a house – and a car. And think what Christmases we'll be able to have from now on.'

'I know how you feel, love.' He put his arm round her shoulders. 'But we mustn't allow ourselves to get carried away. We must be sensible. Look at us. You're forty-five, I'm forty-eight, so our first priority should be to make provision for our old age.'

'Boring!'

'Necessary. Then, at least, we must sit down and work out our priorities.'

'Let's go back to our room, have some coffee and work everything out on a piece of paper.' They went back to the hotel to find their room cleaned, and a fire lit. The coffee they ordered was with them in ten minutes.

'Nothing artificial about the service, is there?' he asked, as she poured their coffee and they both decided that their stomachs might be able to manage a digestive biscuit.

'Right.' Peggy straightened the pad of hotel-headed notepaper and took the top off the Five Oaks logoed pen. 'There's Hazel first.'

'Hazel? What about her?'

'She was supposed to share the cost of the lottery ticket with me. She was shocked I'd spent twenty pounds so I said she could give me a fiver if she thought that was too much.' She wrote down a figure.

'What are you doing there?' He snatched the paper.

'That's her share.'

'Did she pay up?'

'Well, no. She never had it on her when I asked.'

'Then she doesn't get a penny,' he said firmly.

'I'm sure she would have if she'd remembered.' Peggy was wavering for she had begun to doubt that Hazel had intended to. And, when she looked at the sum written down it looked an even larger sum than when she had thought it.

'And do you think if your number hadn't come up she'd have paid you? Oh, come on, Peggy, don't be so naïve.'

'She was really short with me on the telephone last night. She obviously thinks I don't intend to honour my debt. I'd got it all resolved in my mind and now you're confusing me.'

'She was short with you 'cause Bruce has gone bump. They're probably going to lose everything.'

'Oh, no. Oh, poor Hazel, how awful. But they've been doing so well. Why? Bruce managed to keep his head above water all through the worst of the recession. What went wrong?'

'He diversified into an area he knows nothing about – hotels. He sank a lot in some chain in the North bought by a mate of his and it got into hot water. He should have stuck to building – he knows about that. I tried to tell him but he wasn't going to listen to me. To him I was a no-hoper.'

'I didn't know that he thought like that about you. That's horrible. Still, poor Hazel. I've got to share something with her, haven't I?'

'But not a half share, Peggy, for goodness sake.'

'A third of it, then?'

'A quarter sounds better to me.'

117

'You sure that's not too mean?'

'In the circumstances it's bloody generous.'

She screwed up the sheet of paper she'd written on and started another. 'Let's make it a third.' She looked across the table at him.

'Fair enough. It's your loot, after all.'

'Ours,' she said as she wrote. 'You know Daphne offered Cyril's help in advising us?'

'I bet she did. There's another one living beyond his means.'

'Cyril? Good heavens. Am I blind or something? But if that's the case don't you think—'

'We use him? No. If he can't manage his own affairs how's he going to manage yours?'

'That's true.' She sucked the end of the pen. 'Aren't decisions horrible?'

'Yes, but some aren't. What about the kids?'

He was right. They spent a happy half-hour deciding how to help their children. Paul's mortgage to be paid off and him to be set up in a small business. Money set aside for Steph. They could not be as specific about Carol since they weren't quite sure how well Sean was doing, if Dan was right about Cyril.

'Probably best to give her a lump sum to put in the bank,' Dan advised.

'You know what I'd like to do most of all? Buy your mum a bungalow by the seaside. She's earned that.'

'What about us?'

'What do we need? We've got what we want. Pay that wretched bank overdraft off, that's all, some new togs, a holiday in Italy.'

'Don't you want a new house?'

'Whatever for? I like our house. Bet you'd like a new car, though,' she said fondly.

'Please.'

'Heavens, I feel so powerful!'

'How much is all that, then?' He pointed to the paper.

Peggy added up quickly. She looked at Dan with horror and added it up again in case she had made a mistake.

But the sum did not change. She showed Dan.

'Four hundred and seventy-five thousand pounds! It can't be.' She added up the figures again. 'It is.'

'Shit!' said Dan. 'See what I mean, how easily it can go?'

Peggy took up the pen and crossed out Hazel's third share and put a quarter one instead. 'It's not fair on the kids if she gets more.'

The telephone rang. It was Captain Fortescue asking Dan if he could spare him a moment in the bar. Left alone, Peggy thought over the morning's work. It had been depressing, she thought as she packed. How could money shrink so fast? And how to be fair? She was almost relieved when Bill knocked at the door to see if they were ready.

'We've decided we're going to need your advisers' help, Bill. These sort of decisions are too much for us,' said Peggy.

'Where's Dan?'

'Talking to the Captain in the bar. I said we'd meet him there.'

'Well, the account's all settled. Colin's loading the car. I'll give you a hand.' Bill took the case.

'Well, there's a turn-up,' said Dan, as they settled in the back of the Jaguar and were waving goodbye to the Captain and his wife. 'Guess what? Old Captain Reg only wants to know if we'd be interested in investing in Five Oaks.'

'No!' said Peggy as the car swished down the driveway. 'Of course you turned him down.'

'I didn't, as a matter of fact. I said I'd think about it. It might be fun – Mine Host and all that crap.'

Chapter Fourteen

Colin and Bill had been right: Five Oaks *had* made her feel more relaxed. But as the car quickly covered the distance to London and the award ceremony Peggy began to feel nervous again. She wished she could go to sleep, be oblivious of the ordeal ahead, but that was out of the question with Dan wanting to show her lists of figures the Captain had given him.

'You know there's no point in my looking at them, Dan. I've never understood finances of that order.'

'Look, it's quite simple. Here's his outgoings and there's his incomings and that's the profit.'

'If he's making all that money, why does he need us to invest in it?' she said with reasonable logic, after glancing at the figures. Dan sighed as if irritated with her.

'Mrs Alder, it's none of my business, of course,' said Bill, twisting in the front seat the better to see her. 'But I think I should point out that you'll probably find a lot of Captain Fortescues popping up with business propositions. Best to be wary, especially in the early days.'

'You're right there, Bill, it isn't any of your business.' Dan spoke pleasantly enough, but neither the sharpness nor the meaning of his words was erased.

'Really, Dan! Don't be so rude. Bill's only trying to help us, aren't you, Bill? Well, I'll say thanks,' she said, trying to improve the somewhat aggressive atmosphere building up in the leather cocoon of the car. 'I did wonder if something or someone like the Captain would happen. I don't intend that we should make decisions for some time, apart from helping out the kids.' There was no response from Dan, so she did not know if he agreed with her or not, but she sensed, from years of knowing him, that he was annoyed with her and was sulking. 'How did the Captain know about us?' she ploughed on, refusing to let Dan's mood stop her finding out things. Really, she thought, he liked to think he was so smart but he could be naïve too.

'He recognized Colin from when he worked for a football-pools company and put two and two together. Sorry.'

'Not your fault. In any case, we should consider various projects, but it doesn't mean we have to take them up, does it, Dan?'

'Of course not.' Dan's voice sounded irritated, affronted and hurt all at the same time. Abruptly he began to fold the Captain's lists of figures, making as much noise as possible so that everyone was aware of what he was doing.

'Do you like this job? I mean, don't you ever feel a bit fed up seeing all these winners and it's never you?' she asked Bill and Colin, as she continued relentlessly to make conversation.

'Not at all. It's fun – everyone's so happy. We like to think we help ease you into a new life with as little hassle as possible. It's not in our interest for the lottery to get a bad name. We don't want any of our winners being made miserable by their winning – you know, like some of the sad stories one used to hear about the pools winners.'

Dan snorted and settled back on the seat, hands folded in his lap. Peggy glared, but his face was turned away and he did not see.

'But they get advice, too, don't they?'

'They do now. Years ago they didn't – that's when the real problems were. We've learnt a lot from the pools people.'

'How to persuade people to go along with you and your publicity plans for a start,' Dan said gruffly.

'If you hadn't wanted to take part we would, of course, have respected your wishes,' Bill said, looking almost hurt.

Under his breath Dan said, 'I bet,' and Peggy hoped they hadn't heard. She nudged his knee to try to stop him making further remarks. After all, they were only doing their job and had been very kind.

'The publicity keeps people investing in the lottery, keeps the money coming in, makes it possible for winners like you to get the sums you do.' Bill sounded sharp.

121

'We owe you that,' Peggy assured them, forcing herself to smile, despite her nervousness which, fuelled by the tension in the car, was now building rapidly. 'Still, it's an odd feeling, you know. Yesterday I was a nobody and today I lose that – I lose my privacy. It's quite scary, really.'

'People soon forget, Peggy. They get curious about the next winner.'

'Not the people who know us, though.'

'Not much we can do about that,' Dan said.

The London hotel was a modern tower of luxury – nothing false about it – though Peggy could have wished to be on a lower floor, as the wind rattled and the rain lashed double-glazed windows. She was sure the building was rocking, or was that due to her stress?

She was doubly fatigued, from keeping the peace in the car, no doubt. This is how a UN mediator must feel, she thought as she kicked off her shoes with relief and flopped onto one of the pretty pink- and green-striped silk-covered sofas in the sitting room of their suite. Both of them had refused lunch with Bill and Colin, and while waiting for their sandwiches and champagne to arrive Dan was prowling around the room inspecting its contents.

'Imagine us having champagne for lunch.' She giggled at the idea.

'You needn't have made me look such a jerk,' he said suddenly.

Peggy closed her eyes with the resigned manner of one who had expected something like this. 'I don't know what you mean,' she replied, though she did.

'And you needn't use that exaggerated tone with me.'

'I wasn't aware I was using any kind of *tone*.'

'A right fool I felt in front of Colin and Bill – being slapped down by my wife like that.'

'Then perhaps you shouldn't have chosen to discuss the Captain's project in front of them,' she replied, her voice sharp, but she felt too tired to placate him.

'I can see which way it's going to go. Anything I suggest you're going to shoot down in flames,' he said, as he took an inordinate interest in the logo on the hotel ashtray.

'Oh, come on, Dan, that's hardly fair. We'll decide together – of course we will. Maybe even Five Oaks. But we need time. We mustn't rush into anything, must we?' She forced herself to be reasonable: she didn't want the day spoilt by a row.

Dan did not reply but continued his exaggerated inspection of the room, coming to rest at the plate-glass window where he stood staring out at the damp view of London.

A discreet knock heralded the champagne and smoked-salmon sandwiches and Peggy made small talk with the waiter as he opened the bottle. She spoke brightly, too brightly probably, but she wanted to make amends for her surly husband who did not even acknowledge the man. Sensing the atmosphere, he did not bother to lurk for the hoped-for tip.

'Here, drink this, it'll cheer you up.' She had taken one of the flutes and crossed to the window.

'It'll take more than that to cheer me up,' he replied sulkily.

'Dan love, don't make things difficult, please. It's going to be a strain today, anyway.'

'What is? Pocketing a fortune? I could do with such a problem,' he sneered.

'Dan, *I'm* not pocketing. *We* are. What's mine is yours. Haven't we always worked that way? The communal honey-pot?' She forced herself to sound reasonable, but she longed to shake him as she would a petulant, troublesome child. He downed his wine in one. 'More?' she asked, and topped up his glass. 'Come on, don't spoil things.' But there was no response. She did not want to eat now, or drink. 'I think I'll take a quick bath,' she said, and left him to his ill-temper.

In the bathroom she turned on the taps of the whirlpool bath and while it filled she inspected her surroundings. 'Such luxury,' she said aloud to the 'his' and 'hers' basins set in Carrara marble. One wall was covered in mirror-glass sections, one of which she noticed was ajar. She pushed it gingerly and it swung open to reveal a small but well-equipped exercise room. 'Dan, quick,' she called out, her voice so full of excitement that his curiosity got the better of him and he appeared in the doorway. 'Look at this! Our own gym! This is living.'

'Stone the crows,' he said, and leapt onto the large, complicated machine in the centre of the room. Lying back, he began to lift the weights behind him. He was laughing, she was relieved to see.

'Don't put your back out,' she advised, going back into the bathroom.

'It'll strengthen it. Here, maybe we could have it off on this thing – maybe I could tie you up to the weights. Come here.'

'No, thank you, I'm going to have a bath,' she called back, but she was smiling. That was better. They'd made love twice last night and that hadn't happened in years, not since they were young.

'Later then,' she heard him yell, much to her satisfaction.

There wasn't time later. Pippa Ewing, pretty, pert and smart as a button, Peggy's personal style consultant, courtesy of Camelot, arrived to take her to the hairdresser's, the beauty consultant, and Harrods to buy a new outfit – only if she wanted, she was told. Peggy wanted.

Her going out would cheer Dan, she was quick to realize. A group of financial advisers were due; she had simply asked him to deal with them since she was so useless at figures, which restored his male pride in a second. After all, she thought, as she sat in the taxi with Pippa, they were only discussions this afternoon: her signature would be needed. She could decide then while letting Dan think everything was his choice.

Peggy wished that all her life she'd had a Pippa to advise her. It was Pippa who controlled the hairdresser who, against Peggy's wishes, wanted to cut her page-boy short; they compromised with an ear-length bob and a semi-permanent rinse. The make-up was less successful. The autumnal brown and russet eye-shadows, and mulberry lips looked uncomfortable on her, as though they'd ended up on the wrong face.

'Don't worry, Peggy. It'll all wash off and I thought you looked very pretty this morning the way you'd done it yourself.'

'Did you?' Peggy could have kissed the sophisticated young woman, but didn't like to.

An account had been arranged for Peggy at Harrods. Where clothes were concerned Pippa was a wizard. Just by glancing at a dress on a hanger she knew if it would suit Peggy or not, and her eye for colour matching and co-ordination was flawless. They were put in a large, airy room with comfortable armchairs and clothes were brought to them. No traipsing around the various departments for Peggy today.

A Frank Usher dress in black with a sequinned top for tonight and an Armani trouser suit in grey for the morning – something she wouldn't have dreamt of trying on herself – were the core of her shopping. But she didn't stop there. She bought herself lingerie, the like of which she'd only dreamed of before, sweaters, a new winter coat, two new shirts, because she couldn't choose between them, shoes and boots. For Steph and Carol she bought new dresses and hoped they would fit. For Paul's children a pile of clothes; new shirts and a suit for Dan with the promise he could change it if it didn't fit.

Peggy couldn't remember when she'd had such fun – until the bill was presented to her and her smile disappeared sharply.

'It's nearly three thousand pounds! I can't spend that.'

Pippa eyed the assistant, who politely withdrew. 'Peggy, it isn't really that much – not when you see all the things you've got. Good gracious, there are women who'd spend that on one suit.'

'Not me,' she said staunchly.

'This is a special day in your life, Peggy, one that will never come again. If you'll take my advice you'll sign for it and enjoy it, not be afraid of it.'

Peggy squeezed Pippa's hand. 'Yes, you're right. Where's the pen?'

All the same, all the way back to the hotel she was working out how to tell Dan.

He was still in conference with Colin, Bill and two other men who had joined them.

'Dan, could I have a word?' she whispered. He smiled pleasantly, his earlier bad mood completely gone. They went into the bedroom, where her parcels were already laid neatly on the bedroom floor in their dark green Harrods' boxes and carriers.

'What is it?' Dan asked, made anxious by Peggy's serious expression.

'Dan, I've done a daft thing. I'm sorry but all that lot,' she kicked at one of the bags, 'came to three thousand quid, give or take a few pounds.'

'Is that all?' He laughed. 'I'd quite expected you to spend double.'

'You mean that?'

'Oh, Peggy, darling. You're rich! When will you get it into your pretty head?' He kissed her full on the mouth. 'Look, I've got to get back, and I think they want to talk to you – after all, you're the one that's going to have to sign everything.'

'I'll just re-do my face – I don't like this.'

'By the way, your hair's smashing.'

She sat, dazed, in front of the well-lit mirror of the dressing table. When was the last time he'd called her darling? And when had he last said she was pretty?

Chapter Fifteen

Dressed in her new Frank Usher, worrying that she might look like a Christmas tree in the multicoloured, sequinned top, fretting that perhaps the hairstyle was a bit on the young side for her and convinced she'd put on too much make-up, Peggy waited for the evening to begin, for that moment when the cheque would be placed in her hand and she would instantly become a millionairess. The thought made her shiver.

'Do you know who's presenting the cheque?' she asked Dan, who had finally won the battle with his golfball-shaped cuff-links and the stiffness of his new shirt – I could buy him gold ones now, with his initials on, perhaps for his birthday, she thought contentedly.

'No, I think they like to keep it as a surprise until the last minute. That was a knock on the door,' he said, picking at a speck on his new suit jacket.

'You sure?' Peggy teetered towards the door – these heels *were* too high. She'd told Pippa they would be, it was years since she had worn stilettos. 'Yes?' she said cautiously to a young woman in a short tight black Lycra skirt and a scarlet, gold-braided boxy jacket who stood, almost a clone of Pippa, in the doorway.

'I'm Tricia Ballantine-Smith, your PR.' She flashed a wide-mouthed confident smile. 'I'm just checking everything's fine and I'm here to look after you.'

'Where's Pippa?' asked Peggy, not meaning to sound rude but managing to.

'She's finished her job. She was only your stylist,' Tricia said sharply, and Peggy felt she wasn't going to like her much, and certainly with a name like that . . . Peggy was suspicious of embellished Smiths. 'I've brought you these.' She held up a Cellophane-

127

wrapped corsage of orchids. 'Ah, well, maybe not,' she said, taking in Peggy's dress and Peggy decided she most definitely did not like her. 'You look very nice, Peggy,' she said. Peggy said nothing, thinking it would have been more polite if she'd called her Mrs Alder and waited to be invited to call her Peggy. And who wanted to be told they only looked nice?

'You'd best come in,' Peggy said coolly.

'Hi, Dan. I'm Tricia, your PR. My, you look a real dreamboat.' Tricia tittered. 'Isn't that what they used to say?'

'Maybe, but before *our* time.' It was Peggy's turn to sound sharp, glaring at Dan who was grinning moronically at the young woman.

'Now, I've got your schedule here and it's imperative we stick to it. It's being televised live, as I'm sure you know, and we want to catch the evening newscasts.' She handed Dan a sheet of paper.

'Television?' Peggy clutched at her neck anxiously.

'Of course.' Tricia sounded irritated.

'I forgot about it.' Peggy felt confused, and wished she didn't, given the less-than-believing look Tricia shot her way.

'When interviewed by the press we'd appreciate you giving the company's full title and as frequently as poss. It helps us with publicity.'

'What's that, then, when it's at home?' Dan asked.

'Oh dear, haven't you been told? It's Camelot, like King Arthur.' She didn't snap at Dan, Peggy noticed, but bestowed a wondrous smile on him. 'And if you could possibly say how well we've looked after you, the guidance, financial advice, that sort of thing. If you could do that it would be really *dear* of you.' Again the mega-wattage of her smile was directed at Dan, who looked even dafter which Peggy wouldn't have thought possible had she not witnessed it. She coughed, which brought him to his senses.

'I would if it was me who was going to be interviewed. But it's Peggy who's the winner,' he said apologetically, and gave her back the paper almost wistfully.

'No? Really? I'm so sorry. What must you think of me? I'm freelance. This is the first time I've worked for Camelot – their

normal PR is sick. Will you forgive me, Peggy?' She turned her
back on Dan, who looked so downcast that Peggy almost felt
sorry for him, but she managed to resist: silly old goat, behaving
like a star-crossed adolescent, she said to herself. Now the full
power of Tricia's charisma and charm – or what she herself
regarded as such – was focused on Peggy, who was not so easily
taken in. 'A trillion, million sorries, Peggy!'

'Have you seen any of my family?' she asked.

'They've all arrived. They're downstairs.'

'Why aren't they up here?'

'It's easier if we have them downstairs waiting for you. Then
the press can snap you all greeting – we get some lovely piccies
that way.'

'But I want them here.'

'Oh, Peggy, if you wouldn't mind keeping to the schedule?
There'll be plenty of time afterwards. You can have a party up
here then.'

'Peggy, love, we haven't got the time. Come on, co-operate.
I'm sure Tricia knows best.'

And Peggy caved in. She supposed it was inevitable that she
would. Didn't she always go along with what other people
wanted? But she would have liked Steph and Carol to see her
outfit, to tell her whether it suited her or not. She'd have got a
straight answer from them.

'Right then, shall we go?' Tricia beamed.

'Lead on, MacDuff,' Dan said, and Peggy pulled a face at
him, it was the sort of stupid thing he would say, the girl had
made him witless.

They left the suite and walked towards the lift, Peggy feeling
more than apprehensive, in fact like a piglet being led to slaughter
or whatever the cliché was, she couldn't even remember that. Her
mind was gearing up to go into a muddled turmoil. Her hands
felt damp, her stomach queasy, and she knew that if she had to
say anything no words would emerge. She was pretty certain that
if someone asked, she wouldn't remember her name. As the lift
descended it was as if she'd left her brain and reason in the suite.

The lift sighed to a halt on the ground floor and, as the doors
swished open, Peggy could see a gaggle of people waiting in the

hall, all of whom seemed to take a step towards her. She had an almost uncontrollable urge to cower into the lift, shoot back up, pack her bags and run to oblivion.

'Mum! Over here.'

'Steph,' she called, and began to step towards her but Tricia grabbed her arm firmly.

'The cars are waiting,' she said, and guided Peggy towards the street entrance, Peggy looking wistfully over her shoulder for her family.

Later she remembered nothing of the car ride, or her arrival at the theatre where the televised award show was put out on the network every Saturday night. A strange calm had descended upon her and she felt much as though she were in the eye of a hurricane. She watched in an almost detached way as officials rushed about her, and registered their barely controlled panic, but she did not ask herself why they were in such a state. She was spoken to, but heard nothing, rather like the voices that had come and gone in the resuscitation room as she came round from a general anaesthetic after having her appendix out. She wanted her family with her and she could not see them.

The show started and she was vaguely aware of the music, the dancers; she did not laugh as the audience did at the comedian compère's jokes. And then the calm left her as she felt herself being led onto the stage. She was blinking in the bright lights, and she turned round, almost desperately, looking for Dan.

'I'm here, darling,' he said, taking her hand and squeezing it.

'Mrs Alder, or please, may I call you Peggy? It's my great pleasure to meet you. And I'm so honoured to have been asked to give you the cheque. I expect you're a teeny bit nervous – I know I am,' said a familiar voice at her side. She swung round.

'Simon Williams! Never! *You!*' Peggy said in a breathless, gushy sort of voice.

'Well, I think it's me. At least it was this morning when I got up,' he said half mockingly, and smiled his lop-sided smile and arched one eyebrow.

Peggy clutched her hands together. Ever since *Upstairs Downstairs* he had been one of her favourite actors. She had cried when, as James Bellamy, he had shot himself in the series. Peggy felt quite weak at the knees to be meeting him, but refrained from prattling.

'Yes, of course. But . . . if you wouldn't mind . . . when this is all over I'd love your autograph,' she said, throwing caution, and any attempt at sophistication, to the winds. Before he could answer the chairman of the company was on his feet addressing the press, but Peggy did not listen, for out of the corner of her eye she had seen it: a huge, enormous, larger-than-life cheque.

Simon Williams made a charming speech, and then the cheque was in his hands and he was guying about and joking at the weight. Peggy realized Dan was no longer beside her. 'Dan? Where's Dan? I can't accept it without him,' she said, looking about wildly.

'I'm here, Peggy love,' Dan said, pushing his way through a gaggle of grey-suited officials.

It was over so quickly. The money was hers. The audience went officially wild. Simon kissed her cheek and she managed *not* to say she wouldn't wash the spot – Steph would have died with embarrassment, or maybe she would have understood, but Carol wouldn't, that was for sure. She felt immense relief that she hadn't had to make a speech.

Then she was asked to flick the switch that would release the gaily coloured numbered balls which would select this week's winner. In no time at all, she was led from the stage, into the car and back to the hotel, to a room set out with spindly chairs at a table covered in microphones. Again she experienced that strange feeling of floating along as if she'd lost control of her life. The room was full of reporters and TV cameramen, and, with gathering horror, as they pointed their cameras, their microphones and their tape recorders at her in anticipation, she understood that they were expecting her to talk to them.

'How old are you, Peggy?' one asked. Damned cheek, she thought and ignored the questioner.

'Where do you live?'

'Not necessary,' snapped Tricia, who had taken up a position beside Peggy. Dan sat the other side.

'Will you be buying a new house?'

'No. We like where we are,' said Peggy, when Dan didn't answer.

'Are you going to spend, spend, spend?'

'No way,' Peggy said, more confidently. 'We're too long in the tooth for that.'

'A car? What car will you buy?'

'Not a Rolls-Royce, that's for sure.' Dan laughed.

'You must want to buy something?'

'I think I'd like it if we could take a holiday, in Italy, perhaps,' Peggy said, squinting through the over-bright lights and trying to make out who had asked the question. This wasn't so difficult, she decided, and began to relax into her chair.

'Do you think it will make a difference to your life, Peggy?'

'No, why should it?' She sounded puzzled. 'Well, of course, not having to worry about money, that'll be different. And knowing our futures are secure, that'll be nice. But I hope we'll go on as before.'

'How do you think your friends will react?'

'They'll be pleased for us, as we would be for them,' she said.

'And what do you think, Dan?'

'There might be one or two who'll be jealous and drop out of our circle but if that's the case they couldn't really have been friends in the first place.'

And so it went on and on. How could they keep thinking them up? But she did find that as more questions came it became easier to answer them.

The photographers then asked for the whole family to be on the stage. It was Paul who said what was to be repeated in every paper the following morning: 'Our mum is the best in the world. All she cares about is us. It couldn't have happened to a nicer person.' And the photographs caught the moment when all three children, with Candice and Sean in the background, flung their arms about their smiling, yet tearful, mother.

Peggy had thought that was that, but she hadn't read the itinerary that Tricia had given Dan. For almost the next three hours she had interviews at twenty-minute intervals in a small sitting room off the conference area.

Peggy and Dan were interviewed by most of the papers, and several of her favourite magazines, and all took photographs. They stopped at ten to watch themselves on the news and Peggy covered her face in horror at how fat she looked. By eleven it was over.

'Supper?' asked Tricia.

'I'm starving,' said Peggy.

'I'm sorry it went on for so long, so many interviews. I think it was because you have such a charming family – and you're so attractive, of course.'

'Me?' Peggy said in amazement.

'Oh, yes. I thought you all came over very well. And the tabloids love the fact that it's a woman who's won. Up until now it's mainly been men or groups who've banded together, you know – they're not so interesting to the press. But a mum with a loving family becoming a millionairess, well, it's captivating, isn't it? Everyone would want the same for their mother. It's a fairy story.'

Peggy wished she'd go and leave them alone. But Tricia, fussing as always, showed them back to the suite even though Peggy said they could find their way. A buffet had been laid ready for them which Tricia checked – quite unnecessarily – and at long last they were alone as a family. The first time since she had won the money.

Peggy kicked off her shoes, which had been killing her feet for the last couple of hours. 'What a song and dance! I'm glad that's over.' She sank gratefully into an armchair.

'Mum, you were a star!' Paul bent down and kissed her.

'I didn't feel like one.' She looked up at her son and a rather sheepish Candice. 'You two back together?'

'Well, yes,' Paul said, taking enormous interest in his shoes.

'That's the best news I've had in weeks!' Peggy exclaimed.

'What? Better than winning the lottery? Some hope!' Sean laughed.

'No, you're wrong. It is the best news by a long way,' Peggy replied, making a moment of quietness in the general hubbub.

'You were wonderful, Mum. You looked as if you'd been born to it,' Carol said, piling food onto a plate.

'And the dress, it's so pretty, Mum,' Steph said. 'Adventurous for you.'

'I felt like a bit of a sparkle in my old age.'

'You looked very pretty and the hair's lovely,' Candice said.

'Who's looking after Lance?' Peggy asked.

'My sister. She's green with envy that you've won all this money.'

'Not too much, I hope. And you're not letting yourself get too tired, are you, Candice?'

'Me? No, I could go on all night, it's so exciting.'

'Where are you all staying?' Dan asked, through a mouthful of lobster mayonnaise.

'Here. We're one floor down – three rooms in a row. Lovely, too. Courtesy of the lottery people. Flowers, champagne. They certainly know how to look after us.' Carol brought a plate of food over to her mother, flicking a napkin over her lap. 'Here, Mum, I bagged you extra lobster since it's your night and before the mob get at it.'

Peggy thanked her but felt that now she was past needing food. Out of politeness, she ate a little.

'This is all so nice.' Her assembled family were tucked in, some sitting on chairs, others on the floor. Dan, she thought, was on the verge of being drunk. Should she tell him to slow down? To hell with it, she thought. What's it matter tonight of all nights? 'Paul, do you know what I'd like?'

Paul was on his feet in a wink. 'No, Mum, but whatever it is . . .'

'A whisky and soda with gallons of ice. I reckon you can have too much champagne.'

'Careful, Mum, you'll get a hangover mixing drinks.'

'Do you know, Carol, at this precise moment I don't care.'

They all laughed loudly, though Peggy hadn't thought her remark funny. Something was different about them, which puzzled Peggy until she realized they had that look of expectancy which she used to see on Christmas mornings when they were kids.

She beckoned to Dan who wove his way unsteadily to her chair. 'Dan,' she whispered, 'do you think we should say anything about what we intend to do?'

'Not yet, darling,' he whispered back. 'It's all a bit too complicated for this time of night. Best when we've all calmed down a bit.'

'All right. As you say.' And she flashed a smile at Paul and Carol who had stopped talking and chewing, and were, she thought, watching her intently. It was understandable, she reasoned, she'd be doing the same.

The rest began to drink steadily, even Candice, which was a worry, and Peggy considered saying something to her, but didn't. She was tired. This whole evening had been so strange: one minute she was elated, excited, the next she had helter-skeltered into a mind-numbing tiredness.

At about one she stood up, which made everyone else stand up too.

'Please don't – you're flustering me. Sit down, do. If you don't mind, I think I'm going to bed.' But first she crossed the room to where her gigantic cheque was propped up against the wall, and kissed it, which made everyone rock with laughter. 'Carol, Steph, come with me, I've got something for you,' she said, and did not see the glance that Paul exchanged with Candice.

The girls followed her into her bedroom. She had left it in chaos, but some poor soul had come and tidied it while they were downstairs, had turned down the bed and put a rose and a chocolate on each pillow.

'Just look at that, will you? That's luxury!'

'Yes, Mum,' they said dutifully.

Peggy sat on the edge of the bed and looked about the room and felt she ought to be pinching herself again.

'You said you had something for us?' Carol said brightly, interrupting her thoughts.

'Yes, over there, those two Harrods' carriers. I'm not sure which is which. I wish I'd got something for Candice, but I didn't know she was coming.'

They were pleased with their dresses but also, she felt, they were a shade disappointed the parcels weren't bigger. Still, given more time she'd make it up to them.

They kissed goodnight. Peggy undressed, washed and fell into bed and such a deep sleep that she did not stir when a very drunk Dan stumbled into bed three hours later.

Peggy awoke with a start at five and was immediately alert. She lay looking up at the silk-lined drapes – she could see the cherub-decorated corona since Dan had left the bath-room light on. She was thinking of the evening and how it had gone.

In a sudden flash she knew what was different about the children and it made her shiver in the warmth of the bed. They'd been too polite with her.

Chapter Sixteen

Peggy felt as if she'd been away from home for weeks rather than three nights. She sighed a happy sigh of contentment as Dan held open the front door for her. 'It's good to be back.'

'I don't know, I rather enjoyed our little spree,' he said. 'Especially Sunday, just us and the kids.'

'So did I, but . . . I'll just put these in water.' Peggy went into the kitchen with the bouquet of flowers she'd been given the night before last. She stood at the sink filling the vase, gazed out of the window and waved at Pete Henderson, their next-door neighbour, who was pottering in his garden. He couldn't have seen her for he didn't wave back.

'Did you mean that about giving up work?' she asked, carefully carrying the vase of flowers into the lounge. Dan was sitting leafing through the piles of newspapers Tricia had given them.

'Too bloody right. We'll have to get a scrapbook for this lot.' He grinned up at her.

'Don't you think you'll get terribly bored?' she asked with genuine concern.

'Not me. Life's one long holiday. It's everybody's dream, isn't it?'

She did not answer but concentrated on the flowers. She loved Dan dearly but she didn't know if she wanted him around her all the time, every day of every week. For a start he'd be sure to get in the way and she wouldn't be able to get on. Would they irritate each other beyond endurance? She had friends whose marriages had taken a severe bashing – in one case had not survived – when the husband's redundancy forced him to be at home.

'Where shall we go for dinner tonight? Sean was telling me that the Blue Parrot's very good – French, he said.'

'You don't like French food,' she pointed out.

'I'm going to learn to like it. I've decided to become more sophisticated in my tastes, change my image. Bet that surprises you.'

'I'd thought it would be nice if we had a quiet supper here, just you, me and Steph,' she said, wanting to do this with a strange desperation that she didn't let him see. It seemed imperative to her that they go on as normal, just to prove they were still the same.

'As you want. Anything on the box?' He dug in the pile of magazines for the *Radio Times*. She smiled: now that was normal enough. 'Say, how about getting satellite TV now? They've got the movie channels . . .'

'And the sports channel,' she added. 'You're not pulling the wool over my eyes on that one.'

'Okay, and that too. What do you say? And we could scrap this TV and get a really big one.'

'We could have that one in our bedroom. I've always thought a TV in the bedroom would be nice.'

'Aha!' He wagged a finger at her. 'Thinking of getting the adult channel, were you?'

'What's that when it's at home?'

'Porno movies.' He rubbed his hands with glee.

'Certainly not,' she said primly . . . but Hazel had told her the odd blue movie had done wonders for her sex life. Yet look at the state of her marriage – with both of them playing the field it needed all the help it could get. No, that was not a good idea. 'Want a cuppa?' she asked prosaically.

The next day Steph went to school as usual and Dan to work, but unusually he was back by mid-afternoon, noisily jubilant, having handed in his notice and taken the whole of his office to the pub to celebrate.

'I've got to toddle off to the bank. Do you want to come?'

'No, I don't think so. I'll zap round with the Hoover. Would you take the bus so I can go to Sainsbury's? Fancy a steak?' She thus neatly avoided pointing out to him that he'd drunk far too much to drive.

'Lovely idea – with chips? You're going to have to go along to the bank eventually. There's sure to be papers to sign.'

'You know what? It would be a damn sight easier if I just signed everything over to you and you take care of it. You seem to be enjoying all that sort of thing.' She smiled at him proudly as she joked.

'If that's what you want, I'll check if it can be done, shall I?'

'Fine,' she said, suddenly uncertain.

Peggy's trip to Sainsbury's was something she would never forget. At first she had thought it was her imagination that people were staring at her, and she told herself to stop being so neurotic, but after trundling down two of the aisles she had to accept that it wasn't. People *were* staring. On seeing her approach other customers became silent and parted like the Red Sea, and after she'd passed she could hear them whispering behind her. It was a most uncomfortable feeling.

She rootled around in the meat chill-cabinet, selected three fillet steaks and was thinking how nice it was not to be afraid of the price when a woman sidled up to her. 'Of course, you can afford such luxuries now,' she said loudly.

'I beg your pardon?'

'The steak.' She gestured with her hand.

'Oh, I see. Yes, it's a treat, for supper,' she said, kicking herself for starting to explain. Why should she?

'Lucky cow, aren't you?' The woman fixed her with a stare that Peggy found quite frightening. And then she saw that the other woman had wedged her in with her trolley.

Peggy felt a wave of panic. 'Excuse me,' she said, beginning to move the other's trolley so that she could get out.

'Don't you touch my fucking trolley,' the woman screamed. Others turned and looked at them. An assistant, filling shelves, jumped up and ran for the manager.

'Then get out of my fucking way,' Peggy replied, ramming the trolley with hers and scudding up the aisle, head down, to the tills. She paid, and almost ran out into the car park, hurling her groceries into the boot. Abandoning the trolley where it stood, she leapt into the car and found she was shaking from head to toe.

'That was awful,' she said aloud. 'Bloody awful. I won't be going there again!' She put the car into gear. She'd have to find a corner shop, one that would deliver. She looked at her watch. Dan wouldn't be home yet. She needed to talk to someone. She needed to see Hazel, to tell her how sorry she was about Bruce's business; to reassure her she would be sharing in Peggy's good fortune when everything was sorted out; to have her friend rationalize what had just happened, and to calm her down.

She could achieve none of these: Hazel's house was empty, a For Sale sign newly planted in the large front garden.

'You looking for Hazel? She's gone to her mum's.' It was Jennie, the next-door neighbour, ready in her car for the school run.

'Oh, no! I wanted to say how sorry I was.'

'Horrible for them, isn't it? Just as everything and everybody is getting right too. Still, you've had a nice windfall, haven't you?'

Peggy looked up sharply, but Jennie was smiling a genuine smile. 'Yes.'

'Bet that'll take some getting used to. Wish I could have such a problem,' she said. 'If Hazel pops back, shall I tell her you called?'

'Please. You don't have her mother's address do you?'

'Sorry, no. I think she couldn't face us and scarpered. Silly of her – half the estate's in the same boat. Ta-ra.' Jennie waved.

Peggy would like to have delayed her and told her of the incident in Sainsbury's, but she didn't know Jennie well enough for that. She drove home, garaged the car and unloaded the groceries. In the kitchen she searched in the carriers for the bottle of gin she'd bought, and poured herself a large one with tonic. That made her feel better.

Peggy and Steph waited until eight for Dan but still he had not turned up for supper.

'Can't you call the snooker hall he goes to?' Steph queried.

'Hardly. He'd hate me chasing him. No, I don't think that's a good idea.'

'Where's he got to, then?'

'God knows, your father's a law unto himself these days. At least we don't have to worry about him crashing the car. I took it.'

'Can we eat, then? I'm starving.'

Peggy cooked their steak and opened the bottle of wine she'd bought to go with it. She didn't know much about wine, but it was red and expensive, so she'd risked this one.

'Châteauneuf-du-Pape. That's expensive, isn't it?' Steph asked, studying the label on the bottle.

'I thought we'd celebrate tonight. Some celebration.' Peggy was pouring the wine and missed her glass by a centimetre.

'You tiddly, Mum?'

'Don't be silly. I just had a couple of gins waiting for your father.' She didn't say that they had amounted to nearly a quarter of the bottle. To disguise it she'd poured a hefty amount of tonic into the gin and the bottle looked nearly full again. But she was having to concentrate hard on everything she did.

Over the rim of her glass she studied her daughter, proudly admiring the sweet face with its clear, intelligent grey eyes.

'Steph, can I ask you a question?'

'Of course,' Steph answered, as she carefully cut her steak.

'Do you want to go to college?'

Steph laid down her knife and fork. 'What a peculiar question. Of course I do.'

'I mean *honestly* want – for yourself. Not to make me happy or your father. Just thinking about yourself.'

'Who have you been talking to?'

'No one. It was just . . . I suddenly thought how awful if you were only doing this because of me.'

'Come on, Mum! After all the sacrifices you made – of course I want to go ahead with it. Any more of that wine going?'

'That's all right, then.' Peggy settled back contentedly in her chair. Steph helped herself to the remains of the bottle. She studied it for some time as if she was making up her mind about something.

'Mum, can you give me some advice?' she said eventually.

'I'll try.' Something in Steph's tone made Peggy sit up and lean forward.

'At school this afternoon, after we got back from London, Moraigh and Frances were really bitchy to me.'

'What happened?'

'I was bursting to see them and tell them all about yesterday, and Simon Williams, and the dress you bought me and everything. All they said was "Really", turned their backs and walked away. They didn't speak to me for the rest of the afternoon. I think they're jealous.'

'Steph, I'm so sorry. I feel it's my fault.'

'What for? You haven't done anything.'

'No, but if I hadn't won the money then they wouldn't have had cause to be horrible.'

'I'd rather you won the money,' Steph said, with an attempt at a smile.

'It doesn't help take the hurt away, though, does it?'

'So what do I do? If I approach them, what do I say? I can't invite them anywhere – it might be seen as currying favour. It's Moraigh's birthday next week – what then? If I buy her a small present, I'm mean. If I buy her a big one, I'm being flash. That's what'll happen.'

'I think you talk to them, Steph. I think you have to take them aside and say, "Look, it's not me who won this money, it's my mum's. Nothing else is different, I'm still me and I'll stay being me." '

'Maybe I won't, though. Maybe it'll change me.'

'How? I doubt that very much. You, of them all, are the most level-headed.' It wouldn't surprise Peggy at all if Carol put on a few airs and graces, began to think herself far grander than she was, but not Steph.

'I'll try it,' Steph said, not sounding very optimistic.

'It'll be all right, love. Give it time,' Peggy said, with conviction.

Dan didn't come home for his supper. Peggy was in bed and reading when she heard a taxi pull up outside. She waited, but the engine of the taxi ticked over for some time. She put out the light, crept to the window and moved the curtain an inch. Dan was apparently having trouble finding the fare. He stood, in the light from the street lamp, swaying back and forth like a metronome.

'Just look at the state of him,' Peggy said aloud to the Royal Doulton balloon lady on the windowsill. She peered anxiously, as much as the narrow split in the curtain would allow, at the houses opposite to see if there were lights on or if other curtains twitched.

'Good night, mate, thanks,' Dan shouted, and banged the roof of the taxi in farewell. Peggy winced and scuttled back to bed. Should she face him or pretend to be asleep?

'Decisions, decisions,' she muttered.

The front door was slammed noisily, followed by the lounge and kitchen doors as if Dan was searching for her. Then she heard his heavy tread on the stairs, the lavatory door being opened then slammed, the seat being lifted. She leant over and switched on the light. No one could have slept through that.

'Inconsiderate sod,' she said to her book, which she opened at the place she had reached.

'Still awake?' an unsteady Dan said from the doorway. 'Thought you'd be long asleep.'

'It's a good book. Had a nice time?' she asked sweetly, while fuming inside.

'Bloody marvellous – I tell you, I was the most popular man tonight.'

'Buying everyone you knew drinks, I suppose.' She managed to smile – just.

'And anyone I didn't know.'

'Oh, Dan.' The smile had disappeared.

' "Oh, Dan" what?' He sat on the edge of the bed and dropped his shoes one after the other on the floor.

'That's no way to carry on.'

'How would you know? You weren't there.'

'No, true. But you've got to watch it. Just because we can afford drink there's no need to go silly with it, is there?'

'I just wanted to celebrate with my friends,' he said petulantly.

'Fine, but not the whole town and not to this degree.'

'My friends, my own friends,' he said, his voice heavily lachrymose. He flopped back on the bed fully clothed.

She was about to say more about his friends, but he was already asleep. She yanked the duvet from under him, covered him with it and settled back. She wished he'd come home sober so that she could discuss Steph with him and tell him about Sainsbury's. It would have to wait until the morning now.

He woke once in the night, evidently in need of water. Finding himself fully dressed he stripped before climbing back in beside her.

'Dan,' she said softly, feeling for him with her hands, gently stroking the hair on his chest.

'What?' he mumbled.

'Just... Dan...' Her hand slid lower across his smooth abdomen.

'Oh, Peggy, give us a break. I'm still pissed,' he said and turned away from her.

Peggy sighed and lay looking up at the ceiling wondering how the crack was doing. Of course, that was something she could get fixed now. As for Dan, maybe they'd have to go away a little more often. She knew now there was nothing wrong with his performance when he wasn't at home.

Peggy could not get comfortable and neither could she see herself getting back to sleep. She felt the frustrated longing of her body and knew that when she was like this her mind started to whirl and she couldn't stop it. She got up, found her dressing gown in the darkness, and on bare feet quietly descended the stairs to the kitchen. There, she made herself a cup of tea, guiltily opened a tin and cut a slice of Madeira cake to go with it. She sat at the small pine table.

Was it any wonder she couldn't sleep? she thought. Last week she had been unemployed, depressed, lying to her family, afraid of the future – of life. This week she'd won a fortune. All her problems were resolved... and yet, and yet, she had this whisper of fear, like a tendril of smoke, which entered her mind to frighten her about that future. Then, as quickly, it would disappear and she would wonder what on earth *she* had to worry about.

Chapter Seventeen

It was the front door closing on Steph leaving for school that woke Peggy from a deep sleep. She sat up, instantly wide awake, and looked down at Dan who, snoring lightly, was sleeping with a happy smile on his face, one that would preclude her from being cross with him. She leant over and kissed him gently so as not to wake him and then quickly got out of bed, crossed to the window and banged on it hoping to attract Steph's attention. But, head bowed against a biting wind, the girl did not hear her and trudged on down the road.

Peggy shivered in the cold, unheated bedroom. She felt beneath the bed for her slippers, and belted her dressing gown. No hope of Radio 4 now, she thought. She'd try TVam instead.

Tea in hand, Peggy pushed open the lounge door, sat on the squeaky leather sofa and put up her feet. She could get rid of this now, give it to Candice – she'd always admired it – even if the white leather wouldn't last long against the kids' felt-tips. Maybe Carol should have it. She flicked on the television but within a few minutes turned it off again – it was too bright, too colourful, the presenters too slick and professional so early in the morning. She supposed that now Dan would be home every morning she'd never listen to her precious Radio 4 again. She could buy another radio, one for the kitchen; she brightened at this thought. It was an odd feeling after years of having to save for everything – even a new set of underwear – suddenly to find herself able to buy whatever she wanted. She wrapped her dressing gown tighter.

The front-door bell rang. Unusual at this hour. She peered out of the window to see the postman gazing into space with eyes uplifted and the thoughtful expression of one who should be picking his teeth. 'Good morning.' He touched his cap.

'All that for me!' She looked with astonishment at the pile of letters, all held in place by a thick rubber band.

'You're a celebrity now.' He grinned. 'And there's this recorded delivery one, if you wouldn't mind signing?'

His book signed, the letters in Peggy's hand, he cheerily said goodbye and moved swiftly up the path. Peter and Babs Henderson, her neighbours, were getting into their car. She waved. They did not respond. Peggy frowned. 'Babs!' she called out. Babs made a false play at looking about her, as if surprised at having her name called, and searching for the caller. 'Babs. Hi!'

'Good gracious, Peggy, I didn't recognize you. Your hair.' She patted her own neatly french-pleated style and got in the car so quickly that she banged her knee and let out a yell.

'Oh, I see,' said Peggy, not believing her for one minute but unable to think what they had done to offend their neighbours. Ah, well, it's their problem, not mine.

Back in the lounge she began to sort the mail. There were over thirty letters. Once she had separated out the bills and circulars it was down to twenty-five. She slit open the twenty-fifth – the recorded delivery one. She began to read it and within a second her stomach had griped, her pulse was racing and she felt sick. She sat down and, with shaking fingers, lit a cigarette and forced herself to read the letter again.

It was from a firm of solicitors acting for Hazel, claiming half her winnings as her share of the lottery prize on the grounds that in the past she and Peggy had always shared in the financing of any competition they entered, thus any winnings accrued.

'I don't believe it! How could she? How *could* she?' Peggy stubbed out her half-smoked cigarette, lit another and reread the letter again, the paper shaking in her hands. But nothing had changed in it since the last time she had read it. She stood up, aware that her legs felt remarkably weak. She shambled to the hall and, leaning against the newel post, shouted, 'Dan!' There was no reply. 'Dan!' From above she heard an agonized grunt. 'Dan, please. Wake up. Come down. I need you.'

In the kitchen she moved like an automaton as she made fresh tea. She did not need to look for the caddy but put out her hand and made contact automatically. Her mind was racing. There was an unfamiliar roaring in her head as if it was full of panicking birds. She carried the tea-tray back to the lounge.

'Where's the fire?' Dan stumbled into the room, running his fingers through his tousled hair. 'Christ, give me some of that tea.' He flopped into his favourite chair. 'What's up?'

'Read that,' she said, handing him the offending letter and then poured his tea.

Dan whistled through his teeth. 'Bloody hell! Some friend.' He tapped the letter with his finger. 'You didn't promise her the money?'

'No, I told you. She never paid her share.'

'You sure you didn't promise?'

'No, of course not.'

'We need a lawyer.'

'I expect they're listed in the *Yellow Pages*.'

'Who was that chappie who looked after your dad's affairs when he died?'

'Brian Cookson. Some firm in the High Street.'

Dan went out to the telephone and she heard him rustling through the pages of the directory. She heard the rumble of his voice as he spoke into the phone. He returned. 'Three o'clock this afternoon.' He looked down at Peggy who was sitting on the floor, her hands in her lap, looking lost. 'Cheer up. We'll get it sorted. God, my head, why did I do it?' He grinned at her, trying to cheer her up. 'Have we got any Alka-Seltzer?'

'Bathroom cabinet,' she said vaguely.

When he returned carrying a fizzing glass she was sitting in the same position. He sat down on the sofa beside her. 'Come on, love, it'll be all right. Don't look so sad.'

'She's my friend, Dan.'

'Was, more like.'

'But I wanted to share some with her.'

'But not half.'

'No, not half. She didn't pay up, so why should I?'

'Exactly. I wouldn't give her a penny now, if I were you.' He drank his Alka-Seltzer quickly. 'Noisy bloody stuff,' he said to make her laugh, but she didn't.

'I was thinking how quickly we change. Last week we had

nothing. Why, a hundred thousand pounds would have solved all our problems, given us all our dreams. And yet what's happened? Here we are, angry at the thought of giving half of this enormous sum away. We want to hang on to it like grasping misers.'

'Bugger grasping misers! It's your money. It's the principle of it. She's the grasping one. More tea in that pot? Is this the rest of the mail?'

She nodded. She'd forgotten about the other letters. Dan was already slitting them open.

'We should take the nans out tonight to celebrate, don't you think?' he said, as he neatly piled up the letters, throwing the envelopes into the empty fireplace. 'After all, they've missed out on most of the excitement so far.'

'Yes, that'll be nice. Perhaps it'll take our minds off *that*.' She pointed accusingly at the letter on the coffee table.

'Oh, bugger this.' Dan threw the letter he was reading on the table.

'What is it?' She went to pick it up.

'No, Peggy, don't.'

'Why not? I want to.'

'I'd rather you didn't.'

Peggy snatched up the letter. It was on lined paper, and there was no return address in the corner. The writing was uneven and unformed, and it told Peggy she was a greedy cow, a whore, an evil bitch and that the writer hoped she'd get cancer. She screwed it into a ball and threw it into the fireplace.

'I expected rubbish like that. Colin warned us,' she said.

'I forgot he'd told us – too fuzzy-headed. But the first letter I open to be a shitty one—'

'Second shitty letter,' she corrected him.

'Shall we look at the rest or bin them?'

'There might be one in there from someone we know.'

'True. I'll wade through them. How about some breakfast? I need some protein.'

'Bacon and egg?'

'Fabulous. I reckon I'm going to take to this early retirement like a duck to water.'

Over breakfast they debated what to do with the letters. Of

the remaining twenty-four Dan told her that three were from friends congratulating them, four were from relations. Of the other seventeen, two more were abusive, five wished them well and the rest were begging for money.

'I don't want you reading them, you're too soft-hearted,' Dan said, stuffing them into his dressing-gown pocket.

'Are they genuine?'

'Who can tell?' He returned to his bacon and eggs.

'We probably can't judge which are and which aren't. Nor can we help everyone. I think we should choose a couple of charities and donate to them each year. A blanket giving.'

'What on earth for?' He looked up from his plate.

'Because one should give.'

'I do already. I buy my poppy each year. I never walk past a collector in the High Street.'

'I know, but once we know what sort of income we can look forward to, we earmark a lump sum.'

'Perhaps it's tax deductible,' Dan said grumpily.

'I just think we should share our good fortune. If we don't, who knows what might happen?'

'Superstitious drivel.'

Brian Cookson was a pleasant-faced young man who didn't look old enough to be a solicitor. In a way it was a relief to find he wasn't an intimidating, paternalistic type, but it made Peggy worry that he might not know enough to help them. She sat on the edge of her chair and let Dan do the talking. Cookson said nothing but occasionally made a note, for the rest of the time taking a great interest in the right-hand corner of a large bookcase.

'I see,' he said, with a final flurry of notes as Dan finished. 'Now, Mrs Alder, you tell me what happened.'

'My husband just did.'

'I know, but I'd also like to hear it from you,' he said pleasantly. Hesitantly Peggy began to explain. 'And when you were doing the bingo in the paper either of you might buy the newspaper?'

'Yes. Usually whoever got off for coffee first.'

'And why did you stop doing that?'

'Because Bruce – Hazel's husband – said there had been a muddle at the printer's.'

'And then you decided between you to do the National Lottery?'

'No. No, that was me. One Sunday I was a bit fed up,' she glanced across at Dan but he didn't look at her, 'and I bought the tickets on a whim.'

'Then you discussed it with her and she wasn't happy because you'd spent twenty pounds?'

'That's right.'

'But she agreed to pay her share, but just never had the money on her? And you frequently asked her for her share?'

'Well, I wouldn't say frequently, three or four times and then I offered to let her off with a fiver or whatever she wanted to pay.'

Brian Cookson studied his bookcase for what seemed an age. 'I think, Mrs Alder, that there was a form of contract between you and Mrs Hazel Benson. I think a court would find that the decision between you amounted to an agreement. Probably not for half, but for a sizeable settlement.'

'Bugger that!' Dan exploded menacingly to his feet.

'Dan, sit down.' She tugged at his jacket.

He subsided grudgingly. 'I've never heard such rubbish in my life. She's no right at all.'

'I'm sure Mr Cookson knows what he's talking about, Dan.'

'It's only her word against ours that anything was agreed,' Dan blustered.

'That's true, but it would also be perjury if your wife stood up in court and said that. And dangerous. What if someone had overheard them? Then Mrs Alder could easily be sent to prison.'

'Nobody overheard us. Only the last day when I told her to forget it.'

'You said what?' Both men spoke in unison.

'Didn't I mention it?' Peggy said, feeling flustered. 'I was fed up asking her for the money. She obviously didn't want to pay up – I understand why now. It was becoming such a hassle asking her so I said to her to forget it, I'd been stupid buying the tickets in the first place and we'd never win. It was my loss and she needn't give me anything.'

'And she agreed?' Brian was leaning forward intently.

'Yes.'

'And you were overheard?'

'Yes. Young Karen Webber who took over my position at the shop, she was standing behind me. I can't be a hundred per cent sure she heard but she might have – no, she must have heard us.'

'This, of course, puts a different complexion on everything. I'll have a word with her – Karen Webber, you said.' He scribbled the name. 'If she'll make a statement you've nothing to worry about.'

'I wanted to give my friend something, though. I mean, it really is bad luck isn't it?'

'I think she's mad,' Dan offered.

'You mustn't do that, Mrs Alder. Such an action might prejudice your case.'

Dan cheered up immeasurably at this news.

They had decided to take the grandmothers to the Royal, which was the best hotel in town and, being a hotel, was more likely to serve the sort of food which Myrtle, who was a fussy eater, would like.

Fortunately, hidden within the large, complicated and very French menu, they found a roast, grilled fish, and steak and kidney pie – right up Myrtle's street.

'They don't give you much choice, do they?' she whined.

'If you insist on rejecting ninety-five per cent of the menu, Mum, it is a bit limiting.'

'I don't know what's got into you, Dan. You never liked foreign food before – bad meat disguised with disgusting sauces in my opinion.' Myrtle sniffed.

'I think it's a lovely menu,' Jean said pointedly. 'I think I'd like oysters to start with, Dan, and then, since this is a celebration, if anyone fancies sharing a Châteaubriand with me?'

'That's twenty quid,' Myrtle said, rooted to her chair with shock.

'For two, Mum,' Peggy explained.

Myrtle began to scan the menu again, urgently. 'Now what tempts me?' she said, as her eyes raked over the choices on offer but Peggy was pretty sure her mother was comparing prices, frantically searching for something she could eat that would match the ten pounds of Jean's dish.

'I'll join you, Jean, help you out with that Château-thing,' she said finally, laying the menu to one side and beginning to look about her at the large chandeliered dining room.

'But, Mum, you just said you don't like—'

'Well, it's only a tarted-up steak, isn't it? Looks as if they could do with a bit of a paint job, if you ask me.' She dismissed the finest dining room the town had to offer.

'Oysters as well?' Dan asked, cheekily.

'You can take that look off your face, Dan. How could you tease a poor old lady like me? I'll have a prawn cocktail.' She patted his hand affectionately.

The meal began and progressed quite smoothly, even though Myrtle only toyed with her steak. To Peggy's surprise, however, she was sipping wine enthusiastically.

'You're drinking too much, both of you,' she suddenly said.

'What about you, then?' Peggy teased.

'They are celebrating, Myrtle,' Jean said reasonably.

'Well, Jean, my dear, if you don't mind your son dying of cirrhosis, that's one thing, but I care sufficiently for my daughter to worry,' Myrtle said smugly.

'I don't think what we've had tonight is likely to be a death sentence, Mum,' Peggy said, in the patient voice she reserved for her mother.

'What? Two large gins and over half a bottle of wine each, now them brandies you've ordered?' Myrtle rattled off the list. 'And how much have you been drinking since you got the news?'

'Probably too much, Mum, but it won't go on like this. It's all been a bit of a shock.'

'I think it's understandable.' Jean nodded.

'Oh, you would agree, wouldn't you? Always were wide awake for the right opportunity to mosey along,' Myrtle said spitefully, all pretence at pleasantness set aside, whether from impatience with Jean or the result of her unaccustomed intake of wine, it was impossible to say.

'And what does that mean?' Jean asked, affronted.

'I mean you're sucking up to my daughter for what you can

screw out of her.' Dan was visibly shocked at this new side of his mother-in-law.

'Mum, please, that's not fair.' Peggy caught hold of her mother's hand but Myrtle shook it free. She's drunk, Peggy thought desperately.

'It's true. It is. She's always on the look-out for the main chance. She's been turning you against me for ages. Dear Jean, always so modest, always so uncomplaining. Bull! She's been planning this for years.'

'Mum, don't be so silly! How could she have known this was going to happen?' Peggy said, exasperated.

'You mark my words, Peggy, she'll be angling for a pay-out any day.' Myrtle wagged her index finger at her.

'And you won't, Myrtle?' Jean said quietly.

'I wouldn't expect a penny from my daughter. I'm just happy for her good luck.'

'How commendable, Myrtle. But then you've no need, you've been sucking my son and Peggy dry for years. You've nothing left to want.' Jean folded her napkin purposefully.

'You bitch, Jean Alder. You always were a bitch even when we were at school together, but you've got worse. You watch her, Peggy! She and her son – they'll ruin you.'

Oh dear, thought Peggy, she's about to cry. She hated it when her mother cried – always so noisily. 'I think I'd best be getting you home, Mum. Talk about me drinking too much,' she added under her breath. 'Dan, I'll get a taxi. You run Jean back.'

'Safer.' Jean joked, as they kissed goodnight.

In the taxi Myrtle hardly stopped to draw breath as she wittered on and on. When the cab drew up outside her house Peggy got out and put the key in the lock for her. 'And what *do* you want, Mum?'

'What do you mean? I've got everything I need. You've always been good to me.'

'Great. Then you won't mind me helping Jean out, will you?' Peggy said, as she planted a goodnight kiss on her mother's cheek and quickly got back into the taxi.

She collapsed into the seat. She was exhausted – and this was what good luck felt like!

Chapter Eighteen

On Sunday Peggy cooked for the family.

'I don't understand you, Peggy, you were always saying, "Wouldn't it be nice if we could go out for Sunday lunch?" Now we can, you've refused to go.' Dan stood by the kitchen door watching her.

'I want to do it,' she said, whipping up a batter for the Yorkshire pudding.

'I'll never understand you,' Dan said, before leaving for his pint at the Lion and Lamb.

Certainly she must be confusing to him; she had, indeed, often said how nice it would be to lunch out, all of them, like the French do. But, then, he had not been with her that time at the Blue Pig, where reality had not lived up to her imagination. The memory of that awful Sunday assailed her – and yet it had been the day that had saved all their fortunes. She understood herself better now: she *wanted* to cook for them. It was her way of showing how much she loved them. She opened the oven to baste the meat and looked at the large rib of beef with a satisfied expression. How nice it had been to order it and not give a hang for the cost.

What was even better about this particular lunch was that they were all here, including Candice. Later, watching her son with his wife, she felt she could erase that problem from her portfolio of worries – they were behaving like young lovers.

The meal finished, Carol and Sean made as if to move. 'Just a minute,' said Peggy. 'Your dad's got something to say to you.'

'Have I?' Dan looked up from where he was playing with Lance who was sitting on his grandfather's lap. 'Only joking, folks. It's just that your mother and I assume you would like to know what we intend to do with all this money.'

There was a general muttering of 'No', 'No way' and 'None of our business' around the table, which neither Peggy nor Dan believed for one minute.

'Obviously you'll appreciate there's still a lot of sorting out and discussion to be done. I spend a lot of time with the bank and accountants – we're trying to minimize the taxes. The upshot is we intend to give each of you a capital sum to help out with your various problems. Exact amounts? We're still working on it but we figure it'll be around the one fifty two hundred mark.'

'One hundred and fifty pounds?' said Carol, her voice full of dismay.

'Don't be silly, Princess. One hundred and fifty thousand.'

She was dumbfounded.

'Mum, that's too much.'

'I don't think so, Paul. I wouldn't be happy if I didn't see you all secure and settled first.'

'What about you, Mum – and Dad?' Steph added as an afterthought.

'We'll have plenty.'

'What about tax on it?' asked Paul.

'Well, if we do this, then we've all got to look after your mum, treat her real special. She has to live for seven years after the date of the gift. If she croaks it before then, you're clobbered.' Dan laughed, but the others glanced all ways except at Peggy and seemed acutely embarrassed.

Peggy shuddered. 'Oh, shut up, do. Talking like that gives me the shivers.' Then she laughed too, pretending she did not mind, and they were immediately chattering happily at their good fortune. Peggy felt that here, at last, was real joy. Certainly this was a day to remember.

She was surprised when Carol called on Wednesday the following week.

'You all right? You're not ill?' Peggy asked anxiously, when she opened the door to her daughter.

'No, I'm fine. I had some time owing me. I've been into town – looking at three-piece suites.'

'But the one you have is lovely,' Peggy said over her shoulder, as they walked into the kitchen.

'Yes, but it was second-hand – I hate anything second-hand, don't you? You never know who's been using it.'

'I thought that suite came from Daphne?'

'Yes, it did – but it . . . well, it's never felt really mine, if you know what I mean.'

'I'm afraid I don't. I was thinking of offering you our leather sofa, but never mind.'

'Honestly!' Carol's eyes were sparkling. 'Oh, that's different, I'd love that. I won't put it in the drawing room though, but in Sean's study.'

'In his *what*?' Peggy asked. 'Gracious me, don't get too posh, will you?'

'I've always called it the drawing room.' Carol bridled.

'Have you?' Peggy continued to load the washing machine.

'You're moving, then?' Carol asked, as she filled the kettle with water and plugged it in.

'No. What gave you that idea?'

'Sean saw Dad in an estate agent's in town. He presumed . . . I mean it would make sense. You can't stay here now, can you?' Carol took two mugs off the wooden tree.

'Why ever not?' Peggy was amazed.

'Because you won't fit in any more. You've got to start mixing with your own kind now.'

'The people living here *are* my kind.'

'No, they're not. Monied people are now. Are we having tea or coffee?' Carol selected an apple from the fruit bowl.

'Coffee.' Peggy fetched the Nescafé from the pantry while pretending to herself that what Carol had just said was her usual senseless prattling, but not finding it easy to dismiss.

Carol crunched into her apple and stood at the glass door that gave onto the garden where only daffodils were blooming and weeds were beginning their stake-out for the summer.

'I've been thinking I might have the garden landscaped.' Peggy joined her daughter at the door. 'You know, get that nice man at the garden centre in to advise us. Something I could look after myself. I don't think I'll ever get your father interested.' There was no response from Carol, as if she hadn't been listening. 'Anything up?'

'No . . .' Carol looked at her mother as if coming to a decision. 'Well, there is one thing. It's Steph. I'm worried about her.'

'Our Steph? Why on earth?' Steph might never have given them any trouble, but Peggy was wise enough to know that too often the parents were the last to know of any problems with their children. Drugs, pregnancies, abortions, Aids, motorbikes – all her fears paraded triumphantly through her mind. 'What?' Peggy asked, making herself concentrate on the soap powder for the washing machine.

'Both Sean and I think it's unfair giving her all that money!' Carol said in a rush in case she changed her mind about speaking up.

'Why unfair?' Peggy poured the conditioner into its little container.

'She's too young. It's too much responsibility. She might fritter it all away, and then what? I managed without such advantages at her age, it's—' Carol stopped speaking abruptly and Peggy wondered if she was about to add 'It's not fair.' She spun the dial on the washing machine. The water gurgled in just as the kettle boiled on the hob. She spooned the instant coffee into mugs.

'You taking sugar or not?'

'Not – I ate too much in London, put on a pound.'

'Carol, you're as thin as a rake! You make me laugh.' She stirred two spoonfuls of sugar into her own mug and sat down at the table. 'I don't think you should worry about Steph.'

'But what if she spends it all? Then she'll want more.'

'And that wouldn't be fair on you and Paul?' Peggy said reasonably. Carol sat down too, relief that Peggy was being so understanding etched on her face.

'Exactly. I mean I don't want you to think we're not grateful and everything but . . .' Her voice trailed off as she registered Peggy's expression.

'But the gratitude might end if one of you got more than the other.'

'No! Mum, of course not, what makes you think that?' Carol looked indignant at such an idea.

Peggy was on the point of saying 'this conversation' but thought better of it. There was truth, if inadvertent, in what Carol was saying. Money did odd things to people and their attitudes to each other. All the same, she found this conversation made her feel sad.

She looked at her pretty daughter, whose face was creased with concern that she might have gone too far. She put out her hand and touched Carol's almost absent-mindedly. 'I understand, I really do. I want to be fair to you all, all the time – I think I always have been. You needn't worry about Steph. We're going to invest her money and she can have the income, but the capital isn't hers until she's twenty-five. That's fair and sensible, isn't it?'

'Yes. What a relief. I can sleep now and not worry about her.'

'That's right, dear. Now, let's take this coffee into the lounge.'

'Where's Dad?'

'Gone to look at cars, what else?'

A week after this, just as April was storming in, easily mistaken for March, Peggy was invited to have lunch with her bank manager. When he'd called, her immediate reaction was butterflies in her stomach and a frantic searching through her mind for what she had done wrong. And then she laughed at her silliness. Of course, it was the total opposite.

It was short notice and Dan had already gone to London to see someone about an investment plan, had left on the early train. She would have liked him with her. She could not think what on earth she could talk to the bank manager about.

She was back in the Royal. The bank fêted their rich customers well, she thought, as she looked around for Norris Macintyre. She'd only met him twice, once to arrange the overdraft for Carol's wedding and once when he'd hauled her and Dan in to query why they hadn't paid it back when they'd said they would. All she could remember about him was how severe he could be for one who looked so young.

'Mrs Alder, so sorry I'm late. Shall we have a drink?' He ushered her into the heavily oak-panelled bar, which was nearly full of businessmen. She was, apparently, the only woman. She asked for a gin and tonic and they settled in button-backed dark green leather chairs in a window embrasure and talked of nothing in particular, studied the menu and ordered their meal.

'I'm glad you could come at such short notice, Mrs Alder. We've a lot to talk about. I'm surprised you haven't been into the bank before now. I expect you've been busy.'

'Not very,' she said. 'I leave all that sort of thing to Dan.'

'So he says. Which is why I thought we should have a little talk. But we can leave business until after lunch, if you like.'

'No, let's talk now.'

'As you know, Mrs Alder, we arranged a sizeable facility for you and your husband's joint account when we heard the good news. Of course, unsecured.'

'I didn't know that. Well, it must have been only for a couple of days until the cheque was cleared. It has cleared, hasn't it?' She looked wide-eyed with alarm.

'Oh, yes. No problem there. All safely in a deposit account in *your* name. It's just, well, the overdraft is getting rather large. And it does seem silly to pay the interest rates you incur when you have so much on special deposit.'

'Yes, I see that. How big is it?'

'Just short of two hundred thousand.'

'How much?' She looked startled, choking on her drink. 'My God. I haven't spent anything like that. I bought some clothes, but on a store account card. There must have been a mistake.'

'No mistake, Mrs Alder. But you do see the problem?'

'A car! Maybe my husband has bought a new car and that would account for some of it.' She sat up, smiling cheerfully.

'I gather he has. It does account for some, but he's arranging finance on it.'

'On the never-never? What on earth for?'

The bank manager gestured with his hands. 'Maybe he's got exceptionally good terms – quite a few firms are offering nought per cent financing at the moment. I expect he thinks it's better to use someone else's money rather than yours.'

'Yes, it must be something like that. Dan would never get into debt otherwise. It doesn't explain the overdraft, does it, though?'

'I'm afraid not, Mrs Alder.'

'We'd best shift some money over and clear it pronto.'

'I'd hoped you'd suggest that,' he said pleasantly, and she thought he'd rather a good-looking face in a quiet sort of way.

The waiter came to tell them their table was ready. They began their meal and Peggy learnt that Norris – half-way through the meal they'd agreed to use their Christian names – was a keen gardener and she picked his brains on who he recommended she should consult about her garden. Why she'd thought she was going to have a boring time, she could not imagine. Over coffee and brandy she plucked up courage to invite him and his wife to supper one evening.

Norris was helping her on with her coat. 'Peggy, there's just one other thing.'

'Yes?' she asked, as she adjusted her scarf at her neck. She looked up at him expectantly.

'Dan says you want to sign everything over to him. He's had me prepare the necessary papers.'

'I did say it, but it was just a sort of joke really, I mean . . .' Dan had said nothing to her about it since she had first mentioned it. She didn't like to explain to the bank manager that she'd only said it to try to boost his morale a little – she didn't want him thinking any less of Dan. 'I didn't realize he'd taken me at my word.'

'It's an enormous step to take, Peggy, one you should think about carefully, and, as your bank manager, I must advise you to take independent advice on this.'

'I will, but who from?'

'You have a lawyer?' Peggy nodded. 'Then I should go and see him. Telephone me when you have and we'll set up a meeting.'

'Thank you, Norris.' Peggy began to walk across the car park. 'Oh, I'm sorry, thank you for lunch,' she called.

Brian Cookson had a cancellation and could see her immediately. He listened to her explanation of why she needed an appointment.

'You're determined to sign this money over?' he asked.

'The truth is, Mr Cookson, I really don't know what to do. I didn't mean – it was just one of those things one says without thinking.' At the pained expression on the young man's face it was obvious he would never dream of saying anything remotely like this to a living soul, not even under torture. She had horrified his orderly lawyer's mind. 'I'm in a bit of a spot now, though. The handing over to my husband is all set up. But the bank insisted I talk to you first before I sign.' She pushed her hair back from her face with a worried gesture. 'You see, I don't want to refuse to sign and hurt my husband's feelings, do I? Dan deals with all the finances – he always has. Maybe it would be simpler, don't you think?' She did not sound convinced as she asked this. The size of their overdraft kept flashing to the forefront of her mind, like a warning red light.

'I'm not sure you've thought the consequences through, Mrs Alder. You'd be losing control of all your money – you'd be *giving* it to your husband. Should you separate or divorce, you'd have to apply to the courts for a share from him of what is rightfully yours.'

She was amused at that idea. 'Dan and I would never separate or divorce. We've weathered marriage so long that we're not likely to give up now.'

Cookson was still grim. 'I'm afraid, Mrs Alder, that where people are concerned, I've learnt you can never say never.'

Suddenly she felt ridiculous. She twitched her skirt straight and fiddled with the clasp of her handbag.

'Perhaps I should have said – I don't *think* we'll ever separate. But, of course, you're right, one should not presume. Maybe I should think about it a little longer?'

On the way home Peggy was thoughtful. She would trust Dan with her life, she'd always said that, but here she was, reluctant to trust him with her money.

To Brian Cookson, she'd said so confidently she and Dan would never divorce, and yet it was only a few weeks ago that she had worked herself into a state imagining he was having an affair with Hazel. And when Hazel had denied it she had immediately thought there must be someone else. She didn't trust him, or what else could have induced her to think along those lines?

And then there was the overdraft. Even allowing that it included their existing borrowing there was no way they could have spent that amount of money, so where had it gone? Why hadn't he discussed it with her first?

Chapter Nineteen

'So, you don't trust me?' Dan paced back and forth across the lounge carpet.

'Of course I do. It isn't that,' Peggy replied.

'It sounds like it to me. You wait until I'm in London – on *your* business, I'll have you know – before you go to see the bank. Haven't I constantly said you should go, that you should be in on the meetings?'

'Well, yes.'

'Exactly. So why go behind my back?'

'I didn't. Norris called after you had left for London. I didn't know he was going to invite me.'

'You could have turned him down. You could have said you'd rather wait until your husband could come too, couldn't you?' He swung round and glared angrily at her.

'I could have, I didn't think. You know what it's like, the bank summons you and it's like a knee jerk, I suppose. You go.'

'Don't talk so bloody daft, Peggy. Don't you see what you've done? You've made a complete fool of me. Christ knows what interpretation Macintyre and that Cookson bloke are putting on this. I only did what you fucking well told me to. *You* said you wanted me to have the money. It was your fucking idea.'

She winced at his choice of language – so unlike him. She felt her pulse racing, wished she had never gone to the bank, wished she had never got herself into this muddle. 'I know, but I didn't really mean it. I don't think I meant it. I want us to share it, I suppose. Not me to have it, or you, but to go on as we always have – in our bank account, share and share alike.'

'Why didn't you fucking well say so, then?' His face was white with anger, and she saw that his hands were balled into fists.

'Please, stop saying *that* word. I hate it.' She put her hands over her ears.

'I'm saying it because I'm beside myself with anger. How dare you put me in this position? *How dare you?*'

'Hang on a minute. It's not all my fault. You went ahead without discussing it with me. You've run up the overdraft with no explanation to me.'

'What do you mean?' He came forward, ominously it seemed to Peggy. She'd never felt afraid of Dan, never, but this evening his anger was sufficient to scare anyone, but this was no time to give in.

'The manager wanted me to do something about the overdraft. Nearly two hundred thousand pounds, for heaven's sake – and it's not me who's been spending it,' she said stalwartly.

Dan sat down with a thump on his chair. 'I knew this would happen. I knew it was only a matter of time.'

'Of course it would be queried. Don't be naïve, Dan. The bank want their money back.'

'*Your* money, you mean. That's what all this is about, isn't it? Your fucking money, not mine. No one's. All yours. Now the accounting begins. Do you want me to make lists? Each cup of coffee, each newspaper, each pint I have? You want me to account for every penny, is that it?' he shouted.

'Dan, this isn't fair. Please, it's horrible.'

'Yes, it is, isn't it? I'm hurt, Peggy. Christ, you'll never know how much you've hurt me.'

'Dan, please. I didn't mean it to be like this. I just wanted to talk. I wanted to know— ' She knelt by his chair. 'Listen to us, Dan. Listen to what's happening to us. I don't want this, do you?'

He looked at her, his dark eyes bleak with, she thought, an expression of despair.

'No. I want us to be happy, I don't want all this suspicion.' He levered himself up from the chair and went over to the drinks cupboard. 'You want a gin?'

'Please.' She sat on the hearth-rug and felt wretched. She had thought she wasn't in the wrong and now she wasn't so sure. He looked so genuinely hurt. But, she shook her head, she'd started this, she must finish it; otherwise it would smoulder between them, making suspicions grow, forcing them further apart. She accepted her drink. He looked calmer now. 'So what did you spend it on? Go on, shock me.' She forced a laugh.

'I bought some clothes, you know I did. And a watch – you told me to. And your birthday present . . . and . . . I lent some money to a friend. I'm sorry, I shouldn't have done that. It's your money, I should have asked you first.'

'Oh, Dan. How typical of you. Who? Bruce?'

'No, it's someone else. They got themselves in a muddle with the bank. We'll get it back, I'm sure. You're not cross?'

'No, love, of course I'm not. I don't want us ever to argue about money again. It's supposed to make us happy, not miserable.'

They made love. As always it was the best way to bury an argument, she thought, for how could resentment survive such pleasurable intimacy? She lay in the dark and listened to Dan snoring lightly and then became aware of other noises: music, laughter and car doors slamming. A party.

Quietly she got out of bed and tiptoed to the window to see that Jessy and Martin's house opposite was a blaze of light. She could make out people dancing – when the front door opened the sound blasted out into the close. How odd that they hadn't been invited. She couldn't remember Jessy and Martin ever having a party without asking her and Dan.

She climbed back into bed and snuggled up to him. Still, who needed people and parties when they had each other? This was all she needed to be happy. She resolved not to let any misunderstandings over the wretched money get in the way of this happiness.

Sleep was seeping over her when she was suddenly wide awake. She had forgotten to ask him what he was doing in the estate agent's. She lay for a while worrying about that, and then she relaxed. Of course, he'd been getting details of bungalows for his mother – that was it. She settled contentedly into her pillows and drifted off to sleep.

Peggy was still waking each morning at the same time she had when she had been working. Dan was not having the same problem. Most mornings she left him sleeping and after some tea and toast did her housework long before he was up and about. Sometimes, as now, she would pop out to the shops. Since her experience at the supermarket with the unpleasant woman, she had started to use the local shops where she was known and people, she felt, stared less.

April had settled down into a more normal pattern and the winds of last week had dropped. The sun was shining so strongly that, as she walked through the alleyway which linked the close to the main road and shopping precinct, she felt too hot in her new camel-hair coat – something she'd always wanted.

She was coming out of Dewhurst's when she bumped into Jessy going in. 'Hello, Jessy, long time no see,' she said easily.

Jessy began an extensive search of her handbag and muttered something that Peggy didn't catch, but which she presumed was 'Good morning.'

'Nice party the other night?' she asked.

'Yes,' answered Jessy, looking up with a guilty expression and blushing violently.

Peggy felt sorry for her and her confusion. 'Jessy, please, it doesn't matter.'

'But it does, Peggy. We should have invited you. You've always come to our parties.' She looked as if she was about to cry.

'There's no should about it. You invite who you want.'

'It's all so silly. We debated for ages, but then we decided that you probably wouldn't want to come any more.'

'Why ever not?' Peggy looked aghast.

'With all that money.'

'Oh, really! Why should that stop us enjoying one of your parties? Jessy, the money hasn't changed us. We're still the same people – I wish you'd tell the others that.'

'But are you, Peggy? Is it possible?'

'Of course it is,' Peggy replied.

But on the way home, carrying her basket, she pondered the conversation. They might not have changed but others were changing towards them and the end result was the same. Odd, too, how she'd used almost the same words to Jessy that she had advised Steph to use with her friends. How had it worked out for Steph? She must ask her. These days she hardly seemed to see her daughter, who would rush in from school and rush out again. Peggy couldn't imagine when she did her studying.

Opening the front door she called out that she was back. There was silence as she had expected. Dan *was* still in bed. 'Breakfast in twenty minutes,' she called up the stairs. She listened for his customary groan. Poor Dan, each morning, these days, was a rebirth to him. She picked up the pile of mail – it never seemed to diminish.

In the kitchen she quickly sorted through the envelopes. Efficiently she selected a few, the rest she put unopened into the bin. They had soon learnt to recognize the begging letters and the hate mail: cheap envelopes with poor writing and incomplete address. She put the bacon under the grill and heated the oil in the non-stick frying pan.

Dan appeared just as she was about to call him again. 'You been to the shops already?' He jerked his head towards the shopping bag.

'I don't want to sleep my life away,' she said, as she gently flicked fat on the top of Dan's egg.

'You getting at me?'

'No, of course not,' she said patiently.

'Any mail?'

'On the table. I've sorted it. There's a large envelope there for you. It's from an estate agent's.' As she turned she saw him trying unsuccessfully to stuff the large envelope into his dressing-gown pocket. It was too thick so he slid it into his newspaper as if he was hiding it. 'Aren't you going to open it?'

'Later.' He sat down.

'Are they details for Jean's house?'

'Mum's?' He looked up puzzled and still bleary-eyed.

'You know, the bungalow by the sea I promised her.'

'Oh, that. Something like.'

'Let's see, then.' She put her hand out.

'Oh for God's sake, Peggy, stop going on at me, I'm hardly awake.'

'I wasn't aware I was *going on*,' Peggy replied, with the dignity of hurt.

'Well, you were.'

She poured their tea, and sat staring silently at the liquid in her cup as it still swirled around in a vortex from when she had stirred in the sugar. She felt like that, she thought. She would be flat and calm and then someone would say something and she was churned up right through. She blew on the tea to cool it.

'Don't do that, you'll drown a sailor,' he said, as if to make amends.

'No, my dad used to say it's if you blow on ink to dry it, that's what kills them. Tea doesn't hurt.' Her smile told him it was all right again. The telephone rang. She picked up the kitchen extension.

'Margaret, good morning. It's Dan I need but I might as well talk to you.'

'Who is it?' Peggy said, knowing full well but loathing anyone who didn't identify themselves on the telephone but blithely presumed their voice would be recognized.

'Why, Daphne, of course, who did you think it was?'

'Lucretia Borgia.'

'Oh, Margaret, you're so funny.' Daphne laughed. 'I'm calling about the house.'

'What house, Daphne?'

'Why, our house. Aren't you awake yet, Margaret? Cyril and I think that two hundred and fifty thousand pounds is a fair sum.' Peggy said nothing but looked at the telephone as if struck dumb. 'Margaret, are you there? Margaret!'

'I'll tell him. And it's *Peggy*,' she said, as she replaced the receiver. Dan was still eating and was buttering a piece of toast with minute attention to detail. 'You will have gathered that was Daphne.' She stood, one hand on hip, waiting.

'It was meant to be a surprise,' he said, sheepishly.

'What was?'

'The house, Daphne and Cyril's house. It's for sale. I thought it would be nice to buy it for you as a surprise.'

'I see,' she said, and sat down again. She longed to ask with what he was going to buy it, but she remembered her promise to herself. She would not argue with him over money. 'There's just one little problem, Dan. I loathe that house.'

'It's well built, those floors are afrormosia, you know, and all the doors and the staircase are oak.'

'It might be. It might have taken a whole forest of oaks to build it, but to me it would have been a shocking waste of wood.'

'I like it,' he said, a shade sullenly, and Peggy felt her spirits sink. She hated it when he sulked.

'Wouldn't it be better if we looked for a house we both like?'

'I suppose so,' he said, his voice laden with despondency and then he suddenly grinned. 'You agree? You want to look for a house?'

'Yes, I think I do.' A look of sadness flittered across her face but he did not notice. Neither did he ask why she had suddenly changed her mind, so she did not tell him about Jessy and the party.

'In that case . . .' He took the envelope from inside his folded newspaper and ripped it open. Inside were three glossy brochures of houses. ' . . . perhaps one of these?'

She had only to glance at the photographs to give her answer. 'I don't want to live in something grand like that. That's not us. We'd be like fish out of water. Why don't we look for a nice cottage with a good sized garden? Then maybe we could get a dog, now I'm not working. We certainly don't need a mansion.' She tried to keep her voice light so that he would not take it as a criticism of his efforts. 'And the prices, Dan. Look at them. I could never bring myself to spend a sum like that on a house.'

'Don't be silly, darling. We get a mortgage. On your income we can afford an enormous one.'

'I don't want to be in debt.'

'A mortgage is hardly being in debt, Peggy. Honest.' He rubbed his chin, thoughtfully. 'Still, maybe you're right – a thatched cottage with a paddock, by the river, something like that might be nice.' He began to put the brochures back in the envelope. 'Did Daphne say how much they wanted?'

'She said a quarter of a million.'

Dan guffawed loudly. 'She must think we were born yesterday. She'll never get that for it – not in the current market.' He stood up. 'I'll go and have my bath and shave and we'll go and house-hunt, yes?'

'Should I cancel the garden people if we're moving?' she asked.

'No, a tarted-up garden's always a good selling point,' he said as he went out.

Peggy did the washing up with scant attention. She was miles away. She might have agreed to move, but she wasn't sure if it was the right thing to do. Maybe they should stay here. Surely the neighbours would get used to their changed fortunes? But how long might it take? Could she weather their attitude until they came round? She didn't know. What she did know was that it was as if her life had been taken over. Things were happening, plans were being made, and no one asked her. She just went with the tide. But where would the tide take her, and did she want to go?

Chapter Twenty

Finding Jean's bungalow had taken one afternoon. Peggy wished it was as easy to find their own new house. She and Dan had viewed a good dozen properties, but none felt right. She knew every time she said so that Dan looked thunderous, but it was the only brake on events that she had. If she was to move it had to be exactly right.

Jean, on the other hand, had seen two bungalows, both with sea views and close to the shops. She had chosen the second because the bathroom suite was white and she felt she might get tired of the avocado in the first house.

'If you've got a white suite you can change the decoration more easily. You're tied with a coloured suite – and those awful tiles. No, I've made the right choice.'

'Such a decisive woman you are, Jean,' Peggy said, as they drove home. 'You've dreamed about that bathroom for a long time, haven't you? You must have, to have such dogmatic views on colours and the like.'

'A bathroom's been my dream for years. When I get in there, I'm going to have two baths a day and three on Sunday.'

They were silent for a while, Peggy thinking that buying this bungalow was a definite plus factor in a situation which so far had had a few too many downs for comfort.

'You're very kind to me, Peggy,' Jean said suddenly.

'Because I love you,' Peggy replied simply.

'What about your own mother? I don't want to cause any trouble.'

'Mum doesn't want anything. She said.'

'She might have said it, but does she mean it?' Jean asked.

'I think so. She loves her house – and you've seen it, it's a

171

little palace now. There's not a lot more you could do with it, and she'd hate to move away from her cronies.'

'But it's not fair if you do this for me and nothing for her.'

'But I am, I've told her. I'll pay all her bills – electric, gas, council tax – and for a holiday every year. She won't want.'

'I didn't for one moment think she would.' Jean smiled. 'I've been thinking, too. That house we've just seen, I'll rent it off you.'

'Don't be silly, I want you to have it.' Peggy negotiated a roundabout.

'No. It would cause problems if you did. Keep it in your name and I'll pay rent – I do already so it'll be all the same to me. And we'll get a proper letting agreement drawn up by the lawyers, all shipshape.'

'What problems?' Peggy sounded annoyed, but more with the dozy driver in front than with her mother-in-law.

'The children. Your mother.'

'Why should the kids be a problem?'

'Money's funny stuff. They might resent you buying me the bungalow..'

'I'd disown them if they ever thought like that – about their own nan.' She sounded shocked.

Jean spoke seriously. 'Don't say such a thing. In any case, you never know what's going to happen in the future. I mean, you and Dan – well, anything could happen.'

Peggy, changing gear, crashed one and winced at the noise. 'What on earth makes you say that?' she asked.

'I'm not sure, now you ask. But life can be a pig, and if there's one thing I know you can never rely on anything, and you can never say something will *never* happen.'

'That's funny. My solicitor said near enough the same to me.' And Peggy began to tell Jean of the problems she had created by jokingly saying she ought to give all her money to Dan.

'Don't. Don't even *think* of it, Peggy,' Jean said firmly.

'But what difference does it make? We've been together for so long now.'

'Yes, thank God, you have, and I pray it continues. But your life and Dan's have changed immeasurably. This money has ensured that nothing can ever be the same again. It will, given time, change you both. Your horizons will widen, you'll meet new people. You just don't know what will happen. What if Dan had a mid-life crisis and fell in love with some bimbo and had your money? You'd feel as sick as a parrot then, wouldn't you?'

'But he'd give it back to me.'

Jean scoffed at this. 'You think so? With a demanding little lover who's with him because he's rich? Do you really think *she*'d let him give it back to you?'

'That's an awful thought.'

'It happens.' Jean shrugged.

'But it's your son we're talking about,' Peggy expostulated.

'My son, your son, they're all the same. Men can't be trusted, Peggy. That thing between their legs, it rules their lives. I get so cross when I hear them say women are unreliable because of their hormones. Women are ruled by them once a month, men are ruled by theirs all year round. Bah! Men!'

'But you and Fred were so happy,' Peggy pointed out, somewhat taken aback at Jean's feminist vehemence.

'Were we? Fred had at least two serious affairs and I'm not sure how many dalliances. The opportunities were there – as a travelling salesman, he hoped I would never find out.'

'And you stayed with him.'

'Yes, for the sake of the kids. That old chestnut, and what a mistake that was. I bloody well wouldn't now. I'd be off. Any woman these days who stays with a man if he's dipping his wick elsewhere wants her brains tested – what with herpes and Aids.'

'I'm sorry, Jean, I'd no idea. But Dan's not like that. Oh, I had a scare a couple of months back but it turned out it was all in my imagination. But this damn money, that's a different kettle of fish. I don't know what to do. He's so hurt about me seeing the bank and everything.'

'Hurt? What's the great lump got to be hurt about?'

'He says I don't trust him.'

'Too right you shouldn't. Say to him, "I'd be mad to trust you", see what he says.'

'But he goes into a sulk every time it's mentioned, and the bank want something sorted out.'

'Let him sulk. He used to try that one when he was a child.

I'd just let him get on with it. You can't sulk for ever, now can you?'

As she parked outside the estate agent's, Peggy said, 'Oh, Jean, you're a treasure,' and leant over to kiss her. She went into the office to let them know that, yes, they would be buying one of the bungalows, but that there was a minor change and that she would be the purchaser and not her mother-in-law.

Dan's car arrived – a white Mercedes sports with black leather upholstery.

Peggy stood on the garden path admiring it. 'It's a beautiful thing,' she said, but wishing it was black. White seemed a little flash to her and would, perhaps, better suit the image of a more youthful driver. She did hope Dan wasn't going to start wearing tight-fitting jeans, jewellery, and have his hair highlighted or permed.

'And I've got a surprise for you, too. Come with me.' He led her to the garage. 'Close your eyes,' he ordered. She heard him tip open the door. 'Right, you can open them now.'

She did – to see a brand new black Mini sitting there with a large white satin bow tied round its bonnet.

'Oh, Dan! How wonderful! A Mini! The car I've always wanted. For me?' She felt like jumping up and down with excitement but restricted herself to clapping her hands.

'All for you – no sharing.'

'Dan, thank you, thank you so much.'

'My pleasure. You deserve it.' He was grinning broadly.

'I must try it.' She was quickly in the driving seat.

'Hang on,' Dan called out, ripping off the ribbon. 'You'd look like a "Just Married".' He waved her away and she was quickly batting up the road. She looked in the rear-view mirror to see Dan following. She hoped he'd remembered to lock up. He overtook her with much blaring of horns and flashing of lights.

The little car handled beautifully. It really was all she wanted. He was welcome to his souped-up Mercedes, this would be so easy to park. It was kind of him, thoughtful. And then she saw the irony. When would she ever adjust to her new fortune? She'd given the car to herself. Dan had only chosen it. She, probably, would never have got round to buying it – she had him to thank for that. Still, it wasn't just her who wasn't adjusting. Dan wasn't either. He'd been so pleased with himself that he, too, had forgotten that he hadn't bought it, that he was no longer the main wage-earner. This pleased her: it must mean he was getting over all the silly wounded pride he'd made such a fuss about.

'You should be working,' Jean said to her son, over a large slice of chocolate gâteau and a cup of tea.

'What on earth for?' he replied, passing his cup to Peggy to refill.

'It's not natural, that's why. Lolling around the house all day, idling away. You'll rot, that's what'll happen.'

'Mum, you do talk a load of old cobblers at times. Why should I work if I don't have to? You've got a touch of the Victorian work ethic about you.'

'All I know is that people have to have something to do or they start going funny. You'll be drinking like a fish, out of sheer boredom, if you don't watch out. Peggy's still working, why shouldn't you?'

'Peggy isn't. She—'

'Peggy bloody *is* working and probably harder than before, with you under her feet all day. Nothing's changed for Peggy. And look at that.' She pointed at the patio window and the garden beyond where a team of men were busily digging in new shrubs and laying new turf. 'You should be doing that instead of paying others to do it. Give yourself a healthy hobby for a change.'

'I hate gardening.'

'I expect Peggy hates housework. She still does it, though, doesn't she?'

'God, Mum, you don't half nag these days. You never did before.' Dan looked exasperated.

'Why is it when you tell people something they don't want to hear, you're nagging? I'm telling you the truth. Someone's got to.'

Peggy looked anxiously from mother to son. Jean was only saying what she herself had been thinking even if Jean said it with a little more force than Peggy might have. Dan was beginning to worry her. Forty-eight was too young to be retired, certainly for someone who had no other interests – Peggy did not count playing snooker. He had even stopped fixing other people's cars. He was drinking too much and, since one of his pleasures was to drive about in his new car, that was a constant source of worry to her.

'I had been thinking perhaps we could buy a garage or something . . .' she said, her voice trailing off rather lamely at the end of the sentence.

'What for?' Dan looked at her with an irritated expression.

'To give you something to do, you great clot,' Jean answered for her.

'Haven't I made myself clear? I'm quite happy as I am. Why should I go back to getting up at six, getting tired and filthy? I'd be happier if we could find a new house, if only Peggy would stop being so bloody fussy. There's always something wrong with whatever I like.' He was speaking in his petulant voice, the one that annoyed Peggy more than any other.

'If I'm going to move house it's for the last time and it's got to be spot on. I don't want to move again,' Peggy said, reasonably.

'Quite right,' said Jean, helping herself to another slice of cake having asked Peggy by semaphoring with arched eyebrows and a waving knife.

'And I only suggested a garage because you love old cars so. I thought perhaps you could make a speciality of servicing the ones you really like. You'd get millions of customers. Any other kind of work you could employ someone else to do.'

Dan looked thoughtful for a while. 'It might be a good idea, but let's find a house first, shall we?'

And Peggy realized she was trapped. To get him out from under her feet in the daytime, to get him interested in something, she was going to have to commit herself to a house soon. 'It's a deal,' she said, but without enthusiasm.

Still, it was probably for the best, she told herself, as she collected the dirty tea things, forbidding Jean to help her. Dan was difficult these days and living with him was rapidly becoming a diplomatic maze. Perhaps he had always been like this and she had never known; since both of them worked they had spent little time together. Now they were having to learn what the other one was about. She began the washing-up – at least when they moved she'd buy herself a dishwasher.

The money had not been mentioned again. Over a month later it remained safely invested in her name. But she knew he was having his revenge by the simple expedient of buying whatever he wanted when he saw it and rarely consulting her. She, in turn, kept topping up their shared bank account. Because the house was filling up with every imaginable gadget and piece of electronic equipment, a new, and larger, house was now inevitable.

They had the best music system money could buy, with sufficient power to fill a dance hall with sound – no wonder the neighbours weren't speaking to them. He'd bought a gigantic television which loomed in the corner of the lounge. They had a satellite dish on top of the house, electronically controlled from inside, which she knew she would never master. He had personal organizers, computers, printers, photocopiers, all sitting idle since he had nothing to put on them. Boxes lay around that he hadn't even opened. He was like a spoilt child who at Christmas, with so many gifts, doesn't know which one to play with next.

In the cupboard under the stairs were a pair of guns and a clay pigeon trap – though he did not shoot. He'd enough fishing tackle to supply a whole angling club – though he'd only been out once – and a full set of golf clubs, though no membership of any club. He had become a shopaholic, and something had to be done about him, she decided, as she folded the towel neatly.

No sooner had Jean left – Dan driving her in his car – than Daphne arrived. 'Peggy, I need to talk to you,' she said, before she was even in the house.

The correct use of her name put Peggy on her guard immediately. 'A drink?' she asked, since she was dying for one.

'It's too early for me,' said Daphne piously.

'Not for me,' Peggy replied, with a confidence she wouldn't have had some months ago, and poured herself a hefty gin and tonic. Even as she brought the glass to her lips she knew her inner voice was about to tell her that she, too, was drinking too much. She knew it, but for the time being didn't seem able to exist without it. She fully intended to do something about it – when the dust settled, once the move was over. 'So, what is it you want to talk about – Sean and Carol?' She sat on the new chintz-upholstered armchair, which still wasn't right for this room, but which she hoped would look all right in the cottage when they found it, facing Daphne on its matching three-seater sofa.

'It's our house. Cyril and I can't understand why you haven't come back to us on it. I mean, a private sale—'

'Dan did come back to you. He said it was kind of you to think of us, but it wasn't quite right,' she replied diplomatically.

'Was it the price? Did we pitch it too high? That was only a starting price – it could be negotiable.'

'We did think it a bit steep, yes. But—'

'Then we'll reduce it.'

'It wouldn't do any good, Daphne, we still wouldn't buy it.'

'But you must,' Daphne said, too briskly for Peggy.

'There's no *must* about it. We'll buy what we want to buy and not what suits you.' Peggy took a deep gulp of her drink and wondered why everything was so incredibly complicated these days, then saw the question for the stupid one it was.

'Please, Peggy. Please do for my sake.' And, to her horror, Daphne burst into tears.

It was not a pretty sight as the mascara began to roll; neither was it helped by the ugly gulping noise Daphne was making. Peggy sat transfixed at the spectacle. The woman wasn't hysterical enough to slap her, which was a pity. Peggy made do by giving her a Kleenex and saying, 'Come on, it can't be that bad,' which sounded odd, coming from her.

'It is that bad,' Daphne sobbed, dabbing at the tears, making the mascara mess worse. 'We can't keep it. We've got to sell it. Cyril's business, it's—' And the blubbing started again. 'We need the money from the house if we're to survive,' she said dramatically.

'Daphne, I'm sorry.' She was sorry, and she wasn't. She was sorry for Cyril certainly: he'd always been nice to her. She wasn't sorry for Daphne, remembering her autocratic bossing, but then perhaps she was: it wasn't in Peggy's nature to be cruel. 'I really don't see what I can do.'

'You can help!' Daphne spat out. The red-rimmed ferret's eyes even redder-rimmed, peered at her from the folds of a fresh Kleenex. 'You've all this bloody money so why can't you help? Most people like to see their family all right.' She looked evil.

'I didn't know you regarded us in that light.' Peggy felt her face go rigid with shock at the change in Daphne. 'We've hardly seen you since the wedding, for God's sake.'

'We were there. We'd have helped you out in better times.'

'Would you?' Peggy asked, and began to feel for her cigarettes and lighter. Then she remembered she'd put the first of her nicotine patches on that morning and could not smoke unless, as the doctor had warned, she wanted a heart attack. She took another slug of gin instead.

'Yes, we would. There's no question of it.' Daphne's manner had changed again. She was leaning forward earnestly, her voice had dropped a tone, was gentler, wistful almost. 'I'm sorry I spoke so sharply before, Peggy. It's my nerves.'

'That's all right, I understand.' Peggy wished she wasn't such a wimp and had had the courage to throw her apology right back at her.

'Could you and Dan not come over, look at the house again? You might change your mind. Dan told me he'd buy it tomorrow if it was up to him.'

'But it isn't, is it? Honestly, Daphne, I don't know any other way to say this. We're not buying your house because I don't like it and would never want to live in it. There.' Peggy fought the longing for a cigarette and, seeing her glass empty, wished she was on her own and could pour another one.

'I see.' Daphne stood up. 'All I can say is I feel sorry for that husband of yours having a wife who keeps such a firm hand on the purse strings. It must be dreadful for the poor man.'

'I beg your pardon?' Peggy was on her feet, clutching her glass, and at the gin bottle in seconds flat. 'That's a diabolical thing to say.'

'Is it? If the cap fits, I always say. You're causing such unhappiness with this money, Margaret. Look at poor Carol – it's just not fair.'

Peggy held up her hand. 'Hang on a minute, what's not fair? I don't understand.'

'It's obvious. She and Sean have a much higher standard of living than Paul and his little wife – her name escapes me.' She fluttered her fingers in a theatrical attempt to conjure up the name.

'Candice.'

'That's right, Candice. Strange, the names the working classes give their children, isn't it? As I was saying—'

'I wouldn't bother if I were you,' Peggy said with, for her, a surprising degree of menace. That was rich, she thought, coming from Daphne whose own father had worked at the gasworks, and not in a managerial capacity.

'Carol's mortgage is over twice what Paul has on that poky terrace house. It's only fair she has more. And—'

'Get out.'

'I was only—'

'Get out. Now. And don't bloody well come back.' Dramatically Peggy held open the door wide. 'Out.' Daphne, finally registering that Peggy was seriously angry, scuttled past to her waiting Volvo. And Peggy closed the door with a resounding slam.

Chapter Twenty-one

When Peggy heard what Carol was alleged to have said, she should have driven straight round to see her daughter. She should have confronted her, asked her if it was true. Or had it been an innocent remark she had made about her brother and money, which, in the telling, had been distorted into a lie?

Instead Peggy had sat at home by herself and fretted. Alone, with only her bottle of gin for company, she had drunk too much and had worked herself into a hurt heap, remembering every slight, every thoughtless act or remark that Carol had ever committed or said. She had fallen asleep before Dan returned – something that was becoming routine these days.

In the morning, despite the tumult inside her, she knew that she couldn't blurt out much about Carol to her husband. Dan was over-protective of the girl and would defend her to the hilt, no matter what the evidence to the contrary. She would call and see her daughter today, get things ironed out between them.

Over breakfast she told him, instead, of Daphne's tantrum when she had turned her down on the house.

'Still. It makes you think. It's a nice house. We could do a lot worse,' he said, studying his toast and marmalade intently as he spoke. Peggy thought she would clock him one if he ever said *that* again.

Her plan to see Carol was thwarted when Dan blithely informed her that they had an appointment to view a house that morning. 'But I'd plans,' she said, wishing he'd give her more warning.

'Nothing that can't wait, I'm sure,' he replied, with infuriating confidence.

As they sped along in his car, waxed to perfection, Peggy sat deep in thought; there was little need to talk as Dan preferred to drive in silence. She was thinking he must believe that, apart from the time she spent with him, she had no existence of any importance. As she examined this idea, she found it uncomfortably true; now that she no longer worked at the shop and had stopped going to her Italian night classes, she didn't have any other life bar the house, him, her family and the cleaning and shopping it entailed. Without them she felt, with a jolt, she'd cease to exist, as if they were her sole reason for being.

It was odd, really, the ways a woman showed she loved and cared. 'Serve our frozen products, Mrs Alder. Show you care.' 'Clean your bog with this super new cleaner, Mrs Alder. Show the depth of your love.' Such romance! Had it ever existed for her at all? Or had it always been like this? Romantic, passionate love seemed out of place in a semi-detached. Love there was proved by clean shirts in the drawer, and meat and two veg for supper.

Would the passion of Edward and Mrs Simpson or Bonnie and Clyde have survived life in the close? She doubted it. She found herself scratching her hip where her nicotine patch was. They were working like a dream: she hadn't even thought about a cigarette last night – but she wished she could do away with the itch.

The house they had just seen might do, she conceded on the way back. It was neither too large nor too small – with five good-sized bedrooms, the whole family could come to stay, and just ten miles from town, shopping would be no problem.

'Pity about the river,' Dan said. It curled through the valley two large fields away from the house. Peggy said nothing: his idea of a house on a riverbank had given her many a nasty vision: rivers and grandchildren, she couldn't help feeling, were not an ideal mix. 'Good views,' he added.

'If a motorway isn't built in the valley.' It was a lovely, unspoilt valley with beautiful water-meadows – and, as Peggy had noticed, it always seemed to be in the most beautiful parts that the authorities liked to place their roads and cement works.

'The solicitor will sort all that out. Did you notice the Aga? That adds a bob or two to a house.'

'I've always wanted an Aga. Mind you, I'll have to learn how to cook on it.' She watched the hedgerows streaming by. Would she adapt to living in the country after spending all her young life in a large town and the rest in its suburbs?

'You could rustle up a banquet in a billy-can,' she heard Dan say, and glowed at the compliment.

'It was a lovely lounge.'

'I thought picture windows in there would go a treat.'

'Oh, Dan, no. It would spoil the cottage feel of the place.'

'Some cottage!'

'But that's what it's been. I reckon it was once three and it's been knocked into one and the conservatory added. I've always liked thatch, too.' She was happy at the memory of the pretty house.

'There's room for a swimming pool in the garden.'

'Oh Dan. I don't know.' She clutched at her neck. 'What about the grandchildren?'

'We'll teach them to swim, of course. The paddock's included, and the bloke said the copse and adjoining field might be for sale, too. We ought to go for it all.' He slowed down slightly to go around a sharp bend, and Peggy hung onto the car strap to steady herself. 'So, it's decided. We go for that one.'

'Hang on a minute. I'd like to think about it. I want to see it again and check on one or two things.'

'We could go back Sunday or Monday. I'll give them a bell as soon as we're home and arrange it.'

'No, better leave it until Monday. We don't want to appear too eager or they'll never budge on price.'

'Turning into quite the little businesswoman, aren't we?' he said, and she had no illusions that it had been meant as a compliment as she noticed his hands tighten on the steering wheel and his foot press down hard on the accelerator.

'I wish you wouldn't drive so fast. It makes me nervous.'

'Get on with you. It's a straight road. These cars are built like tanks. Safe as houses.' He shoved an Elvis CD into the newly installed player.

*

Peggy didn't have to go to Carol's as planned. Her daughter came to see her – to show her mother her new suit, she said, bought that morning from a shop-within-a-shop in Debenham's. Peggy doubted it. Carol never normally went out of her way to show Peggy her purchases: they did not have that sort of mother–daughter relationship and, in any case, she considered her mother's taste dowdy. Peggy dutifully admired the military-cut suit with its gleaming brass buttons.

'Did Daphne come to see you?' Carol asked innocently, as she refolded the jacket and carefully slid it back into its carrier bag.

Peggy wondered if she'd been sent to persuade her to change her mind about the house or to find out exactly what Daphne had said. She decided to pre-empt her.

'Yes, and if you've been sent to sell the house, forget it. I loathe that house – it's vulgar. And in any case we think we've found one.'

'I like Daphne's house,' Carol said staunchly.

'So does your father, but I don't. And it's not just about liking it or not. It's too big for us, the bills must be enormous.'

'You can afford them now.' There was a steeliness in Carol's voice. Peggy looked across at her, at her perfectly shaped doll-like face, and saw the narrowing of her lips into a tight little line.

Peggy took a deep breath. 'She said something else. She said you felt hard-done-by over the money – that you should have more than Paul.'

'Oh, she never did! How awful. The bitch.' Carol stood, hand over her mouth in an amateurish representation of shock.

'Do you think that?'

'Mum, how could you even ask?'

'Easily, if it's true.'

'Course it's not.' Carol flicked her perfectly coloured blonde hair over her shoulders in an attempt at defiance which failed. There was fear in her face.

'If you think that then I don't know what to say to you. It's so ungrateful and very hurtful.'

'But I don't, Mum.'

'Then I'm glad to hear it,' Peggy said, not believing her daughter for one minute. The door opened.

'Princess!' Dan stood arms wide in greeting.

Carol tripped towards him like a little girl and flung herself at him. 'Daddy!'

'We don't often see you here on a Saturday. To what do we owe this pleasure?' Dan looked at his daughter, his face a picture of pride. Peggy felt the tingling sensation around the area of her heart which often occurred when she saw them together. She did not understand it, and did not know if she wanted to.

'Can't a girl come and see her daddy when she wants?' She giggled. 'Or are you too important now?'

Peggy made a lot of noise putting on the kettle. Odd how when she was upset or edgy, anything really, she always took it out on the kettle. Poor thing, she thought, patted it in apology and lit the gas beneath it.

'We've found a fabulous house – in the country!'

'Mum said. Daphne will be upset – she'd really set her heart on your having her house.'

'I'd have loved it, but there you go – Control here didn't like it and what Mum says goes these days.'

'And what does that mean?' Peggy swung round from the cooker.

'Don't be touchy, Peggy. It's the truth, after all.'

'I thought it was a mutual decision that we'd agreed it was too big.'

'I never did. It's a cracker of a house.'

'It's a God-awful mess of one,' Peggy snapped. She obviously hadn't heard the last about Daphne's house.

'It's got everything, Mum. You needn't do a thing to it. And the carpets and curtains alone cost a bomb.'

'Are you on a commission or something?'

'Peggy!'

'Mum!'

'You needn't look so shocked, Dan. I gather that our daughter is less than content with the amount of money we've given her.'

'Mum!' Carol looked from her mother to her father. 'I didn't mean it like that. I told you.'

'What's the problem, Princess?'

'Yes, Princess, tell Daddy,' Peggy said, and as soon as she had, regretted it. It made her sound petty and vindictive. But then, if

185

she was being honest with herself – hell, how difficult *that* was – it was how she felt.

'What the hell's got into you today, Peggy? Why are you so irritable?'

'Can't I be? Why shouldn't I be? Everyone else has their little moods, so why can't I?'

'I'd better go, Dad.' Carol picked up her shopping bag.

'No, you sit down. We'll get this straightened out once and for all. Tell me the problem,' he ordered.

As if on cue Carol burst into tears. Peggy watched and could not help but admire the way her daughter cried. Little round tears trickled from her cornflower-blue eyes, which did not turn red. Neither did she sniff and blow her nose. She cried prettily, there was no doubt about that.

'Here you are, my love. Take my hankie. Don't cry, you upset your old dad something rotten when you do.'

With the kettle boiling and too hot to bang about, Peggy rattled the mugs instead, but miscalculated and cracked one.

'It's so hard to manage, Daddy. We've this huge mortgage, as you know. And the business isn't coming in as it did. And Sean's dad's going bankrupt and I'm afraid we'll go with him. And what shall I do?' The tears began again.

'Nothing's going to happen to my Princess. I'll see to that. Don't you worry. I'll talk to Sean and I'll sort something out with him.'

'Or even *we*'ll sort something out.'

'Yes, of course, that's right, thanks for correcting me, Peggy. *We*'ll do it.' His voice was heavy with sarcasm. 'Come on, let's do it now, strike while the iron's hot. You coming, Peggy?'

'No, thanks. I'll get on with supper.'

The front door closed behind them and Peggy emptied the undrunk tea down the sink. She poured herself a gin and tonic and sat at the kitchen table with it.

She sometimes wondered if she fell under a bus, or ran away, whether Carol would even notice. Her elder daughter irritated Peggy beyond measure but she wasn't sure if it was Carol who was irritating or the circumstances of their relationship which made her so. Peggy was jealous. Jealous of Dan and Carol. It was a nasty thought, which she liked to keep locked up in the far recesses of her mind. It shamed her but she couldn't seem to do anything about it. She knew that was so from the couple of times a year she took out the idea, dusted it down, contemplated it, analysed it and castigated herself for it. But it didn't stop her feeling any differently about her daughter.

She looked at her watch. It was new – a Rolex, a present from Dan – and she hadn't got used to it, still got a kick out of looking at it. She glanced at it yet again, as she hadn't registered the time. 'Steph's late,' she said aloud to the empty kitchen. She poured herself another gin. 'Just the one, Mrs Wembley,' she said, chuckling as she aped the voice in the TV series – what was it called? – all about a Cockney millionaire living in a big house. If it was out on video, it might be a good idea to sit Dan in front of it, show him that big homes and ordinary people didn't work out. Maybe . . . but the doorbell interrupted that line of thought. Perhaps it was Steph, lost her key.

'Moraigh. This is a nice surprise. Come in,' she said to Steph's best friend, then became aware that three others were lurking at the gate and that Moraigh looked shifty. 'What's up? Where's Steph?' she said, suddenly alert and on guard.

'This is for you, Mrs Alder.' Moraigh handed over an envelope. 'Bye.' And before Peggy could stop her or ask her more, she had joined her friends and they ran quickly up the road.

Peggy returned to the kitchen table, and topped up her glass. She did so because she had recognized the writing on the envelope. It was Steph's, and that frightened her. She sat for some time, the envelope before her. She moved it occasionally, stroked it, but did not open it. It was almost as if she didn't need to: she knew what the note would say and yet it seemed illogical that it should say it. She shook herself, picked up a knife and ripped it open. She read it and slumped in the chair. She had been right.

At midnight Dan returned. Peggy was still at the kitchen table, the level of gin in the bottle much reduced. She should have been drunk and incoherent yet she felt strangely calm and sober.

'Steph's gone,' she said flatly, not bothering to ask where he had been all evening. She had called Carol's at eight to be told he'd been long gone.

'What?' He stopped unbottoning his coat.

'She's gone. She sent this letter . . .' She pushed it towards him. He patted his pocket for his specs.

'Drat. I've left my glasses in the car. What's it say?'

'It's quite short really. Just that she doesn't want to go to university, that she never has and that she wants to travel the world, so she's gone.'

'Alone?'

'No. With that boy Nigel.'

'I never liked the look of him.'

'You never said.'

'You'd have bitten my head off if I had.'

'I never would.'

Dan picked up the gin and, taking a clean glass, poured himself some. He held up the bottle to her enquiringly. 'Just a small one,' she said.

'Little bitch.' He sat down with a heavy thump as if weariness had suddenly drained the strength from his legs. 'She might have said, might have warned us.'

'She says she loves us.'

'Well, thanks a bunch. No indication where she's gone?'

'No, just that she's sorry, after all the sacrifices we made, and that she's grateful for the income that's made this possible.' Peggy's voice faltered there; she had been managing quite well until then. 'I feel it's my fault. I did the one thing a parent must never do and hoped she'd fulfil my ambitions. You can't live through your kids, can you?' She looked up at him, hazel eyes full of tears. She sniffed loudly.

'That's crap. Even when she was very little, she always said she wanted to be a teacher. There was never any question.'

'But maybe we *should* have questioned it. Maybe we *should* have asked her if she was sure that's what she wanted to do. Jean saw it. She warned me and I didn't even listen. I did talk to her when we first won the money but she must have wanted to save my feelings. She sat there and lied, said she wanted to go.'

'Rubbish, she wasn't lying, not then, that's what she wanted *then*. No, it's that subversive layabout Nigel. You mark my words. He's got wind you gave her that money – silly bitch probably told him. He saw his opportunity to do his own thing and sponge off her while he does.'

'Oh, Dan, that wretched money. We always seem to be arguing. There's that scene with Carol, now this. I begin to wonder—'

He put a finger on her lips to stop her talking.

'Shush, Peggy. Don't even think it, let alone say it. It might all go away if you do!' He wiped away the tears that tumbled from her red-rimmed eyes.

Chapter Twenty-two

During the past three months, ever since the win, Peggy had missed Hazel. She was still angry about what she had done, for the lawyers' letters that had winged back and forth had been a worry, even if Hazel's threats had come to nothing. She was hurt that Hazel had never given her time to explain and to make amends. Despite all that, the longing to see her was sometimes almost overwhelming. It could be triggered by the slightest thing – maybe she'd seen something in a shop she knew Hazel would love; or something had happened that she knew would make Hazel laugh – and then she would wish she was here or at the end of the telephone. A best friend was not someone who could be easily replaced, not like an ordinary friend. Peggy missed their special relationship, for Hazel had been someone she could talk to about anything – well, almost anything. Admittedly she had never confessed to the man in the red car, but no doubt she would have got round to it one day.

There was a rumour, gleaned from the girls in the shop, that Hazel had moved to Hatfield way, which would make sense since the head office of Pompadour was there, and another that she was living in a cottage in the back of beyond which Peggy found difficult to believe. A smart estate in a village close to town, yes. The depths of the country for Hazel? No!

Peggy was still bothered by the ethical question of Hazel's right to a share in the winnings. Despite their lawyer writing to say she had no right and that they had a witness who had signed an affidavit to that effect, Hazel appeared to be ignoring it, and a court case was still threatened. None of this, however, stopped Peggy worrying about the unfairness of it all. These attacks of conscience usually hit her fair and square in the middle of the night when there was no one to discuss them with. She would toss and turn and imagine scenarios where she'd arrive at Hazel's door clutching a compensatory cheque in her hand. But by morning she would force herself to remember the high-handed tone of the lawyer's letter and tell herself firmly that she didn't owe Hazel a penny. If Hazel had lost out, it was her own fault. Fine words, but words that did not obliterate the nigglings of conscience.

Peggy was also finding it difficult to come to terms with Steph's abrupt departure. She felt many things: hurt that her daughter should go without a word; fear that something might happen to her; anger at the inconsiderate behaviour. This particular Sunday she longed to see Hazel with an ache that was almost physical. Hazel would talk her through Steph's leaving, she would help her deal with it. She wanted her friend, she needed her.

There was no one else – her mother-in-law now lived too far away and this news was not something she felt she could, or should, discuss on the telephone with Jean. She could not face the litany of blame that Myrtle would hurl at her if she sought solace there. The mutual comforting and understanding which had been herself and Dan had, by Sunday morning, begun to disintegrate. Before and during breakfast, hostilities began with an odd snip of recrimination here, a bullet of blame there. She was glad he'd gone out before it had a chance to explode into a full-scale battle.

She was keeping herself busy. She worked at her cooking, preparing far too much – three veg, two sorts of potatoes, Yorkshire pudding, even though it was roast pork, two desserts. 'Busy, busy,' she kept repeating like a mantra but it did not keep the fears, the dreadful loneliness, at bay.

Peggy was laying the table – Steph's job normally and a task that saddened her even more when she saw she'd laid a place for Steph too.

'Anyone home?' She heard Paul's voice. Lance ran through the door on his little fat legs and grabbed Peggy round the knees and hugged her. She bent down and picked him up, clutching him to her far too tightly for he struggled to be free.

'Anything wrong, Mum?' Paul asked anxiously.

'No, nothing,' she lied, and wondered why she did. They'd got to know sometime.

'Peggy, you look awful,' Candice said, concerned.

'Thanks.' Peggy managed a weak laugh. 'It's Steph. She's left home.' Even as she said the words they did not sound real. How could she be saying them of Steph? Good, sane, reliable Steph.

'Steph? Good God. Where's she gone?' Paul asked, frowning, and Peggy saw a strange look pass between him and Candice.

'We don't know. She left this note.' From her pinny she took the letter, crumpled now from many readings. Candice looked over Paul's shoulder as he read it.

'Little bitch,' he said, as he handed it back to her.

'She told me she didn't want to go to university,' Candice put in. 'But I didn't take much notice – I thought she was just fed up with the work. I got like that with my CSEs. I wish I'd listened to her now.' She looked miserable.

'Silly little bitch,' Paul repeated. 'The sensible thing would have been to wait a couple of weeks and finish taking her A levels and then scarper for a year. This way she's really slammed the barn door shut. How could she be so fucking inconsiderate?' Paul banged one fist into the other with frustration.

'Paul!' Peggy admonished. 'She was frightened to tell me, probably. I know Steph, she'd have been fighting with herself for weeks over this. She won't have reached the decision lightly.'

'Oh, come on, Mum. Don't defend her. It's unforgivably selfish of her.'

'Have you tried the police?' Candice suggested.

'What for? She's over sixteen, she's free to go. She went of her own will. No one has kidnapped her.'

'Well, we've got to find her and that's flat. I need a drink. Anyone else?' Paul asked. Peggy said she would, but Candice declined, indicating her pregnant stomach.

'Your dad's gone to the Lion and Lamb. He said a friend of his has a cousin who's a private detective. He's getting on to him.'

'Where's Carol?' Candice asked, looking at her watch. 'She's late.'

'She doesn't know yet. Still—' She was about to say that the sisters had never been close, but thought better of it.

They had moved through to the kitchen now. Peggy felt happier now that Paul and his family were there for her to fuss over.

They sat at the kitchen table, Lance playing with his Lego. As Peggy came out of the pantry she sensed they had been talking about her and saying something they didn't want her to hear.

'What are you two whispering about?'

'Nothing.' Candice looked uncomfortable.

'It's difficult, Mum, but—'

'Paul! No!' Candice said sharply.

'Look, no time is—'

'Not now.' Candice spoke through gritted teeth.

'What?' Peggy stood holding her lemon meringue pie like a votive offering. 'What are you arguing about?'

'You know Candice has a brother in Australia, Mum?'

'Yes.' It was hard to get the little word out, for she was holding her breath.

'He works in computers.'

'Does he?' Tendrils of fear were crawling in her chest cavity.

'He can get me a job. Mum, we think we'd like to go to Australia.'

Peggy felt her stomach lurch, felt as if the floor had suddenly lost its stability. Carefully she laid the pie on the table.

'Really?' she said, sitting down quickly. Her heart was hammering and inside she was screaming a refusal at the very idea. 'When would you go?' she asked, aware that her voice was wavering. She felt Candice take hold of her hand but she kept her eyes lowered. She couldn't look at them.

'Next month, if we can get our visas done and everything.'

'I thought it took ages and you had to have points in your favour and things.'

'With a job to go to it's easier, and with the money you gave us – that doubles our chances.'

'I see,' she said, and a dreadful bleakness seeped through her.

Carol did not arrive for lunch. Sulking, no doubt, Peggy thought. Probably feeling under the weather, Dan said.

Peggy got through the meal, but how she would never know. She sat rigid, as if that would keep the turmoil she was feeling in check.

Dan thought Paul's Australian plan was a splendid idea. 'Good for you, son. I don't blame you. If we were younger we'd join you. Better life for the kids. All that sun.'

Peggy was thinking about how far away Australia was. Didn't they have poisonous snakes? And all that swimming.

'Lance must learn to swim immediately,' she said, and since the statement was apropos of nothing they looked at her with surprise.

'Of course, Mum. He'll be a little water-baby in no time.'

'Think of the holidays, Peggy. Fantastic!' Dan looked pleased. 'Good job you won that money! We can go when we feel like it.'

Peggy stood up abruptly and began noisily to collect the plates. 'You bloody fool,' she longed to shout at him. Couldn't they *see* her heart was breaking?

Peggy lay on her bed looking at the crack in the ceiling and not worrying about it. She felt exhausted, totally drained. She could hear Dan pottering about downstairs. She wished he would come and join her, hold her, make everything better. Once he'd been like that, so attuned to her moods that he would know instinctively what to say to make her all right again. Now he rarely seemed to notice how she felt. She supposed she could call out to him, tell him she needed a hug. But she didn't. If she had to ask him it halved the comfort he would give her.

'Peggy, want a cuppa?' he yelled up the stairs.

'Thanks.'

She could hear him making the tea, knew where he was in the kitchen as she heard the kettle filled, the lid of the pot lifted.

'You all right?' he asked, as he entered the room with a cup five minutes later. 'Not ill?'

'I feel bereft.'

'You *what*?' He laughed. 'Oh, come on, Peggy. Steph's been stupid, but you heard what that detective told me on the phone. Nine times out of ten they're back within a month, tails between their legs.'

'Yes, because they can't hack it on the streets, can't find work. I'm aware of that. But you're forgetting one thing. She's got

194

money, that's not her problem. She won't be back.'

'You can't say that.'

'No, Steph will have planned this to the last detail. She would have known where she was going and when. This was no spur-of-the-moment thing. She'll let me know she's safe – I know that. It's just all those dreams.'

'Come on, Peggy. It's her life.' He stroked her hair.

'I know. I know. And then Paul. But it's not just Paul, is it? It's Lance and the new baby.'

'I reckon he was being over-optimistic about how easy it would be.'

'Do you?' She brightened up at that.

'Yes, he'll be here a few months yet.'

'Oh,' she said dejectedly, having misunderstood.

'Look, Peggy, you've got to let go some time. He can't be tied to your apron strings for ever.'

She sat up at that, her tea slopping in the saucer as she did so. 'That's not fair. I've never clung to him, not to any of them. I want him to be happy, but is it wrong to wish he could be happy closer to us?'

'I envy the boy. Good luck to him.'

Peggy leant back in the pillows and marvelled at the distance between them. 'That house we saw.'

'Yes?' He looked at her expectantly.

'Let's buy it. Don't let's bother with a second viewing.'

'You mean it?'

'Yes. There doesn't seem much point in staying here,' she said, knowing she could no longer bear this house, and all the memories it contained.

Chapter Twenty-three

Peggy knew the cause of all the upheaval and unhappiness in her life: she hadn't given Hazel a share of the money as she had originally wanted to. Sharing it with her family was not enough to placate the gods. There was only one solution, she decided. If she was living in the Hatfield area Hazel had gone ex-directory, Peggy soon discovered. None of her neighbours had a forwarding address or a telephone number and the new owners of Hazel's house were less than helpful when she rang. Disguising her voice, more effectively than she had dared hope, she rang again, this time pretending she was Hazel's cousin newly returned from a failed emigration to Australia and with a failed marriage to boot. It did the trick, and she was given Hazel's number. She felt sick with apprehension as she dialled and waited for the call to connect. 'Hazel? It's Peggy. I need to see you,' she said simply.

'Well, you're the last person I want to see,' Hazel snapped.

'Please, Hazel, we've got to talk. I've missed you so.' Peggy heard herself pleading, but did not care. There was silence from the other end. 'Hazel. The money . . .'

'If you wish to discuss that I suggest you contact my lawyer. You needn't think you can trick me into compromising my position.'

'Hazel—' But the line had already gone dead.

Peggy had not told Dan that she intended calling Hazel and got scant sympathy when he found out. 'Keep away from her. You'll complicate everything.'

'But I only want to put things straight—'

'You don't think that if you gave her a few thousand that would be the end of it? Don't be daft! It would be the beginning. She'd soon be knocking on the door for more.'

196

'But I feel everything's going wrong because I *haven't* given her anything.'

'God, Peggy, you do talk a load of superstitious twaddle sometimes.' He said it with a kiss on the tip of her nose so that she didn't feel hurt, but she couldn't help wishing he understood better.

It was Jean, sane, sensible Jean, who understood best.

'Peggy, you must stop feeling so guilty about winning all that money. You're looking at everything the wrong way round,' Jean said to her, almost severely, when on a weekend visit from her new home. 'This money will enable you to have a new start, a new life. There's no way you could all have continued as you were. It was inevitable that the money would change things. You've got to learn to change with it.' She paused. Peggy waited for her to continue. 'Just think, a few months ago you had a job, Steph to look after and the others to fuss over. Now that's changed. You've not enough to do after such a busy life. It's giving you too much time to think – and thinking can be a dangerous pastime. Find an interest. Why not buy a shop and sell handbags? You know enough about retail. Travel the world. Only you must stop sitting here in this house worrying about everything. Learn to enjoy your good fortune and get rid of the guilt.'

Jean had only verbalized what Peggy, deep down, already understood. She knew many women like her, who found difficulty in adjusting to their children leaving, and she had not had time before to think about her nest emptying. She had not been prepared for Steph to go so soon. She must find an interest – what interest? Each time she had mentioned to Dan the trip to Italy, he had always come up with some excuse not to go. All his promises, in the past, about the holiday had been a sham: easy enough to give when he was sure they would never have the money to do it. 'You go,' he'd said often enough since, but Peggy hated to be alone, and would not seek isolation from choice.

Still, Jean was right, she told herself in those hours in the night when sleep escaped her, and she made herself think of other things to distract her from her physical longing for the man lying beside her.

Determined to change, the first thing Peggy did was row with her mother. She hadn't meant to. On arriving at Myrtle's house, she had made tea, as usual, and then they had chatted of this and that quite amicably.

'I hear Jean's house is very nice. Got sea views even,' Myrtle said, a shade wistfully, but pleasantly enough.

'Yes, near Brancaster. She's very happy there. You could move, too, if you want. You can have our old house. A quieter area for you, and you always liked it. That's if you'd like?'

'I don't want and I certainly don't like.'

'The offer's there.'

Myrtle indicated that she would like more tea, which Peggy poured and handed to her.

'It's Carol I worry about.' Myrtle took a sip. 'She says that you're looking after everyone else better than her and that's not fair!'

'Then she's lying.'

'What a thing to say about your own daughter!'

'It's the truth. She's had the same as the other two.'

'She needs more. She's moving too, you know, somewhere detached, better class of neighbour.'

'If she chooses a bigger mortgage, that's her problem. I have to be fair with them all.'

Her mother sat up and looked animated. 'You know what, Peggy? You've become hard. You let your own flesh and blood worry herself to death. A right shenanigans we have here. I knew the money would change you. I told our Carol not to worry, I'd have it out with you. I—'

'Mum, do me a favour. Shut up, will you?'

'Well I never!' Myrtle's stout frame seemed to diminish in size like a balloon when the air slowly escapes. 'I never thought it would come to this.'

'Yes, you did – you've just said.' Peggy collected her handbag and scarf. She stood up. 'Look, I don't want to row, but I will if you interfere. I mean it.' She was buttoning her coat.

'You'll regret it when you're old and alone. Who'll care for you then – Steph and Paul gone? Who'll care if your Carol doesn't?'

'For goodness sake, Mum, I can't live my life worrying about my old age.'

'Well, you should. Thank God I've got your brother – the way you've turned out.'

The sheer injustice of this remark made Peggy momentarily speechless. Myrtle, sensing she had the upper hand, went on, 'And what's more, that Jean's buttering you up – she's never had a good word to say about you. She did it to get you to buy that house for her.'

'It's you who the money has affected the worst. Just listen to you!' Peggy would have liked to stalk out but the room was too small for that. At the door she stopped. 'In any case, you've got your facts wrong. I didn't give Jean a house. It's in my name and she pays rent for it.' She nearly added, 'So there,' but prevented herself just in time. She lingered, waiting to see the look of confusion on her mother's face at this information. But it was a tactical error since it gave Myrtle time to recover.

'Well, there, that proves it, doesn't it? You *have* changed. How mean can you get, making that poor woman pay rent?'

Peggy slammed the door. She wished she could walk out on her mother as Steph had walked out on her, but she couldn't – some stupid hangover from a religion she no longer followed, drummed into her years ago, 'Honour thy father and thy mother.' Why, when they didn't deserve it? She'd go back, she knew she would. Back to the carping and the sniping. Peggy had assumed that her love for her mother was automatic, which had kept her going in the past. Recently she'd come to question it. What would suffice now to keep her going? She had no idea, but she'd still go round to Myrtle's, and she knew one reason why: what would people think of her if she didn't? This made her really despise herself.

'Carol still hasn't called,' Peggy said, as she folded the washing ready for ironing. Her voice was controlled, light and conversational, successfully hiding her disappointment.

'What did you expect?' Dan asked, from behind the sports page of his daily paper.

'I didn't think she was serious enough about the money to sulk this long.'

'She isn't sulking, she's hurt.'

'Oh, really! Don't give me that.' Peggy flapped a pillowcase in the air making the linen crack with angry force. 'If anyone should be hurt it's me.'

'Why you?' he scoffed.

'At the risk of sounding like my own mother, after all I've given Carol it seems a funny way to behave.' She grinned sheepishly as she spoke because what she'd just said contradicted her usual view that one should expect nothing in return for something freely given, that the pleasure was in the giving. She *had* thought that and it had been easy until now, for nothing like this had happened to her before.

'You've changed your tune,' he said.

'I could have guaranteed you'd say that.' She felt a flush of irritation with him. 'Are you going to sit there all day?' She allowed the irritation to expand. His being around the house so much annoyed her increasingly, especially when he preferred to loll about under her feet all day and go out most evenings.

'Do women nag for pleasure?' he asked, as he neatly folded his newspaper.

'I'm not nagging,' she said, though she knew she was.

'Where do you suggest I go to stop bothering you?' he asked with an exaggerated sweetness.

'I don't know. Haven't you some business to attend to? What about going to the agent to see if any new details on garages have come in?'

'They'll contact me. Businesses like that don't pop up every day. I told you it would take time.'

'Haven't you anyone to see? That detective?'

'What's the point in spending money on the detective when we know where Steph is?' He spoke patronizingly.

'But a postcard from Greece! It didn't tell us much.'

'She said she'd write – and she will. You know Steph. If she says something she does it. But this doesn't solve what I'm to do to stop irritating you so.'

'I never said you did.' She was defensive, knowing full well that she was being pushed into the wrong corner and that any minute now she'd apologize. 'You could sort the shed out – what you want to take—'

'I could.' He stretched lazily. 'But it's raining. I suppose I could go to Sainsbury's for you.'

'Would you? That would be a help. I've the landing cupboards to sort through. I'll make a list.'

'You know me, anything to help you out. I don't want to get under your feet and make you cross with me.'

'I'm sorry. I didn't mean it like that.'

Once she had made her list and sent Dan on his way, Peggy cleared up the breakfast dishes and set about sorting the linen cupboard. They had lived in this house for fifteen years and had, therefore, fifteen years of accumulated possessions to wade through. In the back of the cupboard she found the pile of blankets, which, since she had bought duvets, they no longer used. Should she Oxfam them or take them? They were best Witney, she told herself, re-folding them and putting them back. It was the same with the piles of white sheets, yellowing at the edges from disuse, she noticed. Still, one never knew when one would want them again and back into the cupboard they went, waiting to be packed. She was left with a pile of lace and crocheted doilies and traycloths, none of which she had made or remembered where they had come from. Each house move she had carted them with her. This time she intended to throw them away, but when it came to it she couldn't and, instead, slid them into an old pillowcase and replaced them. 'They don't take up much room and they might come in handy,' she told herself, as she invariably did whenever she sorted this cupboard.

In her bedroom Peggy started with the drawers in the pillar of her dressing table. In the deepest one were boxes of photographs of her as a little girl with her brother – black and white pictures curling at their crinkled edges. 'I should put them into albums,' she said, as she peered, puzzled, at one sepia-coloured photograph of young women in thirties' skirts and cloche hats, unsure who they were. She ought to take them round to her mother and get her to identify everyone before it was too late.

She paused. What did she mean by that? She shuddered. Before her mother died was what she meant. Then she came across a photograph of her and Dan, on their bicycles, with a group of others from the youth club. She remembered that day as if it were yesterday. It had been blisteringly hot, the roads almost empty compared with today as they had cycled across the flat fenlands, a glorious arc of blue sky above them on their long ride to the sea. The heat had made her tired and she'd fallen behind the others and Dan had come back looking for her, had set his pace to suit hers. They had stopped for a rest and a snack in a cornfield and she had let him kiss her. Her first real kiss and she could still remember how her insides had seemed to turn to jelly. She touched the photograph gently. It was a special one, for that had been the day her crush on him had turned to love, and she'd loved him ever since. She kissed the fading images. How many people had pictures of the day they'd fallen in love? She should get it reproduced for posterity.

Looking at those young people in the photograph had made her feel inexplicably sad. So much love, so much hope. The love had changed, she admitted that. Still, it would have had to. No one could live at the intense level of the first few years – you'd burn out. And the love she felt now, even though it was real, even though she was lucky still to feel it, was a poor substitute for what once had been. A shadow of the glory. But then, she told herself, such love was in the rightful possession of youth.

She felt ashamed of herself now for wishing him out of the way so that she could get on. How times changed! These days she apologized even when she wasn't in the wrong, just to stop an argument that might chip away a little more of what was left of that sublime emotion they'd once enjoyed.

Chapter Twenty-four

Dan had harboured fond dreams of a summer spent at their new cottage, lazing on the lawn, with strawberries and cream for tea. Such plans had been scotched by the surveyor's report: something nasty was wrong with the septic tank and there were difficulties over a dubious right of way.

Dan, frightened that the frustrating delays caused by the lawyers might make Peggy change her mind, concentrated on getting her to shop for the new house. He encouraged her to order new carpets and expensive made-to-measure curtains. They bought pictures, silver, wall-lights, a four-poster bed, cottagy furniture, copper pans for the country-style kitchen – it was a long list and, knowing his wife, he was banking on her being too frugal to waste it all on deciding not to move.

'Good God, have we still got some of this china?' He pointed to a pile of flower-decorated fruit bowls she had unearthed from the back of one of the kitchen cupboards. 'It's not all there, is it?'

'No. Don't you remember when Paul was little and I tripped over his Matchbox toys and dropped a trayful? We lived in Chapter Street then.'

'Yes, I remember. And did you swear!'

'I never did.'

'You did too. I had to cover young Paul's ears.' He guffawed. 'I should bin it or give it away, love. Buy new. You can afford Wedgwood now, can't you?'

'I couldn't do that. Your auntie Daisy gave us that service as a wedding present.'

'Well, she won't know, she's been dead ten years.'

'No, I'd hate to. It would be throwing away a bit of our past.'

He shrugged his shoulders, not understanding how painful

she found this decision-making about their possessions.

He need not have worried about her changing her mind, however. She loathed the house now and the way memories kept popping out at her when least expected. The wind banging the kitchen door shut made her look up expecting Steph to appear. An old pair of football boots in the attic brought back Paul at all of thirteen crying because his team had lost. And stashed away in a box for the granddaughter she hoped for one day was Barbie and her wardrobe of clothes. That made her think of Carol and her obsession for dolls and dressing up, even when she was a tot. Peggy would hold the object and be filled with an agony of longing for a time and a security in her long-gone past.

They'd heard from Steph, an excited letter written from a Greek island called Naxos, which she described in loving detail like a woman writing of her lover.

'You wait. It's summer still – of course it's lovely and seductive. Wait for the winter, bet it gets bleak there too – she'll soon want to come home then,' Dan reassured her. But the summer had passed and then autumn came and the letters continued to wax lyrical about life in Greece. Dan was wrong, for in October a longer than usual letter arrived to say they had moved to Athens, had found an amazing flat in the Plaka, the old part of the city, and that she and Nigel were teaching English. And why didn't they come to visit? Silently Peggy had handed the letter to Dan.

'So much for my theories,' he'd said. 'Sorry, love. Still, it could be worse, at least it's part of the EC.'

She did not talk about it. She reasoned with herself that it was Steph's life and she must do what she wanted. She'd go in the spring, once the new house was sorted.

She'd had to reason the same way when, back in July, she'd gone to Heathrow to wave goodbye to Paul, Candice and Lance. She'd managed well, chatting and joking until their flight was called. Then she broke down and had clung to Paul and he'd looked embarrassed, and Dan had to prise her hands off her son. She never did see them go for the tears blurred her vision. The telephone bill grew alarmingly for there was no point in hoping for a letter from Paul. She tried to ration the calls, but often when Dan was out the longing for contact got too much for her and she'd dial their number. Several times she'd got them out of bed.

She still did not see Carol. They had manoeuvred themselves into a silly trap, had been stubborn to the point that neither knew how to extricate herself. Dan saw her, and from him Peggy learnt that she and Sean had finally moved to the detached house Carol had longed for. When Peggy said she hoped they would manage, Dan said it was no problem, and she presumed that Sean's business was picking up. She missed her daughter far more than she had anticipated. It was yet another disappointment to try to deal with.

So many disappointments! Dan and her, too. That flush of sexuality which had flared up between them when she had first won the money had died. From the frantic lovemaking of the first few days it had slipped to a couple of times a week, then once a fortnight, until now when he hadn't touched her for a couple of months.

Peggy made excuses for him. He was stressed again, not with lack of money this time but by the surfeit of it. Nothing further had been said about her signing everything over to him and they continued as before with Dan looking after her affairs. She preferred it this way. She could have managed, she knew that, she was not stupid, but it was better to pretend she didn't understand it. It gave Dan a sense of pride and she did not want to take that from him.

In September he found a garage to suit him. The previous owner had specialized in servicing older model cars so Dan had a ready list of clients and a staff used to the idiosyncrasies of cars with traditional chassis, beaten aluminium coachwork, ash frames and long-stroke engines. It was further away than she would have wished, near Stevenage.

'The travelling won't be too much for you?'

'Good heavens, no. It's not as if I've got to be there at crack of dawn. The foreman will open up – couldn't be better. And being that much closer to London we have a chance of picking up specialist car owners from a wider area.'

'But what if the weather's bad? When the dark nights come, I'll be worried sick.'

'Peggy, what a fusser you are! Seems to me you sometimes

manufacture a good old worry just to keep your hand in.' He saw the genuine concern on her face. 'That wasn't very kind of me, was it?' He kissed the tip of her nose to reassure her. 'Tell you what, on nights when it's bad I can always put up at a hotel rather than risk the journey home. How about that?'

Of course, she had agreed. The business was bought and put in Dan's name. Peggy had had a real fight to get him to agree to that. 'I can't allow it. It's your money, Peggy.'

'I've given to everyone else.'

'That's different. They don't share everything as we do. It's not right. Both our names, Peggy, I insist.'

'Please, Dan, let me do this. I want to so badly. It will make me happy.' And it would make her happy if he was. 'Regard it as a giant present for all the happiness you've given me over the years.'

'Well, put like that . . .'

September was a special month in other ways. Candice had her baby – another boy so the Barbie doll in the attic would have to wait. Peggy's immediate reaction was to fly out to Australia to see the new grandson, but with the garage just bought and the move to the new house imminent, Dan suggested they delay the trip until next year.

'The new baby will be more interesting then, not just a crying sleeping bundle,' he'd said. Peggy reluctantly agreed.

By mid-October they were in the cottage. There were boxes to unpack still, pictures to hang and shelves to be put up, and with Dan away getting his garage organized, Peggy estimated it would take a couple of months to get truly straight. But in the main the house was liveable-in.

Peggy had allowed herself to believe that, with the excitement of new surroundings, new people to meet, and a new house to play with, much of her sense of loss would disappear. It didn't. If anything it worsened.

Her loneliness was not helped by the amount of time she spent alone, that the cottage was outside the village and there were no immediate neighbours. She could go the whole day without speaking to another soul until Dan returned. Of an evening when she heard the hoot of an owl or the death scream of a wild animal she was nervous in a way she had never been in the town, with Steph upstairs and traffic passing on the road outside.

Loneliness can be a breeding-ground for many ills, and so it was with Peggy. Her longing for her family filled her body in a physical form – like an ingested twin, she thought. It was there in the morning when she woke; it stayed with her through the day. There were occasional moments when she felt she had escaped it, only to have it wing its way back and burrow deep inside her to settle again. Sleep was no release for whispers of it escaped into her dreams.

Seeing less and less of Dan, she had at first resurrected the old worry that he was having an affair, but in a funny way she doubted it. He was still the same with her, still her Dan. It was just the sex thing. *Just* – she grimaced. Such a word made it sound unimportant when it filled almost all her thoughts.

December arrived and, with Christmas approaching, Peggy changed her mind about speaking to Carol – or, rather, not speaking to her. She was being petty, she lectured herself, and this was the time of goodwill. She was supposed to be an adult, and it was time she stopped behaving like a petulant child who had lost a playground argument. Where was all this stupid pride getting them? Nowhere. She telephoned her daughter.

'I was hoping you'd come over here for Christmas – stay the night. We've plenty of room,' she said, fully aware of how she sounded, begging almost.

'I'm afraid we can't.' Carol sounded cool.

'Look, Carol, I'm sorry we had that little set-to.'

'So am I, but it wasn't of my making.' She could imagine Carol's mouth set in a prim little line as it did when she was peeved.

'I know, and I said I'm sorry,' Peggy replied, apologizing again, she noted, and not knowing if doing so was a sign of strength or weakness.

'It doesn't alter anything. We've invited Daphne and Cyril. I can't change the arrangements at this late date.'

'You're doing the cooking?' Peggy asked, astonished.

'I *can* cook, you know,' Carol snapped back quickly.

'I know, I know,' Peggy replied, equally quickly, already rehearsing the self-lecture, the one that told her not to be so pathetically small-minded. 'What about Boxing Day?'

'We're going to Daphne and Cyril's for that. Daphne's doing a goose.'

'Nice for you,' Peggy said sarcastically, and immediately wished she hadn't.

'You see, nothing's changed, you're still being horrible to me,' Carol whined down the line. Peggy bit her tongue, literally, to stop herself making a too smart, slick reply.

'We won't see you until the New Year, then.'

'Well, it can't be helped. I hadn't heard from you so I had to make some plans,' her daughter said smugly.

After she had put down the receiver Peggy felt frustrated at how inconclusive it had been. And, if she was honest, what a waste of time. She looked about her for something to do: experience had taught her that when she was upset keeping busy was a priority. But the house was clean from attic to cellar. Her estimate of two months to get the house straight had been too generous and had not taken into account that there were only the two of them for her to look after. Her Christmas shopping was done, she'd learnt that afternoon television was not for her and she'd finished her book. Now what? Looking out of the window she saw that after days of rain the sun was shining. She'd go for a walk.

Peggy did not kid herself that she was, or ever would be, a countrywoman. She'd lived all her life in towns and whereas she could walk for miles on pavements, window-shopping or peering into others' lighted windows, she was none too sure if there was going to be anything to interest her in the country on a cold day in December.

The chill air was bracing, no doubt about that, she thought, as she pulled her camel-hair coat tighter about her. She slipped on the damp grass in the meadow and made a note that if she was going to repeat this exercise she'd need different boots: the fashion ones she was wearing were quite unsuitable.

She found the silence ominous, yet when she paused she noticed there was noise all about her but not that of people and cars. The trees, even though devoid of leaves, still rustled as the wind whipped coldly about her. The hedgerow creaked and crackled – was it the wind or little animals, hidden but spying on her? Across the fields she could hear the distinct sound of the river, pregnant with rainwater, racing to the sea. She stepped out in that direction and, as she walked, it was brought home to her sharply how little she knew about the countryside. She could only recognize the outline of one tree, and that was an oak. She saw a small hole in a bank, but had no idea what could live in it, and a large flock of birds which she could not identify. She must go into town and buy books on wildlife and plants, she decided. It could be a new interest. This cheered her and she took on a more purposeful stride.

Once at the river she walked along the towpath, but stopped when she saw an old mill, its waterwheel idle, creeper-covered but boarded up, in a sorry state of repair. What a lovely building, she thought, but how sad and neglected. What fun it must be to do up something like that – saving it for future generations.

Beside the river was a fallen tree. Peggy sat on it to watch the cascading icy water. What the hell was she doing here? Why had she agreed to move? How could she expect to settle in an environment so strange to her, and especially when she felt so lonely? Would she ever adapt?

An exuberant and somewhat damp Labrador came bustling up and jumped up at her noisily, leaving large muddy pawmarks on her coat.

'Tristram, get down, you bastard. God, I'm so sorry. Has he made a mess of you?' A tall, erect woman with a headscarf tied round her hair ran up, grabbed the dog's choke chain and quickly clipped on its leash. 'This beast is the most disobedient creature it's been my misfortune to own. Flora Whittaker.' She held out a knitted-gloved hand. 'I insist on paying for the dry cleaning. Such a lovely coat.'

'No, don't worry, it doesn't matter, please,' Peggy said, shy in the face of one so confident. But she was already noting what the other woman was wearing: a dark green quilted jacket, corduroy trousers and green wellington boots. In garb such as this she looked as if she belonged here, whereas Peggy, in her smart coat and polished boots, looked completely out of place.

'But I insist. May I?' Flora Whittaker plonked herself down on the fallen tree beside Peggy. She felt in her jacket and brought out a crushed packet of Silk Cut, which she offered.

'No thanks. I've given it up.' But she looked longingly at the packet.

'Patches?'

'Yes.'

'I tried them, but they made me itch like buggery so I took it up again.'

'They do itch a bit, but not much,' said Peggy, unsure if she was shocked or amused at such language from a stranger. In Peggy's book only close friends swore like that in front of each other.

'You visiting?' the woman asked.

'We've just moved here. About a mile back.' Peggy nodded up the river. 'We've just bought Copse Cottage. My name's Peggy Alder,' she said, embarrassed at saying her name. She did not know why, but she always was.

'What a joy that house is. So pretty. I loathed the previous owner, stuck-up cow. For the life of me I couldn't imagine why she should consider herself a cut above everyone.'

'She was a bit intimidating. She got quite cross that I didn't want her carpets and curtains.'

'Grim, weren't they?' Flora grinned at her. 'All swirls. Revolting if one had a hangover. Tell you what, come back with me and we'll sponge that coat down.'

'No, really—'

'I insist. Then we can have a snort and I'll drive you back.'

'It sounds lovely,' Peggy finally agreed.

Flora Whittaker's house took Peggy's breath away – it was so large. She recognized it as Georgian from the doors and windows. Inside it was gloriously untidy and shabby, and made Peggy think of a full-blown rose when the petals first begin to brown. Beautiful antiques were screaming out for beeswax, heavy brocade curtains needed a stitch, the silver needed a shine, and an attack with a long feather duster on the cobwebs stretched across the high ceilings would not have gone amiss.

'Get your coat off and sit you down,' Flora ordered.

Peggy sank into a sagging sofa covered with a tartan rug that matched nothing else in the room.

'Forgive the chaos, but I never get ahead of myself,' her hostess explained, opening the door to an incessant scratching. Tristram's double, introduced as Isolde, bounded in. 'Sit!' Flora shouted, and to Peggy's surprise the dog did. A grey-haired woman had followed the dog in.

'Nanny, be a duck, see if you can do anything with Mrs Alder's coat.'

'That Tristram's work? That dog should be tied up. I said it the day he came,' the older woman fretted.

'Yes, Nanny. Thanks for the advice,' Flora said, without a hint of irony.

'Now a drink. Too early for a gin? Tea?'

Peggy glanced quickly at her watch. It was four and she would love a gin, but dare she ask?

'I'm having gin,' Flora said, as if reading her thoughts.

'That would be lovely,' Peggy heard herself say and remembered she'd already said something like that.

'Do you like it here?' Flora asked, as she clattered about with the bottles mixing their drinks.

'It's different,' she replied.

'If you're not used to the country it takes time,' Flora said kindly, handing Peggy a tepid gin and tonic. One sip and she thought the roof of her mouth was about to take off. 'Too strong?'

'Bliss.' Peggy smiled.

Flora began to unwrap herself from her clothes. Unwrap was the right word, Peggy decided, as she watched layer after layer of jumpers and scarves being shed.

'It's having no heating, I'm always like this in winter – I hate the bloody cold,' Flora explained, as another jumper was pulled over her head and she unzipped and stepped out of her thick trousers.

'No central heating?'

'My husband refuses to have it, says it will ruin the bloody furniture. Meanwhile, it ruins me.' She finally emerged. She was not nearly as large as Peggy had thought. She had changed from a very plump woman into a mildly plump one and now, with her scarf and woolly hat removed, Peggy could see she was not only blonde but pretty, too, and, she reckoned, about her own age.

Peggy's coat was returned to her, beautifully cleaned, by Nanny. Peggy had thought she was Flora's grandmother, but it transpired she had cared for her as a baby and had stayed with her ever since.

'It's ideal. Poor old Nanny's got a home and I don't have to do the bloody ironing and mending. Perfect!' Flora explained.

By the time Flora dropped her home at about six Peggy felt distinctly squiffy, but also as if she had made a friend. She did hope so.

Chapter Twenty-five

The meeting with Flora had a marked effect upon Peggy. It cheered her. Here again, like Hazel, was a strong, confident woman who could make her laugh, with her somewhat irreverent attitude to life. She saw her twice in the week before Christmas, but it was enough to know that she really had found a friend. They appeared to be opposites, as she and Hazel had been, but in a different way: Flora had the confidence of one born to wealth, position and an expensive education, but, unlike Hazel, beneath the superficial differences of background she and Peggy had much in common. Both loathed domestic work; Hazel's home had run like clockwork. Both loved art and music, whereas Hazel had never quite understood what Peggy was going on about. And, biggest difference of all, Flora and Peggy were 'happily married' unlike poor Hazel who was, no doubt, still battling with Bruce's infidelities. When agreeing with Flora how lucky they were, Peggy buried her lack of a sex life in a welter of self-deception.

'Aren't some men shits,' stated, rather than asked, Flora as she mixed the hefty gin and tonics which she and Peggy consumed with enthusiasm. She had been telling Peggy how a friend of her husband had returned home after doing a bunk with his bimbo secretary, and his wife had taken him back. Peggy had been telling her about Hazel. 'Poor friends. Why do women put up with it? I've always told Lloyd if he strays I'll cut his balls off.'

'Exactly.' Peggy spluttered into her drink. 'I said to Hazel often enough, "Where's your sense of dignity?" '

'Too true.'

'And she's so attractive – smart, slim as a reed and always so well turned out.'

'It would be understandable with old slags like us if our

213

husbands scarpered, wouldn't it?' Flora chortled. 'Overweight and gone to seed, who'd want us?'

'You're only a *little* overweight. I've got more of a problem.'

'It's a bugger, isn't it? I mean, tonight we're going to a dance, and I know there'll be a buffet. I hate buffets. I know what'll happen. I'll be starving, and I'll be afraid to take enough food, convinced everyone's looking at my plate saying, "Look at that greedy cow, no wonder she's fat!" ' Flora squealed with laughter again, but instinctively Peggy knew it was to hide a hurt that Flora could not yet tell her about.

'You feel that, too?' Peggy leant forward eagerly. 'I thought it was just me,' she said, sounding happy.

'Horrid, isn't it? I had a weight problem as a child but I managed to diet it away. Recently, any food I look at seems to fly straight to my hips.'

'Me, too. I was slim until I had the kids and then I suppose I wasn't too bad. But in the past year or two I always seem to be nibbling and it gets harder to shift the extra weight.'

'I think I do it from boredom.'

'And me,' said Peggy, but she knew it was more from sexual frustration. However, she did not feel she could confide *that* to Flora – ever.

'Why don't we go to a health farm, you and me?'

'Oh, yes, why not!' Peggy clapped her hands with excitement. 'In the New Year, let's.'

Peggy and Dan had been invited to Flora and Lloyd's for drinks on Christmas Eve. Peggy, tipped off by Flora that anyone who was anyone in the locality would be there and as she put it ' . . . tarted up – best bib and tucker required . . .', felt almost sick with anxiety, which wasn't helped by the new taffeta dress she had bought for the occasion, or the brand new Charles Jourdan shoes, the price of which still made her gulp. She'd had her hair blow-dried and retinted, and had been to Sadler's where one of Hazel's ex-assistants, now manageress, had given her a full facial. The works, in fact, she thought, as she studied herself in her bedroom mirror and saw her face brightly painted, like a doll. She practised smiling at her reflection: it did not look like her. Her stomach was alive with a plague of butterflies, her skin crawling with apprehension.

'Don't be silly, Peggy,' Dan admonished her, when she confided in him. 'You're as good as the next person – and a darn sight richer,' he finished, and poured them both large drinks. 'Here, have a stiffener.'

'I should be having a bath.'

'Drink it there, then.'

'Will you come and talk to me?'

'In a minute. I've just got a couple of phone calls to make.'

She lay in the hot bath water – a bit too hot for someone of her age. She'd read that hot baths were bad for menopausal women and although nothing resembling the menopause had happened to her yet, given her age *something* must be going on in her body by now.

'Still, just this once,' she said aloud, as she added a little more steaming water. She sank back and adjusted her pretty lace-covered neck-support bath-pillow and her bath cap, which was protecting the new hairstyle, and took another large sip of her drink. It was lethal, she thought with a smile, and combined with the heat of the bath, it had begun to make her feel more than a little squiffy. The bottles of gin seemed to empty with an alarming speed these days and she was finding that, whereas she had once never drunk in the daytime, recently she had started to look forward to a gin at about noon and wine with her lunch. And drinks were poured earlier and earlier each evening. She found herself thinking again, as she frequently did now, that maybe she was drinking too much. Still, it was Christmas, not the best time to worry about alcohol consumption. She'd think about it in the New Year.

Dan, stripped down to his boxer shorts, had entered the bathroom and was standing at the gold-tapped basin lathering his face with his old-fashioned brush. He caught her eye in the swivel mirror over the basin.

'You look deep in thought,' he said.

'I was just wondering if we drink too much.'

'Well, if you're only wondering about it, then we're not.' He started to shave.

Peggy soaped and rinsed herself, then stepped out of the water, wrapping herself in a large white bath towel – huge, soft and new – from John Lewis. She sat on the edge of the bath and watched Dan. He was wearing well for a man of his age, she thought, as she studied his smooth back, his sturdy muscular legs, and admired his tight buttocks.

'Do you remember? I always used to sit and watch you shave when we were young,' she said dreamily.

'Did you?'

'Of course I did.' She wished he had remembered. 'Especially when you did it at night, before we went to bed. I knew then what was coming,' she blundered on. Dan's hand, razor poised, paused in its task. 'That was always exciting.' Even as she spoke she knew she was on dangerous ground, but the memories of the past excited her and urged her on.

'Not now, Peggy,' Dan said quickly, and concentrated on his shave.

'Sometimes I used to do this.' She stood up and in two steps was standing behind him. She reached forward, put her arms about his waist.

'Peggy, I said not now.' He jerked away from her.

'Come on, we've time.' Her hand was at the waist of his shorts.

Deliberately he removed it and turned to face her. 'Peggy, stop it.' He was annoyed.

'Why? We're alone. There's nothing to bother us. But we never do it these days, do we?'

He did not reply but returned to the mirror and recommenced his shave.

'Do we? Why not?' she demanded. He patted his smooth skin with water and dried it. 'Why not?' He opened the bathroom cabinet, took out a bottle of aftershave and poured some into his hands. 'It was lovely earlier this year – you wanted me all the time. What's happened? Answer me!' she said more loudly, feeling reckless, finding the courage, aided by gin and the hot bath, to demand an answer.

'Peggy, look, we're supposed to be going out. I don't want any dramas.'

'I'm not making any dramas, I just want an answer to a

civilized question, which I think I have every right to ask,' she said, sounding more dignified now as she drained the last of her gin and tonic.

He finished putting the aftershave on his face, turned to her and, with an almost weary expression on his face, sighed. 'Because I don't want to.'

'Later, when we come back?'

'I just don't want to. Not now, not any time.'

'What do you mean?' She took a step back from him. Her face, newly, brightly, bravely made up, felt as if her skin was stretched tight across her bones.

'What I said.'

'It's the drink. I said it – I just said it in the bath. We both drink too much – it makes me want it and it turns you off it. That's it, isn't it?' She spoke quickly, breathlessly, anxiously.

'I don't know, Peggy.' He sat down heavily on the lavatory lid. 'I don't know what's wrong.'

She clutched her prized bath towel to her as if it could shield her from words she had demanded to hear, words she now wished had remained unspoken. She felt dizzy. She leaned on the basin and took a deep breath.

'Is there someone else? Please tell me. I need to know.' Before, she had had butterflies in her stomach. Now it was full of writhing snakes of fear. She'd done it again – she'd allowed herself to become smug in her marriage, confident in her man. She was terrified at the prospect of his answer but needed to know.

He put his head in his hands. 'I don't know how to explain how I feel, Peggy . . . I hardly know myself.'

'Then there is someone?' Her voice was raised to a shrill pitch, no dignity now.

'I sound so bloody ungrateful after everything you've done, Peggy. I feel a shit. It's just . . . I thought with this new house I'd feel different, that everything would slot back, that we'd be as we were.'

She felt her spirits easing. He hadn't said there was another woman. He hadn't even bothered to deny it, as if her question had been of no importance. Then it was something else. 'You've hardly given it time, Dan. We've only been here a couple of months,' she said, with as much encouragement in her voice as she could muster. 'It'll sort.'

'I don't know if it will. I just feel so low. Trapped. I lie in bed and think, I'm nearly fifty, is this it?'

'You're run down. You should see the doctor. Get a tonic. Maybe you're going down with something. Maybe we shouldn't go out.' One word tumbled over another in her haste to reassure – who? Herself? Him?

'No, no. We must go. I want to meet your new friend.'

'Then we won't stay long. We'll get you home and into bed.' She inspected her make-up in the mirror to see if it had survived her bath.

'You're not listening to me. It's more complex than that, Peggy. I need more from life. Listen to me—'

She whirled round. 'I don't want to listen to you,' she shouted. He was taken aback by the tone of her voice. 'You've got a touch of the male menopause, that's all. Join the club.' She left the bathroom and ran down the stairs to the sitting room. She crossed the room and sank down in front of the Christmas tree she had decorated, even though there were just the two of them this year. She sifted through the pile of gaily wrapped parcels until she found a slim one. She retraced her steps, in a hurry to prevent any thoughts forming, nagging in her head – thoughts she did not wish to contemplate, to face, not now, especially not on Christmas Eve.

'Here,' she said, thrusting the parcel at him as she entered their bedroom.

'What's that?'

'An early Christmas present. It'll make you feel better, cheer you up.' She was trying to smile.

He ripped at the paper, the gold and silver bow dropping to the floor, revealing a large envelope. 'What is it?' He looked up questioningly before opening it. 'Oh, Peggy. That's nice,' he said, holding up a travel agent's ticket. 'Where to?' He took the brochure from the envelope. 'A cruise? But I thought you longed to go to Italy.'

'I do. But I thought you'd prefer this – more fun for you. Italy has waited so long it can wait for me a bit longer.'

'When do we go?' he asked, and she wished he'd sounded more enthusiastic. Never mind, maybe he was getting used to the idea.

'Two days after Boxing Day. It's a New Year cruise. The Canaries, Morocco.'

'Clever girl.' He kissed the tip of her nose, and she could have wept with relief.

'I suggest we leave on the twenty-seventh. I've booked us into a hotel in Southampton.'

'What about clothes?'

'No problem. If necessary we can buy on the ship.' She was stammering with excitement, thinking of the boxes of clothes she had already bought him, all wrapped and under the tree downstairs. 'Has it cheered you up?'

'Of course it has! What a turn-up!'

'You didn't mean what you said, did you? Not really?' She didn't look at him as she asked – she couldn't, for she was too afraid she might see that he was lying.

'Oh, we all get the hump occasionally, don't we?'

'Was that all it was? Honest?' Her eyes met his now.

'Sorry, darling. I'm an ungrateful old sod. Forgive me?'

'Oh, of course I do. Of course. I love you, Dan. I understand, I've been a bit snappy recently, I'm the first to admit – the hassle with the kids.' She felt suddenly as if all the energy had been drained from her, as if she had been through a storm, but, she told herself, she had emerged the other side, all danger gone. She forced herself to talk. 'And you know, Dan, one thing we didn't realize fully is the shock to our systems of all that money coming our way. We've got to give ourselves time to adjust. Look at how our lives have changed.'

'You're probably right.'

She was sitting on her dressing stool. He stood behind her, looking at her reflection in the triple mirror. 'You're a good woman, Peggy. I don't deserve you.' She put up her hand searching for his and gave it a squeeze. 'I like the hair, but don't you think you're wearing a bit too much make-up? You know, for someone your age?'

Chapter Twenty-six

Flora's drawing room had been tidied almost beyond recognition. The clutter on the mantelshelf had been removed, the books and magazines put away, dog blankets had been whipped from sofas and chairs, the silver was polished, a fire laid, a tree twinkling, flowers in vases – the room looked elegantly pleased with itself.

They were late and the room was already noisily full. Flora swooped upon them, welcoming them expansively, and then paraded them around the room like trophies, introducing them to everyone. That done, she excused herself and scuttled off to be a hostess somewhere else in the large room and left them to their own devices.

Lloyd, Flora's husband, was tall, spare, grey-haired and much older than Peggy had anticipated. He seemed to be loftily detached from his guests, as if speaking to them was a wearisome chore, his mind elsewhere and his body longing to join it. Not one for socializing, Peggy decided, and wondered what on earth Flora, so warm and bubbly, could have seen in him.

At the best of times Peggy was not good at meeting strangers and making small talk but tonight, with so many new faces and such socially confident ones too, it was an ordeal. She always had a dreadful time remembering people's names and while understanding their hurt when she got them wrong, it was nothing to her own mortification. She decided to concentrate hard on the names, and consequently lost the drift of the conversations and was soon feeling all at sea and doubtless regarded as thick.

Apart from a couple of regal elderly women, most of the others were of her own age. This should have been a comfort, but it wasn't. The women eyed her up and down, evidently gauging the cost of what she wore – she did notice with some satisfac-

220

tion that their eyes certainly seemed to linger longest over her shoes.

She was disappointed in their clothes. Most wore long skirts and frilly white blouses, a fashion which Peggy believed had long since gone out. Here it was like a uniform. And Hazel would have had something to say about their too-bright red lipstick and over-use of pink blusher. Their faces, she thought, looked as if they were surprised suddenly to find themselves painted, as if it was a rare event. They had such hard, discontented expressions, despite the social smiles, as if life had been a bitter disappointment to them but they were trying to keep it secret from the world. She did admire how straight they stood and how they moved smoothly as if their bodies were exceptionally fit. They were noisy, that was for sure, as they brayed loudly at each other.

The men, on the other hand, hardly registered her presence, certainly not enough to speak to her. She was not overly upset by this – rather, she had become used to it. Peggy had reached that stage in life, in common with so many women of her age, at which one becomes almost invisible as time has worked its worst.

Peggy thought the men, though somewhat overweight, looked remarkably pleased with themselves. She assumed their pleasure could not be because of their corpulence but perhaps because they possessed the wherewithal to become so. Maybe the size of the tummy was in ratio to the size of the bank balance, like primitive tribes and their attitude to obesity – she smiled inwardly at that thought. They brayed less but rumbled importantly instead, with much rocking back and forth on heels, with thumbs stuck into small pockets which had evidently been tailored for just such a purpose.

She was relieved when the initial flurry of interest at their arrival lessened and, drink in hand, she could make herself scarce by stealing away to sit on a window seat. From there, unobserved, she could watch the party in progress.

All in all, she decided she found both sexes equally intimidating. She doubted if she had anything in common with these people; she wasn't sure she even wanted to find mutual ground. For all that, she had to admire Dan's supreme confidence in company with which he would never normally mix. At parties Dan could usually be guaranteed to be at one end of the room with the men talking cars and football. But here she saw him circulating with a never-empty glass in his hand. His face, she noted, was getting redder by the minute and, curiously, he was beginning to talk as loudly as the rest. He was flirting outrageously, but instead of being annoyed by him, she noticed that the women appeared to be enjoying it and were becoming even louder in their excitement. He was evidently avoiding the men. Watching Dan enjoying himself it was almost as if she had dreamt the conversation in the bathroom, that it had been last night's nightmare. He was the picture of happiness, not a man discontented and querying the point of his life. He looked as if he did not have a care in the world while she still felt lashed by the scene.

'Are you Flora's new friend?'

Peggy looked up, surprised since she hadn't been aware of anyone approaching her, to find a tall dark-haired man, with wide-spaced grey eyes and the slightly sardonic expression of one to whom life has been nothing but a series of private jokes. He was immaculately suited and, for this company, slim.

'Yes.'

'May I?' One eyebrow was cocked, most attractively, in question as he asked to sit beside her. She moved along the window seat to give him room. 'I'm Tarquin Millthorpe, Flora's *much* younger brother, here for the festivities.' He grinned at his emphasis.

'Peggy Alder.'

'Peggy – I do so like non-fussy names. Not like mine! I ask you, Tarquin, named after some bloody Roman. A right plonker's name, as a lot of my friends would be only too eager to tell you.'

'I like it. It sounds, well, sort of romantic. I've never met a Tarquin before.' She would usually feel shy with someone so young and self-assured, but oddly she didn't. And she wondered why he was putting himself down.

'If I ever have a daughter I'd like to call her Peggy, or Polly, or Poppy, even – lovely names. Is it short for Margaret?'

'No. Just Peggy.'

'Brilliant. I'm a purist about names, you see. I don't like them when they're shortened, or instead of. You've done wonders for my sister, you know,' he said abruptly.

'Me?' Peggy sounded her amazement.

'She was getting frightfully boring. She needs more company, different from this lot.' He nodded to the cream of local society. 'All they can talk about is bloody horses.'

'I was surprised when Flora told me she doesn't ride.' Peggy had actually been relieved when Flora said this, since she was terrified of horses.

'That's because a fellow she was particularly fond of when an innocent gal did a flit with the Master's wife and she was put off horses for life.'

'But that was hardly the horses' fault.'

'No, but psychologically, deep down in her mind, she can't divorce the horse from the deception, if you see what I mean – horseflesh and errant men. He could have been the love of her life, couldn't he?'

'But she found Lloyd instead and she's happy with him.'

'Did she tell you that? She lies a lot, my sister.' He wasn't looking at her as he said this so she could not gauge if he was teasing or not – if he was telling the truth, even. If Flora wasn't happy with Lloyd then why did she lie to her? That thought screeched to a halt in front of the brick wall of her own lies. Hadn't she pretended to Flora that all was well with her own marriage? Could she honestly say she was happy? Especially now, after the scene in the bathroom. She glanced about the room trying to see what Dan was up to.

'You seem deep in thought. Am I so boring?'

'Sorry? I was miles away.'

'Why do you keep looking for your husband? Is he the jealous type?'

'I'm not looking for him. I'm just watching the throng.'

'Really?' He smiled, and she felt herself blushing.

'Well, you know, men! Sometimes they can be a bit of a liability.' She giggled at the silliness of saying this to a man.

'I shouldn't worry, you know. All this lot are piss artists *par excellence*.' He rolled his eyes and smiled gently at her. 'Tell me, you're filthy rich, aren't you?'

'Well, yes.' She felt flustered by this bald remark but then found she rather liked his straightness. It was a change from saying nothing about the money or going all round the houses like most people. It was odd the way he kept changing the subject so abruptly, going off at different tangents. He reminded her of Steph and the way she flitted about verbally as if there was not time enough to learn everything she wanted to know. 'Yes, I'm very rich. I won the lottery,' she said, matching his plain speaking.

'I needn't have asked, of course, since Flora told me.'

'Then why did you?'

'I wanted to see if you would prevaricate. You didn't – I admire that. Did she warn you about me?'

'Should she have?' She couldn't help but admire his nerve.

'Oh, yes. I'm a rotter, a right con-merchant. I'll be trying to tap you for a loan before you know where you are.'

'Well, thanks for the warning.' She smiled.

'You know, when you smile, you're frightfully pretty. And if you want my advice – which, of course, you do – you should get your hair highlighted and cut even shorter, it'll knock years off you. Fancy another snort?'

Chapter Twenty-seven

On the drive back from the party – Peggy, as usual, at the wheel – Dan's bonhomie had deserted him and he slumped morosely beside her. She tried once or twice to get him talking but when his answers came as monosyllabic grunts she gave up and they drove the rest of the way, fortunately not far, in silence.

'I thought of going to midnight mass,' she said, as they took off their coats in the hall.

'What on earth for?'

'I don't know, I thought it would be nice. A real Christmassy thing to do.'

'Count me out. I'm going to bed,' he replied, already beginning to mount the stairs.

'Oh, Dan, not now – it's only nine. Not on Christmas Eve.' But either he did not hear or chose to ignore her and continued up. Peggy watched him go, then went into the sitting room and poured herself a large gin and tonic.

She stoked the fire, settled in the armchair beside it and gazed into the flames. Since Paul and Steph had gone away, Peggy knew she had not been the best of company; she had worried that she was getting on Dan's nerves, but she had tried to come to terms with what had happened, had made an effort not to be too much of a drag. And then he behaved as he had this evening and she couldn't think why she bothered. Why did she always take the blame for things even when she was not necessarily the cause? What about the scene in the bathroom? Really, he had a nerve. Did he think he was the only one who woke up and wondered, Is this it? Was the panic of advancing years his prerogative? How often she'd felt trapped, unfulfilled, afraid of time passing, but she'd kept it secret, faced it and fought it. She hadn't always won,

225

but she'd succeeded in kidding everyone else she had.

She did not go to church; instead she sat and drank, not to get drunk but until she thought that her mind was sufficiently anaesthetized for her to get to sleep easily. But once in bed, with Dan beside her, thoughts kept whizzing round and round, and as soon as she had dealt with one another popped up to take its place.

When she had returned to what her mind now referred to as 'the bathroom incident' for at least the sixth time, she made a conscious effort to think about something pleasant for a change.

Tarquin sprang to mind. She had so enjoyed talking to him. He was suave, educated, obviously from a privileged background, and yet she had not felt intimidated by him, or that he was looking down on her – so recently a shop assistant. He seemed to have no side to him. If only Steph could have found someone like him to fall in love with. Still, he'd be too old for her. What age did she think he was? Late thirties, probably. She made an image of his face appear in her mind's eye. He had such a cynical face, but not in a nasty way . . . Sardonic wasn't quite right either. How best could she describe him? He had an ironic expression as if life and everyone in it was a wry joke – yes, that was better. Perhaps the joking and putting himself down was to hide a gentle nature that had been hurt in the past. She smiled into the night. Even if she couldn't match-make him she still hoped she would meet him again.

The following morning, Christmas Day, Peggy had the satisfaction of seeing Dan having virtually to crawl painfully into the land of the living.

'Christ, Peggy, I feel bloody awful.'

'I'm not surprised, the number of glasses of that punch you sank. And was it wise, I wonder, then to go on to Scotch?' She knew she sounded like a million other women the morning after, but she couldn't stop – she couldn't help herself. He had let her down.

'Were you counting? Do you have to nag?'

'I just wish you could have behaved yourself – new people, new friends. What must they think of us? You pissed out of your skull and feeling up the women.'

'I never was,' he said belligerently, eyeing, with suspicion, the bubbling Alka-Seltzer she'd given him.

'If you can say that, then evidently you've got alcoholic amnesia.'

'*You* can talk – canoodling for hours on that window seat with that toy-boy gushing all over you.'

'That was Flora's brother and he was not *gushing*, we were having a civilized conversation.' She angrily opened the wardrobe door and began to search through her new clothes for something to wear. Before, when she'd had half this amount, debating what to put on hadn't been nearly the problem it was now. 'Carol telephoned to wish us *Merry Christmas.*' She endowed these two words with angry spite as she yanked a dark green velvet suit off its hanger. 'I told her you were too comatose to speak to her. She said would you call later. And, if we're to be at the Fox and Duck for lunch in an hour, I suggest you get up.' She slammed into the bathroom, sat on the loo and felt sorry for herself.

An hour later she had to admit Dan seemed fine. Showered and changed, he looked great, whereas if it had been her with the hangover it would have taken her hours to look half-way decent. Another unfairness of life, she thought. And his shower had put him in a better mood, or else he was making an effort for her. If he could, she could, too, she told herself – in any case, she never had been able to stay cross with him for long.

It felt odd to be sitting in a restaurant eating their Christmas dinner instead of being at home at either end of the table, their family around them. The meal was adequate, but not what they were used to. There seemed to be a forced jollity in the large room as if the other diners, disappointed too, and the staff, fed up with not being with their own families, were determined to have a good time, but only emphasizing how artificial the whole set-up was. Without discussing it, neither wanted to linger over coffee and liqueurs, but to get back to the cottage in time for the Queen's speech.

Like every family, they had their routines which never varied from Christmas to Christmas. And so, as always, they did not open their presents until after the transmission. Perhaps they should have changed the habitual pattern for instead of the room being a riotous, chaotic mess of paper hurriedly torn from parcels

as in other years, they folded it neatly. The room remained tidy –
and that wasn't the same either, she thought.

Dan loved his clothes, Peggy her string of pearls.

'Course, it's really your money bought it,' he said. 'I could
never afford anything like that.'

'Don't be silly. How many times do I have to say it? It's *our*
money.' She kissed his cheek and drank the brandy he'd poured
her. 'It's not the same, is it, without the family?' she said sadly.

'I don't know. I think it's rather nice. It's different, but I'm
enjoying the day.'

'Honestly? That's nice. I can't stop myself thinking about last
year, what it was like then, and the thoughts keep getting in the
way of today.'

'No point in looking back, Peggy, that'll get you nowhere.'

'True. And there's one good thing, at least you've stopped
doing a wobbly on me.' She peeped up at him.

'I felt it was my turn. Why should you women have all the
moods?' She laughed at this, glad that he was in good spirits, that
they were friends again. 'What shall we do tomorrow?' he asked.

'I thought I'd pack for us both. Sort everything out so we can
get away early on the twenty-seventh.'

'Fine. Would you mind if I slipped out for an hour or two?'

'No. Where?'

'Oh, I thought I'd pop back into town, see if anything's going
on at the snooker hall – you know, have a game or two. I'd be
back by six at the latest.'

'You do whatever you want, love. I'll be busy here, washing
and ironing.'

'Then I'll be out from under your feet.'

'Yes, you'll be doing me a favour.'

Boxing Day passed quickly for Peggy in a welter of pressing and
packing. At least on a boat it wouldn't matter if she had too many
clothes: they wouldn't be lugging their suitcases from pillar to post.

By six she had finished. She had a long soak in the bath and
by seven had some soup on. She was too excited to eat more
and, no doubt, Dan would have had lunch in town.

228

By eight she began to worry. Should she do what she had never done before and call the snooker hall? By eight thirty she had plucked up courage, only to find that the phone rang and rang and no one answered it. Strange, she thought, and poured herself a large gin for consolation.

When she heard the car engine at ten she could have wept with relief. She rushed to the door about to call out and ask where the hell he'd been. But the words were frozen in her throat by the sight of Dan gingerly being manhandled out of the car by Sean.

'Dan! Sean! What on earth . . .' She scurried down the steps and onto the gravelled driveway.

'Sorry, Peggy. You been worried?' Dan looked up at her from a doubled-up position.

'It's his back, Mum, he's done himself in.'

'Oh, no!' she wailed, taking his arm on the other side and helping move him into the house. It was a long and tortuous business, Dan wincing with pain at every footstep. They lowered him gently onto the sofa where he sank back with relief.

'Christ, Peggy, get me a huge brandy,' he said.

'Should you? We must call the doctor.'

'I've seen a doc. I've been to the hospital. I've strained my back, they don't think it's a disc. Did it playing snooker – difficult shot.' He smiled bravely.

'Oh, my poor darling. Can I get you anything – a hot water bottle, hot chocolate?' She fussed over him.

'No, just that brandy, Peggy, there's a pal.'

'Anything for you, Sean?'

'No, I'd better not, I'm driving, but thanks all the same, Mum.'

She was so overwrought about Dan that she didn't even react to his calling her Mum. 'I phoned the snooker hall, but no one answered,' she said, while clattering about with the bottles and ice bucket.

'They closed early. I was down the hospital for hours, like a bloody battlefield there, it was littered with drunks – some Christmas for those poor nurses. Gory, wasn't it, Sean?'

'What? Oh, yes,' Sean answered vaguely.

'How did Sean find you?' she asked, handing him his giant brandy balloon – another of her Christmas presents to him.

'I called him from the snooker hall to collect me. I didn't want you driving into town all het-up.'

'That was kind of you.' She thought, as she so often did, how lucky she was to have such a fine-looking husband – even in such pain he was still handsome.

'I think I'd best sleep down here tonight, Peggy. I'll never get up the stairs.'

'I'll make you up a bed in here. I can sleep in the armchair.'

'You'll do no such thing. What sort of state would you be in for the trip tomorrow?'

'Tomorrow!' In the panic she had forgotten their trip in the morning. 'Will you be fit enough for the train journey?' Even as she asked him she knew it was a stupid question. Anyone could see he was in agony.

He felt for her hand. 'Peggy, love, I don't think I'm going to make it. In any case, I have to see the quack again in three days. I can't be in two places at once.'

'Oh, what a shame.' She sat down despondently on her new chintz-covered armchair. 'Do you think the cruise company will give us our money back at the last minute?'

'Not a hope in hell. Look, Peggy, while I was at the hospital waiting to be seen, I had plenty of time to work things out. Now, I don't want any argument. I want you to go without me.'

'No!' she shouted.

'You're not listening again, Peggy. There's to be no argument, no discussion. You are going.' He pointed his forefinger, stabbing the air at each word.

'But how can I, with you in this state? How will you cope? No, it's impossible, I'd never have a moment's peace.'

'It's not as bad as it looks, apparently. I'll be a bit more mobile tomorrow. I've been told I should move around as much as possible – I won't be bedridden.'

'Carol and I will look after him, Mum.'

'You could move in?' she asked hopefully.

'They could, but I don't think it'll be necessary. I'll manage. I want you to go.'

'But I'd hate it on my own – you know what I'm like with strangers. And how could I enjoy it without you? It would be all wrong. I'd feel guilty all the time.'

Dan took hold of both her hands this time, grimacing with pain as he leant forward. 'Look, Peggy, my darling, I want you to go, honest. I want you to have a nice, relaxing holiday, really enjoying yourself. You need a break after the move and everything.'

The argument continued back and forth long after Sean had helped her make up a bed and settle him, long after Sean had gone, and long after they should have been in bed and fast asleep.

He had vetoed her sleeping in the chair beside him. 'It's not as if I'm going to croak it in the night, now is it?' So Peggy had gone to bed in the new four-poster, and although she had slept in it alone before, when bad weather had prevented him returning home from the garage, this night she felt particularly alone in it.

She woke early and lay looking at her beamed ceiling – no cracks here. She had made up her mind. Last night just before she had turned the lights out, Dan had said, 'Peggy, I shall feel so guilty if you don't go on this cruise. Please, for my sake, go. I'll get better faster if you do.'

That had been the clincher, Peggy knew all about guilt and how uncomfortable it was, and she did not want him feeling like that over her not going. She owed it to him to go and she did need a holiday. When she'd seen the state he was in last night she had to admit that, after the initial shock, her feelings had been primarily of disappointment. She could make all the arrangements before she left: she'd phone Carol, check when she could come over. She'd get up now and check the freezer.

As soon as Peggy was on the way to London to catch the boat train she began again to doubt the wisdom of going. This time it had nothing to do with staying to look after Dan. No, it was herself. She had never done anything alone, not on this scale, and she did not know if she wanted to try.

The minute she was shown to her room at the hotel, she telephoned Dan. His voice sounded a lot more cheerful and he assured her the pain was easing with the pills the doctor had given him.

'You sound funny,' she said.

231

'Do I? Sorry. It's these bloody painkillers. I tell you, Peggy, I'm wandering around like a bloody zombie.'

'Poor darling.'

The dining room was crowded as she was shown to her single table. From the conversations going on around her it was evident that most of the other diners were, like her, passengers on the cruise. She looked at them curiously: without exception they were all in groups. She was the only one travelling alone.

After dinner, it was far too early to go to bed and she wandered into the bar, which, like the dining room, was crowded and, judging by the volume of noise, the holiday spirit was well and truly in place. The only spare seat was at a table with a sullen-looking couple who did not appear any too happy when she asked if the seat was free. She would much rather have been with the noisy group at the next table. With them, perhaps, she could put a lid on the odd mixture of emotions she was feeling – trepidation at going on this voyage alone, a mite worried about Dan, but excited all the same at the prospect of the ship and the places it was going to take her.

The noisy group were the Rooneys, a large extended family of Londoners. Peggy counted fourteen of them. Aware of her interest and that she was on her own, they soon invited her to join them. Gratefully she turned her chair round as a young couple arrived. Like a light-switch being thrown the noisy jollity ended abruptly and they fell silent.

'Any luck?' one man asked.

'No. Not a hope in hell,' the new young man replied in what she took to be an American accent.

'Never mind, Jim. You're here now and that's the main thing,' the eldest Mrs Rooney said.

'What's the problem?' Peggy whispered to young Tracey Rooney who sat beside her.

'Oh, it's such a shame. It's Gran and Grandad Rooney's golden wedding anniversary next week. We've all pitched in and given them this cruise as a treat and we're all going with them. Jim here lives in Canada. At first he didn't think he could make it, but now he can so he flew in tonight with his wife, Mary-Lou.'

'That's nice.' Peggy warmed to the story.

'But he can't get a ticket. All sold.'

'Oh, no!' Peggy exclaimed. 'How sad.'

The Rooneys continued to commiserate with each other while Peggy sat, deep in thought. Often in life she had found things happened that pointed you one way without you having to think hard about it. This, she was certain, was one of those times. She opened her handbag. 'Here, take these.' She pushed her ticket across the table to Jim.

'What?' He looked across at her.

'Have my ticket – it's a double.'

'But . . . don't you want to go?'

'No, not really. My husband couldn't make it – he's hurt his back. I never wanted to come, but he insisted. We can go later, when he's better.'

'That's mighty kind of you, Mrs . . .' He glanced quickly at the ticket. 'Mrs Alder.'

Tracey Rooney swung round and pointed at Peggy. 'Did Jim say your name was Alder? Peggy Alder?' Tracey asked excitedly. 'Not the lottery winner?'

'Yes, I'm afraid so,' Peggy said. Would a day ever dawn when she wasn't embarrassed at being discovered?

'I thought I recognized you. We nearly cried when you won, you know. Gran said it was nice to see a lovely family getting some good fortune for a change.'

Peggy giving up her ticket seemed to recharge the Rooneys' batteries *en masse*. Finding these high spirits a mite tiring, Peggy went to her room, feeling quite light-headed from wine and brandy, but also, she knew, from the decision not to go having been made so easily for her. It was too late to call Dan and tell him the good news, but she was soon asleep.

Next morning she and Jim had no problem at the steamship company exchanging her ticket and Jim wrote her a cheque to cover the cost. She waved them all off – they were still making an infernal din: maybe two weeks of such exuberance might have been a bit too much to stomach. A later cruise might be quieter. Over her solitary breakfast she had decided to surprise Dan and therefore did not telephone him.

By late morning she was on her way to London. With the

country still on holiday the normal train schedules were non-existent and she had a long wait at Liverpool Street station before catching a train for home. It was late afternoon, and dark, when she reached the cottage.

The house looked so pretty from the lane with what looked like virtually every light blazing. Snow had begun to fall. She had her key, but did not need it since the door was unlocked. Quietly she let herself in. She looked in the sitting room. It was empty. The remains of a meal were still on the dining-table: perhaps he was waiting for Carol to come and clear up after him. In the hall she paused in her step. That was odd: the table had been laid for two.

She went back into the dining room to check. Had she dreamt it? No. The table was set with the best cutlery and glass for two people. Sean had been here, she told herself. But the best cutlery? No. It was Carol who had had lunch with her father. It would be just like her to use the best – and to leave the washing up afterwards!

She began to climb the staircase when Dan, clad only in his boxer shorts, appeared at the top, a cricket bat in his hand, an anxious expression on his face.

'Sorry, did I give you a scare? I thought I'd surprise you.' Peggy laughed happily.

'You're on the boat,' he said inanely.

'No, I'm not. I'm here. I changed my mind.'

'But the tickets?'

'I sold them.' She took a step up. He took one down. 'Well, you might say you're pleased to see me.' She did not say it crossly but lightly, jokingly.

'Who is it, Dan?'

Peggy stood on the staircase, one foot lifted to take the next step. A foot that remained motionless. Everything was frozen. Dan did not move. The clock, she was sure, had stopped ticking. Was she breathing, even?

'You,' she hissed as Hazel, wrapped in one of Peggy's John Lewis towels, appeared behind her husband.

Chapter Twenty-eight

Peggy had no idea how long she had been waiting alone in the sitting room. She could not remember pouring the drink, which she clutched in her hand so firmly that her knuckles showed white. She stood on the hearth-rug, her back to the fire, which was blazing, yet she was shivering with a chill that had burrowed into the core of her bones. Above her, she could hear quick shuffling noises. Drawers and doors were being banged shut. They were whispering fiercely to each other. It was a farce unfolding around her. Would she find it funny one day? It was certainly failing to amuse her now.

She stood stock still. The only movement she made was to lift the Waterford tumbler to her mouth from time to time. And, rather like the victim of an accident, upon finding themselves conscious, feels their body to see what is broken, she began to inspect her mind to see how she felt, how she was faring. Her nightmare had become reality and what did she feel? Nothing, absolutely nothing, just a strange, unreal, icy calm.

One of the logs fell and rolled across the wide hearth. She put her gin on the mantelshelf and bent to tend the fire.

'Peggy . . .'

She swung round, the poker still in her hand. Dan took a step back, alarm on his face. She realized he thought she was going to hit him. She lowered it.

'A log rolled,' she explained, and couldn't understand why she had. Let the bastard feel afraid. That's what he was, after all. 'How's the back?'

'Let's be civilized about this, Peggy.'

'I am. I thought asking after your back was very civilized.'

'You were being sarcastic.'

'I didn't mean to be,' she said, but then thought, Why shouldn't I? 'Did the doctor mean you to take quite so much exercise?'

'Oh, Peggy.' He sounded as if he was disappointed in her. He went to the drinks cupboard and poured himself a large Scotch.

'I shouldn't drink too much when you've got to drive,' she said reasonably.

'Drive? What do you mean?'

'Well, you can't stay here now, can you?' She stood on tiptoe to retrieve her glass from the high oak mantelshelf.

'Peggy, I can explain.'

'What? That Hazel just happened to pop in and was giving your painful back a massage?' She laughed at that, but it was a truncated, bitter sound.

'She did, as a matter of fact.'

'Oh, yeah, and the rest.' She looked down into the flames. Odd, how she was reacting, she thought. She'd always assumed she would rant and scream. Not this – this strange calm. It was almost as if she were watching herself in performance, like an actress in a play.

'Peggy, I want you to understand.'

'What?' She spat out the word. 'What is there to understand? I return home unexpectedly to find you upstairs with my ex-best friend who just happens to be naked under *my* towel. Now what conclusion can I possibly draw from that?' She took a hefty swig of gin, feeling it race through her body, giving her warmth when she was so chill, giving her confidence. 'There was no bad back, was there, Dan? You never went to hospital.'

Dan did not have to answer; the guilt on his face was sufficient.

'And Sean, was he in on this little charade?'

Dan nodded.

'Oh, great. Thanks a million for that. How dignified for us to have our son-in-law helping you in your nasty little tryst. And Carol? Did the little Princess do her bit? Do tell me, Dan, I'm all agog.'

'Look, Peggy, I tried to explain to you the other night. I needed something. I was feeling trapped. I love you, I never wanted to hurt you, nothing like that—'

'Oh, no? Just shove me off on my own for two weeks, so you can have two weeks shagging that bitch. I can see, Dan, that you didn't want to hurt me one little bit.'

'Peggy, why are you being like this?'

'I beg your pardon? *I beg your pardon?*' Her voice rose as she repeated herself. 'Am I to take it that *I*'ve done something wrong? Or I'm *doing* something wrong? What did you want, Dan? That I'd understand? That I'd bring you both a cup of cocoa – tuck you up? Grow up.'

'It's not important, Hazel and me. It's not like *us*. I just need a little time to sort myself out.'

'Do you, now? Still feeling down, are you? Poor you.' She took a step towards him. 'And what's so different about you, Dan? We all get days like that, we all get depressed. The difference between you and me and a lot of other people is that they don't find it necessary to destroy their marriages. Some of us have a little more control than that.'

'Don't say that about our marriage. I can't bear to think of that.'

'It seems to me you should have done a lot more thinking. Some serious thinking about consequences – that sort of thing. Well, hello, Hazel! Come to join the party? Want a drink?' Hazel stood, fully dressed now, in the doorway, a defiant look on her face.

'Are you going to make trouble?' she asked Peggy, cool as ice.

'What do you think?'

'I think you'd be a fool. Can't you just imagine the papers? You're a celebrity now, aren't you?' Hazel said mockingly.

'And Bruce. Does he know? Am I the only person around who didn't? Am I the only fool who believes people when they deny things? Bloody liar, aren't you, Hazel?'

'We didn't want you to find out,' Dan said, sounding miserable.

'How long?'

'Does it matter?' he asked.

'To me it does,' she snapped.

'Nine months,' Hazel said shortly.

'Nine months?' Peggy repeated inanely. 'March! How could you deceive me so? How could you come to my house, Hazel, and sit there denying everything, calming my fears? You must have been wetting your knickers with amusement. You fucking liar!'

'Peggy!' Dan was shocked. 'You don't use language like that.'

'I do now!' she yelled.

'If you must know, I didn't lie to you. I wasn't having an affair with Dan when you accused me of it. He was screwing a secretary from his office, weren't you, sweetheart?' Hazel sniggered, no shame in her face. 'Come to think of it, you're probably to blame, quizzing me as you did. Who's to say you didn't give me the idea?'

That was too much for Peggy. There was no control now, just blind fury. 'I want you out, both of you. *Now!*' She was screaming. 'This minute! Take the bloody car and keep it! There's money in the account.'

'How generous,' Hazel drawled.

'Look, you, you keep your nose out of this. It's none of your damn business.' Peggy jabbed her forefinger towards Hazel.

'Isn't it? You cheated me once out of the money that's rightfully mine. You won't a second time. Dan'll get his legal half share. It's a roundabout way, but I'll get what's mine come the end.'

Peggy knew her mouth had dropped open in amazement at this information. She felt an almost uncontrollable urge to slap Hazel across her perfectly made-up face.

'You bitch!' she said instead, and found one hand holding the other as if to stop it rising and slapping flesh.

'That's right, blame me. But before you do, take a long cool look at yourself. Come on, Dan, let's get out of here. Let's find a hotel and finish what we were so rudely interrupted from concluding.' She flounced out dramatically and made for the hall.

'I shouldn't be too confident if I were you, Hazel. He's just told me you're unimportant to him,' Peggy shouted at the retreating back, and she didn't think she imagined Hazel's step faltering.

'Peggy, I—'

'Get out. Please. Before I smash something over your head and regret it later.' Peggy calmly crossed the room and poured another drink. She lifted the bottle. It was almost empty. 'Before you go, Dan, do me a favour?'

He turned, a hopeful expression on his face. 'Yes? What?'

'Get me a couple of bottles of gin up from the cellar – you know I don't like it down there because of the spiders.'

Was it her imagination or did his shoulders slump as he turned to do her bidding? She congratulated herself: it had been inspired to finish this scene with such a mundane request.

She sat in her brand new wing chair nursing her drink and listening to the sounds in the hall. She had heard him hastily packing a case, had heard it bumping down the stairs. The front door was opened and shut and opened again. There was a final bang, then the sound of his car starting. The crunch of gravel. The roar of its powerful engine. She listened as the sound diminished until she was alone with silence, the only sound the tick of the grandfather clock, bought only last week, another of the things she'd always longed for. The clock and the crackling of the flames in the inglenook. She could feel the silence around her, imagined it swathing her. She wrapped her arms round her and rocked gently back and forth – it was comforting, in a way, like being a baby. And she was in need of comfort. And then the calm, the iciness disappeared. Suddenly, with no warning, her agony began.

'No!' she cried. 'No! No! No!' she shouted. 'Oh, God, what do I do now?' And she began to cry, an ugly, rasping sound. She gulped hungrily and noisily for breath as she wailed. She was full of a searing pain that seemed to travel in her blood to every part of her. 'Oh, my darling, how could you? How could you do this to me? What did I do wrong?'

She sat like that through the evening, rocking, crying, refilling her glass. Her throat ached, her chest was sore, but still she cried. From somewhere came this torrent of tears, this never-ending flow of grief.

At about midnight she got unsteadily to her feet and swayed precariously. Using the furniture as support she made her way laboriously to the door, she hauled herself up the stairs, using the oak banister, an occasional sob escaping from her. She entered the bedroom and stood stock still at the sight of her rumpled bed, semen stains on the sheets. Her hand shot to her mouth as nausea assailed her. She rushed into the bathroom, flopped over the lavatory and retched her heart out.

Peggy sat on the floor, liking, in her misery, the feel of the cool tiles. She dared not move for fear of vomiting again. She leant against the bath – it seemed an age ago that she had sat here and listened to Dan, as he shaved, tell her of his discontent. And she had thought a cruise was all that was needed to set him to rights!

The nausea finally abated. She had hiccups now, but she stood up, splashed her face with cold water, but did not look in the mirror. She didn't want to do that, not yet. Time in the morning.

The morning? How was she to get through the night?

She returned to her bedroom, her defiled bedroom. She only stood for a second at the foot of the bed before she was tearing at it, ripping the sheets off, piling them in a heap. She searched for the towel, her large white John Lewis towel – another on the list of things she had wanted – spoilt now. She found it, on the floor, and kicked it towards the rest of the linen.

With her arms full of washing she made her way down the stairs. She tripped and fell the last six steps and did not feel a thing. She picked herself up and, the linen trailing, made for the sitting room and the wide inglenook fireplace. She hurled all the sheets, pillowcases, the towel into the fire – but nothing happened.

In the kitchen, under the sink, she searched for and found the bottle of methylated spirits she'd bought for the fondue set. Back by the fire, she sprinkled it liberally on the bedlinen. She struck a match, threw it in and the whole thing burst into flames with an angry whoosh. Rapidly she undressed, throwing the trousers and shirt, which must have touched the sheets – might have his semen lurking on them – into the fire.

When all was burnt to ashes she returned upstairs. She went to the guest room and in that bathroom showered, scrubbing herself violently like a rape victim does. Her body had not been touched, but her mind had been violated. She took a clean towel, a blue one, and wrapped it round her. She lay on the bed. She knew she was going to cry. She did not want to. She felt fatigued by tears. But there was no stopping the tears, the pain. She lay in the unfamiliar room sobbing for her man, her marriage, the happiness she had thought was hers. That was how she spent the night, only to be released from the agony near the dawn when exhaustion won over grief.

PART THREE

January

TO

November

Chapter Twenty-nine

In the following days there was no difference between Peggy and a woman after the sudden death of her husband. She grieved for her collapsed marriage. She was swamped by the dark, deep despair of bereavement.

For twenty-five years Peggy had lived cocooned in the certainty that she was one of the lucky few, that her marriage was good, that her family life was strong and secure, that she was happy. Now she felt shattered, shell-shocked, surrounded by the debris of her life. A life where nothing was as she had fondly thought it was.

She drank. She braved the cellar and the spiders, and collected the gin bottles stored there. When they were finished she returned for the vodka. Her evenings were spent relentlessly drinking, trying to rid herself of the despair, but compounding it with the alcohol.

She cried endlessly, exhaustively. She wept from a bottomless well of tears. Her eyes were puffy, her throat ached but, try as she might, she could not stop.

She ranted. She had taken all his clothes from his wardrobe, emptied his drawers, tipped everything into big black bin liners. One night, more drunk than most, she'd got the bags, tipped everything on to the sitting-room floor and systematically ripped everything to pieces with her dressmaking shears. She'd laughed when she had done that: it was not a pleasant sound but, rather, bordered on insanity. She banged the walls with her fists, a tattoo of angry despair. And she would scream, alone in the house she screamed and screamed her anger and her disappointment in him.

She hated. Reserved for Hazel, her perfidious friend, Peggy's hatred boiled up. She would sit curled on her new sofa, drink in her hand, bottle beside her, planning revenge, and what she would

243

say on meeting Hazel again, how cutting her remarks would be, how destructive, how cruel. And, as the alcohol worked upon her system, her thoughts became wilder, racing and scurrying about in her head like a storm of wind, a wind of loathing. Then she would plan dreadful revenge. How she would cut car brake pipes, ram Hazel's car, head on, push her into oncoming traffic, under tube trains, expresses! Could she make an incendiary device? She would put it through Hazel's letter-box. She wanted her dead. She wanted her cruelly dead. With Hazel gone he'd come back to her, she was sure.

To think in this way was not normal for Peggy, she who would weep at television images of suffering people, she who was kind and caring to neighbours and friends. When she allowed one of these rages to take her over, the next day she felt damaged and loathed herself. What if something did happen to Hazel? How would she feel then? Such pious thoughts, though, she could easily set aside the next time the drink did its worst.

It was the injustice of it all that puzzled her. What had she done to deserve such treatment? And why now when everything should be so right? She would wallow in despair and sympathy for herself. She cried a lot when she was like this.

A deep-rooted bitterness threatened to take hold. All she'd done was be a good wife and mother. Fat lot of good that had done her. Where was she left? Alone, unloved, her family scattered, her family betraying her. 'It's not fair', repeated itself over and over in her skull.

She blamed herself. She'd been a size twelve when she married him and now she was a size sixteen. Could she blame him? She'd been blonde, had had pretty silver-blonde hair that he loved to stroke and run through his fingers – the finest hair he'd ever touched, he used to tell her. It was mousy now – she hated the hairdressers, couldn't be bothered with highlights and all that paraphernalia. Could she blame him?

Once she'd loved to dance, go to the pub, even to football matches with him. Then the children had arrived and her life became centred on the house. When she went to work she wanted to spend her free time at home. Could she blame him now?

She had been a good wife, but a boring one. Despite the years, she was not sexually experienced. He was the only man to have known her body. Did her easy acceptance of a lovemaking that never varied bore him? She couldn't blame him if it did. She should have been more adventurous. She should have tried harder.

Hazel, she knew, wore Janet Reger underwear and had sexy nighties galore. Peggy's bras and knickers were white, sensible, Marks and Spencer's most practical. She'd often looked at the prettier stuff, liked it, wanted it, but, then, at her size, she'd reasoned, what would she look like in suspenders and bikini knickers? A bound-up turkey. No, she couldn't blame him.

She cleaned the house. Her mornings were slow in starting – her hangovers saw to that – but, once recovered, she cleaned like a maniac. Not an inch of woodwork, floor or carpeting hadn't been attacked. Windows shone, silver gleamed, worktops glistened. The cooker had never been so spotless. Even the backs of the fridge and freezer were Hoovered and scrubbed. The grouting between tiles was scoured and buffed. Cupboards were emptied and sorted. She wavered only once in the tornado of cleanliness and that was when she emptied the drawers containing love letters to Dan – there were none from him to her since he'd never written any – and old photographs, fading images now of their courting days. Oh, how looking at them had depressed her, how tight was the hurt inside her as she read her young self's outpouring of love. Oh, then how she cried. How she did cry.

Since everyone thought she was away on a cruise no one called, no one came. She had two weeks of isolated grieving bordering on madness. When, fifteen days later, the phone rang, she dropped the cup she was holding from shock, and it shattered on the tiled kitchen floor. Her instinct was to ignore it, but who, even sad, abandoned wives, can ignore a ringing telephone?

'Yes?' she said softly.

'Peggy? Is that you? I thought you might be back by now. It's Flora. Did you enjoy your cruise?'

'Thank you,' she lied, since it seemed the easiest thing to do.

'About our trip to a health farm—'

'I can't think about that now,' she snapped out the words.

'Please your sodding self, then,' Flora answered, but Peggy did not hear, she had already hung up, swamped by feelings of panic. She didn't want to see Flora, she didn't want to see anyone. She needed a drink.

The bottle in the sitting room was empty, as was the one she kept in the kitchen. She ventured down the creaking cellar steps, her arms held tightly about her, her head bowed as she made the area of her body less – less for spiders to fall on was the reason she'd given herself in happier times. She'd laughed at her theory then, but not now.

The case of vodka was empty, too. Looking into the empty carton pulled up Peggy short. She tried to work out how long she'd been here alone and how many bottles she'd drunk, but it was all a bit too complicated. But, whatever the count, she'd been drinking too much and 'That's no solution,' she could almost hear her mother say.

Hell! She supposed she'd have to go and see Myrtle now. She'd be expecting a visit and, no doubt, a present brought from Tenerife or Morocco. Peggy put her face into her hands and shuddered. No, she couldn't go yet, not until she had pulled herself together a bit. She looked a mess, and could imagine how Myrtle would witter on about her appearance. 'Look at you, what self-respecting man would want to bother himself with *you*.' Famed for her dependability and loyalty was Myrtle.

Drinking too much she might be, but she'd have to get more. She would watch it from now on. Maybe she would start drinking later. She would ration the number of drinks in the evening. Or maybe she should switch to wine?

With such decisions to be made, Peggy washed, dressed quickly and slapped on a little make-up. She looked like hell, she thought, seeing the puffy, pink-eyed, lank-haired creature whose image stared back at her. But, then, did it matter now?

She tied a scarf round her head to cover her lacklustre hair. In the back of her wardrobe she found a voluminous old coat she hadn't worn for years, and in the clutter on her dressing table found the Ray-Ban sunglasses she'd bought for her cruise.

A good foot of snow had fallen in the night and she inched her Mini carefully down the drive to the gates and hoped the roads were open. She was glad of the icy bite in the air. It made her feel better instantly and she breathed huge gulps of it. It was the first fresh air she'd experienced for two weeks. Everywhere was so beautiful, so fresh in its pristine white blanket that she felt her spirits rising too.

The main street in Shepherd's Halt, the local village, looked as if a giant had scattered his collection of toy cars willy-nilly about the road. Some cars were slewed sideways onto the pavement, others pointed drunkenly up the hill as if abandoned in a hurry by the occupants. Really, she found herself tutting, a little bit of snow and the English could be guaranteed to panic. She parked her own car neatly and picked her way gingerly across the impacted snow towards the off-licence.

Her transactions were soon completed – mainly gin, she'd weakened when she had seen the familiar and, to her, friendly dark green bottles winking at her on the shop shelves. She'd bought wine, too, more than she had intended. The shop owner obsequiously helped her load the boxes into her car as befitted someone who placed such a large order.

She looked down the street to where the general store's bow-fronted window jutted onto the pavement. Common sense told her she should buy food. She had been eating during the last two weeks, but was surprisingly vague as to what. In the circumstances, it was not surprising. She remembered biscuits, a couple of pizzas from the freezer and a pile of nuts. Maybe she should get some stocks in – some oranges, perhaps, and cheese and yoghurt.

'Peggy! What the hell – what's happened to you?'

Peggy flinched at the unmistakable sound of Flora, shouting for all the world to hear – or at least the half-dozen people on Shepherd's Halt's main street.

'Flora!' she said, and in that one small word managed to convey shock, embarrassment and abject misery.

'You poor old love. Come and have a coffee.'

'I'd rather not.' She half gulped the words down, afraid that the genuine sympathy she could hear in Flora's voice would push her over the edge and make her cry again, and she was so fed up with crying.

'Rubbish, you're coming with me.' And she felt Flora's iron grip on her arm as she was marched towards the Blue Bird tearooms, the twee, gingham-curtained, copper-panned café, which was the local cauldron of gossip and innuendo and the last place she wanted to be.

'Two coffees and two sticky buns, please,' Flora ordered from Megan, the large, comfortable, middle-aged proprietress. 'Now, tell me what's up, Peggy, and don't lie. You look too bloody awful for nothing to have happened.'

Peggy managed a wintry smile. 'Dan's left me for a woman who used to be my best friend,' she replied, and marvelled at how easy it had been to say, at how the catastrophe of her life could be summed up in so few, such simple words. There was a pause as Megan, with talk of the snow, Christmas, and what a dreadful sermon the vicar had given, placed their coffee and buns in front of them.

'You're joking!' said Flora, as if there had been no interruption.

'I wish I was.'

'Your best friend? Not the one—'

'Yes, Hazel, the one with the bastard husband.'

'The bitch.'

'That's what I thought.'

'It's not on, is it? You don't do that to a friend. Just because her own husband's a wanderer there's no need to convert someone else's. Some friend! Where's he gone?'

'I don't know.'

'And don't care . . .'

'Well.' She shrugged as if she didn't, but she was screaming inside to know where he was.

'What now?'

'I don't know.'

'You wouldn't have him back?'

'I don't know.'

'Oh, Peggy, don't be so wet. A shit like that.'

'I don't know.' He's not a shit, she wanted to shout. He's a good man. A good husband – until Hazel got her claws in him.

'Have you been drinking?' Flora peered across the table at her.

Self-consciously Peggy touched her sunglasses, pushing them further up her nose. 'Is that why you're masquerading as a film star?'

'It's the snow. It always hurts my eyes.'

'Oh, yes!' Flora did not sound convinced. 'Booze is no solution.'

'Do you have to sound like my mother?'

'Sorry, but it's true. If you've been allowing yourself to get drunk on your own each evening you've been compounding the problem. Hasn't anyone told you alcohol's a depressant? Why on earth didn't you telephone me?'

'And say what? "Sorry to spoil your New Year, Flora, but I'm in a mess. I found my husband in bed with another woman and I can't cope." Oh, come on, there are some things you can't lumber other people with.'

'Did you? Find him, I mean?' Flora was leaning forward eagerly across the coffee cups.

'Nearly,' she said, immeasurably weary and worried now that she had said as much as she had. After all, how well did she know Flora? How much of a gossip was she? She regretted coming into the village.

'Well, one thing's decided, for sure. The call you so rudely disconnected this morning,' Flora's tone was such that her words could not be taken as a rebuke, 'was to tell you that while you were away I called Shallow Hall, you know, the health farm, and they were fully booked for two months – post Christmas rush, they called it. Well, they phoned this morning and they've had two cancellations starting Saturday. What do you say?'

'Flora, I'm sorry, but I don't think so. How could I face strangers and everything at a time like this?' she said.

'It would do you a world of good. You need it more than ever now – a bit of cosseting and fussing, it'll do wonders for you.'

Peggy looked doubtful.

'Please, Peggy, say yes,' Flora continued. 'I don't want to go on my own and I need to get rid of some of this blubber.' Flora slapped her ample thighs.

'Oh, all right, then. I suppose it's better than being stuck in those four walls on my own,' she agreed reluctantly, but felt she could not let Flora down.

'Good girl. Come on, let's go and phone them.' Flora busily picked up her bags, commiserated over Megan's feet, asked after her aged mother and agreed about the vicar without saying as much and paid the bill – all in a breathless three minutes.

Out on the pavement she suddenly said, 'Look, love, don't worry. Your secret is safe with me. I won't tell a soul, not even Lloyd. Promise.' She squeezed Peggy's shoulder encouragingly, which was too much for Peggy: tears slipped down and escaped from behind her fashionable Ray-Bans. Flora put her arm round her and tried to comfort her, which only made matters worse.

Chapter Thirty

Rather than make a visit, Peggy telephoned her mother. The coward's way out, she told herself, as she dialled the number. She felt ridiculously nervous as she did so, just as she had as a schoolchild and had to confess she'd lost her dinner money or was late home from the youth club. Would she ever stop being afraid of her mother? She had lain awake half the night working out different ways of breaking the news of Dan's departure, how to approach it, what to say.

'What's this I hear that Dan's ditched you?' Myrtle demanded, thus saving Peggy the trouble.

'How do you know?'

'Carol told me.'

'Did she?' Peggy congratulated herself at how normal her voice sounded.

'Oh, I was so hurt. Fancy hearing such news from my granddaughter and not my own daughter, my own flesh and blood! I felt really foolish, I can tell you.' Myrtle's voice, full of doom, issued out of the telephone. And how the hell do you think *I* feel, her telling you? Peggy fumed inwardly but said nothing. She did not dare because she was uncertain now of how her voice would emerge if she did. She forced herself to take deep breaths – she'd read in one of her magazines that that was the best way to calm down in situations like this. 'You there? Have we been cut off?' Myrtle, irritated now, shouted down the wire so that, of necessity, Peggy had to told the receiver away from her ear.

'Yes, I'm here.'

'Well, this is a right kettle of fish and no mistake. Mind you, I'm not surprised. I've seen this coming.'

'Really?' Peggy felt an almost ghoulish curiosity.

251

'Well, just look at you, you've put on weight – no man likes that. And you're such a homebody. There's no spark in you these days.'

Peggy's shoulders drooped with dejection, and she stood nodding agreement with her mother.

'A man likes to get out and take his wife with him, show her off a bit, be proud of her. And—'

At that Peggy's head snapped up. Whose side was her mother on? What on earth had she done to deserve this? '*And*, Mother? What else? What other snippet of loyalty can I expect from you?' she began, anger making her voice shriller than usual. 'I was a homebody for the simple reason I was out at work all day, and when I got home I was tired. I had the meal to cook, the house to clean, ironing to do. When the bloody hell was I supposed to fit in a social life?' Peggy sat down on the hall chair, astonished by her rage.

'Don't you swear at me, Miss.'

'I'm not a miss, Mother. I'm a grown woman with children and I wish you'd start treating me as such.'

'Well, *really*!' was huffed and puffed at her.

'And is it too much to hope that, of everybody, I might have expected some sympathy and loyalty from my own mother?'

'Loyalty? Don't you talk to me about loyalty! Where's yours when it's at home?'

'And what does that mean?'

'It means you're only too happy to shell out money on Dan's mother, and what about your own family? What about me? What about your own brother? Where's your loyalty to us?' she screamed.

'Oh, not that again, Mother.'

'You don't like to hear the truth – you never have. When you were a child—'

'Bye, Mother. Sorry I called,' Peggy said, appalled at how rapidly this conversation had become a row. As she replaced the receiver sharply on its cradle, she smiled at herself in the mirror over the telephone table. She'd never put the phone down on her mother before. She could just imagine her anger and frustration, and wondered who she was now telephoning to complain about her.

All the same, it didn't alter the fact that Carol knew. Had she, like Sean, known about Dan's affair all along? When she had asked Dan if he had told Carol, he had not answered one way or the other. Had he been avoiding giving her a straight answer? The idea that Carol had known made her go hot and cold with embarrassment – and fury. It was inevitable that she would take Dan's side – she shouldn't be surprised that the Princess would side with her daddy. But it didn't make it right. How could Carol take sides when there weren't sides to take? Then, with a jolt, she realized that if Carol knew Dan had left she would also know that Peggy was back from her cruise. That being so, then she must have chosen to leave her mother alone with her misery. She must be aware of how upset and frightened Peggy was. Oh, surely not! This was too painful to contemplate. It hurt, it really did.

Peggy wanted a drink. She stood up to pour one and changed her mind. No, she told herself, it's too early. You've packing to do.

On Saturday morning Flora came to pick her up. Peggy threw her case into the boot, locked the front door and got in beside her friend.

'I'm exhausted. I've been up since five,' Flora announced, putting the car in gear and edging down the snow-packed driveway.

'What on earth for?'

'There's so much to do. Lists for Nanny – she's so forgetful, these days, I have to remind her to do everything, even go to the bog. There were the animals to sort out, leaving instructions for the girl in the village who comes up to feed them when I'm away because Lloyd can't be bothered to do it. And I had her run through all the things to do with the meals I'd packed in the freezer. Lloyd is useless – he can't even boil an egg, and as for heating up a chicken casserole . . .'

'Well, there's an unexpected bonus. I switched the heating down low. Checked the window catches. Turned the water off and I was away. No husband to worry about.'

'No dogs?'

'Not even a cat or a budgerigar.'

253

'You keep it that way, my friend. That way I smell freedom.'
Flora accelerated, more confident of her ability to handle the car
now that they had reached the gritted main road.

Shallow Hall impressed both women. It was a large Edward-
ian mansion built by a rich grocer as a smaller version of Sandring-
ham, set in impeccably tended grounds – even in the winter-empty
garden there were no dead leaves, twigs or weeds. The plants
were neatly pruned and evergreens, judiciously placed, gave colour
to the bleakness.

'Someone knows their *pyracantha* from their *Prunus*, don't
they?'

'Do they?' said Peggy, not clear what she was talking about
but glad to be inside the large house since the wind was getting
up and more snow threatened.

The spacious entrance hall was a blaze of light, a log fire
crackling in the hearth of an enormous elaborately carved stone
fireplace, which soared almost to the ceiling. The house smelt of
pot-pourri, wax polish and burning apple wood and both women
stood in its centre, their noses twitching appreciatively. Vivaldi's
Four Seasons issued mutedly from hidden speakers.

'Oh, God, not that old thing again,' sighed Flora, but Peggy,
recognizing it, enjoyed it. But she did not say she did, and knew
it was a lack of confidence in her own judgement which made her
despise herself.

'It's like a hotel, isn't it?'

'Why are you whispering?' Flora said loudly, as if to counteract her timidity.

'I don't know. It just sort of has that effect upon me,' she
replied, and would have liked to add, 'Because I feel I'm out of
my depth, and I'm terrified of the place and what I'll find here,'
but she didn't. She stood mute and felt foolish.

Flora crossed to a desk which was positioned at a slant across
from the fire and banged a bell that stood on it, aggressively, three
times. Peggy looked about her nervously, picked up a magazine
from the oak coffee table in front of the fire and tried to appear
inordinately engrossed in Strutt and Parker's sale details of an
estate in Northumberland.

'So sorry, ladies.' A voice, steel sharp with accent, cut the air making Peggy jump and drop the magazine back on the table. 'Mrs Whittaker? Mrs Alder?' By the desk, pink-cheeked from rushing, stood a reed-thin young woman with a perfectly made-up face like the girls behind the beauty counters – like Hazel, Peggy thought miserably. She was reminded that her own make-up must have worn off by now and also that she must look a mess in every other department. She was going to hate it here, she knew she was. What on earth had induced her to come?

Flora agreed they were who she said while staring pointedly at the suddenly silent Peggy as if a look might goad her into saying something.

'I trust you had a good journey and you're not too weary. At least at Shallow Hall we're warm as toast. Now, let's just get you both registered . . .'

Within seconds Flora was ensconced in a chair opposite the young woman who, they were told, was called Tania. She had a label stuck on her white blouse that gave them the same information. Soon the two were chatting away like long-lost friends as Tania explained the ropes, and Peggy felt left out. There was so much explaining that it was rapidly going in one of Peggy's ears and out the other.

'Did you get all that, Mrs Alder?'

'No, I'm afraid not.'

'Ah, well, never mind. It's all here in this little booklet.' She waved a gold-embossed red book of stiff card at them. 'Chairman Mao wasn't the only one with a little red book.' She giggled, somehow automatically, as if the weak joke followed by the giggle was her normal welcome to guests, which had been learnt by rote. With a grandiose action, Tania slapped the bell and, like a genie, a young man in white trousers and tunic appeared smiling broadly, perfect teeth gleaming in his perfect face.

'Laurent here will show you to your rooms. 101 and 102, Laurent precious.' She smiled her own mega-watt, white-toothed smile, which encompassed them all and made Peggy surreptitiously lick her own teeth in case any debris from her last meal was stuck there.

Laurent loaded their cases onto a trolley and led the way, at a cracking pace, out of the hall, down a corridor, through a glass-

255

covered walkway and into a modern annexe at the back of the old house, which they hadn't seen from the front. He stopped in front of a door with 101 on it, 'You're better off in the annexe I always think. Easier access, if you get my drift,' and winked broadly at them. Flora winked back, opened her purse and gave him a fiver with another wink, which seemed excessive to Peggy. But when he deposited her at 102 she did the same – she thought she'd better – but she didn't wink.

'Mrs de Belleville will be happy if you could both attend her in her sitting room in half an hour,' Laurent told them, producing a small map from his breast pocket and marking on it where they were and where Mrs de Belleville's suite was. 'And Mrs de Belleville says she's sure you'll be more comfortable in these.' From a wardrobe he produced a white towelling robe with the, by now familiar, Shallow Hall logo on it of a swan rising from water, but which Peggy felt, in her case, should have been a duck. She was relieved to note that the robes were generously cut.

'Haven't I read about this Mrs de Bell-whatever in my daughter's magazines?' asked Peggy, when Laurent had left them alone.

'Probably – she's in all the magazines. She took this place on five years ago, it was pretty seedy then, by all accounts. She's turned it round. She cares, she really cares.'

Mrs de Belleville, Peggy later discovered, was one of the most terrifyingly perfect women it had ever been her misfortune to meet – guaranteed to give anyone an inferiority complex, she thought, as she took the chair offered her in the warm, comfortable sitting room into which they had been shown. She and Flora were two of three, that day's intake. So perfect was Mrs de Belleville that her appearance also guaranteed that her clients would pay out any extras demanded in the hope of looking just a fraction like her.

Her skin shone with health and the inner fire of the zealot almost luminously, as she propounded her theories on food, vitamins, exercise and beauty. The large blue eyes were surrounded by clear whites, not a hint of yellow, or a sign of a broken vein. Her fine, very blonde hair was scraped back from a flawless, line-free forehead, and secured in a large French pleat at the back. She sat ramrod straight, her elegant legs crossed but only at the ankles. She gesticulated with smooth white hands – not an age freckle on them – tipped by pinkly glowing nails.

As she noted each and every part of this paragon, as she listened to her enthusiastic discourse on the treatments available at Shallow Hall, Peggy found herself pushing further back into the comfortable armchair as though, if she pushed hard enough, she could disappear into the upholstery. For with every passing minute she felt grosser and uglier than she had when she first arrived.

Peggy looked at the other two, Flora and a rather handsome man, to see if they seemed as miserable as she was. To her disappointment, neither did – a little anxious, yes, miserable, no.

'Now what I'd like you to do is introduce yourselves to us – tell us a little about yourselves, why you're here, what your goals are.' Mrs de Belleville spoke in the slow, encouraging tones of a primary-school teacher. 'You've been here before, Petroc, why don't you start?' She beamed at the grey-haired, handsome in a flawed way, middle-aged man with a corpulent gut that strained to escape from his white robe and made him look seven months pregnant at least. Peggy thought she recognized him but couldn't imagine from where. Perhaps he was an actor or something.

'Well, I'm here since I'm a recidivist, a fallen soul in need of redemption.' He bowed at Mrs de Belleville who fluttered her eyelashes coyly. 'Too many banquets, too many all-night sittings and too much claret.' He spoke in beautifully modulated tones and as he did he stroked his stomach almost imperceptibly as if absent-mindedly petting a dog. Peggy remembered him now: he was a backbench MP much given to making paternalistic statements on television on any subject; he could hardly be an expert on them all. She'd never liked him on the TV, but she felt quite protective of him now. Was it the robe, and his thin ankles poking out beneath, making him appear vulnerable? Or was it because she was pretty certain that the size of his stomach was a source of great pain to him?

'I'm Flora, bridge and hunting fanatic . . .' Peggy looked up at the sound of her friend's voice and marvelled at her confidence, as she rattled on, finishing with, 'In for a service and oil change.'

The others found this inordinately funny, except Peggy, who didn't know why she didn't or what had got into her to make her feel it was just a plain silly thing to say. And why on earth had Flora said she was a hunting fanatic when she never rode?

'Tut, Mrs Alder, no frowning, it's not allowed – leads to nasty wrinkles and we don't want that, do we?' Mrs de Belleville admonished, still in primary-school-teacher mode.

'Peggy, your turn.'

The faces of the others turned expectantly towards her and she wished she'd had the sense to work out something smart and amusing to say.

'Me? Oh, I'm here to lose weight because I'm fat.'

There was a loud gasping sound as everyone sucked in their breath with shock and regarded Peggy as if she were, if not an alien, at least an undesirable person.

Mrs de Belleville stepped into the breach as a hostess would rescue a difficult situation at a dinner party where a guest had made an unfortunate remark. She launched into an impassioned diatribe on inner cleanliness, her advocacy of the blackcurrant, and the benefits of a twenty-four-hour total starvation.

'What did I do wrong?' Peggy asked Flora as, later, they waited in her room for their appointment with the doctor.

'You said the forbidden word.'

'What word?'

'Fat!' laughed Flora.

Chapter Thirty-one

A week later Peggy sat in her comfortable room with her feet up on the *chaise-longue* as she waited for an appointment for a lymphatic drainage massage, whatever that entailed. It certainly was a rum old world, she thought, when half the population were starving to death and a large number of the other half were, like her, spending a small fortune to counteract the effects of eating too much.

Flora had been right, no one actually said 'fat' or 'obese' or 'overweight'. Rather a 'little needs shaving off here' and a 'tightening up there' or 'a rationalization of body form here,' were the preferred phrases, just as 'death' must never be said in the hearing of a hospital patient.

Closeted with the doctor on her first day had been a more honest experience. He'd suggested she lose three stone and she had said she doubted if she could – and, in any case, she hadn't weighed eight stone since her marriage and couldn't imagine being that size again. And she had joked and said that if she lost that amount she might end up like Rider Haggard's 'She' after she had gone into the flames for the second time and scare everyone witless by the number of wrinkles her fat cells had kept at bay previously. She felt that this was a courageous attempt at humour, but the doctor didn't even smile slightly. Maybe he'd heard the joke before. They had compromised on two stone, though secretly Peggy was aiming at one and a half off by the summer. Why by the summer? she asked herself. For when she went on holiday? And *why*? her inner voice persisted. Because then, perhaps, somebody would fancy her. That thought had depressed her deeply for it only emphasized that she was alone, with no Dan. She was even more depressed by the uncomfortable discovery that she felt she needed to attract a man, which was virtually acknowledging that she couldn't cope alone.

The doctor had congratulated her on giving up smoking and she'd glowed with pride and was glad she'd lied about the odd cigarette she sneaked now and then. But she did not stay long in his good books when, having asked her if she drank, and she said yes, he'd asked how much.

'Oh, on my own a gin and tonic and a couple of glasses of wine,' she'd lied.

'A couple of glasses?'

'Small ones.' She'd compounded her lie.

'Every day?'

'Well, nearly.' She marvelled at the sinner she'd become.

'Then, Mrs Alder, I must warn you you are at serious risk from excessive drinking.' And as she endured the resulting lecture she was glad she hadn't told him the truth.

It was with a great sense of relief on her part and, she was convinced, disappointment on the doctor's, that they found her heart, lungs and everything else functioning efficiently. She'd bounced out of the consulting room, satisfied, and made straight for the dietitian.

This young woman was also depressingly slim but pleasant in a mousy, rather mumsy way for one so young. At a confusing rate she took Peggy through the food maze – what never to eat under any circumstances, what was best avoided, food to treat with caution, and finally – she had almost given up hope of it being mentioned – food it was permitted to enjoy. Peggy confessed that she had been eating disastrously for years, which elicited a sympathetic 'Everyone does.' But when she said, wasn't it odd that something so bad for one could be such a pleasurable experience, it elicited a tetchy 'Well, you're here to learn,' and the dietitian then proceeded to make out Peggy's personal regime. Looking at its meagre calorific intake Peggy wondered if life was sustainable on so little. This woman also avoided the fat word.

For the first twenty-four hours they had eaten nothing, 'clearing the poisons', Mrs de Belleville called it, but were allowed still mineral water which contained Mrs de Belleville's special and highly secret tincture. There was much debate about what this was, what vitamin combination, what herbs. Peggy was certain that she could detect Fernet–Branca, but decided not to admit as much since everyone said how wonderful they felt on it, how much more energy they had. If they thought *that*, it was best to leave them with the idea that there was a secret potion, she decided.

The food, when it was finally permitted, came as a surprise for she had expected to be munching her way through a field of lettuce. In fact, the chef was a genius and though the quantities were minute the quality and taste of the meals he conjured up, for the few calories they were allowed, were wonderful – too wonderful, she longed for more.

They had been advised not to talk or think about food. Peggy joked with the others how every waking moment, when not occupied, she was thinking of food and had even begun to dream about it.

This was another lie. She *did* think about food and she *did* dream about it, but not all the time. Dan filled most of her thoughts. Being alone had become dangerous, for then she mentally slumped into longing for him; going over and over in her mind what had gone wrong, what she had done to make him leave her. Sometimes she allowed herself to dream that once she was out of here and slim again, he'd see the mistake he'd made. He would dump Hazel and come back to Peggy, and all the happiness which was rightfully hers would return.

Peggy had been pummelled and smoothed, massaged and patted. She'd had hot baths and cold. She'd exercised and run and swum and danced. She'd had electrical impulses rework all the muscles that were already aching from the unusual amount of exercise to which she was subjecting her body. She'd had saunas and whirlpools, she'd been plastered with mud and wrapped in seaweed and had been hosed with jets so powerful they hurt. She felt permanently hungry, permanently tired and she was sure she was no thinner.

Mrs de Belleville's much-lauded aims to treat the whole person, inner and outer, failed with both Flora and Peggy. In their self-awareness group, they'd been told to scream their anger at the walls. At the sight of a very overweight man rolling on the floor in a fine imitation of a 'terrible two' having a temper tantrum they had both collapsed in helpless giggles, not anger and had been asked to leave the session. Neither had dared go back.

In the sensory deprivation tank Peggy, far from feeling relaxed and detached from her cares, had a panic attack and had to be let out. Since sitting in the tank or hugging her next-door neighbour did not strike her as the quickest route to weight loss, she dropped all such passive activities and concentrated on the active.

For Peggy, without doubt, the best thing had been the facial. She'd liked that and, scrutinizing her face later, she was convinced her skin looked better. Finally she'd plucked up courage to have the mid-length style hair chopped to a short crop and highlighted and that, both she and Flora were agreed, had done more for her than everything else put together.

'Are you sure old Belleville knows what she's doing? It seems to be a scattergun technique to me – hurl everything at them and something might work,' said Peggy, a week into the regime, as she sat looking at a small bunch of grapes considering whether to eat them all now or just one and keep the others for later when she knew she'd be even hungrier.

'I think it's to keep us on the go, make sure we think we're getting our money's worth,' Flora answered, as she inspected the manicure she'd just had. 'The worst is over, after all – we've done the total starvation. We're on the way up now.'

'True.' Total starvation had been awful, and while doing it Peggy had felt quite odd in a dreamy, floating sort of way, but that had been a week ago.

'There's a group doing a bunk tonight. Are you interested?' Flora asked, almost nonchalantly, as if she was totally uninterested in Peggy's reply.

'A bunk? Where to?'

'The Huntsman. It's a pub down the road about a mile or two. Apparently it does a steak and kidney pie to die for,' Flora said with the rapt expression usually seen on the faces of the sexually obsessed.

'What? You're not thinking of going?' Peggy was shocked.

'Petroc's arranged it. A taxi will be waiting for us at nine, just past the copse over by the tennis courts.'

'That's mad. What's the point in shelling out all this money if you're going to cheat?'

'It's just the once,' Flora said defensively.

'Once too much. It's silly, plain silly.'

'No sillier than drinking that vodka you got Laurent to buy you.'

'What vodka?' Peggy was aware she was blushing.

'Oh, come on, Peggy. Don't lie to me. He told me. He asked me if I wanted some too.'

'And did you?'

'What do you think?' Flora said self-righteously.

'I think you probably said gin rather than vodka.'

'You've been sneaking!' Flora spluttered with laughter.

But it wasn't funny really, it was stupid, Peggy was thinking now as she looked at the offending half-bottle of vodka for which she had paid Laurent an exorbitant sum. It had to be the most expensive vodka in the world. It stood on the coffee table, her tooth mug beside it, and willed her to open it. That inner voice which, in her loneliness, talked rather more than it once had, goaded her to open it. You know you're longing for one, it said.

It was true. She *was* longing for a drink, desperately so. But, then, she was longing for food, too, and a cigarette. The doctor, if she was honest with herself, had frightened her with his talk of units of alcohol, of drink as poison and the female liver's inability to cope. She didn't want this drink if that was the case. She hadn't drunk excessively before – before what? The lottery win or Dan leaving? She couldn't remember now – everything was such a muddle in her head.

'Oh, Dan, why did you leave me? After all we'd been through. And then, just when we'd no more worries.'

She sat up with a start. She'd said that aloud! She was certain she had. She looked about the room as if searching for a remnant of the sound of her own voice, as embarrassed as if she'd been caught out. She stood up abruptly and, grabbing the vodka bottle, walked quickly across the room to the wardrobe and hid it at the bottom of her holdall.

Petroc, Flora and three others escaped that evening for their steak and kidney pie. Peggy wavered several times and almost gave in at setting-off time, but finally raced away from them as if they were the devil and slammed her bedroom door, locked it and had a long, unnecessary bath. It was unnecessary since she'd had one only two hours before.

She joined the lecture which was held each evening an hour after their meagre dinner. That evening's subject was Royal Doulton china, not of particular interest to Peggy, but it kept her occupied and out of trouble, she told herself.

Afterwards she sat in the lounge, sipping a camomile tisane before going to bed and dreaming of the Gaelic coffee she always had whenever she and Dan had treated themselves to a meal at the local Berni.

'May I join you?'

'Of course, please do,' she said, but she didn't mean it, not when it was Sonia who spoke. Sonia Dorking was clever, sophisticated, brittle, hard, and terrified Peggy. She was in the same aerobics and yoga class.

And her initial reaction was the right one. For the next half-hour she sat and listened while Sonia confided her life history. Once it might have been riveting, she thought, but not now. Peggy was the last person who should be told of Sonia's husband's infidelities – not once but three times. It depressed her for she knew that Dan's straying was sufficient for her lifetime; it would be hard enough trusting another man but, listening to Sonia, it would be nigh on impossible.

She frightened Peggy even more when she confessed to her drinking problem – and in consuming a bottle of gin and two bottles of wine each day, she had a serious one. Peggy's fear came from how the drinking had started. Left alone one drink had become two and then three; the slide, according to Sonia, had been inevitable. Warning bells did not ring in Peggy's head, they clanged.

And Peggy hadn't meant to confide in her – someone she hardly knew, and with a drinking problem, who might blab – but she did. It was the sympathy in Sonia's voice, her concerned face when she asked, 'What happened to you? What's making you sad?'

'Me? Sad? Nothing.' Peggy's attempt to laugh off Sonia's question faltered.

'You can tell me. Whatever it is, I'll understand.' Sonia leant forward and gently touched her hand. Maybe it was the physical contact that made her begin to open up, for open up she did to this virtual stranger. Maybe it was her own history that made her tell her more than she intended, more than she'd confided to Flora – even down to the semen-stained sheets.

When she had finished, Sonia relaxed into her chair. 'You're well shot of both of them, husband and so-called friend, if you ask me. And you mustn't blame the money. All that did was illuminate the cracks that were already there and lurking. Take care, though, Peggy. You're far too trusting. Your friend here—'

'Flora?'

'Yes, the hearty one, as I always think of her. Beware of her.'

'Flora? You're joking! Flora's as straight as a die,' she insisted.

'Is she?' Sonia looked enigmatic.

Peggy left her soon after that: she had no intention of listening to any disloyal talk about Flora. In her room she went straight to her hiding place, removed the vodka bottle and walked quickly to her bathroom, uncapping it as she went. She shook it into the basin sharply, helping the colourless liquid on its way. Drinking was no solution. Tonight Sonia had taught her that at least.

'Petroc's dying,' Flora said, as they did their compulsory walk the following morning.

'Never!'

'Yes, sad, isn't it? He's rather a sweetie when you get to know him.'

'What of?'

'Cancer. That tum of his, it'll never go, not now. It's all part and parcel of it. Liver,' she added, in a lugubrious tone.

'I noticed he'd got slim ankles – you know, all the rest of him's normal, it's just his gut.'

'Exactly.'

'How long has he got?'

'They've given him a year at the most.'

'Then what on earth is he doing here? He's wasting precious time.'

'That's what I asked him and you'll never guess what he said. He said he'd got to try and keep fit for the Party, that they couldn't afford to lose another by-election, which they're likely to do, the muddle they're in.'

'You're joking!'

'No, I'm not. Admirable in a way, isn't it?'

'Bloody barmy. You didn't agree with him?'

'No, I told him not to be so unselfish. I said, "Would the Party do as much for you?" He thought not. He's packing and leaving, intent on a short but happy end to his life.'

'That's made me feel so sad. The poor man, and he told me he was a widower too. All alone—'

'Not Petroc, sweetheart. He's got dolly birds crashing out of the woodwork.'

'I was talking to Sonia last night. Her story's so sad, too. Aren't we lucky?'

'Yes, my love, fat but lucky. Race you.' And Flora was away across the grass, surprisingly fast.

'You said *it*!' Peggy shouted after her. 'The F word!'

They always had a rest hour in the afternoon – much needed. Usually she and Flora took it together in Peggy's room which had two beds. At first they had tended to giggle at being tucked up like toddlers at a nursery school, but that had stopped as soon as they learnt how tiring their regime was to be.

This afternoon, though, Peggy couldn't nod off. She was more upset about Petroc than she had realized. She'd begun with thinking him a bit of a buffoon, but now she accepted that he was far more courageous than she would have been in those circumstances. She spent so much time feeling sorry for herself, and yet she had good health – she should be rejoicing in that.

In the next bed Flora stirred and sighed. And that was something else. What had Sonia meant, warning Peggy about her friend? What had she to be suspicious about? But, then, what did she know about this new friend – very new since they'd only met just over two months ago? Was she too trusting? Peggy knew Flora lied: she'd fibbed about her riding, so had she lied about other things?

'Can't you sleep?' Flora interrupted her thoughts. Since they had not been particularly complimentary towards her friend, Peggy felt ridiculously ill-at-ease, as if Flora was reading her mind.

'No. I keep thinking about Petroc.'

'Rough, isn't it?'

'We really are so lucky, Flora.'

'Yes, we are,' said Flora, but there was something in the way she said it that made Peggy look at her with curiosity.

'Anything wrong?'

'No, nothing ... it's just—' And to Peggy's amazement she saw Flora was crying.

'Love, what is it?' She got off her bed and clambered onto Flora's. 'Tell me. Is there something I can do?'

'No one can do anything. I'm sorry, how stupid of me.' Flora fumbled for a handkerchief, which she couldn't find, and Peggy gave her a Kleenex. Flora blew noisily into it. 'Lord, how damp. Must be getting menopausal.' She tried to laugh.

'You can tell me, you know.' Peggy took hold of her hand.

'Oh, I don't know ...' Flora gazed, unseeing, out of the window chewing her lips with concentration as if making up her mind. She lit a cigarette and handed it to Peggy, who absent-mindedly accepted it. 'It was Petroc's news. Made me think. I'm so pissed off, Peggy, with pretending. I'm fed up with the whole sham.' Peggy said nothing, she knew that if she spoke she might interrupt the flow and maybe Flora would never get it off her chest. 'I'm bloody miserable, Peggy. So sodding miserable. It's all slipping past me – time, I mean. It's all going so damn fast and I've left it too late.' She dragged deeply on her cigarette and made herself cough. Peggy waited patiently for her to continue.

'Too late for what?' she prompted, but studied the tip of her glowing cigarette with an exaggerated interest.

Flora turned and looked at her. 'Promise not to laugh?'

'I promise.'

'Love,' Flora said, and pulled a funny face as if saying that word was acutely distasteful.

'But Lloyd?'

'He doesn't love me, never has,' Flora said dismissively. 'I'm a useful object to have around. I popped out an heir for him. I run the house and garden. I'm quite a good cook and I'm brilliant with the accounts, and people, and he's hopeless at all of them. In return I've got position and, a nice home. I'm supposed to be grateful and content but I'm screaming mad with bloody frustration. I still need sex even if he doesn't!' She began to cry again. 'Oh, Christ, I'm sorry, blubbing again. But it's so awful, Peggy, I feel cheated.'

'I know, love. I really do. Dan and I . . . well, we didn't have any sex, come the end. And the odd thing was that although my body wanted it and missed it, it was my mind that was the most frustrated, endlessly asking myself why? What had I done wrong? Was it me? Was there someone else?'

'And getting no answers – and stuffing your face because you aren't, and getting fatter and less chance of it happening. Peggy, you could be me talking!'

'And we both lied and said how happy we were and how lucky we were.'

'And to each other!'

'Why?'

'Pride?'

'Or to protect them – the bastards!' Peggy said with feeling.

Flora trumpeted into another Kleenex. 'Hell, I feel so much better, Peggy. Just to admit it to someone.' And she was smiling again.

'But tell me, why did you say you hunted when we first got here? And you never ride.'

'I don't know.' Flora shrugged. 'I suppose because people expect it – with my arse I look as though I do. I don't know. It's a bit like being jolly because I'm fat.'

'Not any more you're not.' Peggy grinned.

'True. It's an improvement.' Flora slapped her much flatter stomach. 'Have another fag.'

Later in her bath Peggy went over this conversation. You never knew people, not really, she thought as she soaped herself. Poor Flora. Poor Peggy. She admired her slimmer thighs. Well, thinking that way was going to have to stop: a new look and a new attitude, that was what she needed. At least the conversation explained what Sonia had been going on about: she must have sensed that Flora was pretending.

At the end of their two weeks, Peggy had lost over a stone and was still fired up to lose the rest. Her skin felt better, her hair shone. It had been a success. It was an expensive success, though. The floor appeared to move as she read her bill which, with all the extras, was horrendous. Still, she could afford it and it had been worth it. She admired the new Peggy in the mirror and couldn't wait for Dan to see her. 'I'll show you,' she said to her reflection.

'Peggy, help me. I'm in a dreadful mess.' Flora appeared at her door, red, hot and flustered.

'Calm down, Flora, what on earth's the matter?'

'I've done the daftest thing. I've left all my credit cards and my cheque-book at home. It's *so* embarrassing. They like settlement before you leave.'

'Oh, Lor'. What can you do? Phone your bank?'

'It's Saturday morning.'

'Of course. Oh dear. Well, look, I could pay it for you.'

'Would you? Would you really? Oh, bless you, Peggy. You're an angel. I'll give you a cheque as soon as we get home.'

It was later that night, tucked up in her own bed, that Peggy suddenly remembered. There was only one bank in Shepherd's Halt and she'd met Flora in there several times getting cash. It was Barclay's and they opened on Saturday mornings!

Chapter Thirty-two

Without doubt Petroc had taught Peggy a valuable lesson. She returned determined to snap out of the depression that had begun over the children and been compounded by Dan's behaviour. There was so much in her life that she had still to be grateful for and she must keep this to the forefront of her mind.

These were fine intentions, but hard to keep, though she tried. For a start, the house that she and Dan had chosen together, had spent so many hours and so much money on buying what was best for it, now seemed soulless and wrong. No matter what she did, how many expensive flower arrangements she contrived, how clever her lighting, how artfully she arranged the ornaments, her books and magazines, the place felt empty and, worse, she felt like a visitor in her own home.

To counteract this uncomfortable feeling she spent as little time as possible there. Flora had said she was to pop in any time she wanted to and she did. Too often, in fact, for she began to feel guilty about it, so she went to the village church in the hope of meeting someone else to be friends with to give Flora a rest from her. It was not a success. She did not know what was wrong – if she looked too smart, if news of Dan's desertion had got out, or worse, if rumours about her drinking had begun to circulate. The upshot was that, apart from the odd cool nod and a hand-shake from the vicar, no one spoke to her. She walked home and chided herself for a fool. What had she expected? That they all rush out cheering and shouting their welcome? English churches did not work like that.

She spent hours shopping, buying things she didn't need and clothes she doubted she'd ever wear. She bought stacks of books that she did not seem able to read. And she drove aimlessly about the wintry countryside pleased if she chanced upon a National Trust property where a visit would while away a few more of the empty hours that stretched before her.

Her days were incredibly long and she marvelled at how the twenty-four hours she lived through now seemed to crawl by when they used to zip past at an alarming rate. Once she'd never had enough time to do everything; now she was awash with it. It was almost as if she'd entered a different time zone from the rest of the world.

She kept to her diet and lost more weight so that some of the shopping she did was useful, since outfits in her wardrobe were soon too big for her. Those clothes she packed away to take to Oxfam, but her inner voice poured cold water on her jubilation at another half-stone gone and pointed out she might put it all back on again. And the frugal side of Peggy, which still remained, had agreed with her innate caution and she'd put the cases in the loft.

Shopping was easier now that she was smaller; she doubted if she would ever get over the pleasure of entering a shop and making for the packed racks of size fourteen. She began to dare to dream that she might even get down to a twelve. Now that *would* be something.

Flora, in contrast, had put all her weight back on, but it was harder for her with a husband to feed and the gin bottle coming out every night at six. There were compensations to Dan going, after all, she told herself as her grandfather clock chimed six and she poured herself a diet Coke as she settled down to watch the news on television.

Flora had tried to persuade her to join them at several dinner parties but she turned down the invitations. 'I wouldn't be good company,' she explained.

'Twaddle!' Flora snorted. 'You can't mope like this for ever. He's not worth it.'

'I can't snap out of it.'

'Piffle!' was Flora's sensitive reply.

Peggy compromised by accepting an invitation for Sunday lunch. 'Just Lloyd and me. Even Nanny will be away in Eastbourne.'

271

Peggy was livid when she arrived to find Tarquin in the draw-ing room, mixing martinis. She glared at Flora who merely smiled sweetly and said, quite unnecessarily, 'Do you know my brother?'

Tarquin put down the jug and crossed to Peggy. He took one of her hands and kissed her cheek. 'Peggy, I'm so sorry,' he said, which made her throat constrict as she fought the tears which were always just below the surface. 'And might I be filthy rude and say how stunning you look? And I love the hair. Doesn't she look fab, Flora?'

The cause of her sadness was not mentioned again and the lunch was one of the happiest she could ever remember. She was loath to leave.

'Can I give you a lift?' Tarquin asked.

'I have my own car,' she replied, with rather more regret than she thought wise.

Flora had still not given Peggy the cheque for her stay at the health farm and Peggy did not know what to do about it. She'd mentioned it obliquely a couple of times, usually by making some remark about how much it had cost per pound of flesh lost, or the profit margin on each lettuce Mrs de Belleville bought. But Flora had not risen to the bait and Peggy didn't like to ask her outright – it seemed rude somehow.

Nearly two months after she had thrown him out, Peggy still had not seen Dan. She had spoken to him once or twice on the telephone, always about mundane things – odd bills, the bank. She was impressed at how noncommittal she sounded when just hearing his voice made her heart race and her palms sweat. He did not ask to see her, and she did not mind – just a few pounds more off and then she would be ready.

She had to calm down before she saw him, too. She had learnt who the friend had been to whom he had lent the money right at the beginning, soon after she had won. Hazel. It had been used to buy the cottage near Hatfield where she had fondly imagined Hazel to be living with Bruce. This news had made her so angry that had she seen him, she would have started to row with him. She did not want to do that – she wanted him back. It was imperative that she be relaxed and cool when they finally had their reunion.

When she went on her shopping expeditions she rarely went into Sadler's. She debated why and asked herself if it was because she was still embarrassed by her win and by being richer than her old colleagues. But on this particular day she decided she was being silly and turned in through the revolving door.

At the Pompadour stand she lingered awhile but resisted purchasing anything – she'd no intention of helping the company that paid Hazel's wages, she'd be only too happy to see them go bankrupt, she told herself. She stood by the handbag counter, waiting for Karen to appear. No one was about. That would never have happened in her time, she told herself, Viv had allowed everything to get slack. She studied the rows of polished handbags, stroked the glass counter-top and thought how blissfully simple life had been when she'd stood the other side—

'Can I help you?' a voice asked, shaking her back to the present.

'Karen. Hello,' she said.

'Peggy? Is it you? Never! I hardly recognized you,' Karen said, astonishment in her voice.

'I've been reinventing myself,' Peggy said, beaming from ear to ear with pleasure at Karen's reaction. It was then she noticed that Karen's eyes were red-rimmed as if from weeping. 'Karen, is something wrong?'

Those words released a dam in the young woman and she began to sob. 'Oh, you poor girl. Come with me.' Quickly Peggy grabbed at Karen's hand and led her like a child from behind the counter, aware that the sprinkling of customers were staring. 'Let's go into Viv's office.'

'Oh, no!' Karen wailed.

'Come on, Karen. You can't stand on the shop floor in this state,' Peggy said briskly, and in a no-nonsense way marched her into Viv's cubbyhole of an office and sat her on Viv's chair.

'Now, tell me, what's the matter? Is it something I can help with?'

'Oh, please, Peggy, yes. Would you come with me? Some of the others are going but I don't know them that well – they're all senior to me. If you'd come I'd feel better. I'd stop crying, I'm sure I would.'

'Of course I'll come, and of course you'll stop crying,' Peggy said encouragingly. 'There's just one thing. Where are we going?'

'To Viv's funeral,' Karen said, on a rising sob that ended in a jet of hiccups.

'Viv's *funeral*? Viv? *Dead*?' Peggy held onto the edge of the desk. 'When?'

'Haven't you read about it in the local paper?'

'No . . . I don't bother with the papers, they're always too depressing.' She knew she was prattling but couldn't think what else to say or do. 'Was it an accident?'

'Oh, no, Peggy. It was awful. Her mum died last month, you see, then last week she topped herself. Hung herself, she did, from the banisters.'

'Oh, my God. Poor Viv.' Her legs buckled and she had to sit squarely on the desk – Viv's desk. Poor ugly, hung-over Viv. She must have been even uglier in death, certainly the death she had chosen. 'Do they know why?'

'Not really. They presume she couldn't face life without her old mother – they say she was drunk.'

'Then I hope she didn't know much. Of course I'll come with you. When's the funeral?' she asked, deciding it was best not to comment on what was puzzling her, which was why, when Viv had loathed her mother, she was unable to live without her. It was strange but, then, people were.

Karen looked at her watch. 'In an hour. Out at the crematorium. Mr Jenkins has laid on a couple of cars.'

'I can't go like this.' Peggy indicated her bright scarlet wool coat. 'I'll pop upstairs and look for something more suitable, then I'll be back.'

As she made her way to Ladies' Fashions on the first floor Peggy walked as if in a daze. They had all known Viv was unhappy, but had anyone known just how unhappy? Did anyone ever really listen to others' distress? Didn't they just make appropriate noises and move on back into their own selfish lives? She'd talked to Flora, she'd talked to Sonia. Had either of them registered the depths of her despair? How much time had she spent thinking about their happiness as opposed to her own? Peggy shivered at the mental picture of her own isolation, her own loneliness, her own selfishness.

She quickly found a navy blue coat, cut straight with military-style buttons. She decided against a hat. No one wore hats to funerals these days. And her black patent-leather shoes and handbag were fine.

'Her dog – Viv's dog. What happened to it?' Peggy asked Karen when she returned to the ground floor.

'Oh, that was the saddest of all, in a way. You see the dog had died the day before. Viv phoned in, she couldn't come into work – she sounded in a dreadful state.'

'She would have been. That little Peke was her life.' It all made sense now. Without the dog Viv wouldn't have wanted to live. Her mother had had nothing to do with her killing herself. To have her dog to love had brightened the tragedy of Viv's life. How empty it had been – if only, Peggy thought, she'd been kinder to her.

Peggy and Karen took a taxi to the crematorium on the edge of town. The last thing Peggy needed was to share a car with the managing director or other heads of department. She could imagine them all gossiping about Viv and she knew she could not have borne it. Viv had often irritated and annoyed her, but she felt strangely protective of her memory now she was dead.

Peggy had no warning. She sat at the back of the chapel, one person's back looking much like another. She wasn't prepared, at the end of the service, for one of those backs to turn round and to find herself looking straight at Hazel. She felt her stomach turn over and she had to hang onto the pew in front to stop herself falling.

Hazel smiled. She smiled! Peggy was so angry at the sight of that hypocritical smile. Had she not been where she was, she would like to have slapped that smile off the smooth, perfectly made-up face.

'Come on, Karen. Let's slip out the other way. I can't stand the crocodile tears.'

The rest of the congregation were making their way out of a side door at the front. Getting out of the front door of the chapel was not as swift as they had hoped. The door was locked and it took time for someone to open it, and when they did Peggy and Karen found themselves tangled up with the next funeral, the new mourners jostling to get in. It was like trying to get off a tube train in the rush hour, Peggy thought, as they hurried through the throng and found themselves in a cloister, at the end of which were Viv's mourners. Apart from attending the next funeral, which would have looked odd, there was no escape.

'I hardly recognized you, Peggy. What a change!' Hazel said, in a pleasant, friendly manner. This takes the biscuit, thought Peggy. The last time they'd met had been five minutes after Hazel had vacated Peggy's bed and gone off with Peggy's husband. Peggy chose to ignore her.

'Dan will be pleased to know you look so well,' Hazel continued, but her voice was brimming with sarcasm. Peggy had an almost uncontrollable urge to kick her. She turned her back. 'Shall I tell him we met?'

'Suit yourself,' Peggy said, and immediately regretted doing so since she thought she had sounded a bit common. Seeing a gap in the crowd, she grabbed Karen. 'There's our taxi,' she said, pulling the girl with her and sure that she looked most undignified doing so.

'Peggy. How wonderful to see you. Could I have a word?' It was Mr Jenkins.

'Now?' Peggy allowed herself to sound irritated.

'Yes, if you wouldn't mind.' He glared at Karen who, frightened in front of the top brass, said she'd wait by the cab for Peggy.

'A sad day,' he said, unnecessarily.

'Very.'

'She'll be missed.'

'Yes,' said Peggy, even though she doubted if this would be the case, especially by him. Viv had spent her life warring with Jenkins.

'The department . . .' His voice trailed off. Peggy said nothing, since she wasn't quite sure what he expected her to say. He coughed his loud full-of-importance cough. Peggy wondered if he remembered groping Viv all those years ago in Soft Furnishings. Had her relentless campaigning against him gone over his head? 'Yes, the department. I've been wondering . . . of course, your circumstances are now so different and you may not . . . but I thought . . . well, nothing ventured, nothing gained.'

'Yes?' She looked at him, with a puzzled expression, but it

was forced. She had a shrewd idea what he was about to ask, but loyalty to Viv prevented her helping him out.

'Perhaps you'd consider returning to run the department? We could never easily find anyone with your experience. You'd be welcome. I'm sure we could discuss terms. I know Viv would be happy to know you were in charge.'

'I'll think about it.'

'You will?' He seemed perplexed.

'Yes, why not?' she replied.

'And why not?' she asked herself later that night at home. Maybe she needed a job. Maybe if she had a goal it would help her forget, recover, let her fill her life again. But she'd see Dan first. She wanted to see his reaction to her. If he came back she didn't want a job – she'd have no need of it. And what could Hazel's reaction to her have meant? Had she imagined the sarcasm? Suppose she was trying to be friendly? Did that mean she and Dan were finishing and she wanted to be friends again? She'd have to investigate, she thought, as she turned off the light and climbed the stairs to bed. She felt sad for Viv, but more relaxed than she had for a long time.

Chapter Thirty-three

'What on earth have you done to your hair?' Myrtle asked, as she opened the door to her daughter.

'Don't you like it?' Peggy fingered it nervously in the way of one who's still adjusting to a new style.

'Makes you look like a dyke.' Myrtle moved back along the passage to her kitchen where she was baking. 'I'd given you up.'

'Mmm, that smells good,' Peggy said appreciatively, choosing to ignore her mother's remarks.

'I'll wrap one of these up for you when you go.' Myrtle pointed to the nut-brown crusty loaves.

'I'd love one, but I'd better not. I'm on a strict diet.'

'What on earth for? I thought you were looking a bit peaky.'

'You told me yourself I was fat.'

'I never did. I'd never say such a rude thing.'

'You did. You probably did me a favour, made me take stock of myself. I went to a health farm for a couple of weeks.'

'Whatever next? You've more money than sense. I've always said so, ever since you won it. I said, "Mark my words, she'll fritter it away," and so you will.'

'It did me good.'

'You could have done yourself as much good staying at home eating lettuce leaves and drinking water and saved yourself a packet,' Myrtle said, with an audible sniff.

'Not so much fun, though.'

'Oh, yes, and what did you get up to?'

'Nothing, Mother,' Peggy said wearily. 'Seen anything of Carol?'

'Not a lot since they moved. It's a bit far now to pop in. Those parents of his have sold their house for a pretty penny. They're retiring to Spain, last I heard.' She lit the gas under the kettle.

'That's nice.'

'Why be reasonable about them? That Daphne was never anything but grief to you.' Myrtle turned arthritically to face her.

'She didn't bother me that much.'

'That she did. Remember the champagne?'

'Ah, yes. The champagne.' Peggy laughed.

'I don't see what you've got to laugh at. Dan's done a runner, your children are scattered to the four winds, you refuse to speak to the one child who remains close by.'

'I'm not refusing to speak to her, she doesn't want to see me. She's chosen to take sides. If she prefers Dan there's nothing I can do about it.'

'That's that, then. If you're going to be pig-headed, I can't help you.'

'I wouldn't ask you to.'

Peggy picked at a piece of crust, brown and inviting, on one of the still hot loaves. Why was it that every conversation she had with Myrtle was like being on a verbal helter-skelter, one minute talking of inconsequential matters, the next sniping? She doubted if there was another mother in the land like Myrtle, lovely to everyone else and a right bitch to her daughter. The crust finally loosened and she popped the bread in her mouth.

'What you thinking?' her mother asked, pouring boiling water into the teapot.

'Nothing,' Peggy answered, feeling guilty immediately for lying.

'You won't get thin shovelling bread into your mouth like that.'

'Hardly shovelling, Mum.' But as she chewed the lump of bread she found the delectable yeasty taste had gone and she might as well have been chewing cardboard; her mother had spoilt her pleasure in it. 'I've been asked if I'd like to go back to work in the shop – head of my old department,' she said, making her voice bright.

'Of course you turned them down.'

'As a matter of fact I said I'd think about it.'

'Well, you can't do it.'

279

'Why not?'

'Don't be ridiculous! All your money, and working as a sales assistant? It wouldn't do.' Myrtle sucked in air noisily between her front teeth, a habit which always filled Peggy with dread for it indicated that Myrtle felt she was on unassailable ground. 'You wouldn't fit in any more. They'd resent you taking a job from someone who needed it.' She stirred the tea in the pot. 'And imagine the field day the papers would have with that. You'd make us all a laughing stock. Are you taking sugar or not, with this dieting?'

'No sugar. I hadn't looked at it like that.' Peggy frowned.

'You wouldn't. You only ever see things from your own point of view.'

'Mum, that's not fair.' Peggy shook her head with annoyance. She stood up. 'I'll just pop up and do the bath for you.'

'I've just poured your tea.'

'I'd rather do the bath, if you're going to get at me.'

'What a thing to say. Sit down, do. You needn't bother. Carol did it all for me.'

'But you just said you didn't see much of her.'

'I see enough.'

'Mum, look, let's be honest, this house is getting too much for you.'

'What's that mean? You planning to put me in a home?'

'No, Mum.' Peggy felt exhausted with the effort of trying to sustain a normal conversation. 'I just wondered if it's not time to get someone in to help with the cleaning.'

'I can't afford a char.'

'Who's asking you to? I'll pay.'

'I don't like this.' Myrtle's eyes narrowed with suspicion. 'Once my hip's fixed it'll be no problem.'

'But how long's the waiting list? I wish you'd let me pay for you to go private.'

'Me? Private? Not on your nelly. I don't approve of jumping queues from privilege.'

'It could also be argued that it would free your place in the queue for someone else.'

'Never. What would your father say? He'd be spinning in his grave.'

'I should imagine he'd think it made sense. Be honest, Mum, the pain's getting worse and it's making it difficult for you to cope.'

'You mean I'm getting bad-tempered?'

'Well, yes, if you want me to be honest.' Though 'getting' was wrong; 'getting more' might be better but, of course, she didn't say it.

'You've never liked me, Peggy, have you? It was always your father with you. You put up with me on sufferance,' Myrtle whined.

'Oh, Mum, please, not this.'

'You've changed, Peggy. How you've changed in such a short time.'

'So you keep telling me *ad nauseam*. But do you know what the truth is, Mother? I don't think I have changed all that much – but everyone else has. You and Dan and the rest. You're all different. I hardly recognize you any more as the people I loved—'

'Loved?' Myrtle interrupted, grabbing at Peggy's use of the past tense.

'Yes, that's the way it's going. I'm getting tired of the endless whining and carping. There's only so much I can take. And do you want to know the truth? I think I've reached it with you.'

Myrtle's hand sprang up to touch the string of crystal beads at her neck, something she did when nervous. 'Are you deserting me?' Her voice was bleak.

Peggy laughed, but not from pleasure. 'Only you would think to use that word. No, I'm not deserting you. I'll continue to pay your bills. Tell me if you want a char or the op. Our old house is still standing empty if you want a change. When you make up your mind, phone me. I'm just not coming round so often. I don't want these rows. Who needs it?' She stood up to go. 'Maybe you're rowing with yourself – I don't know. All I do know is that I've had it up to here.'

'Don't go, Peggy.'

'I'll be back, Mum. But not as often. Not while you're like this.' She picked up her handbag from the floor.

'I'd like the house,' Myrtle said hurriedly as if to delay her, sounding frightened, as if she thought she had gone too far.

'You would? Good. I'll make any arrangements necessary.'

'You might sound pleased – I'm doing what you want.'

'Mum, it's what *you* want.' She crossed the room.

'You selfish cow! Leave your old mum. What will people say?'

'They won't know, will they? Unless you tell them.'

'Bitch!' was the last word she heard as she let herself out of the door.

She stood in the street of neat, well-cared-for terraced houses and breathed deeply. For her own salvation she had to distance herself from her mother; she could see that so clearly now. She wished she could say she felt different, liberated. She didn't. She felt much as she always did. She got into her car and turned on the ignition. Though maybe there was a smidgin of sadness that hadn't been there before.

Chapter Thirty-four

Peggy's plans to see Dan were no nearer fruition. Having decided that she was unlikely to lose more weight – it would probably not be a good idea anyway since she was now slim enough – she was gearing herself up to telephone and suggest they meet, perhaps for dinner. It did not get that far for she received a curt letter from Dan's solicitor informing her that he wished to start divorce proceedings and that, as was normal, he would be expecting a clean half-share of all their assets.

The letter had made her shake with indignation. It wasn't so much that she minded sharing fifty-fifty with Dan: it was sharing it with Hazel she resented. She made an immediate appointment with her own solicitor. Brian Cookson smiled wryly at the high-handed tone of the letter and pointed out that it would be the courts who determined what her payment to Dan should be, not him. In the circumstances, however, she must prepare herself for it to be substantial, although the letter was probably an exploratory shot across the bows to test the water. Did Peggy want him to reply to the letter, bang her drum a bit? She felt quite confused at so many clichés in such a short time.

'Just acknowledge we've received it. I'd like to try to see Dan first. Maybe we can come to an amicable agreement. I'd always intended that the garage and his new cottage should be his. And I'm happy to make him an allowance. But the rest,' she shook her head in disbelief, 'I just can't believe this is my husband's doing.' Deep inside her she was convinced this was Hazel's work.

Still, she thought, as she drove home from the lawyer's office, she supposed she was no different from a million men who had had to cough up to wives living in adulterous relationships. And, on the other hand, how many times had she said to weeping or

angry friends, 'Go for him, get every penny you can out of him.'
She could regret that now – it wasn't so funny when the shoe was
on the other foot. 'Sorry,' she said aloud, to all the men she had
rubbished in that way over the years.

Once she reached home she called Dan but there was no reply,
and the answer machine was not switched on. Over the next week
she tried several times. It was only when she met Bruce for a pub
lunch – she'd been surprised to receive his invitation – that she
learnt that Dan and Hazel were away on holiday in Spain. She
learnt a lot more too. The cottage bought with her money had
been a veritable love nest for them. No doubt that was where he
had been going when supposedly fixing cars. She discovered that
Hazel had moved out of the flat she and Bruce had rented when
he had gone bankrupt. Peggy thought she should have felt angry,
but instead she felt resigned: what was a bit more cheating?

'He's gone to Spain, you say. I always reckoned he'd only
agreed to Italy for a holiday for my sake,' she said. It was a
comforting thought: it proved he must have cared for her then.

'Sorry? I don't understand.' Bruce looked at her quizzically
over his pint.

'I'd always had this dream of going to Italy. I wanted to see
Venice and the pictures in the Uffizi. I even started to learn Italian,
never got far, mind you. He went along with me, encouraging me,
but we never made it.'

'Hazel said you were a bit of an intellectual.'

Peggy scoffed at that. 'Hardly. Just a love of art and a longing
to learn more.'

'That must be nice, to want to learn. Me, I couldn't leave
school fast enough.'

'My problem is lack of organization – I need to be more
disciplined with my time. Now I have all the time in the world
and I don't do anything about it. Yet there's nothing to stop me
going to London, to the galleries and exhibitions.'

'It's hard, isn't it, to be interested in anything? The evenings
are the worst. Never anything on the television. To be honest, I
just get pissed.'

'Don't go that way, Bruce. Neither of them is worth it. I
started down that path but I pulled myself back sharpish.' She'd
said 'neither of them' but she meant Hazel.

'I loved her so much.' Bruce was becoming lachrymose.

'You played around yourself.' She surprised herself saying that. It was true but why did she say it, almost defending Hazel?

'They didn't mean anything. In any case, it's different for men, there's sex and there's love.'

'Oh, Bruce, that's the oldest excuse in the book.' She laughed at him and said yes, she would like another gin and tonic, after all.

'What sticks in my craw is it being Dan. I thought that bastard was my best friend,' he said, returning from the bar with their drinks as if there had been no break in the conversation.

'I suppose I could say the same about Hazel.'

'Women can't ever trust other women, not like men can rely on men.'

'Or not, as the case may be,' Peggy said sharply. 'What a chauvinist you are.'

'Number thirty-four. Mr Benson,' the Tannoy crackled. Carrying their drinks, they made their way through the crowded bar and into the Duck and Pheasant section of the restaurant. She was having pheasant and he had chosen the duck.

'Red do you?'

'Lovely,' she agreed, looking at her prawn cocktail and thinking what a dreary dish it was with its ersatz pink Marie sauce and limp lettuce leaves.

'Châteauneuf-du-Pape,' Bruce ordered.

'Bruce, you'll let me pay for this lot,' she whispered, when the waitress had gone with his order.

'Certainly not. I might be skint but if Bruce Benson invites a bird out, he pays.'

She was flattered at the idea that she might be anybody's *bird*. 'But that's silly. I'm not your bird and I can so easily pay.'

'I know you can, but I'd prefer it if you didn't,' Bruce said with dignity. She looked at him with new respect.

Dan and Hazel, though absent, managed to dominate the meal. Peggy and Bruce analysed the situation, going back and forth, comparing notes, reaching conclusions, realizing that when both had been absent from their respective homes, they must have been *at it*. They sat over their coffee a long time, pooling their anger, sharing their hurt, taking comfort from each other's similar predicament. Only the sighs of an irritated waitress, and the manner in which she banged some chairs, brought them back to reality and the bill.

'God, what a joy it is to talk it out like this and to someone who understands,' she said, as he waited for his change – right to the end they had argued about who was to pay, but he'd won.

'And to know I'm not boring you stiff.'

'Exactly.'

They offered an apology to the waitress who, from her frozen features, made plain that it was not accepted. In the car park, they stood in the chill late March wind, still talking.

'Fancy a coffee back at my place?' Peggy asked, not wanting to end this conversation for talking about Dan, even in a derogatory way, made him seem nearer.

'You mean it?' Bruce's face lit up. 'I'd love to. I'd like to see your new gaff.'

'You don't know where it is, do you? Follow me.'

She started up her Mini and waited, the engine idling, for Bruce. She was shocked to see him drive up behind in a rusty old banger. Bruce had loved his cars, always the latest, fastest, most expensive. Poor man, she thought, as she let in the clutch and led the procession.

'I like it,' Bruce said an hour later after they had arrived and he had been shown every inch of her property. 'I've always wanted a house like this – every Englishman's dream, isn't it? Beams, lattice windows, inglenooks.'

'But you've always lived in modern houses.'

'Oh, that was Hazel. She hated the old – dirty and musty they were, in her opinion. It was the same with antiques, she wouldn't have them in the house either. Everything had to be spit new, more's the pity. I'd have had a bit more to flog now the going's rough.'

'Dan loves the old, too. Maybe it'll be a problem between them,' she said hopefully. 'He likes grand houses as well. He was all for us buying my son-in-law's parents' place.'

'What, that cock-up over Melbourn way?'

'That's the one.'

'You'd have been throwing your money away. I know the builder who did that one – right fly-by-night and no mistake. Give it another year or two and the problems will start, and the bills will mount.'

The coffee made, the fire lit, brandy poured, they settled down and continued where they had left off. As the light faded, somewhere along the way – though later Peggy could not remember when – they had got off the subject of their erring partners and had talked about themselves.

About eight she made them sandwiches – smoked salmon, 'Just the ticket,' said Bruce – and they opened a bottle of Sancerre. When he kissed her it seemed the most natural thing for him to do.

'That's nice,' she said, as his lips nuzzled her neck and she felt his tongue licking, searching for her ear. 'So nice.' She sighed and pressed her body to him and willed him to search further, to pleasure her more. She almost put up her hand to stroke his hair but remembered in time that he wore a wig and fondled his neck instead. Through the haze of alcohol and sexual excitement she found herself wondering if he took it off in bed. She laughed.

He leant back. 'What's the joke?'

'Nothing, well, I just thought I'd love it if those two could see us now,' she lied, effortlessly after the Sancerre.

His hand slid to the buttons of her blouse. With agonizing slowness he undid one and then paused as if expecting her to stop him, before proceeding, gently, with the next. She longed to tell him it was all right to be doing this, that she wanted him to, that she wished he'd hurry up, but shyness prevented her. She felt she would go mad with anticipation. When his hands finally found her breasts, and he rolled a nipple slowly between finger and thumb, she felt once again the jolt of pleasure slice through her body from breast to vagina, and her body arched from the sheer joy of it.

'Where's your bedroom?' he said huskily.

'Top of the stairs, first left.'

'Better?' He smiled questioningly.

'Better,' she whispered in reply and, clutching her blouse to her naked chest, she led the way up the stairs. They were halfway up when she felt his hands reach up under her skirt. She stood on the stairs frozen like a statue as slowly he explored higher, lifting her skirt as he did so. She swayed as his fingers inched the crotch of her panties to one side. She moaned at his touch as he gently massaged her. She felt his body pressing into her back, felt the hardness of him as he released his penis from his pants, felt its velvety softness caress her thigh. 'Oh, please . . .' She turned on the stairs and looked at him. His dark eyes were already misted with passion, his lips bright red with desire.

'I can hardly wait,' he said gruffly.

'Me too.' She began to inch her way up the stairs, his fingers still in her, so that at each step she took, their position changed, the excitement increased. He did not let go until they reached the bed. There they tore at each other's clothes, needing to feel each other's flesh. Her eyes widened when she saw him naked, and for the first time she thought of Dan. He hadn't got one like that! And she was on her knees and she took his huge member gently in her hands, cupping it as if weighing it. She stroked it almost reverently before, with equal care, she put her lips to it.

She did not pleasure him for long because suddenly his body stiffened and he called out and pulled her roughly up from her knees and pushed her back on the bed. He mounted her body as she writhed in anticipation beneath him. She gasped with pleasure as he entered her, filled her. Quickly she moved her body beneath him catching his rhythm, wanting this to go on and on, but she knew it wouldn't. She was wrong! He skilfully changed his rhythm, she matching it, crying out her pleasure to him. 'It's been so long!' she called. She felt she was split in two as if she was falling; as if her whole body was shot through with an electrical jolt; as if she was dying . . .

Later, she lay, staring sightlessly into the darkness, listening to him breathing. What had happened to her? She had never in her life experienced such a total physical loss of control or such pleasure. There had been moments, in bed with Dan, when her insides had turned turtle, a pleasant feeling, which she had assumed was an orgasm. Never had it been like that – a feeling so intense it was almost too much to bear, too painful in that intensity.

She propped herself up on one elbow and looked down at Bruce. He had taken off his wig and she had not even been aware that he had. His bald head made him look strangely vulnerable,

and, she thought, better-looking. His lovemaking had been perfect
– almost. It couldn't be total – that was impossible for he was the
wrong man. She felt a tear slip unbidden from her eyes and
quickly wiped it away before it could fall. And then she was
aware from his breathing that he was not asleep either.

'Bruce,' she whispered, and wondered why she did when they
were alone.

'Yes.' His reply was muffled as if he had something in his
mouth. In the half-light she put out her hand to touch his face. It
was damp from his tears.

'Oh, Bruce,' she said gently, and the kindness in her voice
made him sob. She put her arm beneath him and held him close
to her breasts as one does to comfort a child. 'It's all right. I
understand,' she said, kissing the top of his head. He sobbed
uncontrollably, and she let her own tears fall unheeded. Together
they held each other with desperation as they both wept for their
lost lovers.

Chapter Thirty-five

The following morning Peggy stood gazing out of her kitchen window, waiting for the kettle to boil, and was not sure how she felt, other than confused. She could have blamed her actions last night on the amount of wine she had drunk, but she didn't. She had drunk a lot, but she had at no time felt she was out of control, and in any case she didn't have a hangover so she hadn't been incapable.

No. She had slept with Bruce because she had wanted to. The fact that she was now embarrassed and wished she hadn't was unfortunate for it was not how she'd felt last night. What had happened in between to make her change her mind, she did not know. All she knew was that she wished he'd got up in the middle of the night and left without waking her.

Now she was going to have to face him. What would she say? How should she act? Should she offer him tea or a full breakfast, or what? Perhaps she should slip out and pootle around in her car for a bit and hope he'd gone by the time she got back. But, then, she couldn't do that – all her clothes were in the room he was in. What if she crashed and was found to have been driving in her nightie? What would her mum say? Worse, what would the press say if they found out?

'Morning.' Bruce was standing in the doorway, grinning sheepishly at her. 'It's difficult to know what to say, isn't it?'

'How about – tea or coffee?' she smiled shyly.

'Tea, three sugars, would be lovely.' He looked relieved.

She was glad she was busying herself with the mugs and teabags, so delaying the inevitable conversation. But eventually the tea was made, the mugs were on the table, and he'd pulled up a chair. She tightened her dressing-gown belt and wished she had had the sense to dress before coming down. She looked at the tea swirling round in a whirlpool as she stirred it.

'I don't know what got into me,' she said, without looking up.

'Me neither,' he said, and then laughed nervously. 'I mean, Peggy, don't get me wrong – I mean, it was great and I think you're great but . . .' His voice trailed off.

'You didn't mean it to happen and I'm not Hazel.'

'Well, yes, that's about it.'

'Don't look so worried.' She patted his hand, finally daring to look at him and seeing the concern on his face. 'We were both lonely, miserable. We've been betrayed. It was probably inevitable we'd turn to each other. But we did, and it's done and we won't repeat it, but I hope we can remain the best of friends.'

'You're a woman in a thousand, Peggy. I was so scared . . .' Again his voice trailed off. Did he ever finish a sentence when faced with an emotional problem?

'That I'd make a fuss, make demands of you?' she said for him.

'Something like that.' He sipped his tea. 'I'd like to stay friends, I really would. I've got mates but I can't talk to them, not about this. But we're both in the same boat, so to speak. You know what it's like.'

She nodded agreement, though she hoped he'd stop talking about it. She didn't want to think of Dan and Hazel together. She didn't want to keep going over the same ground, and certainly not so early in the morning.

'I've been offered my old department back – as manageress,' she said to distract him.

'What, the handbags?'

'Yes. My ex-boss died.'

'And?' He looked at her over his mug.

'I don't know what to do about it.'

'I know what I'd do. The way they treated you! I'd tell them to get stuffed. Then I'd look for premises in town as close to them as possible and I'd open my own exclusive handbag and leather-goods shop – hit 'em where it hurts.'

'But what about the Bag Shop? Old Mr Sutton's got the top end of the market sewn up.'

'He's selling up.'

291

'Never! How do you know?'

'I did some work for him on the shop. He's tarting it up a bit to sell. It's got a fabulous flat over it – roof garden, terrace, very swish it is. And it's freehold. There's not much freehold property to be had in the town centre.'

'It would be horrendously expensive, then. Could I afford it?'

Bruce was incredulous. 'Of *course* you could afford it. Unless Dan managed to pull the wool over your eyes and you signed the money over to him.'

'How did you know about that?' she asked suspiciously.

'Dan talks, Hazel sings – I listen.' He shrugged his shoulders. 'It was way back, when she was about to leave me. I said, concerned like, how would she manage, and she, all airy, says there was no problem, that Dan was about to cop the lot. I thought you were barmy.'

'Not barmy enough, though. I didn't do it.'

'Well, there's a relief. I couldn't understand it – on the one hand there's my wife telling me your husband is crazy about her and yet he stays with you, not her, until you hurl him out. I'd wondered if it was because you hadn't done it and he was hanging on in there waiting. Right?'

'Right.' He had probably hit the nail on the head, and what sort of blind fool did that make her? She shook her head, not liking to think about it. 'Fancy a fry-up?' she asked.

'Too right.'

After Bruce had left Peggy stripped the bed, bundling the linen immediately into the washing machine as if it could wash away her mistake. She then stepped into the shower, washed her body clean and felt better. After all, other women of her age had had many lovers. It was probably because she'd only slept with Dan until now that she was making such a drama about it, she told herself. She felt even better, an hour later when, over a gin and tonic and a slice of guilty quiche at Flora's kitchen table, she unburdened herself.

'Good, was he?'

'Fab.' Peggy felt herself blush.

'Better than the old Duracell route.'

'Sorry?' Peggy looked puzzled.

'DIY.' Flora chortled.

'Am I being thick or what?'

'Your vibrator, silly. Do-It-Yourself.' Flora thumped the table with glee.

'I haven't got a vibrator!' Peggy laid down her knife and fork with shock. 'What an idea!' She was blushing even redder.

'Oh, you should get one. Every girl needs one.'

'I see,' said Peggy, and bent down to pat the Labrador, who was sitting beside her on the off-chance that a piece of her quiche might fall his way. She had to concentrate on the dog for this conversation was getting far too sophisticated for her taste.

'Are you going to continue seeing him?'

'Good Lord, no. At least, not in that way. It was a mistake.'

'Oh, come on. What mistake? You needed a bit of nookie and what better than to do it with an old friend? What about next time you feel the urge?'

'There won't be a next time,' Peggy said firmly.

'Who're you kidding?' Flora laughed again, showing her fillings, and Peggy felt again a bit afraid of Flora, out of her depth.

From usually seeing no one, today was proving sociable in the extreme. Peggy had only been back from Flora's half an hour when a taxi drew up, and from the sitting-room window she saw Jean get out and look anxiously at the house as if trying to fathom if anyone was inside. Peggy banged on the window and waved. At that Jean paid off the taxi.

'My, are you feeling flash or something? A taxi from the station,' she said, as she opened the door to her mother-in-law. 'But what a lovely surprise.' She bent forward to kiss Jean but there was no response from the older woman. 'What is it, Jean? Why have you come all this way?'

'I don't know quite where to begin.' Jean stood in the hallway, clutching her handbag to her as if for support. She seemed to have shrunk in stature overnight.

'Come into the sitting room then. Put your feet up and tell

me all. Does this call for tea, wine or a gin?' she spoke gently, trying to make Jean relax.

'Nothing for me,' Jean said, as she followed Peggy into the room. 'This is lovely. You've got it really nice,' she said admiringly.

'Of course, you haven't seen it since we first bought it, have you? I miss you, Jean. I wish you didn't live so far away.'

'So do I. Then maybe I'd have known what was going on,' she said, as she slipped out of her coat and took the armchair Peggy had indicated.

'Like what?' Peggy took the chair opposite.

'Well, for a start I didn't know Dan had moved in with a woman. He tells me you kicked him out. Don't worry, I wasn't taken in. I told him if you had it would have been for a good reason.'

'It was,' Peggy said, but added no explanation and Jean, being the sort of woman she was, did not pressure her further. 'But I did tell you we'd split up.'

'Oh, I know, but I didn't realize it was permanent. I thought it was probably a reaction to your good fortune, a minor upset which would blow over. But this woman puts a different complexion on it, doesn't it?'

'I suppose so.'

'Well, what are you doing about it?'

'There's not a lot I can do. We spoke a couple of times on the phone, but he's been away and . . . well, then I got the letter from his lawyers. I haven't felt much inclined to see him. And I don't want to call in case I get her. At the moment we speak through lawyers.'

'That's a recipe for disaster. You'll end up not speaking at all, at that rate.'

'That's what I fear.'

'Then why don't you go and see him?'

'And see her?'

'Arrange to meet somewhere else, but insist she isn't with him. Do you want him back?'

'Yes. Very much.'

'Could you forgive him?'

'I think so. I think he's having a mid-life crisis. And at least he didn't run off with some bimbo. Someone our own age is a bit more dignified somehow.' And, she thought, after last night with Bruce, it was going to be a lot easier to forgive.

'I think you're mad. I wouldn't have the selfish sod back in the house if he paid me.'

'You what?' Peggy looked at her mother-in-law with surprise. 'He's your son!'

'Yes, and I'm stuck with him because he is, but you're not. Come on, Peggy, he's behaved abominably. He told me about buying the cottage with your money, gloating he was, thought it was clever. More like stealing, I told him. You should forget him. You're an attractive woman – look in the mirror! You're rich. You could have whoever you want.'

'But I don't think I want anyone else.'

'Then I can't help you.'

'I don't think anyone can.' Peggy crossed to the drinks tray. 'Well, if you don't want a drink, I do.'

'Well, just a small sherry, then. Your mother says you're drinking too much.'

'She would. I'm surprised she didn't say I was an alcoholic.' Peggy laughed and seeing Jean smile, added, 'She did, didn't she?' Jean grinned and the grin said it all. 'My mother's sense of loyalty never fails to amaze me,' she said, as she poured herself a larger measure of gin than she had intended. It was a way of cocking a snook at Myrtle, even though she wasn't here to see.

'You aren't, are you?' Jean asked, a shade anxiously.

Peggy carried their drinks over and busied herself with small tables and coasters before answering. 'When Dan left I went to pot and yes, I was stupid. I went on a bender for a couple of weeks – no one knew I was here, it was easy to do. But I was lucky, I saw what was happening. I went to a health farm and I've got it under control now.'

'Why didn't you call me?'

'I couldn't see or speak to anyone, honestly. I needed to be alone. Obviously I needed the drink, too, or I wouldn't have done it, I'm convinced of that. I think it acted like an anaesthetic on my mind.'

'Could have been dangerous.'

'I know.'

'I can't stay in my house, Peggy, not now,' Jean announced suddenly. 'You do understand?'

'Why ever not?'

'The circumstances have changed. If you and Dan get divorced I wouldn't be your mother-in-law any more.'

'Of course you would. You always will be.'

'But it's wrong, you see.' She fumbled in her handbag, produced a large handkerchief and blew into it. 'Even though I pay you rent it isn't fair. You'd never have bought it if I hadn't been Dan's mother.'

'But you are. Nothing's changed.'

'Well, your mother, stuck—'

'You've been to see her. That's why you're agitated, isn't it? What did she say? That she was stuck in her terraced house, with nothing from her mean daughter? Is that what she's been saying? I told you, Jean, right at the beginning, she didn't want to move. I offered. But what game is she playing? She's just agreed to move into our old house.' Peggy sighed with exasperation. 'Jean, you know my mother, you've known her longer than most, and you know what she's like. She'll never be happy. I've reached the conclusion that she doesn't even want to be. In a weird way she enjoys being miserable and making others the same. That's what she's trying with you. You mustn't let her upset you – if she does then she's won. That's what she's been doing with me for years.'

'She said you'd walked out on her. Deserted her. That's wrong, Peggy.'

'Is it? I haven't deserted her. I pay the bills, see she never wants – I'd pay for her bloody hip too if only she'd let me. I just don't want to see her any more. I can no longer afford my mother's sniping dramas, if I'm to survive. I'm better off not exposing myself to her. It might sound hard but a lot's happened in the last few months. I'm beginning to see things differently.'

'But you were always so close.'

'No, we weren't. My mother kept *saying* we were. I can hear her. "Of course, we're such a close family. Peggy's more my sister." It was crap, Jean. She said it so often everyone believed her –

including me. It's been a charade most of my life, but now I'm not prepared to go along with it.'

'You don't like her much, do you?'

'You could say that.'

'It's interesting. I didn't like my mother either. She was a difficult woman, nothing ever right for her. And yet people are so shocked if you admit to not liking your mother – it's as if motherhood makes them inviolate.'

'It isn't automatic, loving each other, is it? Not once you're an adult,' Peggy said, thinking of Carol but deciding not to mention her. 'Still, I don't want to hear this rubbish about you moving out of your bungalow. If you carry on like this I'll sign the deeds over to you and then what will you do?'

'Of course, Myrtle's turning that against you, too. You should never have told her I paid you rent. She says that's a sign of your meanness.'

'But if I'd put it in your name that would have been wrong, too. You see? You can't win with Mother.'

Peggy persuaded Jean to stay the night and the following day she drove her home. But it wasn't until the last minute, just as she was leaving, that Jean agreed to stay put.

It was a shock to hear Tricia Ballantine-Smith's voice on the telephone.

'Peggy, sweetheart,' she gushed, which immediately put Peggy on her guard. 'It's amazing, isn't it? A whole year gone since you won our lottery. We were wondering if you would like to join us for a little celebration. Maybe you would care to present the cheque to—'

'No, Tricia, thank you but no.' Peggy replaced the receiver with a clatter. There was no way she wanted to be involved. What if the newspapers discovered what had happened to her – and that lovely family of a year ago? No, she was not about to share what had happened with anyone. She picked up the telephone and dialled.

'Sorry, Tricia, we must have been cut off. I'm sorry I can't help you out. I'm going to Australia for a holiday,' she lied. 'Be an angel, keep my whereabouts secret. You know, no press?' Tricia agreed to maintain her privacy. She smiled to herself. How easy it had been.

Chapter Thirty-six

In the following week Peggy made a discovery. When she had been with Dan other men had not existed for her in any way other than as acquaintances or friends. To her it was as if Dan were the only man in the world with a penis, the only one who could ever interest her.

Now, having slept with Bruce, having taken the adulterous plunge, she found she began to look at other men totally differently.

A plumber had come to mend her washing machine. She entered the laundry room with the cup of coffee she had made him and nearly slopped the lot on the floor. He was bending over the machine, fiddling with something at the back. His T-shirt had separated from his jeans, which had slipped to reveal a good three inches of firm buttock. Her stomach lurched, she felt her 'hot-line' activate as a jolt of pleasure rippled through her body to between her legs. She wanted to step forward and touch his flesh, run her finger along the crease of his bottom. Kiss the soft downy hair she could see at the base of his spine—

'You did say two sugars, didn't you?' she asked instead.

'Yes, love, thanks.' He did not even bother to glance up from his task as he spoke. In one way she was sad he didn't and yet she was also glad. If he looked at her, if she had seen even the slightest spark of interest in his eyes, she was not sure what she would have said or done.

She had thought her reaction to the plumber had been an aberration, but shopping in the village store she had noticed a tall, slim, dark-haired newcomer to the village and had found herself contemplating him with an interest that was not merely neighbourly. It was a new state of affairs, and one with which she was not comfortable.

She thought a lot about the Bag Shop and if she should go ahead with buying it. She liked the idea and she didn't. Bruce, Jean, Flora all thought it a good one. Certainly, it was the trade she knew best; the shop was in an ideal position, not only for business but to do one in the eye for Sadler's and Mr Jenkins, who had treated her so shabbily; it was successfully run by old Mr Sutton, but with a younger hand in charge it could be even more lucrative. Everything told her she should go ahead and yet . . . she didn't really want to. Her days were long, admittedly, but they were her days to do with as she wished. Did she really want to go back to a work regime, with its bowing and kowtowing to unappreciative customers?

Then one day over coffee Flora had told her she was 'bonkers' not to go ahead, and put a manageress in, and could Flora buy handbags at cost when it was Peggy's? So dutifully Peggy had made an appointment to view. She had been approved by awkward Mr Sutton who had driven the estate agents mad so far by rejecting as unsuitable everyone who'd been to see his business. A price had been agreed and Peggy had gone home feeling she was walking into a trap. What had induced her to go ahead, and why now, with only herself to consider? Was she still doing what other people wanted?

She spent the following week trying to persuade herself what a splendid idea it was. When an apologetic Mr Sutton telephoned to say he'd changed his mind about selling since his daughter had decided she wanted to take over the shop, Peggy sighed with relief. To Mr Sutton's surprise she said how splendid and how pleased she was for him, and she braved the spiders in the cellar to find a bottle of champagne to celebrate her freedom.

She needed a hobby, she decided, one that would get her out of the house, something healthy. It was Flora who suggested she try gardening, that she'd help out with any problems.

Peggy bought a mountainous stack of gardening books, which she studied wishing she'd learnt Latin so that the names of plants would roll off her tongue as they did off Flora's. On graph paper she planned the new garden she would create around existing shrubs and trees. Flora was right, it was absorbing, and the evenings fairly sped along as she drew her outlines and consulted her books.

Flora then introduced her to the temptations of the garden centre, far worse, she decided, than supermarkets for impulse-buying. Because of the frosts, it was still too early for any serious planting, and Peggy made do with buying statuary, pots and rustic seats. She had a pond dug, a fountain installed and a wooden pergola constructed.

It was at a garden centre on the other side of the city, one she had not visited before and for once without Flora in tow, that she saw him, busily selecting a container of grown shrubs which he was placing on a trolley. It was the man in the red car, the man who had made the waits at the bus stop tolerable on a cold winter morning. Illogically she coloured slightly at sight of him and felt a pit-a-patting of her heart – just like with the plumber and the new neighbour, but this time she was not as anxious at her response. After all, with this man she felt as if she almost knew him. With him it was just like old times. Still, best not get involved, she thought, and turned back to her task of trying to choose between wisteria or clematis to frolic over her pergola. And, in any case, he had probably forgotten her months ago, she decided, as she had almost plumped for wisteria.

'Hello. Have you changed jobs?' a male voice said behind her, and she knew it was him and almost dreaded turning round to look him full in the face. She knew that, if she did, something would happen and was not sure if she wanted it to, but felt an intense excitement at the prospect.

'I took early retirement,' she said, and thought even as she said it what a stupid thing it had been to say.

'I've missed seeing you at the bus stop. You used to make my day for me.'

'That's nice.' She dared to look at him and registered that, yes, he was as attractive as she remembered. Mid-forties like herself, she reckoned. She liked his eyes, dark brown and sur-rounded by laughter lines. With his dark skin and hair he had a Latin look about him.

'Do you come here often?'

They both laughed at the cliché.

'No, usually I go to Proctor's, but this place is good. It has a lot more plants, I think.'

'You like gardening?' he asked.

'I've only just begun. I like the planning and the shopping. I'll let you know about the rest later in the year.'

'They've a café here. Fancy a coffee?'

'Why not?' she said, feeling quite reckless, knowing, even as she turned and fell into step with him as they walked to the kiosk and the café, that she was going to go to bed with him. Even if she tried to shut away the idea it would not go, as if her mind was telling her that she couldn't pretend with it, that it knew what game she was playing.

He was Edward Gault. His father was English, his mother French from Corsica – hence his skin and hair, she thought, and also, how exotic. She'd been about right, he was forty-two. But what was a couple of years between them? He worked as an architect, on his own, and lived at Sutton, a village not ten miles from her own. She knew she should ask him if he was married and how many children he had – she should have, but she didn't, not yet awhile. She wanted to play the carefree game a little longer.

'You look different,' he said. 'Nicely different,' he added.

'I've had my hair cut,' she explained, but did not mention her weight loss.

'It suits you. Shows your pretty face better.' And gently, so gently it was almost as if he hadn't done it, he outlined her cheek. 'Wonderful skin,' he said, and she let him touch her as if it was the most natural thing in the world. 'You know what's going to happen, don't you?'

'Yes,' she replied, lowering her head so that he could not see the longing in her eyes.

'It's been inevitable ever since the bus-queue days.'

'I know.' She was almost whispering.

'You don't know how many times I wanted to offer you a lift but I didn't want to compromise you in front of the others in the queue in case they knew you.'

'They didn't.'

'How sad, then, that we wasted so much time. I was going to stop but you disappeared.'

'A lot happened to change my life.'

'And I should have been part of the change.' His hand was covering hers.

'Do you always talk like this?'

'Like what?'

'Like a 1940s movie.'

He frowned and she feared she had offended him.

'That was rude of me.'

'I'm not offended.' He chuckled, and the dark brown eyes disappeared in the web of laughter lines. 'Maybe it's because when something like this happens it's the only way to talk.'

'Perhaps,' she said, not sure what else to say. She was amazed that she could sit here so calmly, being verbally seduced by a pick-up; amazed that she'd even allowed herself to be picked up. How far had she travelled in a year, or how far had she sunk? She didn't like that idea. But why shouldn't *she* have some fun, too? Okay, so she didn't know him, but he wasn't a total stranger, with all the danger that implied. And why *shouldn't* she take a risk, live dangerously? She'd only herself to think of now. What she did with her life was her business alone.

'I want to go to bed with you.' He clasped her hand tight. 'I can't play games, my need for you is too great.'

She felt flustered at the intensity of his expression, the tone of his voice. No one had ever spoken to her like that. No one, not even – especially not – Dan, had said they *needed* her with such passion. A sliver of sane logic pointed out to her that it was too sudden, that he hadn't known they were going to meet so how real was his longing? But these were issues she did not wish to confront, not now, not today.

'My house?' she said shamelessly.

'We can go to a hotel if you want.'

'No, my place. I'll lead the way in my car.'

She felt impatient as she waited for him to pay for the coffee. They walked quickly along the paths between the plants, to the car park. Peggy felt as if she was floating, and her mind was reeling with the suddenness of this encounter. She stopped so abruptly by the display of pyracantha that he almost cannoned into her.

'Are you married?' she asked, given a moment of reason in this madness. She waited, dreading his reply.

'Now she asks.' He laughed. 'No, I've never taken the plunge. And you?'

'I'm separated.' The word she had been avoiding tripped off her tongue lightly – she had never thought a time would come when she would take pleasure in saying it.

They did not stop for coffee, wine, a tour of the house, any of the niceties. They went straight up the stairs, to her room, quickly removing their clothes before falling onto the bed. It was impossible to say whose need, whose passion, was the greater.

She awoke. She was cold. It was early evening. What was she doing here, naked and chilled? And then she remembered.

'Oh, no,' she said quietly. She looked at the other side of the bed. It was empty. On the pillow a note. 'I'll be in touch', she read. She clambered under the duvet and held herself tight. What on earth had happened to her? What on earth had made her do such a thing? And with a stranger. She covered her eyes with her hands as if shutting out the image of the two of them writhing on this bed, but it would not disappear. Quickly she got up and walked to the bathroom. She showered and then she took a bath, but neither helped. She felt stupid, cheap, and disgusted with herself. Would she dare see him again? And her mind, her traitorous mind, said it hoped so.

Chapter Thirty-seven

Whenever the phone rang she leapt for it. It was never Edward. She wished he would ring even though she knew it was probably for the best if he didn't. She was sure that if he contacted her she would not feel as foolish as she did now. He had said he wasn't married, but what if he had lied? What if she found out too late that he was – after she'd fallen in love with him, as she was sure she would, given the chance. Then she would feel even worse than she did now.

Peggy planned her weekends with care. She tried to make sure she had things to do, especially on Sundays, which, like so many people on their own, she found the most difficult day of the week. If she kept busy she didn't feel sorry for herself, something she despised. Especially when, the week after her meeting with Edward, she read that Petroc had died. Thinking about him in the past months had saved her many a dose of self-pity. On Saturday she invariably went into town to pick up a pile of videos from the hire shop, and on Sunday she bought a large stack of newspapers, all to fill the time. Flora and Lloyd often entertained at the weekends, and sometimes they invited Peggy, but it wasn't something she could rely on.

This weekend she was on her own, and had spoken only to shop assistants and the newsagent, so, when the knocker rat-tat-tatted late on Sunday morning she opened the front door almost suspiciously.

'Stephanie!' she cried with pleasure at the sight of her daughter, slimmer in the face and with her hair longer and hanging loose, but otherwise looking exactly the same. 'You look just as you did when you left.' She hugged her tight.

'Oh, Mum, of course I do.' Steph gave her mother a squeeze. 'What did you expect?'

'Oh, I don't know, some malnourished waif,' Peggy said, feeling stupid.

'Well, I'm starving.' Steph grinned.

'I was just about to cook a brunch.'

'Excellent. You look wonderful, Mum. Years younger. The short hair suits you, and you've lost weight. Clever you!'

She dropped her backpack and a duffel bag on the hall floor and followed Peggy into the kitchen. 'This is a really nice house, but I never expected to find you living in the country. When I got your letter I thought it'd never last.'

'I had my doubts, but don't laugh, I've discovered gardening and I love the house. It's every English person's dream, isn't it? With the thatch, the beams . . . like a chocolate box cover without the bows.'

'Does Dad agree with you?'

Peggy dropped the egg she was holding and it smashed on the floor. 'Tut, what a mess!' She covered her confusion with clearing up the spattered egg, marshalling her thoughts, trying to work out what to say, wishing she'd written the whole truth to her daughter. She got up from the floor, rinsed out the floorcloth and replaced it in the cupboard under the sink.

'Where *is* Dad?' Steph glanced about her as if expecting him to be hiding somewhere.

Peggy slowly sat down on the pine bench opposite. 'Steph, there's something I should have explained in my letters.'

'Dad's all right?' Steph sounded anxious.

'Oh, yes, he's fine. Very fine.' She gave a short, sharp, bitter laugh, which made Steph look at her closely.

'What is it, Mum?'

'Your father left me – in December.' She started to play with the pepper and salt pots, altering their position on the table, like ceramic soldiers. 'I've been on my own these past four months.'

'Mum! No! Why?'

'I still don't really know. Well, not why he needed to look elsewhere. What I did wrong . . .' Her voice trailed off, the hurt still raw and, as always, too close to the surface.

'There's someone else?'

'Hazel.'

'Your best friend?'

'Some friend!'

'Oh, Mum, that's awful. It makes it doubly worse, a double betrayal. Do you see him?'

'No. I've given up trying. At first I wondered if he was avoiding me.'

'Ashamed to face you, more like.'

'Do you think so?' Peggy visibly brightened at this notion.

'What does Paul say?'

'He doesn't know. They're having such a lovely time in Australia. He's not the best correspondent but I've had a couple of letters full of it – the climate, the people. He's coming back next month to finalize all the paperwork. He's leaving Candice, Lance and the baby there. He's got a job. They won't have any problems.' She knew she was rambling but here was another ocean of pain. She rarely thought about Paul living on the other side of the world with his family. She'd locked that idea away in a box in the back of her mind and refused to open it.

'He should know. *I* should have known. What about Carol? Has she helped you?'

'I haven't seen Carol since before Christmas. She decided to take sides and opted for Dan – I'm not surprised, they were always thick.'

'But how *could* she?'

'Oh, it's down to money. She thinks I've been unfair to her. That she should have more than you and Paul.'

'Why?'

'Because of her lifestyle.'

'Oh, sod her lifestyle! Who the hell does she think she is? Mum, if I'd known I'd have come straight back, and if I'd known anything was wrong I wouldn't have scarpered the way I did. I've been riddled with guilt over that as it is, and this makes it worse.'

'I know you were. Everyone was up in arms at the way you went but I knew if you'd faced me with your plans you'd never have gone. Seeing me react would have made the guilt burden even worse. I was upset and hurt – I'll admit that. But it's your life and you must lead it how you want, not how I think is best for you.'

'Oh, Mum,' Steph began to cry, 'you make me feel worse.'

'Doesn't matter now. As long as you're happy. Are you?'

Steph wiped her eyes with the back of her hand. Peggy leant over for the box of Kleenex on the dresser. Steph fumbled for one and blew noisily into it. She looked at her mother. 'It's wonderful, Mum. Really. And when you think it's been the winter and Greece has lousy weather in winter. Just in the past month, it's begun to change and the sun's shining and the people are all smiling and jolly again. It's so lovely there and I've met such interesting people. In summer, when it's really hot and we're swimming, oh, Mum, it'll be paradise.'

'It's an island you're living on?'

'Yes, in the Cyclades. We didn't like Athens – too crowded and the pollution's awful.'

'Are you still with Nigel?'

'Yes, of course. What did you think? That I'd been seduced away by a gorgeous Greek?' She snorted. 'I like them enormously but there's not much chance of that.' She began to fiddle with a ring on her finger.

Peggy watched her, realization slowly dawning. 'Oh, Steph, *no*! Oh, Steph, you're *married*!'

'Afraid so, Mum. We didn't mean to, but well, it was a case of . . .' She patted her stomach. 'I *couldn't* have got rid of it. And, well, when it came to it both Nigel and I are a lot more conventional than we thought. We both wanted to do the right thing for the baby.'

'But you're only eighteen.'

'Nearly nineteen, Mum, you're forgetting. I love Nigel. I know you weren't keen on him, but he's a good bloke and he cares for me and I'm safe with him.'

'When's the baby due?'

'September.'

'You don't look that pregnant.'

Steph lifted her baggy jumper to expose the vulnerable swell of her belly. 'I suppose it's not very big, is it?'

'It's probably a boy, then.' Peggy was finding the idea of her youngest being pregnant difficult to assimilate. 'Where's Nigel?'

'He's back home. I came alone.'

'Don't say that, Steph. Here's home, not there.'

'Not for me, Mum. I'm sorry. That's my home now.'

'So why did you come?' Peggy's voice was cold. How could Steph, of all people, have not seen fit to phone to tell her she was getting married, that she was pregnant? She could have flown out – she could have been with her. What was it with her family that they were all so secretive?

'We didn't want the full catastrophe like Carol's do. We preferred it just the two of us. I'm sorry.' Peggy sensed she had not finished and waited for her to continue. 'We want to buy a bar.'

'A bar,' she repeated as if stupid. 'Oh, Steph, you're so clever, so intelligent. You could do so much better with your life.'

'Mum, please. Don't you see? This was why I went. I've got to do my own thing. I don't want to go to university. I want to live on my Greek island with my husband and child, run our own little business and be happy.'

'Really? And how long do you think the life of a lotus-eater will be attractive? How long before you're bored to death?'

'You don't understand. You haven't been there. The people are wonderful, so simple, so wise. It's a privilege to know them.'

'I'm sure you're right. But be careful, Steph, you could be heading for such disillusionment. How many conversations can you have with them? How many talks about the fish catch? How many discussions on the harvest or the sheep? Their lives are limited, their horizons narrow – not like you. And if you'd been sensible those horizons would have been limitless.'

'There you go – I knew it! Don't live my life for me! That's all you ever wanted, isn't it? "You go, Steph, I'll learn from you." ' She imitated her mother's voice. Peggy banged the table with her fist. Steph looked up with surprise.

'That's not true! I know that's what everybody thought, but it's not so. Okay, I should have kept my cynicism at your simple lifestyle to myself – it's no longer my business. But you must try to understand me, Steph. When you left I thought long and hard, and analysed my feelings towards you. Had I been trying to live through you? No. I know it now. Yes, I wanted you to have what I didn't, but not because I hadn't had it, only because I wanted the best for you. It was that simple. Was that wrong of me? What if I hadn't thought that way? What would you have said about me then? You say that because, deep inside you, Steph, you know you've acted foolishly, throwing everything away on a whim. But, if you can blame me then it's easier for you.'

'That's a horrible thing to say.'

'But it could be true.'

'Could be, but isn't. Look, Mum, I haven't come here to row with you.'

'Nor me. I'm not rowing. Just for once I'm telling it to you as it is. It's all academic, anyway. You've done it – married, baby on the way. You want this bar, you can have it.' She waved her hand in the air in an almost nonchalant gesture.

'You mean it?' Steph jumped up.

'When have I ever not given you what you wanted if I could afford it?'

Steph came round the table to hug her. 'Bless you, Mum. Nigel said you wouldn't agree. You'd try and persuade me to stay here.'

'What would be the point? You'd be restless, miserable. If I'm right and you're wrong you can always sell it later to another couple of lotus-eaters. Meanwhile, I shall enjoy cheap holidays with you.' She laughed at that – she wanted to make light of it, and desperately for Steph to feel better about it. The one thing she didn't want was for Steph to be lumbered with the guilt which had marred so many of her own days.

'Of course you can. Oh, Mum, I'm so excited. It's a wonderful bar, fab position, right on the waterfront just yards from where the ferry docks. Nigel reckons we'll make enough in the summer so that we can come back for a long holiday in the winter.'

'And what about when your child starts school?'

'Oh, we'll worry about that when the time comes,' said Steph dismissively. She studied a sauce bottle with intense interest and then said, 'You know, you've changed a lot.'

'It's hardly surprising, is it?' Peggy got up and began to cook them their brunch.

As she worked, and Steph took a shower, Peggy contemplated what had just happened. She had given her daughter the wherewithal to buy her bar without a second's thought. She should have felt immense pleasure that she could, so easily, make Steph's dream come true. Once she would have been beside herself with joy. Now, though, she felt a sad weariness that she did not fully understand. But the unwelcome thought which nagged at her and wouldn't go away was whether Steph would have come home to see her if she hadn't wanted something. Perhaps it best explained the sadness she felt and the weariness. 'I'm turning into a walking cheque-book,' she said, and at her own words turned guiltily to the door lest Steph had heard her, but no one was there.

Steph stayed for a week. Not that Peggy saw much of her. Mostly she was zipping into town in Peggy's car to look up old friends and returning pleased with herself and her enhanced status in their eyes – married and pregnant.

'Are you going to see your father while you're here?'

'Not likely.'

'Why on earth not?'

'After what he's done to you?'

'But then you're taking sides, like Carol.'

Steph frowned at this, whether at the idea of taking sides, or because it would make her like Carol, Peggy was unsure.

'Do I have to?' she said, and Peggy had to turn her head to hide her smile. Steph might think she was an adult but she still sounded like a little girl.

'I'd like you to. I know he'd love to see you again,' Peggy said simply, and Steph grudgingly agreed.

Perhaps she had been wrong in insisting, for when Steph returned she slammed the kitchen door, and, white-faced, without saying a word, raced upstairs to the guest bedroom, flung herself on the bed and began to cry. Peggy never found out what had been said, because Steph wouldn't tell her, no matter how she pleaded. She phoned Dan, but the answer machine was on. Even as she left the message, asking him to call her about Steph, she was sure he was there listening to her.

On the day before Steph's departure they had confirmation that the money for the bar had been transferred to Steph's bank account in Greece.

'I think I'll go and see Carol and sort her out. She doesn't work on Saturdays, does she? I'd like to see the new house, though how they can afford it beats me.'

'She doesn't work today. And I think your father sees she has enough money.'

'No doubt from your bank account. Mum, why let them get away with it?'

'Fair's fair, and it might help her come round.' As she said this she realized how weak it made her sound. 'Whatever you do, don't tell her what I've done about the bar – she'd be apoplectic with rage,' Peggy said jokingly, unconvinced of who would be sorting out whom when it came to it.

Evidently it was Steph. She returned to say she had told Carol a few home truths, which she hadn't liked and which had led to a monumental row. She did not elaborate, Peggy did not ask; she was working on the theory that Steph would tell her in her own good time, rather as she hoped she would tell her what had transpired with Dan. That evening Sean phoned to complain at Steph's treatment of his wife.

'I don't know why you're ranting at me. I don't even know what was said. I'm sorry it turned out this way but, Sean, I didn't ask Stephanie to see her.' Even as she spoke she knew that the rift between her and Carol had deepened, thanks to Steph who, the next day, was blithely flying away from the chaos she had caused.

'I'm sorry, Mum. Maybe I went too far. I told her she was obviously in love with Dad.'

'You didn't?' Peggy was shocked.

'And if that was the case why was she sucking up to Hazel?'

'Oh dear.'

'And that she was a money-grubbing retard.'

'Oh, Lor'!'

'I've made matters worse, not better, haven't I?' Her innocent eyes looked at her mother with concern.

'It doesn't matter, Steph. Don't worry. I'll survive. I know I can now.'

'You *have* changed,' Steph said, for what must have been the tenth time during her visit.

Chapter Thirty-eight

'Most families are shitty, but yours takes the biscuit, Peggy,' said Flora as, rather viciously, she cut a French stick into chunks, seemingly taking out her anger for her friend on the bread. There had been a warm spell for so early in May and they had planned a pâté and salad lunch out on the terrace, but since it was pouring with rain they were in the kitchen. A cold front had enveloped the country so that even in the kitchen, with its Aga, it was chilly.

'Hang on, Flora, don't cut any more, we're still supposed to be on our diets,' Peggy remonstrated.

'Sod the diets. I need to eat for comfort. I'm *so* upset for you. I know that I didn't know you when you were *en famille*, so to speak, but you strike me as the type who'd have been a lovely mum. They really are the pits, your kids.'

'Oh, I don't know. I mean they've got to do—'

'Exactly – their own thing, but not to tell you she was getting married? As for that little bitch who won't speak to you. After all you've done for them.'

'No! No, Flora, never say that. I did what I did because I wanted to, no other reason. You mustn't do things expecting thanks for the rest of your life.'

'Do you have to sound so pious?' Flora waved the bread-knife dangerously.

'If I don't say that I sound like my mother.' She gave an exaggerated shudder.

'Well, I wouldn't do a bloody thing for anyone unless I was guaranteed gallons of thanks for ever and ever.'

'You didn't have my mum.' Peggy laughed.

'Do you sometimes blame the money for all that's happened?'

'I did at first. I hated it. If I hadn't had the money to give

313

them, this, that and the other wouldn't have happened. But then what would I have been left with? A sham. The kids would have been living lives they didn't want. Dan would, I now know, be longing for his freedom. And Carol's love for her father would still far outweigh her love for me.'

'But you wouldn't have known.'

'Yes – but to live the rest of my life in a charade? And I might have found out the truth in some other roundabout way and not had the cushion of the money to make it easier.'

'Rum old world, ain't it?' Flora did her stage-Cockney voice. 'By the way, I've been meaning to give you this for ages and kept forgetting.' She rootled among the chaos of her pine dresser and produced a cheque, which she waved at Peggy. 'For the health farm. Sorry it took so long.' Peggy thanked her and pocketed it, feeling full of remorse that she'd doubted her for one minute.

'Red or white?'

'Whichever you prefer.'

'Red, then.' Flora expertly uncorked the bottle, something Peggy had not yet mastered.

'We shouldn't be drinking this,' said Peggy, as she took a first appreciative sip.

'Sod it! I'm bored with dieting, anyway. I'm stuck at the same weight. Let's give it up – at least for this coming weekend. My brother's coming – fancy joining us for Sunday lunch?'

'I'd love to. I liked Tarquin.'

'Don't let him seduce you, whatever you do. He's such a creep.'

'I'll remember that.' Peggy snickered.

'I tell him he should write "con-man" on forms as his occupation. How are the men?'

'Nothing to report,' Peggy lied. She'd no intention of telling a living soul of her lapse with Edward. It made her feel both foolish and tainted still – a full three weeks later.

They began their lunch and were half-way through when Flora suddenly laid down her knife, refilled her glass with wine and knocked it back in one.

'Dutch courage,' she said in explanation.

'What for?'

'I want to ask you something and I don't know if I dare.'

'What?'

'You hardly know us – not really. It's an infernal cheek and it's not my idea, it's Lloyd's. He's put me up to it. He keeps nagging me to ask you. Bloody neck, really.'

'What?' Peggy was almost banging the table in frustration. 'Tell me before I go potty.'

'Well, you know the old mill house down by the mill race? The one we saw on that first walk. You admired it.'

'Yes, I remember, a beautiful building covered in creeper and all boarded up. Such a pity.'

'Precisely. That's the one. Well, Lloyd wants to restore it, turn it into flats and do summer lets. You can make a bomb at that.'

'I should think you could.'

'We can get some grants – it's a listed building, you see. But it's only part of what we need.' She stopped talking. Peggy looked at her expectantly. Still Flora said nothing and then the penny dropped.

'I see. And you want me to lend you some money?'

'Well, not exactly. No. We wondered if you'd like to come in with us. We could set up a company and you could take a share of the rentals.'

'How much?'

'Well, we haven't worked it out totally but, well, about seventy thousand pounds,' Flora said at a gallop.

'I see,' said Peggy, aware how nervous her friend must be. She'd never heard her say 'well' so many times. 'I can think about it if Lloyd could get some figures out for me.'

'Would you understand them?'

'I'm not stupid,' she said good-naturedly. 'And if I don't my accountant will.'

'Then it's no good. You see, we have to be seen to put up the money. The banks and the grant authorities must not know we're borrowing more to do it. They know we can't really afford it, you see.' She shifted nervously in her chair.

'So? Whoever's giving you the grant need not know it's me.'

'But if there was a squeak it was you it wouldn't wash. And this is a small area and all the accountants belong to the country

315

club – and they talk, you know. We've already got grants on the barns and a huge bank loan. They'd know we couldn't have borrowed it, since we'd have nothing to pay the interest with. What Lloyd wants, and this is the infernally cheeky bit, is that you trust in us and *give* it to us. I mean, you won't be really. You'll know and we'll know it's just a loan and the money is yours. We just don't want the authorities to know and especially the bank. Have I made myself clear or have I muddied the water even further?'

'I see,' she said, but sounded doubtful about it and found herself wondering if their need for this money was why she'd been given the cheque today, and then not liking herself for thinking that.

'Still, let's not spoil lunch talking boring business. It was just an idea. Forget it. I can see you're not happy with it.' Flora topped up Peggy's glass.

'No, it's not that. Get Lloyd to work out some figures – what you expect to get in rent, that sort of thing. I won't show my accountant, I promise.'

'Bless you, Peggy, you're such a sport.' Flora laughed. Peggy heard real relief in it and asked herself why.

Chapter Thirty-nine

Peggy had been advised that it was a foolish gardener who put out her tender bedding plants before the end of May and the fear of a late frost had passed. She could not wait. The garden was beginning to shape up well: the shrubs she had planted were well established, and the ones that had been there when she bought the house were flourishing. Now she wanted to do her own herbaceous border.

As she dug the rich dark brown soil with her trowel, making neat little holes for the plants, laying them carefully in and wishing them well, she could not think of a task which had ever given her so much satisfaction. Why had she not bothered with gardening before? Lack of time, she supposed, or perhaps it had been lack of patience and now she was experiencing one of the blessings of age. So engrossed was she that she did not even hear a car draw up in the lane outside.

'Well, there's a pretty sight.'

She looked up and towards the white picket gate from where the voice came. 'Tarquin, what a lovely surprise. Flora said you were coming tomorrow, or did she mean Sunday?'

He leapt over the gate rather than opening it. 'It's a secret. She doesn't know I'm here.'

'Why a secret?' Peggy asked, standing up and feeling a twinge in her back as she did, but deciding to ignore it, not even to rub it let alone mention it.

'Why not? I like secrets, don't you?'

'If they're nice ones.'

'This is a nice one, don't you think? We two in this pretty garden, just as the sun begins to set and it's almost time to hear the clink of the ice cubes against the tumbler.'

317

'What sun?' She looked up at the overcast sky.

'You're not a romantic!' He sighed loudly.

'I have had my moments.'

'But, sadly, not with me.'

'Could you carry that garden fork for me?' she said abruptly, feeling uncomfortable, wondering if he was flirting with her – or was it her stupid imagination?

'Did I offend you?' Tarquin looked serious.

'Of course not, silly. Let's put the tools away and I'll clink that ice for you.' She felt all right again as if the moment of danger had passed.

He prowled the room as she prepared their drinks. Every picture was examined, the books were studied, the ornaments appraised.

'So, does it pass muster?' She smiled up at him as she handed him his glass.

'What? This room? Filthy manners of me. Like a burglar, casing the joint. I apologize, but I wanted to know what you liked, what interested you.'

'Why?'

'I like to know all there is to know about the people I like so I don't get surprised.'

'And what have you learnt about me?'

'That you are a woman who wants to know things, too. I suspect you were disappointed in your education – probably truncated by circumstances beyond your control because you're too conscientious not to have worked hard. You're still learning as a result. You like real things – not false, not plastic – and you've a real feel for furniture. You've some lovely pieces.'

'Thank you,' she said, fascinated by his analysis.

'But you lack confidence in your own judgement.'

'How's that?'

'The paintings. They're all new, probably fairly cheap. You're not sure of your taste and therefore frightened to spend too much. And the pictures themselves are diffident, not statements – nice and safe, in muted colours, not a primary to be seen.'

'That's amazing. How did you know all that?'

He grinned broadly. 'They're all dated and I've never heard of the painters.'

'Tarquin! And I thought you were delving into my mind.'

'It's a bad habit of mine. I always assess – it drives Lloyd mad, he says it's vulgar even to look at people's furniture let alone comment on it. For all that, I think your home is delightful, Peggy, almost as delightful as you.' He raised his glass to her.

'Where do you live?'

'A grotty little flat on the edge of Fulham – I can almost say Chelsea and get away with it.'

'Does it matter if you do?'

'I suppose it shouldn't but, then, among the types I mix with it tends to.'

'For heaven's sake, you don't let that sort of thing affect you, do you?'

'It's more a habit than anything, I suppose.'

'When you're not being a con-man, what do you do?' She was astounded at her temerity in saying this.

'I import wine.'

'Really, that's interesting. From France?'

'No, from Eastern Europe. It's cheaper.'

'Are you successful?'

'I don't know, I'll let you know the minute I am. I only started last week.' He threw back his head and laughed uproariously at this and she wondered if he ever took anything seriously.

Peggy looked at her watch. 'I was going to make myself a curry. Would you like to join me?'

'Like to? I'd love to.'

'I hate eating alone. Since my husband left, it's the one thing I find hardest to adjust to – the lack of company – so I tend to avoid meals. I only really eat once a day,' she said, her voice tinged with sadness.

'What, like Labradors?'

'Tarquin, you're marvellous. You always manage to make me laugh.'

'Dear Peggy, there's not much point in tears,' he replied.

He sat on the stool in the kitchen while she prepared their supper. Although he continually put himself down she learnt that he knew a lot about such a diverse number of subjects that not for one moment did she find her mind wandering, neither was she bored for one second.

'I do ramble on,' he said apologetically, as he finished telling her about some frescoes he had seen in Italy. 'Fool that I am, I nearly blubbed, they were so beautiful.'

She told him of her dream to go to Italy one day and to see the art for herself.

'What's stopping you?'

'I hate to do things alone.'

'You wouldn't be alone long in Italy, I can assure you.'

'Don't tease me. You mean gigolos. I don't want ever to get to that stage.'

'Let me save up and then I'll come with you.'

'Would you? But you needn't save, I'd pay,' she said eagerly, without thinking.

'But then *I*'d be a gigolo.' He raised an eyebrow suggestively.

'So you would,' she said, but thoughtfully, and she knew that she would not mind if he was.

The curry was a huge success and Tarquin had three helpings of everything. She watched with pleasure as he ate and managed to blot out memories of other meals and other young people eating them; she was enjoying the evening far too much to let such regrets spoil it.

'Don't you eat in London?' she asked, lightly so that he would know that no criticism was implied.

'Not much if I don't get invited out.'

'Do you get many invitations?' She felt a quite illogical swell of jealousy.

'Not nearly as many as my tummy would like, and few enough to keep my tailor pleased with me.'

He helped her clear the plates away into the dishwasher, slipped a tea-towel into his waistband and insisted on doing the washing up.

'I would have had to be almost dying in bed before I could get my husband to do that.'

'Perhaps he was worried about his sexuality. Thought it made him prissy?'

'Perhaps.'

'A generation thing.'

'You sound like my daughter.' And she felt let down for she

did not want to be reminded that he was too young for her.

Once the kitchen was tidied to his satisfaction they went into the sitting room to listen to music and have some brandy.

'Would you like me to light a fire?' he asked, and as she watched him lay the kindling and then the logs, she thought how nice it was to have a man around the house again. She had put some Mozart on the CD player, which he liked. She sat in her favourite armchair, Tarquin lay back on the sofa, his head on the cushion, a contented look on his face.

'Isn't this nice?' he said.

'Very,' she replied.

'Do you have to sit over there, so far away?'

'I don't think it would be a good idea if I sat there.'

'Why not, Peggy, my love?'

'Nothing.'

'Is wanting to kiss you, nothing?'

'It wouldn't be right.'

'What would be wrong?'

'It's not . . . It's just . . . I'm too—'

'Don't say it!' he shouted. He jumped up from the sofa and was kneeling at her feet, all in one smooth, fluid motion. 'Please, Peggy, my sweet, don't say it, don't think it. We are a man and a woman – that's all that matters. Age is of no importance. Not when you feel as you do, and I feel as I do.'

'How do you know how I feel?' she said breathlessly. She was in a situation she wanted to be in but one that she knew she should not be in and which was rapidly getting out of control.

'A look here, a sigh. Oh, Peggy, I love you, I want you.'

She sat upright. 'Please don't say things you don't mean. It's not fair. It's cruel.' She began to try to distance herself.

'How dare you say what I mean or not?' He sounded cross. She looked at him. He was. 'I know how I feel, deep inside. It's true, I love you. I began to fall for you when I first met you. Then when I saw you again – you can't help these things, Peggy, they happen.'

'How could it have started when you first met me? I was fat, dowdy, middle-aged and boring.'

'You were none of those things. You *thought* you were, that's all. I saw you differently. What does weight matter? Or that your dress wasn't quite right? That you were out of your depth? Good God, Peggy, don't insult me, please. I'm not interested in superficialities. I saw beyond all that to the woman you really are, the one who, that night, was longing to escape.'

'Oh, Tarquin, it would be wonderful if I could believe you.'

'Why can't you? Because we teased you I was a con-man? It was a joke, my love.'

'No, it's not that. It's that I'm frightened of being hurt, of making a fool of myself. You see, there was this bloke Edward . . .' She told him all about the sordid little escapade. Logic told her she was ruining it with Tarquin, but something was goading her into doing so.

'The bastard! The bloody bastard! I could kill him!' Tarquin hit one palm with his fist. 'My poor darling . . .'

If she had needed anything to persuade her that she was safe with him it was this reaction. 'Please kiss me,' she said in a small voice.

He kissed her so well that she felt she was no longer in control of her body. It was his to do with as he wished. First he turned off all the lights and then he led her to the rug in front of the fire, gently he placed a cushion under her head. Slowly he undressed her. Then with an equal, exquisite slowness he began to kiss her body, it felt as if his lips found every inch of her, every crevice, every private place. The warmth from the logs bathed her body, the glow from the fire the only illumination to their passion.

He was a considerate lover, bringing her to climax time and time again before he entered her, and she felt his firm body riding into her and she cried out to him her need and her love for him, too.

Chapter Forty

This time Peggy was not riddled with shame. She stood in her kitchen waited for the kettle to boil and carried the tea-tray back to the bedroom with no feelings of remorse, rather an eagerness to have him awake and talking to her, making her laugh, making love to her.

Last night had been wonderful. She'd had no idea that it was possible to make love so many times in one night and still reach orgasm almost every time. There had been a couple of times where she had faked it, moaning and crying out, but he was so intent on pleasing her that she had not wanted to hurt his feelings.

'Tea,' she whispered in his ear, and kissed him. 'It's a lovely day and the sun is shining.'

'Fantastic.' He sat up in bed and rubbed his eyes with balled fists, and she was reminded of a small child waking. Then she shoved that thought firmly away into the back of her mind. He did not drink his tea, instead he took hold of her and they were making wonderful, free, glorious love, each wanting to make the other happy.

She cooked them an enormous breakfast.

'I thought you only ate once a day?' He grinned up at her as she put their heaped plates on the table.

'It isn't every day I spend a night like that!' she said, feeling marvellously alive, wondrously young.

'That sounds like double Dutch to me.' He leant forward and kissed the tip of her nose and for just a whisper of a second she thought of Dan – he kissed her there – and she found it didn't matter. For once she was free of him, of regret, of sadness.

'So, what shall we do today?'

She would like to have said, 'Go back to bed', but she felt

restrained. That was too forward, it was too soon to talk like that.

'What do you fancy doing?' she countered instead.

'I'd like to have a wonderfully long bath – with you. And then?' He looked at her with a mischievous, sly expression. 'And then I'd like to go back to bed for the whole of the day. And this evening take you out for a wonderful dinner and, of course, telephone my well-meaning sister and tell her I'm not arriving until tomorrow. How about that?'

'I think I could go along with it.' She was laughing as she helped herself to another piece of toast.

That evening she dressed for him with extra care. She was shocked when she saw herself in the mirror, but it was a pleasant shock. Looking back at her was a woman whose skin seemed to glow – she could almost allow herself to believe that she was beautiful, and certainly she seemed younger than her forty-six years. This did not stop her trying to work out how old he was. She had not liked to ask him and she knew why: she was afraid of the answer.

She chose a grey linen trouser suit, which though it wasn't Armani looked very much as if it was. Peggy had always liked clothes even when she had had to budget for them. Now that money was no problem, and she could buy what she wanted, her well-stocked wardrobes were a constant source of pleasure to her. All the same, she hadn't reached the point where she was able to steel herself to pay the sort of prices the designer labels commanded. Perhaps she never would.

'You look ravishing,' he said, when she joined him in the sitting room where he was busily mixing them martinis. She giggled and regretted it, knowing such a reaction was gauche and accentuated the social divide between them.

'I thought we should have one of these before we go, I'm famous for my martini-mixing. I'll just call old Flora, if I may use the phone. I'll pretend I'm still in London, okay?'

She watched him as he dialled the number and chatted to his sister. He always seemed so at ease with himself, so articulate. He had such a lovely voice, although he was scornful of his accent, said it was only useful for selling Rolls-Royces and Bentleys. She loved it, and told him he sounded like a local radio news reader, deep and gravelly and best heard at night! It was funny how he was much taller than she had registered when they first met, but then they had been sitting down most of the time, talking. She was sure he was better-looking, too – or was that because she had now fallen in love with him? At the party she had thought him a little bit too handsome for his own good, but that had been in artificial light. She knew his face well now, had already spent hours observing it when he wasn't aware she was doing so. It had a lived-in quality. It was the remains of a once very handsome face that he now presented to the world, which was much more to her liking. She'd always preferred faces that were a little worn and etched by life; rather like garden ornaments, she thought. They never looked right or comfortable with themselves when brand new from the garden centre. But several frosts chipped away at the smooth stonework, making them less perfect but a lot more friendly.

'What have you been thinking about?' he asked, as he returned from his call.

'I thought you looked like a garden ornament.'

'Is that a compliment?'

'Very much so.'

'Good. I do hope I was a gnome. Flora is devastated that I'm not arriving until tomorrow, but I said I had this dishy bird in tow, whom I couldn't leave. She wants to meet you, all agog, she was.' They enjoyed their private joke, that no one in the world knew about them. 'Shall we go?'

Knowing from Flora that he was always short of money she felt guilty when his car pulled up outside Clover's, the most exclusive restaurant in the area.

'Oh, you shouldn't have booked here, it's dreadfully expensive.' She looked at him with concern.

'Nonsense, best grub in town.' He parked the car.

'Well, at least let's go Dutch.'

'Madame, what a sweet thing to say, I'm moved to me withers. But the day Tarquin can't afford to dine a pretty lady in style then I shoot myself.' He laughed and she noticed again his perfect teeth – could they possibly be all his own? – and then, once again, found herself wondering how old he was. He bent across and gently kissed her cheek. 'Seriously, Peggy, I'm really touched by that offer. But I'm fine, a decent little filly romped home at a hundred to one the other day and I had a packet on her.'

They were soon settled at a table overlooking the river, which flowed close to the restaurant. They had their aperitifs at the table – he'd said the bar was too crowded and he wanted to concentrate on her; she felt quite light-headed at such a compliment.

He watched her as she leant forward to look out of the window at a bird which had landed on the water.

'Do you know what that bird is?' she asked.

'Haven't the foggiest. I can recognize a pigeon.'

'I don't believe you, someone with your background.'

'It's true – ask Flora. I've always hated blood sports, much to my father's despair. I like the country, don't get me wrong. One day I'd like to settle in it, just provided I don't have to kill anything. What about you? Do you like it?'

'I'm getting used to it. At first it seemed like a dreadful mistake – I found the quietness the hardest thing to adjust to. That was until I realized how noisy the country is. It's just that they're different sounds from those in the city. The wind is always making a noise and its repertoire is vast. Then there are the birds. The dawn chorus is deafening and I was never aware of it in the town. The animals are constantly calling or crying out – in the town it was the neighbours' dog who bothered you, but here on a still night it's every dog in a five-mile radius I should think, and I haven't even started about the tractors and farm machinery.'

'And the jets from Lakenheath screaming out of the skies!'

'Yes, and them too.' She paused. 'The best thing about living here for me, of course, was meeting your sister. She helped me enormously. I could have been very lonely without her friendship. The other locals aren't all that friendly – they tend to look down their noses at me.'

'Whatever for? Stupid old drones! Imagine what they're missing.' He smiled kindly at her. 'Dear old Flora, but you want to watch her, you know. She's always on the make and she'll take over your life if you don't watch out.'

Peggy frowned at his words. What a strange family they were, each warning one against the other. Did they not like each other? Was it true? Or perhaps it all came down to sibling jealousy. At least, she hoped so, especially now, when she was proposing to be involved financially in Flora's scheme.

It was a wonderful evening. She could not have been in better company. She laughed so much – she had not done much of that recently and had forgotten the feeling of well-being that a good rib-aching laugh afforded one. And yet, in an instant, he could switch from being the jester and become a quiet, serious friend.

'You know, Peggy, when I was waiting for you this evening, I really got the wind up thinking about you with that creep Edward.'

'Did you?' She knew she should not have told him about that error. Now he would become obsessed with it and it could spoil everything.

'You must watch wolves like that,' he told her. 'You're vulnerable, Peggy. No doubt your old man never told you what a corker you are. You find yourself alone in the world for the first time, and some bastard comes along, gives you the old song-and-dance routine – moonlight and roses all that guff – and you're smitten. Dodgy, Peggy.'

'I know.' She felt let down. She did not need this warning unless, of course, he had no intention of having a serious affair. 'Well, I won't do anything like that again, ever.' She made herself smile as if it did not matter to her what he intended to do.

'I'm glad to hear it. He could have been a serial killer and you might have been chopped up by now and buried in the garden. No, Peggy, my love, you be naughty only with people you've been introduced to properly, like yours truly.'

'Tarquin, you are a fool!' she said with relief.

'Joking apart, though, you haven't had much fun lately, have you? It must have been awful for you when your husband did his bunk, and finding his hand had been in the honey-pot, so to speak. Absolutely awful for you, poor love.'

His concern tempered her annoyance at Flora: who must have told him – natural enough, she supposed, but still she wished she hadn't. She'd talked in confidence to Flora she'd never intended her to blurt everything out to others. Why, she'd promised she wouldn't. 'Flora's gossiping, then?' She forced a lightness into her voice.

'Flora? No, Lloyd told me. Bad luck that. I suppose your husband looked after all your financial affairs?'

'Yes,' she answered warily.

'So who does now?'

'The bank. Hadn't we best be going?' she said shortly, standing up.

'I'm being disgustingly nosy, aren't I?'

'You are.'

'Sorry. It's a family characteristic. Yes, let's go.' And he was on his feet, too, and helping her on with her coat, which made her feel protected again so that she thought she had overreacted.

They went for a walk after the excellent dinner, strolling hand in hand as lovers do – she wished everyone she knew could see her – along the towpath of the river, which danced beside them like a pretty silver ribbon. It was a lovely night: the moon shone round and full, its light softening everything. In the air there was a feeling that summer might not be too far away, after all. She loved him so much, she felt so happy in his company, she felt so proud to have been with him. She wanted the evening never to end and she did not give a fig what Flora said about her brother.

'I'll tell you what I did want to ask you, Peggy.'

'Yes?' She looked up at his strong face in the moonlight.

'Have you made any arrangements about a pension plan? You should have one, you know, and I could fix it up for you.'

Peggy felt as if a bucket of cold water had been thrown over her. How stupid she had been, once again.

'They were set up at the very beginning. We had an army of financial advisers for that but, as my husband said, they were really glorified insurance salesmen.' She said this meaning to be spiteful, wanting to hit back. 'If you don't mind, Tarquin, I'd like to go home. It's a bit chilly for walking.' The moon appeared to have lessened in size, its light white and cold. She could feel the remains of winter in the air, the river looked black as death. He was like everyone else, after all.

Chapter Forty-one

At first Peggy thought she would cancel going to lunch at Flora's on Sunday morning – she could pretend she'd a bug or something, and then she thought, why should she cancel, why should she lie? She had done nothing.

There was no fear of meeting Tarquin there. After she had demanded to go home he had begged to know what he had done to offend her. If he did not know, what was the point in explaining, she asked herself wearily. And he had driven off into the night asking her to tell Flora he'd been called back to London. Tarquin was just another incident to put down to experience, she decided. Forget the pain, forget the lovemaking, he was just someone else on the make. She had to begin to learn that she was not like other people, that she could not allow herself the luxury of trusting them.

She did worry that she might blurt out to Flora the whole sorry tale, for she was feeling whipped with disappointment. Peggy had never been a good liar and knew she might end up letting it all out; she knew herself, once she started confiding. How long would it be before she confessed about Edward, too, as well as Tarquin? After all, she had told Flora about Bruce when she hadn't meant to. She had best not go.

Yet what if Tarquin had already telephoned his sister and told her all? If he had, what would be more mortifying than for Flora, and through her Tarquin, to know she had stayed at home, hurt and miserable? No, she should go.

'No Tarquin, I'm afraid. He phoned early to say he's mortally wounded. Apparently, some bird he sounded very serious about has dropped him. Now that is a turn-up – no one has ever ditched him before that I know of. Here's your gin.' Flora offered Peggy a ready-poured tumbler of gin and tonic. 'Sit you down,' she said bossily.

'Is this one of your normal depth charges?' Peggy sipped gingerly, while wondering if that was a message from Tarquin to her. But remembering how perfidious he had been she concentrated on her drink. Safer, she told herself. 'Heavens, Flora do you want me to die of cirrhosis?'

'Go on, that's not too strong. You're getting to be a wimp in your old age.'

'Just a dash more tonic then, *please!*'

'You realize you cost us a fortune in bloody tonic.' Flora unscrewed the bottle and poured some into Peggy's glass.

'I don't believe him for one minute. He's not in his flat.'

'How do you know?'

'Because I telephoned him back immediately and the boy who shares with him said he'd come down here, late afternoon on Friday.' She looked accusingly at Peggy. 'Do you know anything?' Peggy did not answer. 'What's been going on?' Flora, never one to give up, tanked on.

'Nothing happened. What gave you that idea? Yes, I did see him, if you must know. But I don't know where he is now. He said something about having to get back to London,' she lied.

'He didn't mention it to me. As far as I was concerned he was all set for pigging on roast beef and Yorkshire. So, you saw him last night?'

'We had a gorgeous dinner at that lovely new restaurant by the river. I ate too much and felt guilty as sin when I woke up this morning.' Flora did not react to this but continued to look at her questioningly. 'Your brother is great fun. I can't remember the last time I laughed so much.' Flora stood with arms akimbo her eyebrows arched in query. 'Nothing happened,' Peggy repeated, in the faint hope that Flora would believe her.

'Something *always* happens when my brother is involved. What was it? Did he try to grope you?'

'Of course he didn't. The very idea!' Peggy relaxed, her whole body sagging into the sofa cushions with relief that Flora was barking up the wrong tree.

'If it wasn't that, then, what was it? Something to do with money I'd bet.'

Peggy groaned. She had meant it to be an inward groan, but it emerged out loud.

'There you go. I knew something had happened. How did he upset you? Am I right? Was it something to do with lolly?'

'No, of course not.' Peggy studied the drink in her hands with a deep attention.

'You're fibbing. Come on, out with it. It's me, Flora, I shan't repeat it.'

'Well, if you must know . . . I was stupid, I suppose. I thought it was because of my new looks and my charm that he had invited me out to dinner. That he wanted to get to know *me*. Instead, he tried to sell me a pension plan.' She tried to make light of it, make a joke of it, send herself up, but she failed miserably.

'Oh, my poor love. The prat! I told him not to mention even the tiniest squeak about money to you. That someone in your position could be paranoid about gold-diggers. I warned him, I said you'd take to the hills. I told him you'd have had a pension all set up ages ago. What a nerd he is.'

'Oh, great! So you worked out some sort of strategy between you before he even invited me, I suppose. I can imagine the nice cosy chat. "You know her, sis. What's the best way to screw some cash out of her – straight out, or soften her up with a dinner?" Some friend you are,' Peggy said angrily, standing up as she did so.

'Peggy, what's got into you? What do you mean by that? That's a horrible thing to say.'

'It's all so bloody pat, isn't it? God, what a fool you must take me for.' She put down her glass with a bang, uncaring that some of the contents had spilt over the side and onto the polished table.

'Look, Peggy, I don't know why you're so upset with me. Yes, I can see why Tarquin has pissed you off but what the hell have I done? He likes you, he really does. He's always asking after you. In fact, I think he fancies you – not that he's ever said anything to me, he wouldn't, you understand. He did mention the pension thing to me, why not? What's more natural than that he should ask me, your friend, the best way to approach you? I said, "She's very vulnerable, she gets begging letters by the truckload, don't talk business, not at a nice dinner, or she'll think you're just like the rest." '

'Like you?'

'What does that mean?'

'Come on, Flora, you know damn well. The project you and Lloyd want me to invest in. What's in it for me? What's in it for you? Most convenient, wasn't it, that you should pay me for the health farm the same day you ask me for seventy thousand pounds?'

'That's a shitty thing to say. I apologized to you for being so late with the cheque. Okay, I'll be honest. I was late because I didn't have it and I'd had to juggle things a bit, but I did pay you. It was just coincidence that it was that morning. Hell, I never wanted to ask you in the first place but Lloyd persuaded me to.'

'That's right, hide behind Lloyd. You expect me to believe you? You're your own person. You never do a bloody thing you don't want to.'

'I'm hurt that you should think like this, Peggy.' Flora's eyes filled with tears. 'I thought you were my friend.' For a second Peggy wavered but then bent down and picked up her handbag from the floor just as the door opened and Lloyd walked in.

'Ah, Peggy, I want to introduce you to two friends of mine.' Peggy, standing straight, found herself looking directly at Edward Gault. In that fleeting instant, as their glances met, she had the satisfaction of seeing that he was embarrassed but, more than that, he was afraid, too. The reason for his fear was standing beside him. 'Peggy, this is Daniel Gault, our architect on the Mill House, and this is Florence his wife. We thought we could discuss plans and ideas over lunch . . .' Lloyd continued blithely, oblivious to the atmosphere in the room and the looks passing between them.

'We've met – I mean, *Edward* and me.' She could not resist it, enjoyed the look of terror on his face, the puzzled expressions of the others – let him sort it out. 'I've never met Mrs Gault.' She was surprised at how normally conversational her voice was, just like any polite and inconsequential party chatter. In fact, she longed to shout, he picked me up and screwed me and the bastard lied and said he wasn't married. She wanted to, but she didn't. This woman had done nothing to her so why should she hurt her with the truth? Didn't she know better than most how painful a husband's unfaithfulness was? And this man didn't matter to her any longer. What he had done to her was nothing compared to Tarquin's behaviour.

'How do you do, Mrs Alder.' Florence was smiling pleasantly at her. 'You live in that lovely cottage down by the water meadows. I see it often when I'm walking the dogs.'

'That's right, the thatched one.' She saw her opportunity. 'You must pop in any time you're passing. I'm usually there. We could have a cup of coffee and a good old gossip about things,' she said, with a smile. Had Florence been looking closely, she would have seen that the smile fluttered about her mouth but did not reach her eyes. She glanced quickly at Edward, who was called Daniel, in time to see him looking aghast at her suggestion. Peggy allowed herself another little smile at that, but this one was genuine, before she walked towards the door ignoring Edward completely.

'Peggy, you're not going?'

'Sorry, Lloyd, I am. Flora will explain everything to you.' And with a conscious effort to look as dignified as possible Peggy opened the door and stalked out of the room.

She was getting into her Mini when the front door burst open and an agitated Lloyd appeared, waving a sheaf of papers. He leapt down the moss-covered stone steps two at a time. 'Peggy, I don't know what's happened, what's been said, but at least look at these. I meant to give you these figures weeks ago, but I was waiting for the drawings.' He bundled what were evidently plans for the Mill House conversion on to the seat beside her. 'Please, Peggy.'

'I can't promise anything, not any more.' She switched on the engine. 'And in any case I wouldn't put a penny of my money into a project where that fornicating bastard of an architect is involved.' She put the car into gear, stuck her foot on the accelerator and swept the car in a wide arc on the driveway before the house, leaving Lloyd with his mouth wide open in astonishment, his face a picture of anguish as he watched her drive away. Me and my cheque-book, she thought, as she swung the car on to the main road.

Peggy was making a sandwich in the kitchen. She had had a gin when she got home and, still full of anger and mixed emotions,

333

had drunk it too quickly. Combined with the one Flora had poured her it had soon gone to her head. She had calmed down a little; the seething of this morning had dissipated to be replaced by the lingering emptiness of rejection. It was different from Dan's renunciation of her, and though the same degree of anguish was absent it hurt all the same. Edward, Tarquin, Flora – quite a list she was building.

As she buttered her bread she heard the roar of a powerful car on the lane, a familiar rumbling noise. The butter-knife clattered on to the work surface. She was holding her breath, waiting for the car to sweep past. It stopped. She clutched at her throat and leant against the kitchen unit, her pulse racing. Was she imagining it – the car door slamming with an expensive clunk, the footsteps on the gravel of the path – because that was what she had longed to hear? No, it was no dream, it was real, very real, as the front doorbell rang. She took a deep breath, walked like an automaton towards the hall. She paused to look at herself in the mirror, patted her hair, licked her lips and, feeling sick with nerves, opened the door.

'Hello, Peggy.'

'Dan,' she said simply. They just stood with Dan scuffing the gravel and she playing with the door handle, neither looking at the other. 'You'd better come in.' The words sounded ungracious, but what else was she to say? She opened the door wider to make amends and managed to smile. Dan smiled back tentatively.

'House is looking nice. You do, too,' he said, clumsily.

'Thank you.' They both stood in the hallway, feeling shy of each other, uncertain what to say, how to proceed. 'I was making myself a sandwich. Do you fancy one?' she asked eventually, after a silence that seemed interminable.

'No thanks. Carol cooked us a huge lunch,' he said. She stiffened at the use of the word *us*. He must have noticed for he suddenly added, 'She's a good little cook, she must get it from you, but she's still not a patch on her mum.' And he smiled what Peggy thought was one of the falsest smiles she had ever seen.

'Come into the sitting room.'

'What about your sandwich?'

'It can wait. A drink?'

'Have you got Bacardi and Coke?'

'Nothing like. You don't drink stuff like that, do you?'

'Picked the habit up on the holiday we took. We went to the Canaries, had a wonderful time, great weather when it's all murky here. You should go.'

'Gin do you? I'm not into exotic drinks.' She turned and busied herself with the glasses, glad to have something to keep her occupied for the few minutes it would take her to calm down. Had the man no sensitivity? Why mention his holiday? Correction, Peggy, she told herself, *their* holiday. 'I'll get us some ice.'

'I'll get it.' He stood up.

'No, you won't know where anything is, I've moved things.' She felt better for saying that, and even better when she noticed his slight frown, as if she had touched a raw spot. Alone in the laundry room she took the ice tray from the freezer and smashed it on the side of the sink imagining it was Hazel's head, and that helped relieve her tension a little.

Back in the sitting room she had the distinct feeling that he had not been sitting still but had been looking around her things. She did not like that – it was not as bad as the violation one feels from a burglary, but all the same it made her uncomfortable.

'Why have you not answered my letters and calls?'

'It's been difficult, Peggy.'

'I don't see why. A pen and paper is all that's required or one active digit,' she said sarcastically.

'I thought it was best if we talked through lawyers.'

'A lot worse, more like,' she said with feeling, and couldn't think why, if he believed that, he had turned up unexpectedly on her doorstep. The paradox made her edgy and on guard.

'Have you heard from the kids?' he asked, as she handed him his iced drink.

'Steph writes regularly. She seems very happy.'

'She doesn't write to me. But then I'm not in her good books as she made plain to me last time I saw her.'

'So you hear from Paul, then?' she asked, completely ignoring the remark about Steph. She would love to know what had been said between them, but she was not going to give him the satisfaction of discovering that their daughter had not confided in her.

'Not often. Not the greatest of letter writers, is he? He phoned when the baby was born.'

'I'm meeting him off the plane this week.'

'Shall I go for you? You hate the motorway.'

'That's kind of you but I'm getting used to driving anywhere now, and, in any case, I'm looking forward to meeting him. Of course, you're fully aware that Carol doesn't contact me.' Since they were checking up on the children they might as well check them all out, she thought.

'You don't contact her.' He sounded defensive.

'I have, but I've given up trying. If she doesn't want to talk to me or see me, so be it. I don't intend to beg her for an audience. Still, I think you could have talked to her about the situation, told her not to take sides. She listens to you, she'd have done what you want her to do. But come to think of it, maybe she did.' He had the decency to look ashamed – so she'd got it in one. He didn't look well, she thought, studying him more carefully, now that the first shock of his arrival was wearing off. He'd put on weight and he had the puffy look of one who drank far too much. She hoped the number of gins she sank weren't etched on her face too. He looked tired – well, more than tired, exhausted would be a better word – no doubt caused by Hazel's sexual demands. Such a thought precluded sympathy.

'You look fabulous, Peggy,' he said, almost as if he was reading her thoughts.

'You needn't sound so surprised.' She didn't mean to sound bitchy, was cross that she did, but thinking of Hazel had made her.

He chose to ignore the remark. 'I like the hair. It suits you, makes you look really pretty again.'

'Again?' She gave a short laugh totally devoid of mirth. That word said it all, she thought. She had been pretty but then she had stopped being so for him and now she was pretty again. Had he always sounded so patronizing?

'You know what I mean.' He had the grace to look embarrassed.

'How's Hazel?' She was not sure what had made her ask that.

'Difficult. A very demanding lady, our Hazel.'

'Didn't you realize that? I'm sure Bruce could have told you. Do you mean sexually or in other ways?'

He looked at her with a shocked expression, that she, of all people, should ask such a thing. 'I meant materially.'

'Ah,' was all she said. So that was why he had called. He needed a larger allowance than the one she paid him. 'Doesn't she like the cottage?' What devilment had made her bring that up?

'I'm sorry about the cottage. I should have told you about it. So you found out?'

'Of course I did. What did you expect? It was only a matter of putting two and two together to work out that it was the reason for the large overdraft, and that *poor* Hazel was the friend in need and recipient of your largesse. I just hope you had the sense to put the house in your name and not hers.'

'What makes you say that?'

'I don't know, just a feeling.'

'What, that we might split up?'

'Perhaps.'

He leant forward in his chair, still clutching his drink, an anxious air about him. 'We have split, Peggy. She's gone back to Bruce, took a packet with her, too.'

'I'm sorry,' she said, and marvelled at how hypocritical she could be when her heart was singing with pleasure at the news.

'It was when I refused to pursue you over the money. I said to her you had been more than generous in the circs. We had the cottage, you'd bought the garage for me, you gave me the allowance. Anything else was just piggy.'

'I suppose it was the lottery ticket business that still rankled with her.'

'Really vicious she's been. Nag, nag, nag. I'd had enough. I'm not used to that sort of thing. I don't like it. You were never like that about anything.'

'No, but then I hadn't lost out on half a fortune, had I? I can understand how she felt.' Her smile seemed to embolden him for he visibly relaxed and when he smiled back it was the first genuine one since he had arrived. He put his glass carefully on the side table, leant even further forward and took her hand. She let him.

It seemed strange that his touch should still feel so familiar.

'Peggy, I've come here to ask you to take me back. I'm sorry, I've been a bloody fool. I won't stray again, ever. It's out of my system now. You see, Peggy, I love you. I want to spend the rest of my days with you.' She removed her hand from his grasp. He sat back on the cushions, a look on his face she could not quite identify before his expression changed and he looked questioningly at her.

'Do you? That's nice,' she replied sweetly. 'The problem is, Dan, I don't want to spend the rest of my life with you.' It was not what she had intended to say. These were not the words she had gone over and over in her mind when she had dreamt of this moment, practising for the day it would come. She had longed for his return with every fibre of her body. But, even as she spoke them, even now as they hung between them, she discovered that she meant every word she had said. She did not relish it and she derived no pleasure from the incredulity on his face. In a way that she did not truly understand she wanted to comfort him: for a split second she imagined taking him into her arms. But she saw immediately that such an action could so easily be misconstrued and would cause him even more distress. 'It wouldn't work, you see.'

'No, I don't see. I know you love me, Peggy. Why else have you been trying to see me? Your letters, the phone calls.'

'That was then, this is now.'

'There's someone else?'

'Why do men always presume that? No, there's no one.'

'Then why, Peggy?'

'To be honest, Dan, I don't know.'

'Then you *will* come back, it's just a matter of time. And I'll fight for you, I will.'

'No, don't. It would be a waste of time. I'm happy, you see, as I am. I wouldn't want any more pain between us. I'd like us to be friends.'

'You've turned into a cold fish, Peggy.'

'I don't think so – a realist, more like, for the first time in my life.' She stood up and opened the door for him. 'It's better if you go. Please.'

Shaking his head with disbelief and muttering to himself, Dan left her.

As she closed the door she acknowledged the reason she had turned him away. Tarquin had let her down, betrayed her, but he had made her feel like no other man had ever made her feel. She could not settle for second best, not now. Dan was that, no doubt about it. Maybe she would find the magic again one day, maybe not. But one thing she did know: she was better off with nothing than a make-do.

Chapter Forty-two

In the following days Peggy frequently considered what would have happened if she hadn't still been seething against men. What if Dan had arrived on a miserable Sunday, with rain dripping down outside and no good black-and-white movies on the television to watch, and found her feeling lonely and depressed instead of angry? Would there have been a different end to the story? If so, she told herself practically, they could not have had that much of a relationship if the absence of a Bette Davis movie could bring her back into his arms.

She had surprised herself, though shocked might be closer to the truth. She had looked at him sitting in front of her, making his little speech, and she remembered that anger, triggered by something in his expression, which took her days to identify. It was smugness. He had trotted out his words, no doubt carefully prepared and practised in advance, perhaps even in front of a mirror – she wouldn't put it past him, he was vain enough. He had had his fun, his fling, but now he wanted the solidity of their relationship back. He expected to slide into her bed because she would be waiting for him. Her reaction had completely cocked up the touching scenario.

There should have been a big gap in her life – had she not, for the past few months, spent hours of each day longing for his return, planning how to make it happen? But that space in her mind had disappeared. That was another shock, that so many hopes and longings could vanish without regret. When he left, last December, and she had gone on her bender and had cried herself sick, she had thought then that she had no more tears to shed. She had evidently been right.

Of course, her memories remained. There were times when

she liked to think about them – those times when the kids had been young and when she and Dan had been truly in love, when they had no money and everything had to be saved for and was appreciated the more.

Money! Such a little word for something that could cause such anguish. The lack of it caused nothing but worry, created misery and broken homes. Too much, and what happened? A warring family, now torn apart and herself left alone to count the stuff. Would she have been better without it?

This made her sit down and think. Would not having the money have altered anything? Dan might still have fooled around – not might but probably would, she corrected herself. Which did she prefer: to have been innocent of the knowledge or to have the truth? It was an impossible question to answer.

The past. Her past. Her supposedly happy past. But hadn't she fallen into the trap of so many women? Because she had wanted to have a happy and close loving family, because that had been her dream and ambition, perhaps she had constructed it in her mind, when in reality such a state of affairs had never existed. The whole 'happy-Alder-family saga' had been a figment of her imagination.

And since, what had she done for herself? She had done little, except lose weight, feel sorry for herself and allow herself to become too vulnerable. Some things were going to have to change around here, she told herself seriously.

During these days, try as she might the image and memories of Tarquin kept intruding. She was no longer angry with him. Now, she was left with the regret at what might have been, had it not been for the money. But then, she had to ask herself, what was the likelihood of her having met Tarquin and Flora if she had remained poor? Zilch, was the reply.

Peggy hardly recognized Paul when she stood at the barrier at Heathrow and watched her bronzed, fit and fatter son appear pushing a trolley with a large stuffed koala bear on the top of his luggage.

'G'day, good on yer, Ma,' he said, in an excruciatingly bad Australian accent, grinning from ear to ear.

'All you're lacking is a big hat with dangling corks,' she said, when she eventually emerged from his bear hugs. 'No wonder the Aussies loathe the Poms if you go round talking like that, taking the mickey.'

'Mum, I've found bloody paradise.'

'That's nice,' she answered, her heart sinking at the realization that he'd never come home now.

'Shall I drive?' he asked.

'Don't you trust me?'

'You hate motorway driving.'

'I don't any more.' She got into the driver's seat.

'This is for you, Mum.' He handed her the koala.

She looked at its nose with its shiny leather tip, at the black beady eyes. 'Paul, thank you, you know I've always wanted toys like this and never had the nerve to say.' She hugged the bear to her before carefully putting it on the back seat.

'Why didn't you?'

'Seemed too silly for words, a grown woman like me.'

'I'll buy you a teddy next.' He clipped on his seat-belt. 'Love the car. What happened to the Mini?'

'I've still got it, I use it around town – it's so easy to park. But, last week, I was a bit down, and I decided to treat myself, so I bought this as a sort of consolation present to myself.' She reversed competently out of the parking bay.

'Consolation for what?'

'Oh, odds and sods that annoyed me.'

'Must have been some big annoyance to warrant a Porsche! And you just swore, Mum! You said, "sod". Tut tut!'

'It's second-hand – it didn't cost that much. It's only a cooking Porsche,' she said, as they cleared the tangled outskirts of the airport.

'What's that?'

'Like cooking sherry, the cheap one. I could never have bought a new one, or a 911.'

'Mum, you don't have to justify yourself to me, if you want to hot-rod around in a Porsche – a right old *motor-granny*!'

'Old habits die hard. And you needn't hang on for grim death like that. I can handle it – and well.'

The rest of the journey, as if by mutual consent, they talked only of Candice and the children and how happy they were, general things. Dan wasn't mentioned once.

'Lovely little cottage, Mum. The kids will love it when Candice and me dump them on you and swan off.' He laughed, but she had a sneaky idea he might mean it.

'Oh no you won't! I've no intention of becoming a knitting sort of grandmother.' Best to nip such ideas in the bud, she thought.

'You've changed, Mum. Steph said you had, and it's not just because you look a dream. I mean you do, but I'd no idea . . .' He stopped in mid-sentence and looked away from her in confusion.

'That I could look like this? Was that what you were going to say?' She smiled broadly at him so that he would know she was not offended.

'You're still so pretty and with such a nice figure.' Again he looked shy and uncomfortable as if he should not be saying such things to his own mother. 'Dad must be mad.'

'He got a touch of the male menopause. It happens to a lot of men of his age, this urge to rush off and prove that time isn't running out on them as it is on everyone else.'

'Yes, but it's usually with a much younger woman not an old over-made-up hag like Hazel.'

'Oh, I don't know, I think she's a very attractive woman.' They both looked at each other and burst out laughing at this statement.

'Still as nice as ever, aren't you?' He smiled at her with pride.

'No, I'm not, and certainly not over her, but it's the truth. Saying she looked like the back of a bus wouldn't alter the situation, would it?'

'It might make you feel better.'

'I don't need to, I'm all right as I am. Don't think I've turned into a saint – many's the curse and fearful end I've wished on her, but it's past.'

'I thought I was going to find you all twisted and bitter. Steph said you were pretty pissed off.'

'You spoke to Steph about us?'

'Yes, she was upset. She thought she might have made matters worse for you, rowing with both Dad and Carol.'

'Nothing could have made it worse, bless her. I must call her and reassure her.' She was making tea and there was a pause in the conversation while she concentrated on filling the pot with the boiling water. 'What *did* Steph say to your father that upset him so?'

Paul guffawed. 'Didn't she tell you? No? She said he'd told her to mind her own business. She saw red and told him it was her business and to take a long look at himself, that he was behaving ridiculously, that he was nothing but a menopausal old fool and that, when he was old and senile and Hazel had ditched him, not to turn to her 'cause she had no intention of wiping his arse.'

'She never did?' Peggy's hand had shot to her mouth.

'Straight up. And I know how she feels.'

'Don't be too hard on him. I doubt if he could have helped himself at the time.'

'Mum, you're too reasonable by half. He broke your marriage up, aided by that tart. Don't tell me you forgive her too.'

'No, I'll never do that. What she did was tacky. But she didn't break us up. I honestly believe that no one can break up a good marriage. If it hadn't been Hazel it would have been someone else. He'd done it before you know. He'd had an affair with a secretary at work.'

'Hell! He never did? And I thought I knew him.' He shook his head with disbelief. 'You didn't stray, though, did you?'

'No, but it was enough for me. I was happy. I'm now mortified to discover that others weren't as happy as I was – especially your father.'

'You were such a good wife, though. He could never have complained.'

'To be fair to him, he never did. Your nan says it was my fault, that I had become fat and boring.'

'Nan can be really spiteful when she wants, can't she?'

'You saw that about her?' she asked, almost with gratitude.

'Still she's old, you have to make allowances, don't you?'

'I thought I was the only one who saw through her.'

'You know the problem with this family? We never talked, not really talked – you know, cards on the table and let it all hang out. Everyone was always too afraid to say what they were thinking.'

'So as not to make a crack in the "happy family" façade. Of us all, Carol is the most honest. She says what she thinks a lot more than the rest of us.'

'Only because she's more selfish than the rest of us. And she can keep mum when it suits her. Mind if I smoke?' he asked. 'Of course! That's something else different about you – you've stopped.'

'It's a miracle, isn't it? Mind you, I have sneaked the odd one. I don't think you ever really give up. I'm a bit like an alcoholic, you know – one day at a time. I've had enough tea, fancy some wine?'

He drew the cork. 'Steph said you'd bought Dad a garage business.'

'Yes, that's right, before we split up. He was too young to retire. He specializes in fifties and sixties cars. You know how mad he was on them.'

'And the old house? Have you sold it?'

'No, we decided against it – before the split, that is. We never discussed anything after it.' Sadness flickered momentarily across her face. 'I'm trying to persuade Mother to move into it. I think she will once she thinks she's made enough fuss.'

'So where's Dad now?'

'He bought a small cottage near Stevenage. It's close to his garage workshop and it was easy for Hazel to get to her company's head office, but that's irrelevant now. She's scarpered back to Bruce.' She couldn't keep the satisfaction out of her voice as she said this. She was still hoping to hear that Bruce had seen sense and had told her to go.

'You mean, you bought it for them,' he said bitterly.

'Don't forget, in a divorce I would have had to have given him half of any house, wouldn't I? So it all works out the same in the long run.'

'He's asked for a divorce, then? There's no hope of a reconciliation? Would you like me to go and talk to him for you? I will.'

'Darling Paul, thanks a lot, but it wouldn't help. You see, it's me who won't have him back.'

'Honest? Heavens! That's not quite what I expected to hear.'

He smiled twistedly, and she felt sorry for him – and the conflicting emotions that must be raging in him. 'Does this mean you've found someone else?'

She laughed at that, too loudly, but at his words Tarquin had sprung to mind. 'You men are so funny. That's what your dad thought, too. It's as if you think no woman can be happy unless safely tucked up with a man. I thought that once, but I'm learning. It's not been easy but I'm beginning to realize I can function by myself, and I shall continue to do so, if I want to. If *I wish*. You could never imagine what those words mean to a woman like me – of my age and with my background, you know, brought up to think that marriage was the only option.'

'Have you really thought this through, Mum?'

'Oh, yes. That's the whole point. If I were with someone else I wouldn't be able to see everything nearly as clearly as I do.'

The week that he spent with her went too fast. It seemed no time at all before she was back at Heathrow and watching him disappear into Departures – he had more luggage to take back, though: she had had a wonderful time shopping for her grandchildren and for Candice.

'Carol's really upset, Mum,' he'd said, as he kissed her goodbye. 'Give her a bell.'

'Perhaps,' she'd replied. And now, roaring back along the motorway she was still debating whether she would or not. Could she face any more drama or pain? For that was what she risked. Or was she becoming strong enough now to weather anything her family chose to hurl her way?

Chapter Forty-three

Over six months had passed since Dan had left her. She knew herself better and had gained confidence but she was still undecided what it was she wanted to do with her life; however, she was certain a day would dawn when it would all be clear to her. Although she enjoyed a drink, she had learned to cope without the crutch of alcohol, which she now knew made matters worse and not better. She could be in the house of an evening and not jump at every noise. She had learnt to deal with the occasional downturns in her moods. Perhaps most importantly, she knew that when she felt sad and lonely it would not last.

One morning she awoke and was suddenly aware that she had moved without noticing into a stage where living alone had become the normal way of life. She was enjoying the unexpected freedom brought by having no one to consider. She said to herself that perhaps she would never again want to live with someone else. This was brave and not totally honest for at night, sometimes, she lay in bed and wondered how it would have been with Tarquin. She still had difficulty opening a bottle of wine, balancing the household budget and fumbled when changing a plug. And the spiders in the cellar remained a constant fear.

For well over a year she had been rich but she still knew little about money and how to make it work for her. She relied heavily on her advisers. And in that year she had become accustomed to having money and being able to buy whatever she wanted. The time when she had been afraid to spend, when she bought the house and her Porsche, had gone. She knew now that she need never worry again. On the other hand, she had learned caution in handling money and a healthy distrust of most schemes put her way. She had learnt that the world was full of people who

347

felt they could spend her money more wisely than she. She realized now that there was power in its possession; it could also be used unscrupulously; and, even, those who had financial good fortune could be weakened by it. For to lose her trust in family and friends was one of the saddest things that had ever happened to her.

With the arrival of summer Peggy's garden was the constant pleasure she had hoped for. She fussed about her plants like so many babies. She spent as much time as possible waging war on slugs and weeds. It was tiring work but satisfying as each day she could look at her borders and enjoy the explosion of colour she had helped create.

Perhaps regarding her plants as small children had made Peggy think of her own and of the care she had lavished upon them. Frequently she remembered Paul's parting words. She decided not to telephone Carol, as she had in the past, which had proved so unsatisfactory. It is the easiest thing in the world to be insulted on the phone. This time she drove round to Carol's new house.

As she parked the car on the new estate Carol and Sean had recently moved to, Peggy looked about her. The houses in different sizes and styles made the development look more like a village – a spanking new one, but a village all the same. There was even a pond on a green, and the houses had been positioned so that mature trees had been protected. Carol and Sean had chosen a mellow red-brick replica of a small Elizabethan house with mullioned windows. As she walked up the crazy-paving path to the front door Peggy couldn't imagine why people would want to buy a reproduction house when a few miles back she had passed several genuinely old houses for sale. Perhaps this was a cheaper way to purchase a dream. She was filling her mind with such inconsequential thoughts to try to keep at bay the nervousness, which was lurking, waiting to pounce and swamp her, make her turn and walk away, back to the peace and calm of her cottage and garden. She could just imagine her mother telling her not to be so silly, on edge at the prospect of seeing her own daughter. Easy for Myrtle to say, hard for Peggy to do. What if Carol opened the door and closed it pronto upon seeing her? She'd feel a right fool then. She rang the bell. Maybe this was a fool's errand and she would find them out. She looked at her watch: five thirty on a Saturday. They should both be in – Sean back from cricket and Carol from the shops. She'd chosen this time, this day, for she wanted Sean here: she couldn't face Carol alone, as recriminations were more likely to fly.

Sean answered the door. His face was a picture of confusion and surprise mingled with embarrassment, all tangled up with a flicker of welcome. 'Mum! Well, this is a turn-up. Thank God you've come.'

'Is Carol in?' she said, thinking his welcome a little over the top.

'Upstairs.' He held the nail-studded door wide open and she stepped into a pleasant hall in which stood a very dusty oak chest. As she followed him up the stairs she noticed that the stair-carpet could have done with a good sweep. And then, come to that, why were they going up the stairs and not to the sitting room? Was something wrong? She stopped, one foot on the next tread.

'Sean, what's the matter? Is Carol ill?'

'Dreadfully, Mum. We're waiting for the doctor now.'

'What is it?' Peggy's nervousness disappeared in a second to be replaced by concern and a different kind of anxiety.

'We don't know. I thought . . . When I saw you . . . on the doorstep, I thought you knew. That Dan had told you. Given you a bell.' Sean spoke in short bursts as if his own fears had made him unable to string a sentence together.

'No. I came because I thought it was time I sorted things out between us. I'd decided all this silliness had gone on long enough. Thank goodness I did.' Her palms were suddenly sticky, her stomach was fluttering with her apprehension, and her heart was pounding.

'In here,' said Sean. 'Darling, I've got a surprise visitor for you,' he said, in the hearty tones so often used by the healthy when speaking to the sick – the very sick, Peggy realized, and her heart plummeted.

'Mummy, oh, Mummy.' At sight of her a white-faced Carol put up a thin arm beseechingly and began to cry. Peggy quickly crossed the room and sat on the edge of the bed. She took her daughter into her arms and was immediately aware of how little there was of her to hold. Something was very wrong here.

'It's all right, Mummy's here.' She soothed her, in the time-honoured way. The years had slipped away and Carol was no longer a determined young married woman who was not speaking to her mother, she was Peggy's little girl, the one who'd been afraid of the dark. Nothing changed, not really, she thought, as she hugged Carol and wished she could make whatever it was go away or suffer it for her. She looked up at Sean. 'What's wrong with her?' she mouthed at him, in case some dreadful truth was being kept back from her daughter.

'We don't know. The . . .' He began to mouth back at her when the doorbell rang. 'That will be the doctor,' he said, and raced down the stairs two at a time.

The doctor was a small, brisk woman who looked no more than a couple of years older than Carol. She had the smug smile of one who is well pleased with herself and has no doubt that, due to her profession, she is a cut above everyone else. She was dressed in jeans and a baggy sweater with large teddy-bears knitted on it, a style of dress that did not impress Peggy, who preferred her medics older and soberly suited.

'So what have we here?' she said with evident irritation.

'I'm sorry to bother you, Doctor, but Carol's worse,' Sean apologized, motivated by the doctor's tone of voice.

'Surgery's in an hour.' Her attitude was snappy and annoyed.

'I know, I'm sorry.' Sean was worried and sheepish in equal measures.

'You surely didn't expect him to get Carol up and take her to your surgery? Just look at her.' Peggy felt compelled to interrupt.

'And you are?' The doctor looked at her questioningly.

'I'm Carol's mother, and it's obvious to me she's in no fit state to go anywhere,' Peggy said, standing up as if to affirm this statement.

'You're qualified, too?' The doctor smirked.

'Of course not, but anyone with a pea brain can see she's extremely unwell.'

'There's a lot of this around. I'll rewrite your prescription.' She opened her black bag, revealing its pristine interior, and took out her pad and a pen.

'A lot of what?' Peggy asked.

'This bug. Most of my patients who have it are managing to wrap up warm and get themselves to the surgery,' the doctor said, still miffed, while she scrawled on the pad.

'Is it the same medicine? The last lot didn't work,' Sean, apparently emboldened by Peggy's stance, dared to ask.

'No, but you have to learn patience with treatments. You can't expect overnight miracles. Give it a couple of days and she'll be feeling a lot better.' The doctor packed away her pen and pad, clicked shut her Gladstone bag, and stood up. 'Bring her to the surgery on Thursday,' she said, as she turned to leave the room.

'Hang on a minute. Aren't you going to examine her?' Peggy said from beside the bed.

'That won't be necessary. I know what's wrong with her.'

'You might not think it is, but I do. I want my daughter examined.'

'I'm sorry, Mrs . . . ?'

'Alder.'

'Mrs Alder, I don't think it is up to you to tell me what to do.' The doctor fixed Peggy with a superior steely stare, which was intended to make her wilt into submission. It had the opposite effect.

'Oh, no? Well, you listen to me, young woman.' Peggy advanced threateningly upon the doctor who took a step backwards until the closed door stopped her moving further. 'If you don't give my daughter a thorough examination I shall report you for unprofessional conduct and negligence. What is more, I don't think you have a clue what's wrong with her. You're simply treating her with words. Well, Doctor, it's not good enough. If it transpires that there is anything seriously wrong with my daughter, I shall sue you in every court in the land – and don't think I can't afford to.'

'If you insist.' With an expression of frustrated fury, as if she wanted to hit Peggy, the doctor returned to the bedside. An hour later Carol was in hospital, in the private wing, and emergency blood tests were under way.

Sean and Peggy, having stayed as long as they dared at Carol's bedside, were finally shooed away by the nurses, and lingered in the hospital car park saying their goodbyes. Both delayed getting into their cars, taking comfort from each other. Sharing their concern gave them strength. They agreed that already Carol had more colour, looked better – perhaps a tiny sparkle had returned.

'I can't thank you enough, Peggy. You were wonderful,' Sean said, and in the moonlight she was almost sure his eyes were full of tears. She smiled, not at him, but because, in his stress, he had called her Peggy for the first time. She hoped it would continue.

'It was nothing. That doctor needed talking to like that.'

'She's always the same. She hates touching people, we've all decided.'

'And she's a doctor! Ridiculous.' Peggy began to unlock her car door. 'What is she? Clairvoyant? Why didn't you get another doctor in?'

'She's the only one in the practice. I still can't get over you, though. Honestly, Peggy, I didn't know you had it in you.'

'I surprise myself sometimes,' she said, as she got into her car. 'Are you sure you don't want me to come back with you, or do you want to come to my house?'

'No, thanks, Peggy, you've been a brick. Now I know she's safe I'll crash out. I'll give you a ring in the morning.'

But was she safe? Peggy thought worriedly as she drove home in the darkness. Poor child, she had looked so desperately ill, so tiny in the hospital bed.

Back home she allowed herself a large brandy – the only way she would get to sleep. She sat in her favourite chair, her mind racing, a dozen thoughts clamouring noisily for attention. Was the hospital competent to cope? How did she find out who was the best man to care for Carol? Should she be in a big hospital in London? What if she did . . . Abruptly Peggy stood up and crossed to her desk. If she did something, wrote some letters, paid some bills, maybe the racket in her mind and the terror would subside. Among the clutter of papers she noticed her electricity bill and final reminder. Dan would have done that in the past. She was late paying everything – pathetic, she told herself. She made a mental note to go to the bank and ask them whether she could do a direct debit for things like that. She picked up the bill from her desk and, as she did so, noticed the pile of papers Lloyd had given her two Sundays ago, which she had not even bothered to look at.

Carrying her drink and the folder back to her chair she settled down to look at them, just to see how big a fool they thought her.

Ten minutes later she put them down. 'Oh, no,' she wailed to the empty room. She picked them up again. She had rowed with Flora, lost her only friend here, and for nothing!

The figures drawn up showed they intended to repay her over a ten-year period using the holiday-let rentals, and half those rentals would be hers as a partner. For security Lloyd was offering the pictures in the drawing room and a pile of Georgian silver. And she'd doubted them!

Chapter Forty-four

Peggy looked at her watch. Nearly half past ten – dare she telephone at this hour? Lloyd, she knew from Flora's moans, was very much an early-to-bed type. Would the noise of the telephone wake him? She was pretty sure that Flora would still be glued to the television or, if not, reading. She'd have to risk it. She couldn't let it rest till morning. She was agitated enough already without this and she needed some sleep. Unless she spoke to Flora sleep would be out of the question. She dialled the number quickly before she came up with some good excuse not to.

'Flora, it's me, Peggy,' she said in reply to the abrupt information that this was Flora Whittaker speaking.

'Yes? So?' Flora's expressive voice conveyed both curiosity and suspicion.

'Flora, what can I say?'

' "Sorry" might be a good start.'

Peggy was not sure how to carry on. Flora sounded so cold and angry – she could hardly blame her.

'I can say I'm sorry until the cows come home but I'll never really make amends for what I said, and for storming out as I did the other Sunday.' She paused but Flora said nothing. 'It was unforgivable of me. I overreacted. If you want to know the truth I'd been badly hurt by Tarquin. I – well . . . he'd been at my cottage since the previous Friday, and you were right. We did. All romantic and lovely and then he tries to sell me some flaming insurance thing.' She was amazed that there was still silence at the other end – it was so unlike Flora. 'I guess all that money has made me paranoid. It's something I know I've got to deal with – and quickly. Your scheme for the Mill House is nothing but fair to me and I'd been thinking . . . Oh, I'm too ashamed even to tell you what I'd been imagining.' Still there was silence. 'Are you still there, Flora?'

'Yes,' was the uncommunicative reply.

'And the last straw was seeing that creep Edward, or Daniel as you seem to know him, all cosy with his little wife.' She hadn't wanted to say that but since she was getting nowhere fast perhaps she was going to have to confess all. 'The bastard told me he wasn't married.'

'Really?' Flora spoke at last and sounded curious.

Peggy took a deep breath. 'Otherwise I would never have slept with him.' She closed her eyes as she said this as if by shutting out the world she could make the whole unfortunate incident disappear.

'You never did? How riveting. Tell me, it's rumoured he's got a huge dong, is it true?'

'Oh, Flora, really!'

'This puts an entirely different complexion on everything. I intended to disappear you from my life for being so bloody suspicious and horrible, but for gossip like this I'll forgive you anything.' Flora roared with such a loud laugh that Peggy had to hold the receiver away from her ear. 'Tell you what, come to lunch tomorrow and tell me *all the gory details*.' She spoke in a spooky voice, still bubbling with laughter. 'I always had a feeling that friend Daniel— What did you say he said his name was, Edward? That's strange, you know. That's his wife's father's name – Freudian! Well, anyhow, I always knew he was a two-timing bastard, and poor Florence is such a sweetie, and filthy rich, of course. The creep!'

'I'd love to see you, get everything sorted, but I can't. Carol, my eldest daughter, was taken to hospital this evening. I dare not leave the telephone and, in any case, I'll be visiting her, I hope, if she's not too poorly.' She had tried to sound calm and collected but 'poorly' was such a sad little word and so inadequate for the serious straits her daughter was in. She was fighting the tears and her voice emerged harsh and tense.

'What's wrong with her?'

'They're not sure. She's got a dreadful fever and if she tries to walk she falls over. She'd been treated for a flu bug, would you believe? I met her GP, an incompetent if ever I saw one.' She blew her nose, delaying what she had to say next. Illogically she felt that if she said it aloud it would come true. 'The doctor who saw her tonight . . . he couldn't be certain . . . there's a thousand tests to be done yet . . . a brain tumour,' she blurted out, and her whole body slumped with despair. There she had said it now.

'You poor old scone,' Flora said, and then the phone went dead as if they had been cut off. Just as well, thought Peggy, as she replaced the silent receiver. She felt she did not want to talk any more and, anyway, she wouldn't be able to find the words. She would probably end up crying down the telephone. She searched for her handkerchief and, not finding one, went into the kitchen for the roll of kitchen paper. She tore off a couple of sheets and blew her nose, consciously controlling herself.

Absent-mindedly she put the kettle on. Dear God, please let Carol be all right. Don't let her die. She sat on a kitchen chair. Why should God listen to her? When was the last time she had prayed or been to church? She inhaled sharply. Air caught in her throat; a groan of despair escaped into the empty kitchen. Apart from her failed mission to the village church, she had last set foot in a church at Carol's wedding. The tears she had tried to control escaped and cascaded down her cheeks. Did God mind people like her, only praying in an emergency like this? Would He listen?

She stared at the kitchen sink, the stainless-steel draining board glistening like diamonds through her tears. Why had she allowed the stupid row to escalate as it did? She knew Carol, how dim she was, how easily she took offence and then managed to multiply it into a great mountain of injustice. She was still a child. It had been up to Peggy to calm things down, to talk things through and find a solution – she was the mature one. She had failed Carol and she had failed herself. If only the split with Dan had not happened the way it did. If only her pride had not been so hurt. If only Carol and Sean had not decided to take sides. If, if, if . . . She slumped forward on to her folded arms and sobbed. Her grief was such that she did not hear the kettle whistle, the car draw up, the front doorbell ring. She looked up through tear-filled eyes only when the back door opened and Flora, in a haze of night chill, burst into the room.

'You shouldn't leave the back door open like that, I could have been anyone – a burglar, a rapist. Oh, my poor darling.' Flora stopped her lecture at sight of Peggy. 'Oh, sweetheart, it'll be all right. Come on. Christ, what a racket.' She crossed to the cooker and took the kettle off. 'It's not tea you need but a stiff drink, and don't say you're off the stuff. There's a time and a place and this is most definitely both. In any case, I need one!'

'I didn't say I was off it, just cutting down, and yes, please, I'd love a brandy. The bottle's in the sitting room.'

Peggy sat at the table, clutching her sodden wodge of kitchen paper and waited for Flora to return with the drinks.

'This is the daughter you fell out with?' asked Flora, as she banged and crashed in the dishwasher searching for two glasses.

Peggy nodded and gulped. 'Yes.' The word, becoming trapped between two sobs, emerged almost incomprehensible.

'I assume that was yes.'

Peggy nodded again and, still clutching the kitchen paper, got up, crossed the kitchen wearily and opened the cupboard containing the glasses.

'I can never remember my way round this kitchen. That's the trouble with these fitted ones – too many cupboards to make into a muddle.' Busily Flora poured large measures and placed a glass in front of Peggy, who was not responding to her chatter. 'Come on, old love. This won't do, you know. You've got to stay strong for everyone.'

At these words, Peggy lifted her head sharply, her face suddenly animated. 'That's what we always do, isn't it, us wives and mothers? Stand firm and strong. Well, I don't bloody well feel I want to. I'm not sure I'm capable of it. Oh, Flora, I'm so afraid,' she said in a panic-fuelled rush.

'And fear of fear is the worst of all. I bet you've been sitting here alone making all manner of pacts with a God you never normally believe in? Am I right?' Peggy did not answer: it was as if the last thing she had said had drained her dry for the time being. She took a mouthful of brandy and choked on the burning sensation in her throat. Flora jumped up and whacked her on the back, which only made matters worse. 'I trust you haven't been making Him any silly promises – like "I'll give all my money away if only you'll make her better"? I hope not, because when she's as right as rain you'll still feel you've got to keep to your side of the bargain just in case or something even worse comes scudding out of the skies with a Peggy-Alder label on it. It would be too silly for words.'

'You got here before I could. I was working my way up to it.' She managed a wintry smile, which encouraged Flora.

'And I suppose you've been sitting here working yourself into a lather of guilt about having the damn stuff in the first place. Thinking if you hadn't won none of this would have happened and you'd still be playing nuclear families with the unspeakable Dan?'

'Something like that, yes. You have to admit that everything in my life went well until I did win.'

'What a load of old cobblers!' Flora puffed out her cheeks and poured even larger brandies for herself and Peggy. 'That's the direct opposite of what you thought a few weeks back. Why, Lloyd and I both thought how sensible you were being in *not* blaming the money for all that had happened to you. "That's an intelligent woman thinking," I said. Now, don't go and prove me wrong, will you?'

'It's difficult not to.'

'It's all been a shock, too much of one. You'll see it clearer in the morning. And you weren't thinking of taking that creep back? Never! Don't even say it.' Dramatically, Flora clapped her hands over her ears.

'I did think it would be nice if he was here and we could share this together.'

'You phoned him?'

'He was out.'

'Thank goodness for that.'

'Oh, Flora, you don't understand. You can't possibly know how alone I feel.'

'Who's her quack?'

'Someone called Stanton, he's a senior consultant.'

'My cousin Toby's a bone-crusher. I'll give him a bell, get his advice.'

'At this time of night? Won't he mind?'

'He's used to me calling at all hours. I'll use the telephone in the drawing room – can't have the sound of your sobbing in the background. Pour us another.'

'Another?' Peggy asked. Surely she couldn't drink any more – she could never drive home. She need not have worried. Flora didn't go home. She returned from her call to tell Peggy that Toby said the only man was a Braithewaite in Harley Street and he would arrange it all, together with Carol's transfer to the private wing of University College Hospital, and also announced she had called Lloyd, who was 'awfully sorry and all that', and told him she was staying the night.

Peggy assumed she would sleep in the spare room. No. Flora insisted they slept together. 'Nothing like a cuddle when you're feeling miz.'

Peggy was falling asleep when Flora suddenly nudged her. 'There's one thing, old scone. If you hadn't won all that lolly you'd never been able to afford old Braithewaite and UCH. So there.' Peggy could imagine her putting out her tongue in the darkness like a little girl.

'You win,' she said sleepily.

Chapter Forty-five

Peggy woke, stretched lazily and enjoyed that pleasant moment between sleep and waking, neither a dream state nor yet awake, but a gentle, floating feeling, like lying on one's back in a balmy sea. She was suddenly aware of a warm shape beside her and of a knee digging into her behind. Gingerly she looked over her shoulder. Flora lay on her back taking up a good two-thirds of the bed, with her mouth open and snoring. For a second, as her sleep-soaked brain tried to work out what Flora was doing in her bed, she was blissfully ignorant of what had happened the evening before. Then it came flowing into her mind, a black, swirling horror like the darkest flood-water. Carol! She sat up with a jerk that made her head reel. Of course! The brandy. How could she have been so stupid to drink too much and at such a time? She looked at the clock. It said ten. She had overslept – the alarm had not gone off. She picked up the offending clock only to see that it had worked and she must have switched it off in her sleep. She swung her legs over the side of the bed and rested for a moment, allowing the world to regain its equilibrium, then shuffled to the bathroom. She avoided looking at her face in the mirror over the basin, dousing it instead with cold water to try to get some sense into her brain.

What on earth would Sean think of her? Flora's cousin might already have intervened and she should have warned her son-in-law first. Maybe they had already moved Carol – but surely not. Wasn't the medical profession awash with etiquette? Surely this would take time to organize. How would it be approached? She did not want the staff at this hospital upset only to find the London man refusing to take Carol on as a patient. That could be sticky. Maybe they shouldn't even contemplate moving her but leave her where she was. She sat on the loo and piled worry on top of worry. At least there was one glimmer of hope: she hadn't heard the telephone. Or would that, like the clock, have been ignored?

She threw on a dressing gown, left Flora snoring, and raced downstairs. Without waiting to switch on the coffee percolator, she quickly dialled Sean's number.

'Sean, thank goodness you're there. I overslept. Is Carol all right?'

'She had a good night's sleep. I think she looks a little better. You just caught me, Peggy. I came back to get a nightie and stuff for Carol before the ambulance comes to move her to London. Thanks for that, Peggy.'

'You don't mind my interfering? Oh, thank goodness. It was Flora who arranged it all in the middle of the night. I woke with such a start and thought what will you think of me not even consulting you?'

'The sister was a bit miffed about our moving her, but the registrar said the bloke in London was marvellous, the best in the country, and she'll be better off there. But a private ambulance? This is going to cost an arm and a leg, Peggy. We've no private insurance – silly, isn't it, me in insurance? But, well, we're so young and you don't expect anything to happen when you're young, do you? It'll take me for ever to repay you.'

'Don't be silly. I don't expect you to repay me. Whatever next? What's money for but to help those you love? Just thank heavens that I can do something.' She smiled at that. She must remember to tell Flora.

Peggy was to repeat that expression time and again during the nightmare which had begun to envelop them. Carol did have a brain tumour; whether it was benign or not could only be confirmed from a biopsy, but due to her raging fever an operation was out of the question. The virus causing the illness had to be isolated – and as quickly as possible if she was to stand a chance. Working as the doctors were, in the dark, treatment after treatment failed, and Carol's condition deteriorated rapidly.

Any family that receives the sledgehammer blow of such horrifying news seems always to turn inward, relying on its members for the emotional support necessary to help the patient and to survive themselves. Friends congregated and offered words of advice and help, but they were outside the inner circle – they had to be, for they could not begin to comprehend the agony of those in the centre, who could only stand by in a state of frustration and impotence.

Peggy rented a large flat near the hospital and Sean moved in. Dan, who had been away for a weekend's fishing, rushed up to London as soon as he received the news and joined them at the flat. Steph flew in from Athens. Poor Steph, thought Peggy, as she watched her youngest, stomach swollen now in the seventh month of her pregnancy. This should have been a happy time for her, calm and placid, not one of all this drama. She felt even sorrier for her when Steph confided how guilty she felt that she was so happy and pregnant while Carol suffered, and how afraid she was that her happiness would be punished in some way.

'Steph, if you never listen to another word I say, for goodness sake listen to me now. This is not your fault – this is fate at work. Your happiness must not be marred by unnecessary guilt. Don't get like me, larding my life with it, carrying the flaming burden with me for years.'

'It's hard, Mum,' Steph said, holding her belly as if protecting the baby from life.

'I know, sweetheart.'

'I mean, we never got on and all that. Look how we were always rowing. I thought I hated her, but now . . .'

'You find you love her? Families are funny. No doubt if the tables were turned and it was you who was ill I'd be having this conversation with Carol.' She took her daughter in her arms, trying to comfort her.

'I should never have called her a retard.'

'Probably not, but I doubt if she's holding it against you now.' Peggy released her. 'And if you think you should feel guilty, how do you think I feel? I should have patched things up with her months ago. Rows left to smoulder are dangerous. And now . . .'

362

She felt the tears that were never far from the surface pricking her eyes, demanding to be released. 'Still, this won't do. Let's get you sorted out,' she said briskly. 'Do you mind sharing a room with me? There are twin beds so we needn't kick each other.'

'But Dad?'

'He's in the single down the hall,' Peggy said, with a set to her mouth that brooked no argument.

Myrtle arrived, thankfully on a cheap day-return. 'Well, this is nice,' she said, settling herself into an armchair after visiting Carol in the hospital. Peggy was pouring tea and Steph came into the sitting room with a pile of toasted crumpets. 'Just like old times, isn't it? This is how everything should be, the family united.'

Peggy concentrated on her teapot, Dan looked out of the window. Sean handed round the cups and sugar.

'I hope all that separation nonsense is over between you two, and that you've come to your senses, Peggy.'

'Oh, yes, Mum, I've done that,' Peggy said with feeling, neatly skating over the question. Myrtle seemed to accept her reply and concentrated on her tea.

'Are there enough for me to have two crumpets? Your gran's very partial to a crumpet,' Myrtle said sweetly to Steph. 'What do you think Carol's chances are?' she demanded suddenly, taking them all by surprise. Sean dropped his teaspoon.

'I'm sure she'll be fine. Her temperature is coming down, and they think they might be able to operate in a day or two. Then we'll know,' Peggy said in a relentlessly bright voice, looking anxiously at Sean who, with the strain of the last few days, was looking as if he, too, would soon be hospitalized.

'A friend of mine had the same – dead in three months, she was,' Myrtle announced before finishing off her crumpet. Sean set down his cup with a clatter and raced from the room. 'Where's he gone?' Myrtle looked up.

'Mum, really! Do you have to be so insensitive? The boy is beside himself with worry. What a thing to say!'

'I didn't say it would happen to Carol, of course it won't, a strong girl like her. I was just telling you about my friend. I thought you might be interested.'

'Well, we're not,' Peggy said emphatically.

'Have you thought to let Paul know?' Myrtle helped herself to another crumpet.

'Of course we have. We call him every day with progress reports.' Peggy tried to keep her irritation under control.

'I should think this place is costing you a pretty penny. Just look at those curtains – swags and tassels like that don't come cheap.'

'It works out less than a hotel for us all,' Peggy answered wearily.

'I'd have thought you'd have sent Paul the fare to come. She is his sister, after all.'

'You do that when people are dying, you stupid old bitch!' Dan shouted, and he in turn raced from the room.

'What on earth's got into everyone?' Myrtle was affronted.

'You have, Mother. Are you enjoying all this – enjoying upsetting people? Are you getting a kick out of it? Do you *like* being so morbid, torturing people?'

Myrtle hauled herself to her feet and collected her handbag. 'I never came here to be insulted, I must say. You do talk rubbish sometimes, Peggy. Of course I'm not enjoying myself. I happen to love my granddaughter, which is more than can be said for you. I don't understand how Dan wants you back with your spiteful mind.'

'Let's get one or two things straight here, Mum. Dan and I are not back together. And,' Peggy held up her hand to stop her mother interrupting, 'before you say it, you're wrong, it's me, I won't have him back.'

'Then you're mad, a good man like him. Still, I'm obviously not wanted here. If you could come with me, Steph, and help your poor old gran get a taxi.' She pointedly didn't kiss Peggy goodbye as she left the apartment.

'Heavens, I didn't know Gran was capable of being so horrible. What got into her?' Steph asked, when she returned from her errand.

'I think maybe she's finally got bored with pretending to be the sweet grey-haired granny to the rest of the world. I'm rather relieved she has. Now you'll all understand what I'm dealing with.' Peggy grinned.

Jean came, and was a tower of strength. For her they pulled out the put-u-up in the sitting room. She spent a lot of time with Steph, and Peggy could see the young woman relax visibly. Not once did she pry into Dan and Peggy's affairs, but accepted what they had decided without question.

'How's the guilt?' she asked Peggy one night when, the others in bed, they were sitting on Jean's bed having a mug of cocoa and looking at the latest batch of Paul's photographs of his family.

'I believe it's getting controllable. At least I query it now. Why do I feel like this? I ask myself. Be gone, I say when I'm feeling particularly strong,' she asserted.

'Poor Peggy. This must have been an awful blow.'

'Do you know, Jean, in a funny way I'd been waiting for it. I've been so lucky, three kids all fine, two perfect grandchildren. You hear such tragic stories. What was so special about us that, apart from measles and things like that, nothing serious had ever happened? How long could my luck last?'

'Dear Peggy, all mothers think like that.'

'Do they?' She looked surprised at this: she'd been certain this had been her burden alone. 'Then I'm being silly?'

'No, just normal. Grans have a bit of the same problem too, you know. And the nasty thing about life, I've always discovered, is that just as things are going smoothly something comes along and throws a spanner in the works.'

'Like God is saying, "Don't take too much for granted." '

'Oh, God, I haven't a lot of time for Him. He seems to have a perverted sense of humour, if you ask me.'

'Oh, Jean, don't talk like that. I mean . . .' Peggy's voice trailed off.

'What? I mustn't say what I think because at my age it won't be long and I'll be meeting Him – in person so to speak?' Jean chuckled. 'Well, if I do get to heaven I shall say the same to Him. I've never believed in saying anything about anyone that you're not prepared to say to their face.'

'I've no doubt you'll get to heaven, and I can just imagine you giving Him a piece of your mind.' Peggy laughed, too, and it felt strange. 'Gracious, that's the first time I've really laughed since all this blew up. It feels odd.'

'As if you shouldn't?'

'Well, yes.'

'There you go again – G-U-I-L-T. What are we going to do with you, Peggy?' Jean looked at her affectionately. 'And what are *you* going to be doing, Peggy – with your life, I mean?'

'I don't know for sure. I've spent my life thinking, You must do something. The last few months I've thought of buying myself a business, or going back to college to finish all those courses I started and never finished. And you know what, Jean, I don't think I could confess this to another soul, but I'm beginning to think, Why can't I just do nothing? Just try to enjoy myself – be happy, if I'm lucky.'

'At last! Now you're talking sense.' Jean clapped gleefully.

'Just look at Carol, the poor kid. All she's ever wanted was to have babies. Instead she's always having to work. If she gets through this I'll make damn sure she can have as many babies as she wants.'

'After all that's gone before?'

'You know Carol. She and her daddy . . .' Peggy laughed again but this time it did not feel so strange.

'You're a good woman, Peggy.'

'Oh, get away with you, Jean. I'm not. They're my kids, that's all.'

Chapter Forty-six

The agony of waiting was over. Carol's mysterious fever had abated of its own accord and she had been wheeled off to her operation. The time she spent in the theatre and afterwards, when the family were waiting for the results of the biopsy, was, without doubt, the worst.

The tumour was benign.

It took a long walk in Hyde Park and several hours wandering aimlessly in the streets of London for Peggy to adjust to this state of affairs. She had been worried sufficiently long for it to have become part of her life. She felt unsure of herself, unsure if she dare believe that Carol would be all right. Afraid that if she did it might prove wrong. Without it, a void was opening inside her and what would fill it became another fear.

She began to look for a church. She had done no bargaining, as Flora had feared but, on the other hand, God, if He was there, had certainly come up trumps. What was wrong in her finding a church just to say a polite thanks?

The church she eventually entered wasn't peaceful and quiet like the one at home, surrounded, as it was, on all sides by its graveyard and sheltered by large, centuries-old trees. This one, set in the heart of the City, was filled with the rumble of the traffic outside, the tramp of tourists' feet. In the Lady chapel a party of French teenagers giggled away their boredom. But for all that, sitting quietly in the pew, Peggy felt a sudden peace, a tranquillity that had been missing from her life for some time – since long before Carol's illness, she worked out. While it was pleasurable, and a relief, it also made her wonder if she had spent all the previous years of her life being wrong about God. If that was the case, then she'd have to negotiate with Him to agree to her talking to Him in her own house or garden. One thing was clear, she could never face going to church – not in the village. That one attempt had been enough for her; she could not bear the self-satisfied, snobby clique who made up the congregation, and she had no need, or desire, to become one of their number. In the past, had she been confusing the Church of England with God? Perhaps He thought there was room for improvement, too. For how could God be a snob, worried about status and its symbols, like houses and cars, and how people dressed? She was not alone in thinking this way. Hadn't she heard Myrtle say often enough, 'There's more sinners in church than out.' Perhaps He would understand how confused she felt; maybe they could work something out between them.

The sun was shining as she emerged into the bustling street. She was momentarily blinded after the darkness of the interior and could not see who was calling her name from the other side of the street. 'Peggy, it's me! Hang on.'

She might not be able to see, but she recognized the voice. She stopped walking and waited, aware of a change in her heartbeat. 'Hello, Tarquin,' she said, wishing she was anywhere but here, as if she had been caught doing something not quite nice. He bent and pecked her on the cheek.

'I thought I saw you go into the church. I lurked about for a bit but when you didn't mosey out I presumed I'd missed you. I'm so glad I didn't. Fancy a drink?' He smiled his slightly crooked smile which she found so attractive.

She meant to say no, but instead she said yes.

They entered a wine bar, dark, musty and noisy. 'Red or white?' he asked.

'Red would be lovely.'

'Claret or burgundy?'

She made a face. 'I haven't the foggiest – the one with the long neck.'

Sitting waiting for him to return from the bar she took time to look about her and registered that she must be the oldest person there. The place was full of the young, winding down from a day's work, she assumed. She felt suddenly drab and dowdy against all the bright, short-skirted young women, aware that she hadn't any make-up on – in fact, hadn't bothered with it the whole time Carol had been in hospital. Judging by the number of people he greeted and who said hello to him, Tarquin was on familiar territory. Watching him, she knew for certain what a fool she had been over him. It would never have worked: this was his environment, these were his friends, she was years too old for him. It was one thing to know this, quite another to deal with it when she could see him and know she still wanted him.

'You look dour. Ten p for them – inflation.' Tarquin grinned as he plonked a bottle and two glasses on to the table.

'We can't drink all that.'

'We can give it a try. I'm game if you are.'

'Oh, Tarquin, it is nice to see you again.' She gazed at him.

'Thanks for that, I thought you might hit me with a blunt instrument.'

'Too much of importance has happened since then. I can't hold a grudge.'

'Poor darling. Is that why you have such a doomy look?'

'No, it wasn't for that. I felt old. Everyone here is so young.'

'I suppose they are. Never given it much thought. I like it, and the plonk is good and cheap.' He filled her glass.

'How old are you, Tarquin?'

'If I said forty, would you believe me?'

'No, not for a minute.'

'Ah, well. I'm thirty-eight – and three-quarters,' he added seriously, and it reminded her of the children when they had always insisted on their important half or three-quarters on their age. 'Why?'

'Just curious – or nosy, if you prefer.' She had been right. Eight years – it was too big a gap. What would the children have had to say about that – and Myrtle? At that thought she smiled.

'What's the joke? Care to share it?'

'It's nothing. I was thinking of my mother – it made me want to laugh.'

'I always want to cry when I think of mine.' He grinned, and then the grin disappeared as quickly as it had come and he looked serious. Such a demeanour did not suit him. He reminded her of a small boy who has been caught out and is trying to appear grown up. 'I heard about your daughter. I'm awfully sorry. Grim.' He shuddered, and topped up their glasses.

'She'll be fine now. The tumour wasn't malignant.'

'Hence the church. Thanking the old codger upstairs?'

'Something like that, I suppose. It's been hell – a sort of hell.'

'Then it helps, doesn't it, to have a natter with God? Sorts the mind out, gets everything back in its right place again. A good dollop of medicine for the spirit.'

'Why, yes!' She knew she looked at him with a surprise which was less than polite.

'I often pop in and say a prayer or two.'

'So you believe in God?'

'Believe in Him? I rely on Him! What with the messes I seem to get into.' Though they both laughed they also understood and Peggy wondered how long you had to know Tarquin before he dropped the clownish, undergraduate façade behind which he hid when facing the world.

Tarquin asked her this and that and, as before, he made her relax. Soon she was telling him about her fears, the terrors that had haunted her in the past weeks. He took hold of her hand and squeezed it. At his touch she felt a familiar, dangerous jolt.

'It's over now, sweetie. You can relax. You know, hearing you talk of something as awful as this happening to one of your children, makes me think it's probably why I always knew I didn't want to be a parent. I would never be able to deal with such trauma.'

'Is that why you've not married?' And then she added, 'Yet,' purposefully.

'I've never felt the need, let alone met the right woman. Or maybe no one wanted me. I used to get lonely but not any more. If I've got a cold I think how miserable I am, and wouldn't it be nice to have someone look after me? But then I go and see Flora, married to that miserable old sod Lloyd, and I think maybe I'm better by myself.'

'I've never found Lloyd miserable. I rather like him.'

'Takes all types.' He shrugged his shoulders. 'You'd have to live with Lloyd to know him as he really is. He's got a good line in social graces, which ends the minute he shuts the front door on his guests.'

'My mother's just the same. The world thinks she's such a sweet person—'

'And the family knows differently?'

'Actually it's me who knows what she's really like but I'm living in hopes that the others are learning.' She paused. 'Why did you say Flora was grasping and for me to watch out for her?'

''Cause she is, she gobbles people up if she can get away with it. She needs people to fuss over and boss. She'll gobble *you* up as quick as a wink.'

'I wish you'd made yourself clearer. I nearly lost her as a friend. You fuelled my paranoia. I thought she was about to cheat me. We had the most dreadful row.' She was embarrassed confessing this.

'Sorry, didn't mean to.' He put his arm round her shoulders. 'I didn't mean to do a lot of things. I mean, I loved that weekend, I still dream about it. I didn't want you to think I was after you to invest in some scheme. I was just worried about you. I don't even sell the bloody things, I have a friend who does – and I was worried about him, too. He's desperate for some business – his wife's pregnant, you see.' His open face creased with a frown. 'I really blew it, didn't I? Any chance . . . ?' One eyebrow was raised in question. She found him so attractive when he did that. Peggy felt her pulse race. How easy it would be. How exciting, and fulfilling. But what would the children say? How Dan and her mother would laugh.

Instead she said, 'Maybe it was just as well you did. The way that weekend shaped up, it probably saved us both a lot of grief later.' She looked at her watch. 'Good heavens! Is that the time? I must get back. My family will be wondering where I've got to.' The last thing she wanted to do was to leave him, but she must. She did not trust herself to stay.

'I thought you'd given up on your family?'

'Does one ever?' She grimaced as she stood up to go.

'Can I see you back to wherever you're staying?'

'That's kind, but it won't be necessary. Thanks for the wine.' She bent down to kiss him on the cheek.

'I wish you wouldn't go, Peggy. There's so much still to say,' he said appealingly as he stood up.

'What?'

'There's stuff to straighten out – you and me.'

'Oh, Tarquin, just look about you.' She nodded at the crowd milling around the bar, the young women with their equally young men.

'I don't know what you mean.'

'I'll explain another time. Bye.'

'Promise there'll be another time,' he called after her, but she slipped through the throng and did not answer him.

In the taxi she felt not only that the burden of worry over Carol had lifted but she felt happy too. A rather light-headed happiness, which she could put down to the effect of the wine but, of course, it might also have been because of the hour she had just spent with Tarquin. He was, after all, one of those people who exuded good humour, who made one feel better from just being in his presence. If only she could keep their relationship to that of good friends. Anything else, in view of the age difference, was out of the question, she thought regretfully, as the cab drew up outside her rented flat.

Chapter Forty-seven

After what seemed like weeks but only involved a couple of visits, Myrtle agreed a date for her move to Dan and Peggy's old house. Helping to pack the accumulation of fifty years took an incredible amount of Peggy's time. It was not a happy experience either, for there were too many memories for Myrtle to pass over lightly. Hours were spent listening to her reminisce as an ornament, picture, a long-forgotten postcard caught behind a mirror, or the inscription in a book suddenly jogged her mind and made it scuttle back into the past.

During this process Peggy learnt a lot about her parents that perhaps she'd have preferred not to know. The father she had worshipped, and for whom she had only ever felt sorrow, turned out to have been quite the womanizer. Myrtle had let it slip when a faded group photograph of a coach trip to Cromer fell out of the back of an old copy of Mrs Beeton.

'See that smirking bitch there.' Myrtle stabbed the photo with one stubby finger. 'Ida Trewin – thought herself a cut above the rest of us since she lived in a semi-detached by the park. She'd set her cap at your father. That day it was disgusting the play she made for him.'

'What happened?'

'Oh, she got him. They usually did. The problem with your father was he never worked out that his fly buttons were for keeping the disgusting thing in, not just for taking it out.' She snorted her disdain for matters sexual.

'But you never said, Mum.'

'What would be the point? It was nobody else's business 'cept ours,' she said, with the determined set of her mouth that Peggy knew so well. 'Still, Ida had a terrible life I'm pleased to say –

married a right bugger of a husband, who kept her short of everything including the how's-your-father.' She sniggered at that. 'Then she died young. Good riddance, say I.'

'Mum, you're supposed to forgive.'

'Forgive? Me? Never! I believe in revenge. It's a very sweet dish, especially when eaten cold.'

'Were there many like Ida?'

'Too many, that's why we were always so short of cash when you were kids. Having a bit on the side is a rich man's sport, not for the likes of him. I told him enough times but would the selfish sod listen? Never.'

'But then, Mum, if you didn't like sex, what was he to do?' Peggy hated to hear her speak in this way of the father she had loved and cast around desperately for any form of defence.

'I liked sex well enough. It was your father. He was no bloody good at it. Wham, bam, thank you, mam. Would you put up with that? Of course you wouldn't. Better off without was my motto.'

Peggy forbore to ask her how she knew that it was bad. 'Shall we do this one?' She lifted a cardboard shoe box from the back of her mother's wardrobe on to her bed. 'What have we here?'

'Memories.' Myrtle said softly as she picked up a pile of letters tied with a faded ribbon. 'What do you think of him?' She thrust at Peggy a photograph of a handsome young man in the uniform of a naval rating.

'He's very good-looking. Who is he?' But even as she asked the question she already knew the answer.

'I'd have married him, got a divorce from your father, and all the hassle that would have caused in those days – divorce was frowned on then. But he didn't come back from the war. So that was that. I only ever fancied him.'

'Oh, Mum.' Quickly Peggy put her arm around her mother's shoulders, noticing for the first time that she was a lot thinner than she once had been.

'I met him a year after marrying your father. It was love at first sight. I'd never felt like that about your dad. All jelly-like inside when I thought I was going to see him. Your dad was away at sea, and in those days, what with the war and the bombing, you never knew how long you'd got to live and so we did it.

Here.' Gently she stroked the crocheted bedcover. 'You needn't look all shocked. Yours isn't the only generation to get up to a bit of hanky-panky.'

'I'm not shocked, Mum, I'm sad. I'd no idea you were so unhappy with Dad. I didn't know he was a philanderer. It makes everything so much clearer.' She looked at the hopeful face of the young sailor. She was glad he did not know how his Myrtle had turned out, how bitter and twisted she was. God, what people did to each other, she thought, sadly.

'Why did you stay with Dad?'

'Where was there to go? And your brother came along, and then you. Then I was trapped. Who'd have taken me on with two brats in tow? So I stuck it out – for the duration, as they say.'

'Mum, do you really want to move?' she asked.

'Of course I do. It's time I lived in a nice, convenient, modern house. Nearer you lot, too. What makes you ask that?'

'Well, all your memories are here. Maybe you don't want to leave them. Maybe I've been wrong to insist.'

'Memories are in here,' she tapped her head, 'not in bricks and mortar. We'd best get started on that case over there. And don't drop it. Good God, Peggy, you are clumsy, always was.' The older woman fussed and fretted over an old cardboard attaché case, which was also filled with papers. She sat back, a pile of them in her hands. 'Why? Don't you want me to move to your old house?' Myrtle looked up at Peggy, her small brown eyes alert and suspicious.

'I didn't say that. I just wondered . . .'

'That's what the question implied.'

'It did no such thing, Mum.'

'It did to me. Want to hang on to it, perhaps, and sell it? Make even more money for yourself.'

'Mum, really! You can be so exasperating. I was concerned for you, can't you believe that?' Peggy spoke slowly, with an exaggerated patience that she knew was rapidly wearing thin.

'With difficulty. It would be the first time.'

Peggy inwardly sighed but did not bother to answer. What was the point? 'I'll go and make us some tea,' she said, jumping to her feet, wanting to get away from her mother if only for a few minutes. And people wondered how grannies could get themselves battered, she thought grimly, as she ran down the narrow stairs.

That was the first and, it would seem, the last time she was to be permitted to see the soft, sentimental side of her mother. It was as if Peggy had seen her mother through a window, just for a tiny moment, and had a peek at what might have been. But the curtains had been sharply pulled across and they were soon back to Myrtle's normal carping. In a way, Peggy felt more at ease with the bad-tempered, nagging mother than the sad, dreamy one. And at the back of her mind lurked the image of her father: she found what her mother had said so hard to believe. But, then, who ever knew anyone totally? Hadn't she found that out with Dan?

Had there been a time, just a few short months ago, when Peggy did not know how to fill the hours of the day? When she had worked at the shop she had found it a struggle to fit everything in. But now, as she took on more and more, she discovered a strange phenomenon: the more she did, the more she was able to do. That was odd, she thought. Of course, as a result, she was in a perpetual rush. The great advantage was that she could keep all silly mooning about Tarquin at bay. She tried to get to see Carol, who was home now and convalescent, at least once a day. Sean had given up his job temporarily to look after her but she was not the easiest of patients and he needed the breaks that Peggy's visits gave him, even if it just meant he could pop out for a pint.

'Men are impossible, aren't they, Mum? Always down the pub.'

'You can hardly say that of Sean. He's an angelic husband.'

'You don't know the half of it,' Carol said ominously.

'Shall I peel the potatoes for your supper?' Peggy asked, not wishing to get into an argument with her daughter over her husband.

There was a restlessness about Carol that worried Peggy. She never seemed able to sit still, and roamed the house, tidying the tidy, dusting the dusted. Peggy sensed a discontent in her, as if her illness had made her look at her life and find she didn't like it. To help, Peggy told her of her plan to help them with their mortgage so Carol need never work again and could concentrate on having the family she longed for.

'I don't want babies. I can't think of anything worse than constantly being pregnant and ugly,' was her response, much to Peggy's surprise.

'You never used to say that. You were desperate to start a family, if I remember correctly.'

'I can change my mind, can't I?' Carol said shrewishly.

'Well, it's all a bit sudden. But if that's all that's worrying you, you needn't. I'm sure you wouldn't be ugly – pregnancy can make some women look beautiful. Look at how wonderful Steph looked.'

'Gross, more like. I'd much rather have a car.' She looked slyly at Peggy, unaware how transparent she was, like a child who thinks it's outsmarting an adult.

While helping her mother and visiting Carol, Peggy was also engrossed with Flora and Lloyd on the conversion of the Mill House. Lloyd had enlisted a new architect – of Edward there was no sign and he was never mentioned, not even by Flora – whose plans had been finalized and passed, and work was starting.

'Peggy, we've been talking, Lloyd and myself. Neither of us is any good at wallpapers, colours, that sort of thing – just look at this place. We've never really had to choose stuff, we always inherited the lot. You wouldn't fancy doing that side of it, would you? Look how nice you've got your cottage. We'd just make a pig's ear of it.'

'I'll have a go, but I've never thought I was any good at interiors. The cottage sort of told me what it wanted.'

'There, exactly. Just as I said to Lloyd. The woman's a born interior decorator.'

'You should have seen my other house. You wouldn't have said that then.'

'That was different. You never had time before, now you do. And don't forget, you had others imposing their taste and opinions on you. You probably listened to them which, of course, can be fatal. Left to your own devices, I think you're a whizz at it.'

With such faith backing her, Peggy soon found herself in a happy welter of paint, wallpaper, fabric samples, and began to find confidence and to believe that maybe she was quite good at putting things together. So much so that she dreaded the project coming to an end. What was she to do then? She suggested to the Whittakers that they set up a company converting old houses: Lloyd was good at seeing the potential and getting architects to realize his ideas and she would do the interiors.

'And what about me?' Flora demanded.

'Obvious. You keep us enthused and you landscape the gardens.'

That week they formed their company – at Flora's insistence it was called Second Chance. 'Something we should all have,' Flora said, as they raised their glasses to toast the new venture.

'I'll drink to that.'

'If you'd see my brother – instead of avoiding him – then you might get one.'

'I'm not avoiding him but between my mum, daughter and you I don't have much time left over for any socializing.' Although she joked, it was true. She was avoiding him. He called her often on the phone and she enjoyed talking to him, but she always turned down his suggestions that they meet, no matter what promises he made not even to touch her. She was frightened of the effect he had on her, and the disappointment that might lie ahead if she allowed their relationship to return to that of lovers.

Chapter Forty-eight

With Carol on the way to recovery, Myrtle finally moved and settled in, the Mill House nearly finished and a new property not yet bought, Peggy thought if she was ever to take a break, now was the time. Seeing Tarquin in the wine bar had shaken her far more than she had at first realized. Even keeping as busy as she had, thoughts of him constantly intruded. Nothing was helped by his constant telephone calls and, as much as she enjoyed them, she knew how vulnerable they made her, how close she often was to agreeing to see him. Carol had been through so much recently – her illness, the break-up of her parents' marriage – that it was too soon to expect her to accept her mother with another man, and especially a younger one. Steph might have been able to deal with it, but Peggy knew Carol too well: what her friends would think was important to her. If Peggy was to maintain the new calm relationship she had with her daughter, any silly thoughts she had about Tarquin had to remain that – thoughts. It was not so hard a choice, she told herself frequently. After all, what could be more important than how one's family saw one? Anyway, as she had lectured herself time and time again, it was an affair that was doomed. The eight years between them could never be eradicated as any other problem could. She should get right away, if only to protect herself from her own foolishness.

Where to go was decided for her when Nigel called to say that Steph had gone into labour. Peggy, who had never flown in her life and whose experience of 'abroad' amounted to a long-ago day-trip to France with Dan, ventured off to Athens and, admittedly with some difficulty, took a boat to Steph's island.

The ferry-boat, yawing drunkenly on the aquamarine-coloured water of the Aegean Sea, approached the island. She shaded her eyes against the intense glare of the sun which, even in September, was painfully bright, until she could make out the little white houses with their blue shutters clustered together as if for comfort against the sea, and sheltered by olive-covered hills. At that moment she understood why Steph had wanted to come back here to stay.

Nigel, changed now from boy to man with his added responsibilities, was waiting for her on the quay. She hardly knew him, had met him only twice, and did not know quite how to greet him. Even if he was her son-in-law, kissing seemed a bit over the top. And then she thought how formal she could be, how middle class and restrained, and threw her arms about him, pressing a kiss on his cheek. She laughed at his surprise and gave him another for good measure. Later he asked Steph if her mother drank.

Seeing her youngest child – who, in Peggy's eyes was still that, a child – holding her own baby, was a moving experience.

'I can't believe it,' she said. 'You with a son of your own.'

'Don't get damp, Mum. It comes to us all.'

'I'm not crying, but if I do they'll be happy tears. Happy for you and the baby and Nigel and me.'

'But you've been a gran before.'

'Yes, I have, haven't I?' She did not say what she was thinking – she did not want to be unfair, to show any favours – but this time was different from when she had seen Candice holding *her* baby. This was Peggy's daughter, that child had grown within Steph, within Peggy's own flesh and blood. There was a huge difference. Lance she had grown to love, this baby she would immediately die for.

She stayed two weeks on the island, not with Steph but putting up in the local hotel.

'We've plenty of room, Mum. Stay with us.'

'No, this is a very special time in your lives. The three of you should be alone as much as possible to get to know one another.' She would have liked to spend every waking minute with her grandson – Alex, named in honour of the country of his birth – but she rationed herself, only appearing at around noon and leaving at six. She dined in the local tavernas, sat of an evening in Steph and Nigel's bar watching the passing scene, walked on the beach, and flirted with the Greek men – but that meant nothing.

She could not fault Nigel. Steph had chosen well. Not only did he work hard in the business but he was a tower of strength at home with the baby. Steph had been right and she wrong: men willing to live as truly equal with their wives did exist.

When she left it was with promises that she would return before six months were up, but it was still a wrench to go.

The trip had whetted her appetite. All timidity about travelling solo had disappeared, and with so many new experiences and images to keep her occupied she found her longing for Tarquin was more easily kept under control. She could go whole days now and not think of him – well, hardly! She wanted to see Paul, her grandson and the new baby, making it fair and square in a silly way. Emboldened now, as soon as she landed at Heathrow from Greece, she booked a flight for Australia the following week. She just had time to check that all was well with Second Chance, managed not to talk about Tarquin with Flora, cleaned and aired her house, washed and pressed her clothes and was off again.

As she settled in her seat on the plane she could not understand various friends' complaints or fear of flying – she loved it. Of course, she thought, as the stewardess fussed over her, travelling first class might have something to do with it.

Australia was welcoming, beautiful, but not a place she wanted to tarry. The impression she had as Paul drove her around was that it was too big. Beyond the lovely, sophisticated city lay an untamed, unforgiving and frightening wilderness. She could never forget it was there, and its presence made her feel uneasy. Perhaps one should come here first when young and unafraid of anything. She told Paul this, but he scoffed at her fancies and then she knew she had been right.

This was not to say she did not enjoy the month with Paul, she did. It gave her infinite pleasure to see him so happy, so comfortably settled, and him and Candice once more in love with each other. She was sad to say goodbye to them but she did not feel the same wrench she had felt at leaving Steph's island. Had it been the island, or was it Steph? She refused to contemplate such a thought for then everything she had ever claimed about herself as a mother would be false. At the airport, however, she told Paul she would be making this an annual trip now, and was astonished by the ease with which she could say this when, for other people, it was a once-in-a-lifetime trip.

On the return flight she stopped off in Hong Kong and Singapore. She enjoyed shopping but nothing prepared her for the scale of products here, the endless choice. On her last day she called Flora from her hotel. 'The shops here are amazing. It's given me an idea. Why don't we open one of our own?' she said excitedly, after they had both agreed how close she sounded, and weren't modern telecommunications marvellous and what was the weather like where the other one was.

'What sort of shop?' asked Flora.

'One selling lovely things for the home. Jade, vases, ornaments, carvings and fabrics, furniture, even. Everywhere I look there are things I long to own. What do you think?'

'Great idea. Who'd run it though? Neither of us has the time, not with Second Chance. I certainly don't want to be tied to shop-hours and you'd be mad to go back to that,' Flora, always practical, commented.

'We can get a manageress in.'

'And what about the buying and importing side? It sounds jolly glam now but I bet the travelling might pall after a bit. What about your garden?'

'I suppose you're right.' Peggy could see her plan being squashed at its inception.

'How about Tarquin? It's right up his street,' Flora asked, and Peggy recognized she was trying to sound nonchalant and failing. For all that, despite the miles which separated them, Peggy felt her heart give a traitorous flip at the mention of his name.

'Isn't he too busy with his wine-importing business?' She congratulated herself that she had instilled a lack of interest into her voice.

'Absolutely dire! Gone down the tubes, like everything he does. Come to think of it, I'm not so sure we want my brother involved – he's absolutely the kiss of death to any business,' Flora bellowed down the line.

'With us involved he could only succeed,' Peggy said, unaware how confident she sounded, already forgetting how she would never have spoken in such a way barely a few months ago. And then she realized what she had said and how awful it would be to be in constant contact with Tarquin, seeing him often, knowing any relationship was doomed. She shook her head defiantly. 'We could always advertise for an agent. I bet we'd get loads of replies. Maybe I should delay my return, see what I can sort out this end.'

'No, don't do that,' Flora said quickly – too quickly, Peggy thought. 'I need you here. There's a wonderful property I want you to see.'

Peggy was suspicious. They did not need her there; they had arranged that any property they found could be bought without her go-ahead – she trusted them implicitly now after seeing the meticulous accounts that Lloyd kept for her. Flora was up to something, match-making, no doubt, and since it had been she who had mentioned Tarquin and not Peggy, it must be something to do with him. Well, she could plan away. It would not get her anywhere.

On the long flight back, when she was settled with her champagne and the latest copy of *Chic* magazine, the stewardess approached her diffidently. She smiled apologetically. Peggy gave her an encouraging look. 'Yes?' she asked, when the woman didn't seem to be going to say anything.

'Mrs Alder, I do hope you won't think this an infernal cheek but there's a young journalist back in Economy . . . well, actually, she's my kid sister – Josie Kingston. She's trying to make a go as a freelance but it's tough. So, she wondered if she might have a word with you?'

'Me? What on earth for?'

'An interview.'

'But after all this time?'

'I'm sure people are still interested in you, Mrs Alder. I know my mother is. When she sees the new lottery winners, it reminds her that she'd love to know what happened to you and your lovely family – you were the same age, with the same number of children, you see. You stuck in her memory in a way the others haven't. I'm sure she's not the only one who has remembered you.'

'Why not, then? For your mother.' And why not? she thought,

as she waited. It was only a matter of time until it got into the tabloids that she and Dan were divorcing. She could imagine the meal they'd make of it. Would it not be better if she let it be known in her own way? At least she could meet the journalist first: if she liked her she would talk to her; if not she'd finish reading her magazine.

'This is very kind of you, Mrs Alder. I know you don't like giving interviews. But it would mean so much to me if I could talk to you.' Peggy had been joined by the journalist. She was tiny, with a mass of black hair, large expressive grey eyes, a lovely face, and she looked sixteen. She wore large imitation-horn-rimmed spectacles; Peggy wondered if she hoped they made her look serious and older. If so, they failed on both counts. They merely made her more appealing. Peggy liked her instantly.

They had soon talked about her children and what they were doing, what she was now doing, and then Peggy forced herself to tell of the breakdown of her marriage. 'Would you blame the money for that?' Josie asked, sipping her First Class champagne.

'No. All the money has done is make me see things more clearly. And it's given me a luxury denied most divorced or separated women of my age – independence, the wherewithal to look at the reality of my life and say, okay, that's how it is, but I can manage.'

'So you don't regret winning?'

'No way!' Peggy said emphatically. 'Because of the win, I've had the thrill of helping my children out. When my daughter had a suspected brain tumour I was able to pay for the best advice and immediate attention. I don't have to worry about bills as I used to. I can travel the world on a whim. Honestly, Josie, I'd rather be a middle-aged woman with my winnings in the bank than with nothing, becoming bitter and seeing how much I can screw out of an erring husband.' She laughed merrily at that.

'And have you lost many friends? You know, through jealousy, that sort of thing.'

Peggy looked out of the window at the duvet of cloud beneath her. Hazel sprang to mind. Just the thought of her spoilt the moment. 'Those friends I lost weren't true friends in the first place,' she said, and young and inexperienced as she was, Josie was bright enough to pick up the thin trace of sadness and bitterness in her voice.

Peggy stopped off in London for a few days to do some shopping. She resisted the urge to telephone Tarquin. She finally returned from her travels to a garden leafless and sodden in a damp, foggy November. It was going to need a lot of attention and how to fit in the work would need thought. What had happened to her dream of doing nothing? There was a pile of mail and Flora was soon on the telephone to say she had found a new house for them to look at, sixteenth-century and a wreck – in other words perfect.

'Saw the article in the *Mail*. Super. Lovely picture of you, too. Where was that taken?'

'In Greece. I gave it to Josie, the reporter. She wanted to send photographers here, but I didn't want that. A picture of me at home might give a clue to where I live – and that would only lead to more begging letters, and I find them impossible to deal with. When was it in? Can you save it for me?'

'Yesterday, I think, or was it the day before? But I've got it, I just managed to stop Nanny using it in the cat litter – such an ephemeral thing, fame!' Flora laughed loudly at this. 'Who's the fellow?'

'What fellow?'

'In the picture – dishy, dark-haired Romeo-type ogling you.'

'Oh, no!' Peggy groaned. 'That was Steph's barman – randy little so-and-so, all of twenty-two. I asked Josie to cut him out.'

'Well, they haven't. They imply he's a bit of a special friend, if you get my drift.'

'No! Can I sue, do you reckon?'

'I wouldn't bother. If everyone lands up thinking that at your age you can pull a gorgeous hunk like that, it's a bloody compliment.'

Carol did not agree with Flora. The next day, when Peggy arrived with the presents she had brought back for them, she found her daughter incandescent with rage.

'You've got a nerve!' was her welcoming shot while Peggy was still standing on the doorstep. 'How could you? It's so cheap and tacky. God knows what my friends will think.' By now Peggy was in the hall and being ushered into the sitting room while the tirade continued. 'And with a greasy Greek. Really! How could you let him even touch you?' Carol slammed the door shut with such force that the Swiss cheese plant in the corner quivered as if cowering from her fury.

'Thank you for your warm welcome, Carol,' Peggy said sardonically. 'As a matter of fact I didn't do anything with the boy – certainly not what your dirty little mind thinks I did.' From her expression Carol was obviously taking umbrage at this, but before she could get a word in edgeways, Peggy continued, 'It was a snapshot your sister took of us on the beach. He works for Steph, that's all. And don't cheapen yourself by making remarks like that about the Greeks. They're a kind and charming people.'

'Well, you should know.' Carol's face had the self-satisfied look of one who feels she has the upper hand in an argument. She spoke in a tight, spiteful voice, one that Peggy had hoped had gone for ever.

Peggy felt it best not to answer her – she did not want to get into a row. She sat down on the white leather sofa, which had once been hers, and looking about her at the faux-beamed ceiling, the York stone fireplace, she thought the sofa looked as out of place here as it had in her own home.

'And why did you say such horrible things about Dad in that newspaper? He loves you, you know. He hasn't left you – he needed a break. He'd do anything to have you back.'

Peggy should not have been surprised by this since it was Carol speaking, but all the same, she was. '*Needed a break!*' Peggy's voice rose dangerously. 'What rubbish you do talk, Carol. I only told that reporter what was true – that your father left me. I didn't say why and with whom. He got off lightly, if you ask me.'

'You called him erring.'

'A very mild word, in the circumstances.'

'And how do you think he feels with a picture of you smooching with a toy-boy in a national newspaper?'

'Quite honestly, Carol, I don't care.' Peggy had one of those moments, becoming rarer, when she would have given anything for a cigarette.

'And why did you have to say you paid for my op? I don't want my friends to know that. I told them we paid for it, not you. You spoil everything.'

'If you hadn't lied in the first place then you wouldn't have been upset now.'

'Gran says everyone will think I'm nutty, having to have a brain operation.'

'Fortunately, not everyone is as ignorant as your grandmother.'

'Honestly, what a thing to say about your own mother. You never have liked her – she's right. Like you've never loved me, always preferring the others.'

'Carol, don't start that, please.' Peggy sighed. 'Of course I don't love the others more than you, mothers aren't like that. But quite honestly, Carol, sometimes you make it easier to *like* Paul and Steph more than you. They don't make fusses like this. They're pleased with what I do for them.'

'I suppose I'm going to have to say thank you for ever. I thought you were supposed to do things because you *wanted* to, not because you wanted us to spend our lives thanking you!' As if on cue, Carol's beautiful blue eyes brimmed with tears.

'Carol, I don't know what to say to you. Of course it gives me pleasure to give to you. You're my daughter. But I don't understand why you have to spoil everything. And after your operation I'd have thought you'd take stock of your life and be grateful—'

'There you go again – gratitude.'

'Not to me, you stupid child, grateful that you survived, that it wasn't cancer. Oh, what *is* the point?' Peggy said, exasperatedly, and she picked up her handbag and prepared to leave.

'You're not Mum any more. I don't know you any more. You've changed so.'

'Don't be so dramatic. Of course I'm still me. I'm just a bit smarter, that's all.'

'See? You'd never have said *that* before! You'd have said you were thick.'

'Don't be so dim! I meant appearance.' Peggy, in the midst of the drama, managed to grin. She moved towards the door.

'And I think it's disgusting of you to flaunt your boyfriends on Dad's backyard,' she shouted across the room.

Peggy paused and slowly turned to face her daughter. 'I beg your pardon?'

'A friend of Sean's saw you slobbering over each other.'

'Who? When?'

'Some man, at Clover's restaurant. Shameless!'

'If I was, so what? Why shouldn't I do whatever I want, when I want? Your father did.'

'With a man half your age? Our friend said he could have been your son,' said Carol in a sing-song voice more suited to the playground. 'And what are people going to say, our friends, for goodness sake, when they see you with a gigolo, behaving like an old whore?'

At this both women stood in shocked silence as if time itself was frozen, Peggy unable to believe the words she had just heard, and Carol shocked that she had even said them. Peggy continued to the door, her face set rigid with hurt, and began to seethe with rage. She paused, her hand resting on the handle.

'Give me a ring when you can see things with a little more sense, and when you feel ready to apologize. Until then, don't bother.' And Peggy slammed the door, which was the only indication of how angry she felt. The Swiss cheese plant was all aquiver again.

Peggy let the silence of her home wash over her. Normally she would expect to feel herself calming down in the peaceful surroundings that she had made her own, but not today.

She crossed the hall, went into her sitting room and poured herself a drink. She stood on the rug in front of the unlit fire and felt cold, although the room was warm. She felt sick to the pit of her stomach. Her mind was reeling, thoughts flying in all directions. It was a mind in shock, which was trying to regain its equilibrium.

She sipped her drink rhythmically and stared into space with eyes that did not register what they saw.

What more could go wrong? Why, when everything should be so good for them all, did this spiteful carping still go on? Why could they not live in peace like other families? She had loved, cared for and nurtured them, shared her good fortune with them, and yet she was in the wrong. Always, where Carol was concerned. Would that ever change? No, of course not. How long would her patience last? Why should she bother? Suddenly these thoughts, tumbling through her mind, out of control, screeched to a halt. So that was how Carol saw her: not as her mother, not as her friend, but as an old whore! A strong word, an unusual word to use even in the heat of the moment to one's mother. An unforgivable word. If this was how Carol felt why should Peggy bother any more with her – with anyone? That inexcusable, grievous word was, in fact, liberating.

Suddenly she put down her glass. She stood, her hands on her hips, thinking, reaching a conclusion. She did not walk to the telephone but, rather, strode purposefully. 'Families,' she muttered to herself. She picked up the telephone and dialled a London number.

'Tarquin? It's Peggy here.' She paused, allowing herself to enjoy the obvious pleasure in his voice at hearing hers. 'I wondered if you were free this evening, whether you would like to come to dinner?'

'I should love to. Where and when? Just give the word.'

'Here. Seven?'

'You mean your cottage.' His voice was surprised.

'Yes . . .' She clutched the receiver until her knuckles showed white, and took a deep breath. 'And, if you like, bring your toothbrush.' She cringed mentally as she said that, and had no idea where she had found the courage. She was almost sure she had not meant to say it.

There was a moment's silence. 'I've a brand new one.' He laughed, but then his voice changed and he was suddenly serious. 'Just one question, Peggy. Are you all right? What's happened?'

'Nothing. I thought you wanted to see me.' She was fighting to sound light, jolly.

'Sweetheart, something's happened. You're hurting – I can hear it in your voice. You sure everything's okay?'

'I'm fine.' Here was the serious, sensitive Tarquin others never saw, the one who lay so deeply hidden under a disguise of glib remarks and self-mockery.

'I could come now, if you want me to. I'm worried. Is it serious, the thing that's made you change your mind about seeing me? And why won't you tell me?'

'I don't mind you knowing. It's not a secret. And it isn't serious – I mean, it depends on the way you look at it.' Could she explain and would he understand? 'I think for too long I've been living a certain way because I was taught to behave like that. It's as if I was programmed, like a computer, to be a certain person. I've spent too long thinking of myself as *Mother* and not *Peggy*. I've decided to live my life how I want to live it, not how I think other people want me to.'

'That's excellent news. So, what was the calamity that made you change so radically? It must have been something enormous.'

She hesitated. He knew her better than she had realized. 'You've heard of the last straw which broke the camel's back? Well, this camel's last straw was followed by the whole hayrick.'

'Poor darling. You sound as if you need a lot of loving to get you right again. Peggy,' his voice softened, 'my love, I'm so glad I'm included in the new scheme of things.'

'There's just one other thing, Tarquin. Bring your passport. I was thinking of flying to Florence for the weekend – that's if you like the idea?' She was smiling at her own audacity, at her own freedom to decide. 'I've skirted round my money, Tarquin. I've been afraid of it, paranoid about it. I've even blamed it for things happening. But now I know they would still have happened. Having the money has set me free from my past and from the expectations of others. That money can and will bring me happiness, I know that now.'

And she did, she thought, as she cradled the phone in her hands, loath to replace it and disconnect them. Happiness meant Tarquin, she was sure – well, almost. She touched wood. A little of the insecure Peggy of the past still remained.